LIFEAHOLIC

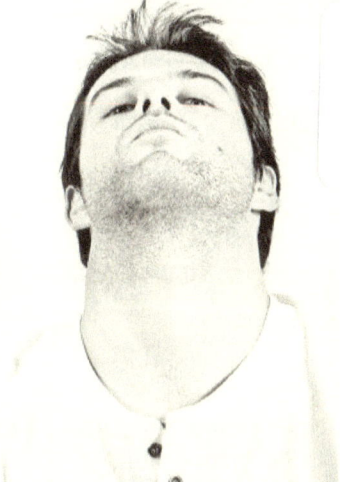

Stephen "Talent" Brocklehurst is an actor, writer, director, singer and producer based in London, England. He believes anything is possible, and has spent over 5 years producing a 360 degree project consisting of: a book (this one), an album ("ImmorTalented"), a TV show, and several films ("Radio London," "Morning Tea") to do his best to prove it. He currently is or has been:

- o   A represented actor, playing the lead in feature films, TV pilots, music videos, commercials, and more
- o   On national TV on more than 10 occasions
- o   Top 2% National IQ - admitted to British MENSA (though it took two attempts, and he is unsure as to how this happened at *all*...)
- o   In the top 1% of 2012's "Britain's Got Talent"
- o   In Steven Spielberg's movie 'War Horse'
- o   Twice nominated for music awards for his album
- o   Published in Canadian spiritual magazine *Synergy*
- o   A T.A. Parachute Regiment soldier
- o   A broker at the World's top broking firm
- o   An actor in the UK Best Feature "Love Tomorrow" at the Raindance Film Festival

 New Generation Publishing

LIFEAHOLIC

For Trystan Edney

For Layla Birch

For Reiss Aikins

For Hilliam Wale

For a Jedi

For my Little Sister

For my Brothers

For my friends

For my Family

For Pari

For my Mother

For You

WORDS OF WAR FROM OTHERS

"Stephen's range and skill as an actor are evident to anyone who has seen him at work in front of the camera, but when coupled with his immense musical talent and writing ability, he becomes something of a creative powerhouse. On sets, he's constantly seeking to learn and refine and was also astute enough to assist less experienced actors in honing their performances, without them feeling they were being taught. A true 'Everyman,' Stephen blends skills and passion and fires it all with unwavering dedication. I whole-heartedly recommend him."

Leon Loay Hady, novelist, writer

"A fine example of how a leading male actor / writer / musician / producer should conduct business in this difficult industry."

Alex Macaulay, CEO Blackbull Productions

"First time I met him it was hilarious, listening to his epic journey of trying to get to the 'Captain America' shoot without fouling himself publicly on a train. The second time was a blast as we hit it off whilst having the pleasure of auditioning as giants on 'Jack the Giant Killer.' Then it was yet more fun as we couldn't get out of the place; the code for the gate wouldn't work and even if it had there were no trains. I won't go on. Just my thoughts."

Jason Beeston, actor and colleague

"He's quite strange. He's talkative as you like at times, but then others, he'll just keep himself to himself. Know what I mean? There was days when he was laughing and joking, a real sport, and the life and soul of the whole shoot. But there was several whole days, where he didn't say a word at all, far as I know."

Contributor kept anonymous by request

"An original, one of a kind, cannot be replicated, mastermind;
A devil in disguise, a phoenix from the ashes about to rise,
The man whose star is already risen with a driven need to succeed, whose ambition will fuel his mission;
A complete and utter head-case, but still one of my favourite men in this thing we call the human race."

Margarita Mitchell Pollock, actress, model

"He's an absolute bastard. And I mean that as criticism and honest observing. For what he did to my friend Mandy, and you know what I'm talking about, y'all, he ain't nothing but a piece of white trash who can't control himself. If y'all's a girl who's ever got mixed up with the so-called 'Talent,' then y'all know. He don't raise a hand to a girl, least not so far as I know, but the way he beats is with them words of his. He was a man I loved, and that don't tell y'all nothin' but how blind a person I used to be."

Contributor held anonymous by request

"He fired me and I hate the prick."

Former Employee, held anonymous by request.

"Stephen is a push when you have stopped, a chat when you are lonely, a guide when you are searching, a smile when you are sad, and most of all a friend who is always there for you! Like every man, he has needs and sometimes girls take advantage... but being a man he can't let them down, so in a way it's a win-win situation and if that's OK with him then it's ok with me! Sometimes he does get caught in a moment of rush, work and perfection in all what he does, and as a friend I miss having him around as he is always so busy these days! But I got to admit that he is doing what it takes to make the dream come true, so sacrifices have to be made and I, as a friend, have to stand by him! The only bad thing I can say about Stephen, is stop being a workaholic! But I am here when you need me!"

Goddaughter Kenia Martins, Maxim Cover Girl

"He's a liar. He's become a liar who can't help but lie, like an addict. Tell him to come up here, and I'll show him. Fight my son? Who does he think he is?"

Father of Former Friend, held anonymous

"Stephen: my first love; an all-consuming love catalysed by hormonal teenage lust: an attraction and desire that lasted past our school days and into times when we both should have known better. Two paths, designed to separate but destined to cross, resulting in epic failed attempts at self-control. Distance and time have allowed clarity, perspective and, most of all, true happiness."

Former Girlfriend, held anonymous by request

"I met Steve during the filming of "War Horse;" now, I am a very good judge of character, and I take people as they come. The first thing I found Steve to be was an approachable person; he seemed to want to be noticed, not for being the centre of attention, but as a person who anyone could approach. He had a way about him that made him stand out. Firstly, the way he does his job: he was 100% professional. One thing that really stood out about Steve is his personality; it's like a lighthouse, but sometimes he can turn that light off, like on the day when I was called to translate something into German and I told him I knew the answer, but he seemed to ignore what I said and still continued to text someone (really all I wanted him to do is save money, lol)... but hey, some people do forget that others do know the answer and are only slower to respond. Then one day he was writing something, and I asked him "Steve, what you writing there?" and he responded, "I am writing a book." I said, "What, can *you* write???" (being sarcastic as I could), but he was like a rock and continued to explain it to me; until I decided to contribute to it, when he asked me about the 501st Legion, and I believe you will see what I said when you read the book. My overall opinion about Steve Brocklehurst:

1) He is a very genuine and nice guy
2) He is professional in what he does (on set)
3) He can sometimes be overwhelming in his personality
4) He is willing to accept any person, but often distances himself, and falls in to his own world for peace and silence
5) He will sometimes retreat in to his own world to think of projects
6) He, in my opinion, would be one of the best people to have if it came to someone doing a job in front of the camera
7) He has a heart
8) I believe that he can be very outspoken in such a way that even would surprise himself

Overall Steve is a great artist with his own ghosts, and I believe he will be a great artist, and a great person to be around and work with. And also someone whom I would serve with in an operational theatre under fire!"
Jason Cook, former British Soldier

"Raving narcissist, utter gent,
Easy to wind up, and 1000 percent
Genuine, driven, passionate and bold,
Occasionally lost, can never be told,
Lusty and loveful, tempter and tease,
Won't ever stop till the world's at his knees..."
Jim Hatton Brown, artist and writer, friend

CONTENTS (TENTS FOR CONS?)

FOREWORD – by METIS of THE BEYOND TALENT EXPERIENCE

Insofar as this book is a testament to and a celebration of an ethos and a code, this foreword is intended not only to provide context *on* the author, but also context *for* the author (yes, I'm talking to *you*). It is a reminder to the journeyman who wrote it of the strength that he himself embodies in undertaking to walk this arduous path. It is also an invitation to enjoy it, *sans* 'lash,' if only for a moment. To relish what it means to be the kind of person who does the kinds of things that he does.

It requires deep conviction to live your life by your own principles. It is a conviction rooted in a belief that is more fundamental than even conscious belief itself. It is the footsteps of a soldier who finds himself moving forward despite hearing the words "I can go no further" ringing so loudly in his head that he thinks others might hear it too. They cannot - all they can see are the progress of footsteps, and the weight of footprints left behind. It is a belief, and a knowledge that is somehow deeper than the belief of your own beliefs, or the knowledge of your own knowledge.

Trust me, this is not an easy road to walk.

So why do it?

It is done for two reasons: first, because if you apprehend dreamchasing, or 'lifeaholism,' clearly, then any alternative is merely second best. And a distant one at that. Second, because the pain, enormous though it may be at times, still only hurts up to a point, and one of its many rewards are moments of exceptional lucidity where you are able to make statements which honour that which is great within you, such as the following:

I have, and never have had, and never will have, any intention of giving up.

I'm not that bothered whether you read my book. I'm bothered that I WRITE it.

I enjoy describing Steve to other people. There is the character, the honesty, the mania, the extremism, the boundless generosity towards friends and family… and then of course, there is his sometimes occupation, on which I'll let him elaborate. But what tends to intrigue people most, I have found, whether they 'agree' with his methods or not, is the fact that these snapshots form a tapestry of a man who does the things that they are afraid to do. They tell me that he must be 'fearless'. In fact, this isn't the case at all. The truth of the matter is much more impressive.

Everyone has fears, but not everyone has the courage to face them. Bravery is not the absence of fear; it is action in the face of it. Steve *is,* in fact, an everyman. We all are, and that is precisely what makes him so inspiring: that and the fact that he genuinely sees the same limitless potential in you as he sees in himself (well, maybe not quite *the same*…), even if you don't. This is something. In fact it may be one of the only things that people who know him well can all agree on. He brings out the best in the people around him.

It is ironic, perhaps, that one of the most generous people I have ever had the pleasure of knowing would birth a philosophy entitled 'Selfism' – but it is *not* paradoxical. I don't need to explain that here. I'll let him do that.

I've had the privilege to see Steve at some of his most fearful moments, and to have him present at some of mine. I saw him take the stage for the first time. I was there with him. Even before that, I saw him lay the gauntlet down before me, and make me rise to the challenge myself. In all likelihood, had it not been for him, there would be no 'Metis,' and there would be no 'Talent.' There is no greater gift a friend can give you than to help you bring the best out in yourself. Steve does this for all his friends. Even those who count themselves amongst his 'past' (although he has never looked at time and distance the same way others have) will admit to the fact that he changed their life profoundly, and for the better.

There is a thin line between opposites: love and hate, genius and crazy, heads and tails…and there is no doubt that Steve has many opposites inside of him. Sometimes I pretend to ask myself if Steve is too crazy to understand his own limits. In reality, I know he's one of the only people I've ever met who's genuinely smart enough to understand that there is no such thing. I love that about him.

There is a cost to being a dream-chaser that spectators to this great race will never realize. It is the cost of measuring yourself against a horizon of infinite possibility and potential – there is always a long way to go, no matter how far you have already come. This can be an overwhelmingly sobering thought…the only remedy is to drink in the moments deep enough to make up for it.

Luckily for Steve, he's a Lifeaholic.

Metis

- *4 time EMA (Exposure Music Awards) award-winning rapper*
- *City of London CDS trader*
- *Published writer and spoken-word artist*
- *Co-founder of "The Beyond Talent eXperience"*

THE INTRODUCTION TO A SINNER

"This is what I do, this is Who I am,
Your Honorary Lifeaholic Blue-eyed Man..."

- Talent -
"Lifeaholic"

- IMMORTALENTED 2013 -

I'll be honest.

I didn't know how to begin this. Nor do I know why it has taken so long.

I suppose a large part of me felt it was too self-indulgent.

Another part of me still believes the story is not a big deal, or that it is not worth telling in the first place.

But that's not the truth.

The truth and nothing but the truth *is*, I've been scared.

To come clean, to 'fess up, to air my laundry in public.

Or whatever.

And if you believe *that*, you'll believe *anything*.

No, the biggest issues stopping this particular piece of shiterature have been mostly (1) having no time and (2) a lack of certainty about where to start.

And then I thought, *screw* it. Just start.

Just start writing and see what happens. (To all aspiring writers, that's all you really need to know...)

So, on that note (a B sharp, in all likelihood), let's get on with it.

My name is Stephen Clifford Brocklehurst.

I am a bog-standard 30-year-old male caucasian homo sapien human being, hailing from the London region of the United Kingdom on a continent called Europe, which is itself located in the Atlantic ocean in the Western Hemisphere of planet Earth, itself the capital of the Milky Way solar system within the universal self we call the universe.

Hi.

How's it going?

Britain, the country in which I live, has controlled the largest Empire to date in the history of the known universe. So it's an amazing country. Capital, in fact. And London is the Capital of England, which is kind of the Capital of Britain, which I'd like to think is a contender for the Capital of Europe, which I'd like to think is the Capital of the World, which is deffo the Capital of the Solar System, which is without doubt the Capital of the Universe.

So, in a sense, I'm lucky enough to live in the Capital City (true) of the Capital Country (arguable) of the Capital Continent (*never* getting away with that) of the Capital planet (ah, finally, agreement...) in the Capital Galaxy (sorry E.T.) of the Capital Universe.

(I may have to call this book "Capital".)

[Or "Overly repetitive waste of paper from massively long winded Midlander"]

I am son to a woman who was a sportswoman, a musician and a teacher, and to a man who was a soldier, a boxer, and a construction / surveying specialist.

I am one of six billion people who live on this planet in the year 2010. The planet we live on is itself roughly six billion years old, and is part of a solar system that is part of a galaxy that is part of a *universe* that is itself approximately thirteen billion years old. There are approximately between 100 to 500 billion *other* galaxies in the known Universe.

Makes you feel pretty small, doesn't it?

I do not consider myself special.

I am an Everyman, through and through.

To my oldest and best friends in the world I am known simply as Brock. I got six As at A-level and a degree from the best University in the country as him.

To my inner circle I am a member of the Beyond Talent eXperience called Talent. As he I was nominated for two EMA 'Best Artist' music awards.

To others I am called Dr. Invictus Schadenfreude. It is not good to know this man. He has attacked people and been hospitalised on more than one occasion. He is reputed to be a Class A drug user and a male escort.

To some I am called Stephen Axim or Axim Reds, from my days in Clubland. I ran thirteen club-nights a week and put 1600 people into a club on a Tuesday for more years than I can remember.

To some I have been Abdullah the Preacher. I preached hatred and died on the streets of London as he.

To more I have been Milan, the Slovakian manic-depressive. While I was Milan, I tried to kill myself, and encouraged terminally ill people to take their own lives. I succeeded.

To a few I was Cap the Commander. As Cap, I failed my troops in my mission. I also apparently managed to sweat on command.

Briefly, I was Dom the Bully. I picked on my employee and slept with the girl of his dreams.

For days I was Kent Mansey the Debt Collector. I kidnapped a man and put a gun in his face.

For twenty-four hours I was the Nameless One. I ate food out of a public bin and cried for a long, long time.

I was for a time The Witness to Jehovah. I had doors slammed in my face.

A long time ago I was Michael the Redeemer. I went insane and lost my mind.

For one, amazing, tears-in-my-eyes weekend I was The Everyman. I was Chad the surfer, Billy Bob the Redneck, Boris the Russian florist, Agent 00Jesus, Delroy the Jamaican beachwear salesman, Lavio the gay Italian hairstylist, and Lord Harris Cobblebottom VII the Urban Aristocrat.

I repeat: I am an Everyman.

Just like you.

I am by trade a represented actor and writer.

I am also a director, a poet, a friend, and an award-nominated singer. At present I am also a represented model, an only child, a lyricist, a father-to-be and husband-to-be (someday), a male escort, a former TA Parachute Regiment soldier, a former dance instructor, and a son. But above all things, I am a man.

17

I have written scripts, books, poems, and a belief system.

I have betrayed those I love and caused near-irreparable harm.

I have made and been in twelve feature films, eight short films, five music videos, eleven commercials, and been the subject of five documentaries.

I have run my own PR company with my best friends, which ran thirteen nightclubs a week in central London, putting over 1,500 people into a single one on a Tuesday night.

I have been a male escort and had my time be financially procurable.

I have been a salesman and known what it is to hate oneself with venom.

I have been in a Hollywood blockbuster on the same screen as Tommy Lee Jones, Samuel L Jackson, and Agent Smith from the Matrix.

I have been so intoxicated that I could not control my own actions and put the fear of God into my own family and friends. This I can and will never forgive.

I have been a Territorial Army Parachute Regiment soldier and felt fear of failure, and then pride beyond measure in success.

I have been a martial artist and have been beaten into unconsciousness.

I have tried to get into MENSA to find out if I am what they call 'a genius.' I failed. Then I succeeded.

I have impregnated women without meaning to and without their knowledge or consent and without my knowledge or consent.

I lost my first child.

I have kissed men. And more besides.

I have had former friends of mine turn nemesis and cast stone after stone at me from across a street in broad daylight.

I have performed onstage before a thousand people.

I have given £100,000 I did not own to a man I did not know.

I have encouraged my girlfriend to bed my best friend. Which she then did. While I was in the House.

I have sprinted a mile and a half whilst roped to a telegraph pole.

I have seen my best friend near-throw himself from a twelfth story balcony.

I have traded millions and millions of dollars of CDS contracts.

I have found over a hundred people work.

I have fired over a hundred people.

I have smoked cigarettes, drank alcohol, smoked weed, and worse.

I have worked three jobs at a time.

I have performed my album onstage as the opening act for Memphis Bleek (Jay-Z's act).

I have lost the love of my life. Three times.

I have been a dirty secret.

I have founded and lost a corporation.

I have lived for three decades.

I have failed, and failed, and then failed some more. And then succeeded.

I have, and never have had, and never will have, any intention of giving up.

I am an Everyman.

But I am also a Lifeaholic.

And I have no fear of death. (Although it scares the *shit* out of me.)

This is my story. The part where it all gets put on the line. The shot at the title.

Or as much of it as I can tell. (Without getting nicked).

(Again).

"So," asks the informed reader (think: friends, family, women with a grudge) "with your literature degree and your lifetime of writing and creativity, how exactly are you going to put this thing together?"

To which I can only say, I have no idea.

I suppose the obvious way is chronologically. Tell you the deets (details) from the beginning through to the end and build it up so you might give a shit.

Or, I could reverse the order and claim some kind of literary device is being used. I'd be reversing time in order to give the reader blah knowledge of the current time, blah, and thus frame the past as more important, blah, and thus I'm so blah clever, blah, and please read my book.

Blah.

Crap.

Waste of space.

I'm not that bothered whether you read my book. I'm bothered that I *WRITE* it. I am bothered that it serves a *purpose*.

I'm bothered that people who wish to chase their dreams, but who have been told they cannot do so, realise that this is not so.

Literary time devices?

Screw *that* for a game of soldiers.

I reckon I'm going to start with my favourite place, and for my favourite reason.

We're going to start with YOU.

Yeah.

We're starting with YOU.

And the reason, beloved reader, is the most important of all reasons.

Especially to us human beings.

It is the "why."

I'm going to tell you WHY I am doing this, and WHY I am doing this for YOU.

Or more accurately, because of YOU.

WHY?

YOU.

See, the problem is - despite my absolute commitment to manhood, to inner warfare, to the Parachute Regiment, to bare-knuckle brawls with the East Texan Tae Kwon Do champion, to running my own company, to a constant alliance to the truth, to drinking single malt whisky, to being the best friend I can to my friends, I have to confess:

I completely, absolutely, entirely and utterly, madly, absurdly *love* you.

Why?

Well.

Let's take my opinion *out* of it.

And let's just look at the statistically most likely, most scientifically accurate evaluation of who and what **YOU** are.

You.

Are.

The single most complex and highly evolved organism in the known and possibly the unknown universe. You are an impossibly fortunate cosmic winning *lottery ticket* of a being; a child born of the stars, from the womb of the Big Bang and in the loving arms of the oceans of planet Earth.

By all rights, you are so cool and against-the-odds that you should not exist.

You are part of a race of beings that have survived war, torture, genocide, apartheid, more war, rape, pillage, fast food, and all the savage beasts and animals of planet Earth.

You are the sole known beings to have stepped foot on another world (the moon), are at the top of the intellectual food chain, and are wired into the very fabric of the universe the same way stars and suns are wired into it. You can do anything you wish. No, that's not quite right. You can do *everything* you wish. And this is *you* that we are talking about.

We are all made of the same stuff.

Which kind of means *you* are *me* and that *I* am *you* and that we are all linked and all the same.

Kind of.

Ask the Buddhists and Quantum Physicists if you don't believe me.

You have near-limitless potential to invent, create, discover, innovate, conquer, liberate, and optimise.

Disagree? Then contemplate that Neil Armstrong stood upon the moon before you were born, that we and *only we* invented the internet and Facebook, and that before us, there was no such *thing* as a Big Mac.

Human beings *ROCK*.

And, given that we are all born of the Big Bang, or of some kind of God, and that we share the same ancestors and evolutionary chain, we are, of course, family.

YOU are the *why*.

Because, basically, I want you to be the best you can be. And I want you to be the happiest you can be. And in order to be that, I think you need to know something.

21

I think you need to know that you have the right to be everything you want to be and to be as content, satisified, and happy as you can be.

I think you need to know *what* you are and what you are *capable* of.

Which of course, my brother, sister, friend, whichever you may be...

...is *anything*.

Or rather, as I said above, *everything*.

Don't believe me?

Heh.

I was *hoping* you'd say that.

Sit back. Put your feet up. Grab a beer. Roll a spliff. Run the bath. Do whatever you do.

And get ready to be AMAZED...'cause the whole point of this, is that you and me get *PROOF*.

I repeat: there is **nothing** you cannot do.

As for me?

I think I must have decided when I was about ten or eleven.

I'd always been creative. I'd written, drawn pictures, sung in the choir, played the piano.

I got lucky by having the most supportive parent you could ask for.

As in, *lottery ticket* lucky.

I'd always read comic books. Captain America, Spider-Man, the Hulk, Transformers, everything.

'Course, the one that reigned supreme, truth be told, was Thor. But more on that later.

I reckon I just loved being inspired: the firing of my imagination; the colours, the names, the action, everything.

But most of all?

I loved the *code*.

The hero's code.

The idea that if you fought hard enough and worked hard enough, you could set the world to rights and do anything.

This is either called 'optimism' or 'naivety.' Or maybe even just plain 'stupid.'

Either way, I knew the comics and stories inspired me to try to do better.

And to try to *be* better.

And then movies and cartoons did the same.

Thundercats. Transformers. The A-Team. Knight Rider.

('Course, I didn't know back then that half the characters in these things were real people: actors and starlets who were probably alcoholic, or high off bleach, or whatever. Wouldn't have mattered if I had, to be fair...)

[Note - to all budding film directors or directors of any kind - all you need to know about directing or storytelling can be found in old cartoons, comics, music videos and the like. Simply show something in its best, most positive light or worst, darkest shadow. And then pick where on the scale it works best.]

And so I began to think, that surely the most rewarding act in the world, and also the most fun you could have with your clothes on, and actually also the most logical and humane thing to do as a person, was to take the most positive message you could, the most powerful and liberating Truth, and then spread it.

Paint it.

    Write it.

        Sing it.

            Act it.

                LIVE it.

                    BE.

                            It.

So I did, and so I do, and so I am.

Or at least, I'm *trying*.

Storytelling is my game.
And it's an underrated art form.

In days gone by (my father could say this far better, but he's not here at the minute), kings would pay for the greatest tale-tellers in the land to attend court, and to regale the Lords and Ladies with the greatest epics, the most magnificent tales, the most extreme love stories and romances.

Why?

Because storytelling is the oldest art form in humanity that has been kept and honoured since time immemorial. And because people love to be inspired, to be moved, and to be made to see and feel things they cannot see and feel.

How do parents teach children?

How do teachers instruct their classes?

Why do we still go to the movies?

Because we learn and we become inspired through stories. The moral of the tale becomes the tale of the moral.

We *learn*: through storytelling; the sharing of vision.

New experiences passed on to us from other people, to whom we are most grateful for transporting us, even if just for a moment, for one tiny second, to a place we never dreamed of but CAN SEE AS IF WE WERE THERE.

And, on that note, to people who hate "Star Wars', or who think "Lord of the Rings' is pretentious, or who consider "Avatar" to be overrated:

Fuck. *Off.*

And grow up.

Have the humility to admit what you are: a *child*. A child in awe at what you see.

You think seventy years old is old?

You had a look at a tree lately? Had a think about a planet?

The universe is thirteen billion years old.

Seventy years old?

Seventy years young.

As I said.

Fuck. *Off.*

I'd be sat somewhere, unimaginably bored.

My mum had taken me to an aunt's house, or to her school, and like most bored-out-of-sheer-idiocy-and-ingratitude children, I needed something to occupy myself.

(Laughable, isn't it?)

My mother, in an act of both mercy and sheer genius, would pass me toy soldiers, or a piece of paper and pens or pencils.

And then magic, genuine *magic*, happened.

Something that had never existed before suddenly existed there and then on the page.

Technically speaking, in our universe, matter / energy can neither be created nor destroyed.

It can only change form.

("Yes, hmmm, yes that's *right*, hmmm," go the scientists. I *know* that... *freaks*...)

And yet, it happens every day.

Our minds, those unfathomable and infinite pools of abundance, conjure up on paper or in audio form or visually or however, things that have never previously existed.

I saw the contents of my mind spill out onto the page.

My *imagination* could apparently *create* things. From *nothing*.

I nearly laughed myself into hysterics.

(You ever seen "The Incredibles?" There's a bit where the kid runs away from the bad guys, and legs it towards the ocean, terrified, thinking he can't walk on water. So he runs faster and looks up at the sky away from the water, so scared is he of drowning or being caught. Then he looks down and sees he is pegging it across the surface of the sea, against everything he believed possible. The laugh he then emits is precisely how I felt, is one of the greatest sounds ever produced by man, and is also well worth watching.)

[To whichever gifted fuckers made "The Incredibles," you can *pay* me now...]

So I kept drawing. And writing.

Then it was music. Then it was poems.

And then, joyously, it was ACTing.

One of my parents has bad rheumatoid arthritis. From the age of thirty, they were in, and still are in, more pain on a daily basis than you or I have felt since we were six.

This was one of my more painful lessons: that some things in life, you cannot change. Not within your lifespan.

I fucking **_HATE_** that.

As in, not the kind of hate like "I hate cricket" hate, but the kind of vitriolic, venomous snakebile that makes my eyelids curl upwards and my teeth vibrate.

However.

I found out that laughing made them forget the pain for a second. Made them smile.

So I copied every character on TV ad infinitum, and that seemed to make them laugh (you should _see_ my Scooby-Doo).

I might have been ten? Eleven?

And there's not an acting school on the _planet_ that'd get a more enthusiastic pupil.

I was hooked.

Music.

Drawing.

Acting.

Poetry.

Short stories.

Long stories.

Mimicry.

Makes my parents laugh? Makes pain go away?

Takes what is in my mind and makes it real?

That's called alchemical magic.

It's called imagination.

If you have ever done any of the above, you are, like me, a member of the imagiNATION.

I hail you and bow before you.

And I love you to the point of insanity.

You are the healers and sorcerers among us.

As am I.

Now. Having cleared that up... let's get to the _point_...

26

DECEMBER 2009:

"THE END IS THE BEGINNING"

"My vocation's
Flowing in a basement
For a transformation
The whole race faces..."

- Talent -
"Flowtation"

- IMMORTALENTED 2013 -

So.

Here we go, people.

Let's begin at the most sensible place: the beginning. That way you'll get it.

It happened to be the beginning of the end.

And I suppose it all started when my life in the city came to an end of its own...

I'd been there two years, partly by accident, partly by design.

And mostly because I have the best friends in the schnigging *world*.

Anyway.

Two years I'd been there as a broker. And I'd been on, shall we say, good money. As in, free porn and whisky good.

Yeah. I know. Why would you leave, right?

I'd had a corporate card that meant I had to spend almost no money so long as I was out with my client, who was actually my best friend for nigh on a decade. I'd had a job with the best broking firm in the world, and I worked with some of my closest friends. I made £35,000 a year basic plus bonuses that totalled up to *a lot*, and I had a crew around me of about thirty guys who were, to be frank, safe as houses. Houses with CCTV and guard dogs. Guard dogs with *uzis*.

I'd funded my music video, my website, my life, my bills, my dating, my whole world, by working at a broking firm. The world was, I suppose, my oyster. Card. As in, it let me get through Life's gates.

And so, I repeat, why would you leave?

Well, you've probably got the gist by now.

Believe you me: I was *shitting* myself. I'd had numerous conversations with my mum and my friends about whether this was wise.

One of my best friends, a bearded legend who would outdo himself later in Ibiza, told me he thought it was the wrong move. *"Stay another year in broking, man."*

I couldn't *believe* it. I was heartbroken. After all the support I'd given, did he really think I could not survive on my own? Did I not deserve the same support I had given him?

(Note to all - don't hold it against people who try to put hurdles in your way or talk you out of your dreams - just remember that what they're saying is about as important to your future as the thoughts and feelings of a mosquito are to an oncoming car windscreen...)

See, I'm the guy who freely admits he's shooting for the stars and often gets pretty damn close, and also the guy who advocates never giving up.

For instance: after years of hearing various people's opinions on my intelligence, I wanted to see how smart I actually *was* (or more likely, wasn't). So I tried to get into MENSA. The first year I failed by two points, getting 138. To be fair, I did pretty well finding the place, I was that hung over. But even so, I was fucking *pissed*. As in, insanely so.

I do not. Like. *Failure.*

Did I give up?

Did I *fuck.*

I took it again the next year, and you are now talking to a MENSA man.

'Nuff said.

I suppose my friend was giving me good advice, truth be told. Sound advice. Safe advice.

To stay in a secure place with a lot of job security.

And yet. I knew it wasn't going to happen.

So I left.

And I was *terrified*.

I'd had job security. I'd had future security. Hell, I'd had my father actually *happy* with my life choices. I was going to be a millionaire if I just *stayed where I was*. I could have bought enough whisky and a big enough pad to live large for pretty much *ever*.

And yet.

AND.

YET.

I couldn't stay.

Staying made me feel like a coward. Like a cop-out.

I felt, in an nutshell, like this:

Like a person who is looking at two boxing rings. In one of them he can play it pretty safe (still harder than 99% of people *ever* play life, but pretty safe nonetheless, to his mind), taking on guys his own size and shape, and doing that he can win some decent titles.

This was me staying at my broking firm, running my own company, and so on.

In the next one is a fucking MONSTER with boxing gloves on each of his *teeth*, he's that huge; behind which is a treasure trove so big that when you simply *look* at it you go blind. This was me actually manning up and going after what I regard as "The Prize."

(Note to all - "The Prize" - this is whatever you value and desire most, in terms of career, relationships, and life - not always related to fame, fortune, money, women, and often very mundane and simple - all of which is *irrelevant* - work out what your "Prize" is, and life gets a lot easier.)

[And a lot, *lot* harder.]

I'm the kind of guy who wants the treasure.

And I will go to war with Godzilla to get it.

The City was amazing, but it was not for me. And to be frank, I'd been pretty unhappy the whole time I had been there. While the people there were good people, *decent* people, and my boss had been a good man, I had simply not been enjoying my life.

I worked with my best friend in a professional environment and at one of the world's most prestigious companies. But I was miserable.

Which to me proved a moral I had always had some doubt about, that being: money does not buy you everything.

It does, however, buy you everything *else*.

But *everything*?

No. That takes, shall we say, a little *more*.

My first day on the job one of the senior brokers had been reviewing my CV and asked, "So why the fuck do you want to get into broking? You could do anything, looking at this."

I replied the only way I could.

"Erm. This is the biggest broking firm in the world, right? People at this desk make more money than God. Right?"

He replied the only way *he* could.

"Well, yeah. But money ain't the world," he observed. "And broking's a shit job."

Now I'm not saying that's strictly accurate. It's not. Broking can be more fun than interactive porn and a chocolate-scented bubble bath for one. But fuck me, was it a revelation to hear.

I had made good friends at the company, and one in particular.

But my life, my heart, my soul, had always been in the same place since I was twelve or younger.

And at some point, after being:

- A student (UCL - best university in the country now, beeyatches...)
- A barman (Boundary Hotel, eat ya heart out...)
- A security guard (Brown's nightclub, Holborn, in the Spring of '01)
- A parachute regiment TA soldier (That's *right*, people...)
- A nightclub promoter (CC Club, Elysium, China White, Cafe De Paris, Opium, Saint Bar, Trap, Propaganda, Maya, 24 Club, Pangaea, and more...)
- A recruitment consultant (Huntress).
- An entrepreneur (Mischief)
- A male escort (None of your damn business...yet...).
- A dance instructor (JRP London)
- A writer (Synergy Magazine)
- And, as we've established, a broker...

I knew I had to step off the safety net and actually man up to do what I knew I had been blueprinted to do.

So I left.

I'll rephrase that: actually, first off, I got made redundant. This, to anyone who's had it happen, doesn't feel like a bed of roses.

I then had various offers to take new jobs doing the same thing for other companies. Three months after leaving I still got emails and offers asking me to come back.

I asked people for advice.

I did not take it.

I got made redundant from my job, but I left the City.

I made the industry redundant to myself.

And that of course meant, with less money coming in, that I had to move apartments.

As well as adapt to a new career, just before the New Year.

Merry fucking Christmas, genius.

My name is Wicksy, and I am a financial broker and male escort in London in 2010.

I am about to get made redundant from a six-figure (including bonuses) a year Cityjob, and also lose my £350 an hour escorting work; oh, and also my Playmate girlfriend. I am about to be unemployed, homeless, and without partner or any form of income. I am also soon to be murdered.

Over the next twelve months, in fact, I am to:

- **Travel the world**
- **Get tortured and then waterboarded whilst chained to a bed in a cellar**
- **Be unemployed and homeless**
- **Turn thirty**
- **Be stabbed to death in the street by a man I barely know**
- **Flee from eighty charging men on horseback**
- **Watch the world's greatest living director make a movie**
- **Become manic-depressive and encourage terminally ill people to end their own lives**
- **Bully my own employee and sleep with the love of his life**

- Get nominated for two awards, and then lose them both
- Sleep with an international football player's ex-wife
- Take over the top two floors (Penthouse) of a building near the Olympic site with my friends
- Get dumped by a Sony singer-songwriter
- Punch a sex doll off a nineteenth floor balcony
- Have to watch the person I love most in the world be hospitalised for almost four months
- Get caught holding a gun in the face of a man who owes me and my crew money, and
- Film my own TV show and then have to spend four days recovering from the shoot.

It is almost Christmas when this is happening, and my world feels like it is coming down on top of me.

And despite my best efforts, I am no Atlas...

My name is *actually* Stephen Clifford Brocklehurst, as we established.

That was just the Everyman in me coming out.

Wicksy was the nickname I was given at my broking firm. And he was my City persona.

As we said, these past two years I have been a CDS broker at the world's largest broking firm trading hundreds of millions of pounds of CDS contracts. That's a jargonistic term used to sex up the idea of insurance contracts. And these are also sentences I never thought I would say.

I have also, rumour has it, been a male escort in the city of London, providing 'companionship services' to women who wished to pay for my company and time at the rate of £350 to £550 an hour. I have been dating a playmate who is nail-bitingly beautiful and who has modelled in men's magazines and tabloid newspapers.

Some might say my life is peachy, thanks to job one, job two, and a playmate.

I am about to lose all three.

And much, much more.

I have no degree in finance. I had no previous experience in broking. I have worked here during the greatest financial crisis my generation has ever seen: the 'credit crunch.' I was twenty-seven years old when I started and have had to learn a whole new language to survive: "brokerspeak". I have traded over a billion dollars worth of CDS contracts for my best friend, who is also the single most prolific trader at a top investment bank.

I have friends in high places. I also have friends in low places, but then more on that later.

And now, after my boy has left to pursue his own dreamchase, as well he should, I have been let go, since Citywork requires clients.

No clients, no work. No work, no money. No money, no job. No job, no income.

Summing up, I thought *I'm fucked*.

This meant I was either to get another job in the city for an equally ridiculous paycheque (the safe route) or I was to take the leap into the perilous world of full-time film and music, as an actor, writer, and singer (the Lifeaholic route, but possibly also the stupid one).

I walked out of work as usual on a Friday having lost (I shit you not):

- A six-figure a year job at the world's largest broking firm
- The daily company of forty safe-as-houses brokers, one of whom is one of my best friends
- A £36,000 a year expenses card
- A £350-£550 an hour escorting job, companioning women (mostly married) out to dinner, theatre, drinks, and clubs
- All my regular clients from escorting, since my agent is returning to Oz to reunite with her husband
- My flat, since paying a grand a month for accomodation with no basic salary makes *no* sense
- Possibly my studio, which I've had for three years, for the same reason as above,
- And my woman, who is a glamour and underwear model and page three regular, due to me having worked three jobs over the last year and not having seen her enough...

Typical.
So to be frank, I'm a tad scared.
I am not, by nature, a financier. In fact, quite the opposite.

A friend of mine observes quite rightly that the world markets were doing just fine and dandy until yours truly stepped into the breach. At which point, well, it all went a bit Pete Tong. As in: galactically so, as by now you know.

I am in truth what they now call a Raptor: a rapper and actor.

This is alongside being a writer and director, and a bunch of other stuff. And I am definitely a general pain in the arse.

I am a creator, to give the craft its proper name. I am a vocabulayman, a grammapprentice, a performer, a brickie of words and music, a scriptplumber, a cinemaniac, and a lyricist.

A creator.

Being in finance was never part of the plan. However, to swim against the tide, I am immensely, immensely grateful to the City, and specifically to Messr Gibbs and the members of what I call "the Preditors" (predators of credit), since that particular job allowed me to pay for:

- My studio (The Chocolate Lab)
- My music video (Everyman)
- Three documentaries
- My first website www.immortalented.com
- A gift for my best friend's birthday; a film starring all his closest crew
- My album "**ImmorTalented**"
- And most importantly, above all, two years of me doing what is most important to me...

And that, ladies and gentlefolk, as we know, is ACTing and making Music. The combination of which we call "cinemusic." Making me "the cineman."

I have believed for as long as I can remember that I was built for the world of film and music, of entertainment and inspiration, of soundscaping and storytelling.

Not because I'm special, or different, or a unique snowflake, or any of that crap. No. (In fact my first video and album track "Everyman" was made precisely to state this fact... I am a bog-standard, normal, run-of-the-mill human being. Just like you. Because however amazing you *think* you are, trust me, there are people out there who would send you packing without batting an eyelid. Lesson One: employ humility, as there is always, *always* someone better...) But because I am most in love with the creative arts, specifically those of film and music.

34

I believe both have the capacity to entertain, to teach, to inspire, and to change for the better, or optimise.

My soul and my mind are most keenly attuned to these two industries or vocations. I love them beyond measure. I have since I could walk, talk, or read comic-books.

Were someone to cover my expenses, I'd do it for free.

I also find creativity to be a female I am in love with.

She is the art form through which any human being may give birth: to their own ideas, their own thoughts, and their own *creations*. And, since I am hugely sexist, believing women to be the superior sex, (fellas, I love ya, and I love being one of us, and god knows I'd never want to BE a woman. [screw *that*] I just prefer the look and taste of womanhood.) {Although I do harbor a suspicion that we are all, to some extent, bisexual} [how many times did I just contradict myself...?] she is the one by whom I find myself completely bewitched.

I'd probably be a politician, truth be known, had I the stomach to tolerate such brazen dishonesty, such repulsive corruption, and such grotesque deceit (to improve things, to make a difference, in whatever manner I could). Or if I just thought someone of my particular nature would be tolerated for longer than twenty-four hours in such a snakepit.

But on both counts, I don't.

I choose not to enter such a viper-nest and I don't think I'd last twenty-four hours in it anyway unless I was willing myself to become a viper.

And believe you me, you do not want that.

At *all*.

So I find that my Youprint (the blueprint of You) is to be a storyteller. That is what I love most. And because the line I come from is a working-class one, half-teacher and half-builder.

(For those of you out there with no idea as to what you wish to become, permit me to help. Just imagine every job in the world paid twenty grand a year, and resulted in no fame and no fortune - what then would you choose for your craft? To what then would you choose to dedicate your mind and soul? To what actual ACTivity would you commit yourself?)

However. I live in London. I am not *from* London. I have had to earn, fight, beg, borrow, work, cajole, plead and battle like a madman to stay in this city whilst chasing my dreams.

I aim to get the most from my life.

I aim to get as far as I can.

I aim to live the most fulfilling life I can, that might then help others find their Way.

I'm not saying I'm fit to be some kind of example.

But I'm certainly nuts enough to try.

I enjoy every second I am given, no matter how painful.

I am an Everyman.

But I am also a Lifeaholic one.

So: I spend all weekend on the phone to my nearest and dearest, finding out what they think; whether I am ready to become the person I wish to be, or whether I need yet more day-jobs to fund my existence in this beautiful woman of a city.

I listen to the advice of the wisest people I have ever met, and what they would do were they in my shoes.

Opinion, frustratingly but unsurprisingly, is divided.

"You're not ready," say some.

"Do it now while you have the chance," say others.

"Get another job in the City," advise a few.

I am lost.

I know what my heart is telling me, but if there is anything I have learned from the wisdom of my dear Metis, it is that the mind is more to be trusted.

My beloved Loki tells me different.

"If you don't do it now, you'll regret it for the rest of your life."

He is, to my mind, on the money.

You might be thinking that I have the most unusually named friends in the world. That would not surprise me. The situation is this: I rechristened all those for whom I care with new monikers- BTX names (more on that later). This name reflects their personality and what they mean to me. So: "Merlin" is called so because (1) he goes out of his way to educate me, (2) his work benefits the environment, and (3) he has a beard the size of Winnapeg, Minnesota.

It also allows me to speak of them without revealing their identity. But they know who they are.

The BTX (Beyond Talent eXperience) is so named because Talent will only get you so far. You need the discipline, perseverance, guts, fortitude, determination and discipline to translate your Talent into a career, success and rewards. And this is what our collective does. It features:

- Shanghai - former club promoter and doorgirl turned state educator
- Metis - 4 time EMA award-winning rapper and writer
- Blaqmale - top UK producer and hitmaker
- Rooster - award-winning film producer and actor
- Unia - Glamour model and actress turned psychologist
- LL Fortune - entrepreneur, surfer, former Club magnate
- BTP - a snowboard-instructing, world-travelling heiress of a party animal...

And many more.

I heed Loki's words. I step from the city with terror in my gut and I decide that I will give it a go, that I will chase my dreams.

This, I know, will mean I lose my home and have no money coming in, for maybe a year, maybe two. Maybe more.

I head home, afraid. I get the impression I may be making a grave mistake. But no matter. Rosie is coming over, and this will surely lighten my mood, since she's one of the most stunning women I have ever laid my eyes upon.

We've been together a happy three months. Several of my friends advise me to marry the woman.

Sod's Law.

Rosie and I are apparently ending it.

She believes, ironically, that I have been seeing other women. It's ironic because she is about the only woman in nigh on a decade I have seen exclusively, and the chances of her believing this are roughly nil.

Oh *goodie*.

She is hurt that she did not get to live with me for a week as we had discussed. She says I did not care for her as she cared for me.

I am so numb from working three jobs and from losing the most lucrative one, and from having to move home, that the loss of Rosie barely registers. It's only when my agent calls (for escorting) and tells me apologetically that she is leaving to Australia to give it another go with her husband that it all sinks in.

I sit in the living room in my King's Cross flat.

I am on the floor up against the radiator, having switched my phone on silent. I cannot handle speaking. In one swift week it has all fallen apart. I sit with a bottle of whisky drowning my sorrow.

I wonder if I am making a colossal mistake.

I swig the whisky and light a cigarette, and try not to cry.

I go to the gym the next day to work my frustrations out.

I hammer the punchbag so hard my knuckles bleed. The trainer tells me to ease off.

I am exhausted. I run for five miles. I lift weights. I let my iPod bang at me until, shattered, I think, "fuck it," and walk out.

I'm almost at Angel station when I see Rooster.

He's a diminutive British Asian who, bluntly putting it, saved my ass.

I saved a lot of money at the City job to make a music video I had envisioned for years. The producer and I fell out because the edit was not completed to my satisfaction, amongst other things.

I was left not with a music video, but with the wreckage of one.

Rooster is the guy who saved it for me. I owe the man a lifelong debt for that. I see him at the tube, just as I decide to walk back to King's Cross, since I need more time alone with my thoughts.

He tells me he's just been asked to produce a new feature film.

While I am elated for him, my heart breaks. I would dearly love to be involved in something like that. That's the whole reason I left in the first place. Feature films have been my dream since I was old enough to know what dreams were.

The movie is apparently something to do with assisted suicide, so he says, and stars a Slovakian lead character. I try to conceal the hurt and tell him I wish him all the best with it, and that if I can help, I'd love to be involved. But I'm a long way off playing the lead in feature films.

For many actors this takes years: years of background work, of scraping and living on the edge, or working for free and then working for free some more, and then working for free again.

I thank Rooster again for all his work as we have done almost ten different projects since my music video.

I start the walk back to King's Cross.

I absolutely *love* this area.

It is going to kill me to leave it.

When I first came to London to study at UCL and join the TA Paras, I did my runs (five to ten miles) round this area. It was, back then, a total shithole: full of drugpushers and more brass than a school band.

Now with St Pancras and King's Cross being regenerated, it's had millions of pounds put into it and is looking slickalicious.

Plus I can get to Euston to get home to see my family in very little time. And from King's Cross tube you can get *anywhere*.

The flat, despite being the size of a shoebox, is very good for me.

I am entirely independent and need or require no one. I have become more organised and disciplined than ever before. I've even sent off my first ever self-written, self-produced, self-performed track "Lost Tribe" to a music awards organisation (the EMA's: Exposure Music Awards) to see if my music is as good as I think it is.

See, music and film have been the goal for quite some time.

Well, actually, for my entire my life. I've owned a one-fifth share in a music studio for the last three years, in which, unbeknownst to my fellow brokers, I have been producing my first album after two years on the spoken-word circuit that saw me get to the finals of the UK Unsigned competition: not once, not twice, but thrice. All while I lived at King's Cross.

Yes, the area and I are in love.

But I trudge down the hill with heaviness in my heart and a post-gym knackered body. My City job never made me happy, but right now, the uncertainty and the constant losses are just making me *miserable*.

And there's still that niggling itch that says I am doing the wrong thing, that perhaps my father is right and this is all some childish impulse to see my own name in lights, or some other fatuous, idiotic craving.

I'm feeling blacker than night and am halfway home when my phone goes.

"Steve, are you home yet?" It's Rooster, bless his little cotton socks.

"Nah man, I'm about halfway there. Why, wassup?"

"I'm having a meeting with Milan about his feature, near Angel tube."

"What, the assisted-suicide-Slovakian-depressing one?" I ask.

"Yeah," he replies. "I've suggested he look at you to play the main character. I think you've got a shot at the lead."

I do my first about-turn in almost ten years and start running.

I sit at the pub table, dazed and confused.

I've been out of the City for less than a day, nearly had a breakdown, and this was *not* what I expected.

It marks a true first for me. I am being interviewed as to my suitability to play "Milan", the lead male in feature film "Morning Tea", written and directed by Milan Sebo.

The story and character (based on Milan himself) are both based on real events. Milan the character is a manic-depressive Slovakian, and has been sent to a kind of self-help group at which he meets a group of terminally ill people: Salwa, Serge, and Andrew being the most prominent.

Milan the character finds the therapy group pathetic, and takes the three off to form their own unit, whereat he encourages them all to take their own lives as an act of defiance - "retake control of your life by ending it yourself - don't die wasting away in torment" type stuff.

I can't believe this is happening. Milan the director is clearly a little discomfited at the idea of an Englishman playing a Slovakian.

And at *me* playing *him*. I commit his body language and accent to memory for future reference.

It seems he wanted to play the lead role himself but Rooster wouldn't have any of it. He's not a fan of people doing multiple things on a film. Stick to what you are good at, is his ethos.

Next day Milan the director sends me the script to look over. The film is *heavy* - with the Milan character being morally questionable, if not downright insidious. He encourages terminally ill people to kill themselves.

Which of course means I *love* it, which of course means *I want this fucking role*. Especially as I've read a lot of stuff recently about the Dignitas clinic. Assisted suicide is very 'now,' and is a matter on which I have no shortage of passion.

We go to the first script-read.

I read the script along with twelve other actors and actresses. I do it in the Slovak accent that I have worked and re-worked for nearly a week.

In the rehearsal, director Milan tells me to drop the accent as he thinks it might be "blocking me." That is until three cast members go up to him and ask "Is the lead guy *actually* Slovakian?" At which point he looks at me funny and then talks to Rooster.

I get the text message from Rooster later and nearly throw myself knacker-first out the window, I'm that happy.

"You got the part."

"Are you OK doing some method acting things?" Milan the director asks.

"Erm. Sure. Absolutely," I reply. Then, carefully, "Like what?"

Milan the director has had a brainwave to help me get into this whole "manic-depressive" shindig: crash-course-calorie-limitation dieting and sleep restriction to 4 hours a night.

You've got to be fucking *kidding* me...

"Really...?" I ask, a little unsurely.

"Really!" Milan the director replies, smiling.

I try not to cry.

So, I limit my calorie intake to 400-500 kcl per day by eating apples and slim-a-soups only, and altering what drinks I consume.

This, boys and girls, is *not* fun.

My weight drops by a stone in 4 weeks. I get less sleep than homophobes in prison.

I've memorised the script and know what my costume will be.

Ludicrously, whilst preparing for the movie, I also receive an email saying I am now nominated for the Exposure Music Awards "Best Artist - Out of Area" award for my "Lost Tribe" track.

I've just gone from being unemployed and homeless to a feature film actor and award-nominated musician. I'm so happy I nearly soil myself.

Now all I need is a place to live.

I'm about to go onset for ten days in a feature film production, and I play the lead. Suddenly, walking out of the City seems not so foolish after all.

I'm not a particular believer in fate, destiny, or astrology.

But I'd like to believe this is a sign.

"How would you feel about moving in together?"

The question takes me a little off guard, but to be honest I am grateful for it.

Rooster told me only weeks before that he and Chow Bella (a close friend of his and mine, a costume and wardrobe girl who also worked on my music video) had been burgled whilst living in Angel. So they had to move anyway.

We've been on the set of "Morning Tea" for almost a week, and everyone had heard about the burglary. Rooster suspects an inside job by someone in the building. Optimism is not his forte. However, knowing the sharpness of his game, he may well be right.

"Where you looking?" I ask.

They haven't started yet, is the upshot.

They know I was about to be looking due to the whole lost-all-my-income-and-needing-a-cheaper-place thing. So they want to see if I'd be a prospective new flatmate, since we all know each other and work in film and music (cinemusic).

I'll be honest: after living on my own for two years, it seems like a risk.

I often don't play well with others, and I can be a lot for people to take. I'm highly self-reliant, independent, and I like shit done my way. I can be foul-mouthed (no shit?), keep irregular hours, and let's face it, would you want to live with a male escort?

(If so girls, the number is 07779... heh, yeah, *right...*)

So I'm not sure. But there can be no harm in looking. And I do need a new place, pronto.

I do *not* want to go home to see my family for Christmas (a lifelong tradition - my family are *everything* to me) without having a place to live in London. I've been here ten years and survived.

Having to move home now (though not in a bad way) would be difficult for me to swallow professionally, and would be a kick to the nuts of my pride.

"Sure," says I, "let's have a look for something."

"Morning Tea" is a *blast*.

Playing the lead in a feature is even more than I hoped it would be.

I'm making amazing friends: Milan the director, all the cast, Serge the axe-ent, Salwa small, Andrew Iced-Tea-Chunderer, Amanda the makeup Queen, Eduardo the Latino location manager, Steve-O the camera guy, the sound man, and all the rest are just amazing to work with. Bartholomew the Schenk is a soldier, heaving the Red One camera (the size of a small village, and amazing, apparently, cause it's 4k, something to do with how many colours it picks up) around on his shoulder where others would end up in hospital with a dislocated life.

Smugz Malone proves to be a dark horse, and one of the funniest people I've ever met in my existence. Chen looks like a Chinese skier crossed with a five-year-old chef with a fake 'tache. And the art designer Popus ends up being a female rapper and singer of immense proportions who I will work with (and do other things with) [maybe] later.

And I'm left holding the bag with the character Milan, who I strike gold with in one sense and drop the ball on in another.

The following is Stephen Brocklehurst undercover secret material on the art form known as "acting". Actors of the world (which is really *people* of the world) take note:

DEFINITION – The Verb: "To Act"

1. To do something; exert energy or force; be employed or operative: *He acted promptly in the emergency, dousing the flames with his urine.*

2. To reach, make, or issue a decision on some matter: *I am required to act before noon tomorrow, or, say the kidnappers, my goldfish gets it.*

3. To operate or function in a particular way; perform specific duties or functions: *to act as manager, of a sex shop or bar, for example.*

4. To produce an effect; perform a function: *The medicine failed to act, but the amphetamines did just dandy.*

5. To behave or conduct oneself in a particular fashion: *to act well under all conditions, except when drunker than a priest in a nursery.*

6. To pretend; feign: *Act interested even if you're bored, no matter how roadkill-just-been-roadkilled she is.*

7. To perform as an actor: *He acted in three plays by Molière, who's as exciting as watching the extreme choir channel.*

8. To be capable of being performed: *His plays don't act well; the cast are all too busy shooting up.*

9. To serve or substitute (usually fol. by *for*): *In my absence the assistant manager will act for me; just provide him sufficient kleenex and a phone on vibrate.*

Notice: only on definition 7 is there anything to do with "pretending" or "feigning."

ACTing, ladies and germs, is not about pretending. It is about *doing*.

You cannot get out of bed or do *anything* at all without performing an ACTion or ACTing.

ACTing is not deception; it is ACTion.

Remember that.

So anyway: first up, here's how I drop the ball.

I know that this character isn't entirely likeable. Which is fair enough, given what he does. But he has to be watchable. And given that I'm playing him, I'm confident enough in that regard.

I'm not an arrogant actor, mind. I am just very, very, *very* confident.

I can do accents. I can change my body language. I have a repertoire of characters stored away for rainy days. I can do slapstick. I can do drama. I've done eight documentaries, four music videos, and a load of short films. I can act. I can even do presenting, if needs must.

However. This is my first feature film in which I play the lead. I want it to be something *special*.

So: I do the whole film in a Slovakian accent, for starters. I do the 400-calorie diet (apples and slim-a-soup) until I've lost a stone and am so tired I can't stay awake even if you try electro-shock therapy and occasional bouts of amateur dentistry. I keep a suicide diary (*not* light reading). I write a thirty-six-page backstory for the character. I begin depriving myself of sleep.

Not enough.

This has to be so good that when people look back at the line of characters I played, the reaction, whether they like him or not, is that the character Milan showed precisely what I was capable of even back then.

So I think I need two more things: hair and music.

So, Amanda (wonderful, wonderful, *wonderful* makeup girl and friend) and I come up with a hairstyle that is a bit nuts. It's all Wolverine-meets-someone-who-lives-in-a-wind-tunnel. I think Milan the director will hate it. Milan the director loves it.

To be fair, it looks wicked. It's a game changer.

And *yet*: here's how I drop the ball.

You only see the hair in a few scenes (thankfully one is the opening), and therefore the effect is hugely marginalised.

I had previously seen Milan the character as a guy who wears beanies (gives him a slight "is he ex-military?" look to him): which, when I watch the film back, reduces the impact of the hair and therefore the character.

Translation?

I fucked up: by not going with my gut and by playing it a little safe.

Rule number two: always admit your own mistakes, and only forgive them if you learn from them or fix them.

Then we have the music.

This is how I strike *gold*.

I see Milan as a very cerebral person. He's sharp as a tack on the inside, but just a little misguided.

I want to bring the complexity out through a kind of melancholy, a wistfulness that will make him harder to write off as a nutter, but will also make it more possible that he is seen as a psychopath (in the film he encourages terminally ill people to take their own lives as a reclamation of control - however it is never made explicitly clear that he is not doing it purely because he is a bit of a twisted bastard...).

So I want him to hum. Regularly.

I want him to hum something extremely profound and moving.

Not Beethoven's 23rd, mind, but something so potent that it actually glues itself to the observer's mind and gives the character real gravitas.

Brilliant idea, albeit a tad ambitious. Do you have any idea how accurate a piece of music must be in order for it to magnetise you to a psychopath?

I walk around my shoebox flat for over a week (not kidding) listening over and over to my entire CD and iTunes collection whilst making notes and drinking whisky (still not kidding) and humming over thirty-two melodies as sample ideas, tons of which going down the phone to my friends to see what they think, and some to my new woman Tasha (met her in the local dirty chicken shop) [*still* not kidding] who thinks I am literally mental (*so* not kidding).

It took me a fortnight to come up with the melody for my "Everyman" chorus. This is just as bad, if not worse.

Nothing works. Which pisses me off because I'm now seeing epic potential here: if I get this right, the score (soundtrack to the movie [interesting word for it, no?]) takes care of itself. If it is something the audience hears from Milan the character and also the film itself, people might walk out the cinema humming the tune to themselves and thenceforth no matter what they thought of it they would *remember* it.

This would give the film more impact, more weight. Milan might get hailed as a visionary director.

But nothing comes. I'm almost tearing my nasal hair out with a clamp, I'm so annoyed at myself.

And then, as if by magic, something happens.

I'm in the kitchen washing up, having left the TV on.

My mind, as ever, is preoccupied with a million things and is missing my mum and my Parimosita, when suddenly (my sense of direction or "the right way to go" is acute) the beautiful sound of the answer assails my ears.

I leg into the living room and stare at the TV.

It's the scene in "Shrek" where the Princess is singing in the forest.

It's a melody I've always had a lot of time for. It's wistful, loving, and speaks of profundity of character. Also (wonderfully) if I simplify and alter the melody (I'll not steal someone else's work - not now, not *ever*) the new "Morning Tea" version may still have historechoes (historical echoes) of its origin, meaning people will subconsciously think of certain elements of Shrek when they hear it.

"Shrek" of course is a comedy, but it also deals with a complete outsider, an ogre, the kind of person who just does not fit in. He's the kind of person who makes few friends and is perceived as being highly dangerous.

Perfecto *allstars*.

We're getting halfway decent here.

I rework the melody and start humming it, working out where in the script I can drop it in.

I'm over the moon with it.

It's so effective on set the makeup girl and the costume girl come up to me after the toilet scene and tell me they've been humming it themselves in between takes because it's so catchy.

That's what I'm talking about.

I'm ecstatic. I now feel I have done my job and that the director will be happy.

I'm onset talking to the crew (I make a point of helping the crew carry stuff and making tea for people - actors who won't get their hands dirty? You can fuck *off*...) when I get an email from Chow Bella.

She's just looked online and seen an apartment in Stratford (where?) that we apparently *have* to see (why?) according to estate agent FLKing (who?).

I ask Rooster if he's seen it. He says no. So, we agree to go take a look, reckoning it's a waste of time.

I'm a central London kinda guy. I love King's Cross. And the only good thing I've heard about Stratford is that it's a great place to go if you're suicidal but don't have enough cash for decent cyanide.

So my hopes are not exactly high.

"Fuck it, Roo," says I, "let's go have a look."

Stratford is not the Stratford you think it is.

It has bugger all to do with Shakespeare, for example. (If you don't know why I said that, put this book down, Google-map your nearest school, and then go there this instant. For ages.)

(As in, fucking *ages*...)

It does however have the new site for the Olympics, which is the biggest building site in Europe. It does have the location for the new Westfield shopping centre. It does lie on the East side of the capital.

The Stratford station itself is serviced by the jubilee line, the central line, an overground, and the DLR (Docklands Light Railway, for non-Londoners). And the station itself is next to the main bus station.

There is already a huge shopping centre next to the station, and when we get there it is crawling with police. London is making sure it is safe and dandy for 2012: the year Olympian.

Rooster and I get to the station and walk our way to the building that houses the flat we are here to see. I pray to myself silently that it is bigger than the shoebox I have lived in for two years.

As we walk and get to the street of our destination, I see a magical thing:

The building is *huge*. And it's only five minutes from the station. And more importantly, some weird but highly slick green laser fires out diagonally above the building. It looks like the bat signal fires up above over this magnificent work of man.

And then before you know it, we're in, past the concierge, in the lift, and up to the flat that may change everything.

My name is Milan, and I am in a mens' public toilets pretending to take a piss.

It stinks in this place. I hum the song of Milan quickly to calm some kind of... excitedness? Is it right? Can you say this?

Ah, *forget* it.

The man to my left wears a leather jacket. I like it, I think.

This is what I am thinking when I take the gun from my jeans and point it at his fucking head. His face goes white and he stares at the barrel. I smile.

His name is Will. He left Salwa when he found out she had bowel cancer. I saw the photo of the toilet. There was more blood than shit. It was disgusting. But you should not leave a woman when she is sick.

I tell him to get on his knees. He gets on his knees.

I tell him Serge and I have AIDS and that we are going to fuck him.

I don't have AIDS. But Serge does. Soon Will will.

Will cries. I smile. Serge laughs.

Will is now shaking. I point the gun in his face and tell him to tell me his fucking name.

He does not believe us. Serge chucks his HIV card on the floor.

I tell him we are going to fuck him in this filthy public toilet.

He scampers across the wet floor and cries in the corner.

He believes us *now*...

The apartment is *not* what I expected.

It is a duplex (split-level) *penthouse* apartment on the eighteenth and nineteenth floors, with three double bedrooms, a kitchen, two bathrooms, storage space, and a wraparound balcony.

It is amazing.

Roo and I are clearly thinking the same thing: something has to be wrong with this.

"So," Roo goes, "how much is it?"

I calculate at speed. Three bedrooms at say 200 apiece times four weeks per month is 2400 a month. So I'm thinking somewhere between that and three grand a month, which means I'll be hit for about 800 to 1000 a month, or 200 to 250 a week.

Net result: that's too much. I need a place way cheaper.

Rooster and I look off the balcony and the view is stunning. I can see all of London; the Dome, Canary Wharf, the river, everything.

"It's 1300 a month," the FLKing person says.

Rooster and I look at each other.

"What?"

"Pardon?"

"*EH*??"

Again I calculate: 1300 divided by 3 is 325 a week, which is 108 each. And apparently it includes water. I nearly laughwank there and then.

We look at each other again and both think something must be wrong.

There's space here to do some *shit*.

I can bring my music recording equipment here, Rooster can have his film-editing suite, and we can throw house parties like a mowfowe.

If we felt like it, we could start a *zoo* in here.

That means we don't just have a residence; we'd have a music studio, a film suite, a photography set, a party location, *and* an apartment.

This house is *hot*...

If Rooster and Chow Bella are down, then fuck me running, I'm in like sin.

We look off the balcony as it gets darker, and yet another coup the estate agent forgot to inform us of: cutting across the first green laser that *literally* shoots directly above the building, far off in the distance, is another laser directly opposite.

The building points skyward from the baseline of the Earth's surface up into the point of a triangle that forms above its peak. The first laser must come from the Greenwich Observatory or something very close to it.

This must be or be damn near to the Greenwich Meridian. That means...

The flat lies as near-as-dammit-is-to-swearing directly upon the line that defines time.

I'm so sold I may as well have a white post sticking out of my head with a sign on it.

I speak to my parents about the wisdom of it all; the notion of having housemates still seeming like a risk. One of them is as eloquent as ever:

"Steve, don't be stupid: you go somewhere on your own and it'll cost you twice that, and this way you'll have a flat full of people who do cinemusic. How can you beat that? Don't be a twat."

'Nuff said.

Chow Bella, Rooster and I discuss it all and agree: we're having it.

There's only one week to go till the end of "Morning Tea," and I'm about to move into a duplex Penthouse in London at the age of twenty-nine with a line producer and a costume and wardrobe girl, both of whom are friends, in a building next to the two biggest sites in Europe that is situated on the line of time.

'Nuff said yet again.

Wanna help yourself out at the end of a year?

Will the court please note: Exhibit T - my list of resolutions.

For the last three or so years I have made resolutions every New Year's Eve on a variety of subjects, but in general:

- Health related
- Women related
- Family related
- Film related
- Music related
- Writing related
- Fun related

There's usually about six or seven per category.

Of those resolutions I have pretty much knocked 80-85% out the ballpark.

And considering they normally number around fifty or sixty in total, I'd say that ain't too shabby.

This year, for example, I'm hoping to complete the following (in their respective groups):

WRITTEN (4)
- ImmorTalented / Lifeaholic (my book)
- A TV show (TBC)
- My first short (Loveblind)
- My first feature (TBC)

MUSICFILM (9)
- Finish my album mix
- Master my album
- Sell my album / get signed / get management
- Do five feature films
- Do a Hollywood feature
- Do first film score music
- Get your own agent
- Complete your album art
- Write a Clubland Treatment (wrong category, dipshit)

HEALTH (4)
- Quit smoking
- Stay at thirteen stone
- 180 gym visits
- 1000 calorie a day diet

LIFEAHOLISM (7)
- Bungee jump

- Go to LA for a fortnight
- See a Darksky
- Do a standup comedy show
- Have a thirtieth birthday holiday
- See the Cannes Film Festival
- Take Driving Lessons

FAMILY-WOMEN-MISCELLANEOUS (6)
- Make six trips home minimum
- "Meet" twelve new women
- Sign up to Ray Knight extras agency
- Sign up to Casting Collective extras agency
- Sign up to Mad Dog extras agency
- Save the 10k you need for next year's rent and bills

TOTAL RESOLUTIONS = Thirty

I record these in my diary (my absolute life to me) and I monitor them weekly, monthly, yearly.

As I also do my weight, my calorie intake, how much I do or don't smoke and drink, and more.

Er, what?

Are you fucking *crazy*?

No chicos and chicas, I'm not. Ever since I had to calorie diet for "Morning Tea", I liked having my weight under my control. As in, *control*.

Now, I've been a lot of shapes and sizes – I've been sporty slim, kickboxer lean, drinks-too-much chubby, outright fat, parachute regiment fit, citybroker loose, dance-instructor cut, and weightlifter built (and I have the pics to prove them all). But often these were not deliberate choices but the results of circumstance or work: the lack of deliberate choice, to put it plainly.

Not any more.

Now I monitor my calorie intake meal by meal so I know what I burn and I know what I consume.

A page in my diary contains the following information on a daily basis (this is a sample from "Morning Tea" time, assuming on set working all day is the equivalent of one gym session burning 550 calories [also assuming I burn 550 calories a day naturally] <which is WAY too low> {but this is how you get it done, people}): -

Weight: 13.1st 82kg

53

Breakfast Cal:	100 cal (two apples)
Teas Cal:	150 cal (three teas)
Lunch Cal:	50 cal (one light soup)
Snack Cal:	100 cal (one banana)
Dinner Cal:	100 cal (one apple and one light soup)

TOTAL CAL: + 500 cal

Cal Burn Work: - 550 cal

Cal Burn Life: - 550 cal (total burn 1100 cal)

NET CAL: - 600 cal

And that's how you lose a lot of weight quickly.

And probably also how you die very stupidly.

In my diary I also monitor my daily finances, my goals, and several other KPIs that I deem essential to my life.

I have lost my keys, my phone, my shoes, and once even on one occasion an entire pair of jeans with all of that lot in at once (don't ask).

I have, however, *never* lost my diary. Ever.

At work they used to call me "The Machine" because I'm basically an organisational psychopath. I like shit organised to the point of lunacy.

Because organising yourself means you are efficient and in control. And only then can you be fit to organise or manage or direct others.

I look back at the results of the month.

I've been cast in my first feature. I've found a new place to live. I've been nominated for a music award. And it's not even Christmas…

Speaking of which, it's time to go home.

Home is in the West Midlands, the very heart of the country, two hours away by train to the North.

Christmas is my time to head home and see my family. I could write an entire book about my family but the odds are if I did that I'd not have any family left.

So we'll avoid that.

It's been a lifelong tradition for me to go home at Christmas. I use the time to regenerate and have some personal time to recuperate from a year of battering my body to batshit.

My mum, my nan, my dad, and my friends all assist in making me human again.

My mum above all brings me back down to planet Earth and reminds me what life is actually all about, and is the reason I do all this in the first place.

I take immense pride in being a good son. Or at least in being a decent one.

I have made cardinal errors and committed unholy sins.

I have lied, betrayed, chickened out, got drunk, got high, broken laws, started fights, had my ass kicked, lost money, gambled, failed to turn up, not answered my phone, threatened people, quit jobs, fired people, quit hobbies, smoked, fucked, impregnated, aborted, and done all kinds of things I am not proud of.

In some ways I suppose you could say that the battle I fight is some karmic method of seeking atonement.

If that is the case, I am nowhere near good enough at what I do.

Do I have a guilty conscience?

No.

Because all of the above are things I admit freely and am fighting to correct.

I make no claims of perfection. I am not a martyr. I am not even a particularly good role model.

The day my best friend announced me as the godfather to his son, he said he did so because he wanted someone 'reliable,' who had 'good timekeeping' and 'solid communication skills.'

My own frickin' mother yelled out "you sure you're talking about the right person....?"

Cheers, Mum.

However: in one aspect above all others, I'll take you all on right *now*.

If you find someone who works harder at their craft than I do then I'll kneel before them happily. I have no ego issues other than with myself.

If you can find a better friend to his friends than am I, I'll eat my own toilet.

If you can find someone who dreams bigger and works harder to manifest those dreams than me, then bring 'em over here.

I could do with a week or two off.

There is no shame in admitting and celebrating the greatness of others. And this means there is no shame in admitting and celebrating one's own greatness.

The trick is becoming or getting or achieving it in the first place.

So I head home a bag of mixed emotions.

The year ahead is to be my first true foray into the only industry in which I believe my happiness and fulfilment may be located.

And that shall be the main subject of my writing.

The year ahead.

The year:

- I turned **30**
- I left the City and quit trying to play it safe (**SafePlay**)
- I began my career full-time in film and music (**DreamChasing**)
- I moved to the East Side of London, and for the first time ever made it my *home*
- I starred in my first lead role in a feature film: **Status & CV Update - Feature Film Actor**
- I completed my album – and am now a **two-time award-nominated** singer and rapper

I sit on the train with a head full of questions and a chest full of resolve.

Twelve months.

I have twelve months to get as far as I can.

With the money I have saved, I may just be able to last two years instead of one.

I have that long to get what I need.

Am I going to succeed?

Sirs and Ladies, I am not psychic. I cannot answer that. I can only tell you I am going to go to *war* for it.

I believe life and the universe are mathematical. If I work hard enough I should receive that for which I toil.

But how can I check it?

How can I prove I have done what I need, and avoid the necessity of 'trusting myself?'

Lightening strikes while I am on the train.

As a writer I've written over fifty poems, twenty short stories, twenty-five songs (hence the album), loads of scripts, a novel (almost) and a belief system. I love writing.

Aha.

Light bulb moment.

I'll keep *another* diary.

I have my normal diary for my time and organisation. I'll start a new one that covers what I do during the year.

Twelve chapters. One for each month. I'll even integrate it with my album and with my forthcoming films.

It'll be the most ambitious thing I've ever done: a 360-degree project that pulls together:

- **"Lifeaholic"** (the diary / novel of my first year in entertainment and music full time)
- **"ImmorTalented"** (my album that encapsulates what I feel)
- The first music video I ever made: **"Everyman"**
- **"Talent 2009"** (my documentary by Dennis Lowe)
- Some kind of feature film, probably "**Radio London.**"
- My first ever feature film: "**Morning Tea.**"
- Some kind of TV show, and...
- **Cartel Clothing** (a clothing brand for others to show they share similar beliefs / tastes / ideals)
- **"Parimosita":** my second music video
- And a new venue, yet to be confirmed...

I start laughing at my own craziness.

No wonder people think I'm nuts. The phrase "that can't be done" jumps involuntarily into my mind.

It sounds like too much to do in twelve months. Hell, it sounds like too much to do in twelve *years*.

It sounds, even to me, like it's impossible.

I don't even have an agent, or a manager, or any form of help outside family and friends, and bluntly put, it's not their problem.

But fuck it.

I didn't come into this world to be some pussy that sticks to job description only.

Screw that.

I'm going to do it or get as close as I can without hospitalising myself.

I head home with a new sense of purpose.

I now have a method of checking my own progress that will also give me a new product that people might find interesting, and that would also serve as a kind of manual for aspiring musicians or actors.

And that would act as my mission statement.

The train passes Coventry. I am almost home.

And I know exactly how the novel might end.

It'll be me going home at the end of 2010 to see my mum and my friends and my family.

And the distance between now and then, whatever ascension or fall I have gone through, will be my judge, committed to print.

I smile.

The idea has merit.

If I can stick to it then the world's my oyster:

The first year doing film and music full-time.

This is also the year I turn thirty.

This is also the year my school friends turn thirty.

This is also the year 2010.

I begin scribbling notes to see if this has any significance (train journeys are immensely useful for this - take out a pen and pad and see what happens) [I've written some of my best material on trains... see the track "Only Son" for proof].

My scribbles, once translated, look a little like this:

The year is 2010. 2010 if you split it is 20 and 10.

If you add 20 and 10 you get **30**.

So now we have 2010 and 30 as their total.

2010 is the year and **30** will also be my age.

Hmm. That's convenient. How about my date of birth?

The 5th of July 1980. Nothing there. Wait, what if we write it numerically?

5 - 7 - 1 - 9 - 8 - 0.

What happens if we add those together?

$5 + 7 + 1 + 9 + 8 + 0 = $ **30**.

Hmmmm.

Now we have 2010 the year, 30 my age, and 30 the sum of my birthdate.

That's even *more* convenient.

That's 3 numbers that lead to 30. 3 points being made. Three points being made is a triangle. Three sets of 10.

If you take the zeroes away from the year, my age and the birth-sum you have 3.

And 3 is the number of triangles. So 30 would be the number of 10 triangles.

Hmmmmm.

3 numbers that lead to 30 and triangles and a year of trinities.

I walk from the train and through the station. The sight I see outside the station makes me feel a hundred million times better about the world in general.
My home and my reason for being are sat in the car before me.
I head home to sleep and prepare for the year ahead, which is apparently to be the year of Trinities and the first year I chase my dreams with no distractions.
Bring.
      It.
         On.

QUARTER ONE – WINTERSPRING:
The Opening Salvo

Stephen "Talent" Brocklehurst

As "Milan" in "Morning Tea"

In the "Everyman" video – award-nominated

"Dr. Invictus Schadenfreude"

JANUARY 2010:

"RETURN TO LONDINIUM AND OHHH, BROTHER..."

"And When My Primal Roar, Steals From Out My Lungs,
Then Up On Wings I Soar, Until My Time is Done..."

- Talent -
"Lost Tribe"

- IMMORTALENTED 2013 -

So I'm coming back to London, and I'm armed to the teeth with several things.

First up is my new MacBook, which is so the nuts I think it may actually have pubic hair. I'll soon be able to record my own music and vocals.

Secondly is a new sense of freedom. I am returning to my city with fire in my guts.

Seen the family? Check. Had a little break? Check. Sorted the flat out? Check. Time to attack film and music as you have dreamt of doing since you were a boy? Check city, babycakes.

And I'm looking forward to getting back in the new flat; the new hotspot at Studio 107 that is destined to become "The HOTHouse."

But more on that later.

For now, I can't wait to see the view, the East side of London (heh - I'm an East Sider now... makes me feel like I should throw up gang signs and walk like I recently stepped toe-first into a paving slab), the Olympolice, everything.

I then recall our flat is on a pre-paid meter, and is all electricity.

We have no gas. OK, cool, no worries. I enter the flat and grab the prepay card, bomb it round the corner shop and ask for 40 quid's worth. May as well light up for a week, right?

Right. So: 40 quid goes on it, and I then step into the building, enter it in the metre, and get ready to chill out till the cows come home.

Except there *is* no light. There *is* no electricity. There is therefore no *heat*. And this is not like being at ground level and being somewhat chilly. Oh *no sir-ree*.

This is being perched naked atop the eighteenth and nineteenth floor in the bleak midwinter with frostwinds howling past your glass-walled flat and thinking you'd rather be back home in Kansas.

Wherever that may be.

It's nut-shrivelingly cold, and I am unamused: as are Rooster and Chow Bella when they return days later.

We are all of us sat in the flat huddled up and freezing. Possibly to death.

I put on a big jacket. Nothing.

I try wearing another pair of socks. Bupkiss.

I have a shot at another jumper and pair of underwear (though obviously not in that order) [may actually have been more fun...]. I may as well have put on a napkin.

I head downstairs and grab a duvet. I now feel slightly better, however the temperature is dropping. I can now see my own breath.

The electricity firm (who shall remain nameless... but they're French, if that helps...) explains the situation.

"Your former tenants at that property have an outstanding balance on the meter. This must be cleared or the meter itself changed and reset before you can get your electricity working. Sir."

"N-n-no p-problem mate... h-h-h-how much... izzz... itt?"

A pause. I can still see my breath in the air.

"It's considerable, Sir," the teleguy tells me.

"I... d-d-d-d-d-don't... f-f-f-f-fucking.... c-c-care..." I reply. "H-ow... m-m-m-much... ?"

"Their balance is two thousand one hundred seventy-six pounds and seventy-six pence. Sir."

Fuck.

"F-f-f-f-fuck..." says I. "I s-s-s-s-s-s-s-see..." I hang up.

Now, I've never worked for an electric company. And I'm not much of an engineer. In fact I can't even rewire a plug.

Technologically speaking, if your choice was either to get my advice or to get assistance from a sack of wet hair, I'd choose the latter.

But surely, *surely*, the point of a frickin' prepay metre is to avoid this problem entirely? I.e. no payee, no lightee.

Geddit?

Apparently not. Over two grand. What a fucking shambles. I have to go downstairs and sleep with a girl in the building just to get a warm bed. It's nonsense.

We have days of literally freezing our asses off. I see more of my breath than I am comfortable with.

When the engineer finally does come over to sort all this mess out, I'm so grateful for this basic kindness (even though I know it is his job) that I nearly shed tears and start hugging him. We've been fucking cold.

He's even kind enough to refund my £40.00, which I find difficult to believe he does, but he does, nonetheless.

Next day we at least wise up a bit. We get candles, or tea-lights, or whatever the hell they're called. We get loads. As in, like fifty.

I'm not sitting there like *that* again.

I've been back in London a couple weeks and all I've been doing is setting up my flat.

Time for that to change.

Rooster and I sit and talk at length about acting, and about where best to advertise online. If you're an actor you have to have your shit together, or life will chew you up like dogmeat.

I book in a photo shoot with a friend called Abdul Basit who is both a fellow Cityman and a photographer. On both counts, due to my history, we understand each other. It's nice to see other Cityfolk who have more than just making money on their mind.

My friend Roger Birch, who'll be getting engaged later this year, is a similar cat. We've got designs on a clothing label. Plus he's safe as houses, and used to be built like one.

I get some headshots and start putting together my CV. I've just been in "Morning Tea", a feature film, and have done a decent number of projects before that.

So at the very least, the CV won't embarass me.

I advertise it on Starnow, CastingCallPro, and Spotlight. For good measure I find another six sites and advertise there too.

Rooster gives me a copy of the actor's handbook so I can get my emails and info sent out to agents.

I decided I wanted an agent in my first six months, so we gotta get cracking. If you're an actor, you have to have an agent. If you want a decent agent, then you probably need to interview with ten, which means you need to advertise to about a hundred.

I decide therefore to send my stuff to 250 agents and see what happens. This is *not* likely to get done in a week, since I also have to compose the actual email, get the headshot and CV attached, and somehow get my showreel done.

For which I currently only have:

- My music video, "Everyman"
- My documentaries
- My short, "One Way Street"
- And hopefully soon a cut of "Morning Tea"

And getting a showreel done isn't cheap. This is all going to be expensive.

To give you an idea of what "expensive" means, I'll explain:

- My music video and website cost me roughly 15k last year
- My rent for the year just to *survive* is going to cost me 7.5k
- My costs for the year if they stay at 500 a month (which is not a fortune in Hotcity [London]) are also going to be about 6.5k
- My documentaries cost me about 2k
- For a total of 15k this *year* before I even buy a *pint...*

So you can see, being in my line of work is expensive.

Truth be told, this is why so many creatives don't make it. It's devilishly expensive here: you often have long periods of no work, and all the people who are meant to help you (agents, managers) want you to prove yourself before you do.

You kind of have to make it without them, and then they sweep in and take a lot of the credit for "finding" you.

It's a *long* road.

So my days ahead need to ensure all my correspondence is top notch.

I'm composing my email and checking all the agents in London one day whilst Rooster, Chow Bella and I tidy the flat, when I get an email from someone at a TV production company.

This particular TV production company is one I recognise; hell, it's one *you'd* recognise, as they make probably the biggest reality TV show in history.

I immediately know it for what it must be: a prank. Some friend of mine has found my profile and sent me a wind-up.

The email, or as much of it as I can retell legally, reads:

"Dear Stephen,

After reading your profile on Starnow, we would like to invite you to audition to be a ********* on *** *******, as your bio makes you sound like the perfect candidate. We have a few questions about your profile, i.e. how much of it is accurate and how much of it is "artistic overselling". Please get in touch with us on the details below asap.

Dionne
****
For Channel *."

Yeah.
Right. Cause I was born yesterday.
My reply reads:

"Dear Whoeverthefuck

Nice try. Whichever mate of mine this is, believe you me I'll get you back a thousandfold. If you're going to yank my chain, at least pick a show I *might* at least bite at, as you know that I absolutely fucking *despise* *** ******* and all it stands for. Go schnig yourself.

Yours,

Brock"

I smile and put the laptop away to get back to cleaning.

66

Rooster and Chow Bella and I have almost got it licked when my phone rings. I pick it up.

"Yeah?" says I.

"Hello Stephen? This is Dionne from *******. We just received a rather colourful email from you. Do you have a minute?" says her.

My guts nearly drop out of my arse. I freeze.

"Erm. Haha. *Ha*. Er. Sure? Is this a piss-take?"

"Ah, no Stephen, this is not a, as you call it, piss-take."

I eventually put the phone down and see Rooster and Chow Bella collapsing in fits of laughter.

"You're never going to do it?" Chow Bella asks. "Are you?"

I shrug my shoulders. I see Rooster still chortling his buttnuggets off.

My voice is vinegary as hell.

"Shut *up* yer laughin'. Bitches."

I spend a good deal of time writing a short based on my experiences as a male escort.

I alter the events enough to avoid being sued and change the main character slightly from me to a blind man to give him more character.

Rooster introduced me a while back to a gifted director by the name of Garrett Millerick, and I'm thinking he's the guy to direct it, primarily because he has a heart of gold and is highly sensitive, and the film needs someone sensitive at the reins if it's not me.

Garrett and I meet several times, and while we have a tough time agreeing on "Loveblind," we both love movies, TV and women, and have a great many things in common.

He's also, like Smugz, one of the funniest people you can ever meet. Having people like this around keeps me both grounded and sane.

His background is mostly that of being an actor, and he has a great understanding of how actors work.

This at present is important, because between him and Rooster I'm digging up all the information a man can possibly get on auditioning and being an actor.

And make no mistake; this profession is highly sought after.

Lead actors in Hollywood productions get paid a fortune for what is perceived to be one of the most exciting jobs in the world in return for worldwide fame and fortune.

Music and film are recognised as glitzy and glamorous to pretty much everyone who doesn't work in them.

And that's still not why I'm doing it. But it's important to know.

So I get my boy Abdul to do my first photo shoot to get my headshots.

The issue is that I hate having my headshot taken, because that *does* feel like self-indulgence. I go to Abdul's place and meet both him and his lady, who ends up being something of a creative herself and a lovely person.

We talk about prospective films and how everyone has been doing, and then move onto me getting my headshot done.

This is trickier than said due to the fact my mind is mostly occupied by my boy Metis, and by Tasha.

Metis is one of my very, very, *very* best friends. It's thanks to him I've been doing music for the last four or so years.

I've spent much of my life developing the kind of group of friends you'd sell your own 'nads for. Kev, Shanghai, Loki, Chrissie E, Sharvitsu, Lope, BTP, Merlin, Ayan, Thiscock, TnT, LL, Rooster, Flowgirl, and Rosemania are amongst the very closest.

Metis is my joint best friend and is an uber-legend.

He's conquered the worlds of basketball, finance, and music, and is in the dictionary under various phrases including "success story" and "determined" and "prodigy."

He's got a listening session coming up at Bungalow 8, which is one of the coolest clubs in one of the coolest cities in the world.

I'm nervous on his behalf, not because I have any doubt about how it's going to go, but because I want it to go so well it smashes everyone out the building.

Which I'm sure it will, but I send everyone on my Facebook an email and message about the listening sesh anyway. When it comes to screwing up, if it's between underdoing it or overkill, I'm overkill central.

And to be fair, I suppose I'd better explain.

Metis and I started in music at the same time.

I was a nightclub promoter in central London for some of the hottest venues in the world and he was the world's best banker-to-be at the world's best bank.

Again, being honest, when I met the man I couldn't stand him.

Predominantly because he was the most similar man to me I'd ever met, and because my little sister (by life, not birth) was enamoured of him and trying to get me to like him.

Note to all: you want me to like someone, put them near me and shut the fuck up.

Let me judge for myself.

The best way to ruin a person or a movie for me is to spoil the ending or make me miss the trailers. I'll pick who and what I like, thank you.

So he and I over the course of years, nights out, and many, many conversations, become friends.

I realise more and more that he is like my mirror image, except from a different place and DNA strand.

He ends up introducing me to hip-hop in such a way that its impact on me is massive.

As in, it occurs to me, despite its massive global success, to be one of the most highly evolved art forms of civilisation and to have been somewhat ignored by millions of people.

It's poetry put to cutting-edge music. It's like Shakespeare played to modern day Tchaikovsky. In a sense.

We end up going to a show to watch a guy called Saul Williams, after watching his extraordinary film "Slam."

It finds its origin in a craft called 'Spoken Word'. This art form is best summed up thus: it's performance poetry mixed in with freestyle and rapping, usually performed acapella.

We go to see this man, Saul Williams, at Scala in King's Cross, after watching his movie.

69

Ever since watching it a thought had been germinating in the hive of my mind. The thought had been something akin to the fact that I needed to get in the entertainment game sooner rather than later.

I'd back-burnered it since returning from the States ten years ago, and the hip-hop education and spoken word intro had made me think that perhaps it all needed to begin *right now*.

We watched Saul Williams smash the living daylights out of it.

By which I mean he took simply his voice and the occasional bout of background music and had made almost a thousand people go *crazy*.

Me included.

The sheer force of the honesty, of the realness, moved me profoundly. This is not ordinary speech. It's speech with all the bullshit and fat cut out of it.

And this, we call Realspeak.

Metis and I walked home, and on the way we said almost nothing to each other. Sometimes the mark of good company is the lack of any need to speak.

When speak we eventually did, the only sentence I could think of that made any sense was:

"We need to do that."

"Hm?" he more than understandably replied.

It took me a minute to summon the courage to say it again.

See the thing is, sometimes you have to give breath to truth to actually be able to externalise it and look at it.

And saying it and then externalizing it means acknowledging it.

And that means actually having to *do* it.

That, or, be a pussy.

And I, Ladies and Gentlemaniacs, am no pussy.

"We need. To do. *That*."

He looked at me.

"Yes. Yes, we do."

And here's the thing about friends.

There's two kinds.

The first kind will tell you the truth whether you like it or not; compliments when you don't think you deserve them and criticism when you are scared to hear it. And even if everyone else on Earth says you are smashing it, they come back to you and *still* raise the bar to places you aren't sure you can even reach.

They challenge you to be the best you can be.

The other kind of friend? I don't know a great deal about them, but from what I hear, it's pretty much everyone else.

So literally weeks later we were preparing our first performance at a bar called Motion that held a night called "Poetry In Motion."

I'll not recount all the events, but suffice to say I was scared out of my wits to the point I couldn't read my own writing or hold the paper on which it was written without my hand shaking. I had to improv my first ever live freestyle just to hold it together.

My mother summed it and me up pretty well that night.

"Your freestyle was better than the poem."

She was right. The crowd had given us a decent reaction. But the thing about a 'decent' reaction is, it makes you want a fucking *animal* one.

I took one look at Metis's face and saw the exact, precise, identical reaction.

This needs *practice*, is what the look said.

I smiled and nodded.

I'll not forget that night.

Ever.

And when a friend raises the bar, it's only polite to raise it back.

And on that note I head with Tom, Kev, and Chrissie E to my boy Sharv's thirtieth birthday.

Sharv is one of my oldest and closest friends from my secondary school, and in life in general. I can't say I made a massive contribution to his birthday, but I was there and that's what matters.

My mind, typically, was Otherwhere, occupied with notions of my boy's listening session, and a documentary that was likely to cause me no small degree of pain.

Rooster and I spend forever trying to get the flat in order.

We fix up the door-phone, we order internet, and after we spent hours upon hours on the phone we get our electric sorted.

By 'sorted,' I mean we do the following, so pissed off are we at the fact we spent nearly a week at the top of a tower with no heating or lights:

We make a list of every electrical company in the city.

We call them.

We tell them we are unhappy with ***, our current supplier, and that we want to know what deals they have for people who wish to switch.

They offer us deals ranging from 10 to 15% off.

We call all the other companies back.

We tell them we have been offered 10 to 15% off for the first year if we switch.

They offer us better deals, ranging from 15 to 20%.

We calculate which companies charge the least per megawatt hour (at this point I am nearly gnawing off my own face in sheer boredom) and we draw up a shortlist.

We call them all back again, explaining we have been offered discounts of 15 to 20%.

Most of them say they cannot match this kind of saving.

Four of them can.

They offer us up to 25% off the first year, and even more if we pay online, and even more if we have a fixed rate.

We sit and discuss this.

Rooster and I are now close to nasal bleeding from the sheer volume of phone calls and call time.

(It's all "Dial 1 for a pointless answer phone message; dial 2 if you just want to hear shitty elevator music; dial 3 to enquire about your bill; dial 4 to order my cousin Roger's pizza for him; dial 5 to tell us how great we are, or dial 6 if you want to speak to an actual human being, in which case we'll just play you all the options again...")

After almost an entire day on the phone, we have our chief two candidates, both of which will give us 28% off the first year and will love us long time.

Now: it's 'Moment of Truth' time.

I don't like to leave someone or something out of anger without first giving them a chance to rectify it.

So, Rooster calls ***, our current energy supplier, who left us at the top of the Eiffel Tower in winter with no heat and electricity, and tried to charge us over two grand we didn't owe to turn it back on, to offer them a last-ditch chance at salvation.

"Yeah. Yeah, we're looking at cheaper alternatives. We've spoken to fourteen suppliers and at least two of them are offering us 28% discounts on the first year's bills. We thought we'd call you to see what deals you might offer existing customers in such an instance to encourage them not to leave your company.... yes... yes I understand that..."

I watch with fascination. Rooster has that thing that I do not and never have possessed - a natural inclination and tendency towards negotiation.

"... yes... we had no electricity for a week... yes we were freezing... no, I mean *literally* freezing..."

I can imagine a guy at the other end starting to feel the need to loosen his collar.

"... that's right... no lighting either... we actually had to buy fairy lights... no, fairy *lights*..."

I just need popcorn and some music and this'd make a wicked show.

"... that's correct... we've had discounts offered of 20 to 25% from a lot of your competition... two of whom... yes I said two... two of whom are offering 28% off the first year with online payments and a fixed fee monthly..."

I'm almost applauding. Give me five minutes and it'll be a standing ovation...

"... yes... yes... uh-huh... yes we'd like to know what discounts you can offer to encourage people to get them to stay so you don't lose all your customers... yeah... yes I'll hold..."

I'm dying to hear this. Surely it's gotta be "If you find a price to beat ours, we'll match it", right?

"... Uh-huh... yeah... uh-huh... erm... how much?"

I'm still as night.

"2%? I'm... I'm sorry... you can offer us a discount of 2%?"

I collapse into an immediate fit of outright belly laughter.

Rooster hovers at the brink of losing his shit and then finally also collapses into a riot of laughter. While he's still on the phone.

2%. In this day and age. I laugh so hard I fear I may just burst a lung.

I realise while we're sorting things that the documentary I am about to see scares me to no small degree.

The documentary that is concerning me was made by Daniella Alencar. She is going out with one of my best friends, Jimmy Jam.

Jimmy Jam was kind enough to work our till for us back in the days of Clubland, and was Loki's best friend at the time. He became one of mine. Not too many people can be trusted with running your till without nicking money. Jimmy Jam can.

Dani studies film and wants to work in it in the future. She's asked if she can do a documentary on me (why do these people ask for such trouble? Are they gluttons for punishment?) and natch (naturally), I've said yes.

The issue is, the documentary was about Metis and I being nominated for our first music awards. And while Metis slam-hammered it, the documentary I'm sure is going to be an "Awwww...he almost made it" kind of film on Yours Truly.

Cause I was nominated, but I didn't win. Twice. And this kind of sympathy-evocative, lost-but-almost-won piece I may well be able to live without.

However, Dani is a generous and sensitive person, so I'm hoping I don't come out like a complete moron.

We'll see. And even if the documentary bites a big one, what I want to see *more* is the "Morning Tea" cut.

I go to an initial "Morning Tea" screening with Rooster, but my mind is elsewhere. I'm trying to work out how best to finish my album *and* get an agent *and* score a new feature *and* stay sane.

It's not easy.

I get accused of juggling too many things at once by a lot of people.

If I were a less agreeable man, I'd accuse them of doing far too little and far too infrequently. However. I don't.

Right now my mind is populated by the words I heard during a recent encounter with my new girl, Tasha.

"You're supposed to be this man of passion, this artist, this guy who's living for such a cause, but you're not. You're full of shit."

Tasha is the kind of girl that by all rights, you'd marry. She's beautiful, sexy as hell (most women who dance at Secrets tend to be), and better read than I am.

"You're colder than any man I've ever met, and I can prove it."

See the thing is, I actually *am* in love with this stunning young woman. I don't spend my time with women unless I'm in love with them. I just happen to fall in love pretty often because I reckon, at heart, I'm a romantic.

I love most people I meet and certainly everyone on the planet. My respect and loyalty, my intimacy and closeness, on the other hand, are not easy to come by. And I know, for sure, *any* second, we're gonna go through...

"...Why it is you won't introduce me to your friends? If I'm that important to you and you're all about the truth like you say, then tell me why you've met all my friends and I haven't met any of yours? Why haven't I met Metis? Eh? EH?"

I can't help but smile. I've had this conversation a hundred times before and I'm sure that until Miss Right walks in I'm going to have it a hundred times again.

"What is it? Am I not enough for you? I get guys asking me out all the *time*. I'm not some chavvy illiterate who can't spell her name without a dictionary."

I actually laugh out loud. And partly because she's right. My friends would probably love to meet her and I'd love to take her out, but until there's proof that she's going to survive the shitstorm that is my life, I see no point in that.

"I mean, I know we're compatible sexually because, I mean come *on*, but I don't actually know anything about you."

Here she's wrong. She knows so much about me it's ridiculous. I tend to accelerate the get-to-know-each-other process as much as possible as a matter of habit.

Attraction equals comfort multiplied by interest. And we know a load about each other. What she means is that she knows very little about me *as a person*. She can't tell what I'm *thinking*. She can't predict what I'll do. And I'm *actually* pretty simple to understand.

What's irking her is that while she cannot do this to me, I've been able to do this to her since pretty much the moment we encountered each other.

"You're one of the most complex people I've ever met. I'm surprised you've not been locked up. With your history you ought to be in a mental facility, and I'm thrilled you're not, but Hoots Magoo (*eh?*), you're not the easiest guy to cope with..."

OK maybe simplicity isn't my strong point. My Parimosita used to say a similar thing. I really can't see how I'm that complic...

"And the open relationship thing's just bullshit. Bull-shit. No one does that (Actually, both my best friend and I do. And the people at Killing Kittens... and the...). You want to have your cake and eat it. That's you. That's what's going on."

Fucking hell, Tash. Easy does it.

She's a stripper, so her bullshit levels are way lower than normal.

Strippers get enough bullshit at work. They don't need it at home. She also volunteers to work with the elderly, which is part of why I find her so attractive. And of course, the surgery helps.

"You're just scared."

Ah. Here we go.

"You're just scared of being made happy."

As per usual, what people cannot understand, they make up stories for. I'm pretty convinced this is how most deities were created.

"And you're especially scared of being made happy by a woman."

Oh for the love of *Pete*...

"And you're especially scared if that woman is me."

For fuck's *sake*...

"You're just scared."

Will someone...

"Scared to death."

... Please...

"Scared of being happy."

... Shoot me...

I sit and watch the documentary with Metis, and Dani has laid out the works.

She's done a cracking job, and it all looks pretty good. It needs work and it could use sharper editing, but it works.

On the other hand, I watch myself losing out on my award *again*.

Oddly, there's no pain. Partly because the man sat next to me is my brother-in-arms and BTX founder and he smashed it so hard it may never get fixed.

I congratulate Dani and her team and head out. Part of me is in mourning for an award I may never have deserved anyway, but the majority of me is exultant. Because if you can take all that and watch it back again, then you can take anything. Still. I feel an odd wistfulness.

I get home and watch a *lot* of "Studio 60" to chill myself out.

May Odin be praised, it works. That show is the *nuts*.

My CV is almost done.

And on it, I've covered everything except theatre. I've done music videos, documentaries, been nominated for awards, done short films and commercials, done some voiceover work, and just had my first lead in a feature.

We're on the way.

The listening session is a hit, as I knew it would be.

We have round a hundred people show up and they're a mix of music industry people, friends, lawyers, women who want to be at a glitzy event, and, you know, other people.

His (Metis's) album is going to be like mine: off the chain. It's a mix of hip-hop, spoken word, old school jazzy beats and a load of the most cutting edge lyrics you'll ever hear.

I have a few drinks and say hi to a few people, and watch my best friend rock the house like none other.

There are moments in life and then there are Moments. Actually, his poetry collection was called "Momentary Eternities," with a foreword by Yours Truly. I might actually include that later on, come to think of it. This right here is what you call a Moment.

We've gone from doing Spoken Word at a club no one's really heard of to an album-listening session with music industry managers and music lawyers at a venue that plays host to the most famous celebrities in the world.

He's got his friends around him and a crew that are getting more professional looking by the minute. And I've got Luckiya dancing like a maniac, and her lips fused to mine.

I'll not forget this in a hurry either.

The end of January sees me doing more of the same.

I'm basically a battle-machine; headshot, CV, email, album all my stuff to be made ready to market.

My New Year's resolutions are done; my aims are set, my job is clear. If I am to turn thirty this year (which I am), depending on how lucky or unlucky I am - I am either halfway (please no) or thirdway (more like it) through this game we call Life.

I know I have a bad habit (several, actually) [in fact screw having one, I probably *am* one] of trying to bite off more than I can chew, but then it hasn't let me down too bad so far.

To be fair, I feel a little David-esque in the face of Goliath.

The entertainment business has conquered and broken hundreds of thousands of people. It has executed millions of careers. It may mean the stupidest thing I ever did was leaving the City: that may come to be my only and biggest regret.

Thing is, I have this little sling in one hand, which is my will to ascend, my drive, and my Self; and then a perfectly smooth rock, which we may call our Talent (whatever that may or may not be worth) in the other.

The Goliath before me is titanic; his weapons are bigger than am I.

But if I put this stone into this sling, it fits well enough.

And as Goliath approaches, if I swing this missile faster and faster, and if I focus on the clean target of his forehead, and if I pray to all the Gods that have ever existed to bring me Fortune, and if I release it just at the right second...

Well... we may just be able to give Goliath a bit of a headache, and knock him stone cold out. That or kill him in one sharp blow.

That, or die trying.

I hope it will not be the latter.

The first month of the year of Trinity has almost passed.

An amazing amount has happened. I feel like the past four weeks were well worth all the time and effort.

And yet.

I have a mountain to climb. The mountain is neverending. We cannot reach the pinnacle until the day we expire. We can only judge ourselves thus - by the distance between where we were at our point of birth and how far we have come at our point of death.

I care not how scared I am.

I will not buckle. Not now. Not ever.

I have my family to think of: I have my mother, my nan, my father and my friends, for whom justice must be done. In which case I shall give all I have. And I've been scared the whole way through.

Has it stopped me?

Has it *fuck*.

There endeth the lesson. We never, *ever* give up.

We never.

Give up.

Ever.

It's the last day of the month when I get the call.

*** ******* wants to see me next month.

A show I hate but that has it's last airing to its millions of viewers wants to give me a chance to be on it.

And I don't know which is greater.

My distaste for the show, or my curiosity as to what would happen if I were on it.

Well, only one way to find that out.

All right then.

Business as usual…

Bring it *on,* homechisel...

FEBRUARY 2010:

"VALENTINE'S MONTH AND "RADIO LONDON""

"She's the most incredible thing,
I think I've ever seen, in my entire life,
And I've been around here, once or twice,
This woman makes me adore my own eyes..."

- Talent -
"Parimosita"

- IMMORTALENTED 2013 -

February normally starts out weird for me.

First week of the month I'm manic after nuking the place in January. Week two I normally try to chill a bit (just to remember what chilling is actually *like*) and then avoid Valentine's Day.

Being polyamorous or polygamous and a fan of Valentine's Day do not go hand in hand. Don't get me wrong; I love it, if I'm in a relationship serious enough not to be working. But I'm not.

So this year it's work central.

And I have applications to send.

The target for this month?

Fifty.

Send out fifty applications to agencies across London and see what comes back. My guess (from years of Clubland experience) is that about 5% will be willing to see me (from what we call a "cold" introduction, i.e. email) and of that I'm hoping around 80% will be interested in representing me.

I tell myself if it doesn't work, every month going forward, I'm just doubling it. So if all else fails, next month I'm sending 100.

I've signed up to all the necessary sites, and that alone has cost me nearly a grand. You wanna be an actor? Fine.

Then you have you pay your way onto the following:

ACTING
- Spotlight (essential, every actor on planet earth is on this - get on it)
- Casting Call Pro (also good, the Robin to Spotlight's Batman)
- StarNow (*way* better than they say)

EXTRAS
- Casting Collective (asap, shitloads of paid work, feature films, major studio movies)
- Ray Knight (tv, paid work, some movies, very hard to get in to)
- Mad Dog (features, paid)
- 20/20 (same as above)

That's a *lot* of sites and there's no guarantee of paid work. But then, that's why you have a headshot and a showreel.

You compete. You battle. You get in the ring and you fight.

I'm sending ten applications a day, ten introductory emails a day, and applying to thirty castings a day. Let's see what the deal is and how hard this shit *really is* to crack.

The Huntress job taught me that life is a numbers game. You want an acting job? Then do not just apply to one. Apply to a hundred. Be everywhere. Turn the rules against the rulemakers.

Make the system work for you.

Pickup operates on the same system. You want to take a beautiful woman or a hot guy home? Then get used to talking to ten or twenty on a night out.

And peacock your ass off.

I had a PUA instructor for about a month (because remember *Rule 1*, **no matter how good your game is, someone else out there would put you on the bench...**) and my *God* was it a learning experience.

And here's why: beauty, you will discover, makes us lazy.

Now, I'm not saying I'm the best-looking dude. That'd be pure arrogance and totally un-me (cue hysterical laughter and bouts of pointing and giggling from at least twenty people I know).

However: I'm not roadkill, either. The celeb comparisons I get piss me off but could be far worse: Tom Cruise (with long or spiky hair), David Beckham (with a skinhead, and you can fuck *off*), and previously Robbie Williams (spiky hair dyed black, and now you can *really* fuck off).

However.

My looks for good or bad are no thanks to me. They came free with the genes. And if something comes easy to you, you get lazy about it.

Easy, for example, approaching and talking to women. Or so I thought.

But when you *actually* go back through your memory banks and reflect on the number of complete strangers you have spoken to or picked up or seduced, the number is irritatingly low ("low" of course means different things to different people. Natch. [Natch, again = naturally] <natch.>).

With pickup you get trained to approach complete strangers and practise getting the results you want - which, whether work-related, personal, or for nocturnal Olympics purposes, is usually for them to like you, which is always about one thing: gravity.

Increase your gravity, attract more. More of everything.

The more you attract, the more you can dismiss.

So, attractive women usually have zero game. They just have a shitload of built-in gravity, which, let's be clear, is entirely by accident and not of their own making.

(Although makeup helps. And surgery. God *bless* you people.)

So they attract a truckload of people, but have no training in discerning the good from the bad (except what they see on TV; men too are equally guilty of this, but then who is there to teach either sex?).

So they simply develop a filtering system. Anyone who sounds, looks, or acts normal? Fuck off. Unless you're staggeringly good-looking / funny / charming / sexy, in which case, as above, you're not "normal."

Gravity - the extent to which you draw things to you, or perhaps better put -

Your human magnitude.

Humagnitude.

So.

My game went up a few levels. Mostly by simply putting into practice the notion of the numbers game, which is simply the *law of mathematics* (and once you get used to this, accept it and try it, you will love it and adore it and thank the Lord for its simplicity and thence become a *mathemaddict*).

So. My applications state clearly who I am and what I have done and that, opinion aside and personal shit aside, I'm the nuts.

Not only do I elevate my status in the emails, I peacock like a mofo.

"Peacocking" - to strut, to flair like a peacock, and act / dress like an absolute maniac (though a cool-as-ice one), thereby attracting more attention than a bearded person in a hijab holding a suspicious suitcase outside the White House.

It's just a method of forcing yourself to be who you are. You wear white t-shirts and jeans all the time? Fuck *off*. Try wearing some shit that Prince wears and watch the difference. You'll be amazed.

And you'll get a sneak peek later in the Cannes film festival section.

I've been hitting the gym like a maniac.

By which I mean, an hour of cardio and an hour of weights each time. If I took protein shakes I'd look like a wrestler, but that ain't the point. I just want to be resilient enough to handle what's about to happen for the rest of the year.

That's my primary goal: just to get through the year in one piece, or as close as I can get to it.

You'd think this workload combined with so much gym time and admin work would send a man crazy. But it doesn't. It makes me stronger. What *does* drive me batshit is the fricking internet companies. I thought we had it bad with the electric companies, but next to these internet goons, the electric people are pure thoroughbred pros.

We've tried to install Virgin, and then BT, and it's all gone pear-shaped. My good friend Garrett Millerick has had ludicrous problems with these guys and warns me it'll take up to seven months for us to get wireless internet sorted.

Hah! Seven months! Doth he know not to whom he speaketh...?

...

(In the end, Garrett, so you know, it took us eight months. I lose. Conclusively.)

Anyway. The reason you need wireless internet to do any of what Rooster, Flowgirl and I do on a daily basis is pretty simple: you have to have email and internet access for communications, for uploading footage, to get samples for costume and wardrobe, and for me to apply to like a thousand agencies. It's not a maybe.

It's a must.

February kicked off with a bang.

There's a few things still on my plate, however, and it's important I deal with them as well as possible.

First off is an audition for "You Need Help", a short film / TV pilot for a show by a gent named Daniel Foss. Smugz and Rooster get me the audition and it's not in my capacity to turn them down on pretty much anything.

So I go. I head out to nuttbuck fowhere and appear at a massive studio building. The auditions are being held with Rooster, Smugz, and Lord Foss, along with Twiglet who is reading with the applicants. I've learned the lines and am pretty confident at how it is to be played.

The guy is looking for a young Ewan McGregor. Now, a young Ewan McGregor isn't so much something you can play as it is something you are, so I have to go in a different direction.

I try my own version of the character but the director hates it, I can tell. Which is fair enough, since it's his movie.

I meet Twiggers and Smugz here and we have a laugh as usual. I even add a touch of my own to a particular scene and though it puts the final nail in my coffin job-wise, it does give everyone in the room a real good laugh.

There's a scene where the lead guy is getting dumped, and needs to take a leak before he leaves his now-ex-girlfriend's house. He asks to use the bog, the sink, anything he can drop trou on. She tells him to fuck off, and then he begs for a goodbye hug.

Now, it ain't in the script, but as I give Twiggers a goodbye hug, I make a noise and quiver a bit as though I've just had a slash all over her leg.

The people in the room erupt with laughter. I mean *everyone*.

Except for the director. Who now hates me.

Typical.

Oh well, worse things happen at sea...

Suffice to say, I didn't get the job.

Knackers to it. Rooster and I go to a screening of "Morning Tea" with a load of the crew.

My heart jumps and sinks when I see the edit.

Watching yourself onscreen is somewhat unnerving, by the way.

And if you are like me, then you are uber-critical of everything you're watching. So I see the hair mistake and a hundred other things I did wrong. To be fair, I am also proud of the accent and the performance in general.

The edit, however, is not what I had hoped. Rooster and several others share my sentiments. We aim to get this into the Cannes film festival, and to do that, in my humblest opinion; the cut needs to be better.

Still, perhaps the Cannes guys will see things differently.

It's reality TV time, folks.

I get to Wembley arena, and to be honest, I'm pretty nervous. I've spoken to all my friends and family about this and it's about 50-50 down the middle as to whether I should actually be doing this at all.

The view from the station is immense.

No wonder people love coming here. I'm reminded again of my Spanish Marbellan girl from the hotel telling me that as she saw me by the pool I "looked at everything like I love everything". That's blatantly true. Most of my time when I'm not working (which is seldom) I'm a kid in a candy shop.

Dani arrives with her camera crew and we do a few interviews before I approach the building. I'm trying to relax.

I force myself to remember that I didn't start this whole process and, truth be told, I don't really even give a shit about being on *** *******.

I walk to the building and the camera crew is barred. Go figure. I walk in.

There's more security here than you'd get at Area 51. They take my name and give me a number. There's random people walking around with radios and mics, and the logo for the show is everywhere.

I'm led into a room that is reminiscent of a school hall.

I'm given a fifteen-page application form and told to sit and fill it in. There are maybe a hundred or so people in the room. I sit and start-speed writing, answering the questions pretty much vanilla until it starts getting detailed about family.

"What are the names of your closest xyz family members?"

- None of your fucking business.

"Where do they live?"

- REALLY none of your fucking business.

"How would you describe your relationship with them?"

- Listen to me, buttweed; I wouldn't.

It takes me about half an hour to fill the sucker in. I then get assigned a new number and told to wait.

There's security all over the shop.

I then get called with about twenty other people out of the hundred (more are still streaming in) and we are off.

I'm led into the bowels of Wembley arena - it's all underground tunnels and passageways. You could make an amazing film here.

We finally come to a long corridor of a tunnel, and we wait in groups of three outside a door.

I see extremely unusual but eccentric individuals: an army guy in a wheelchair with an eye missing and two fake legs, two essex blondes who are louder than a pair of tiger tanks and who *must* be mother and daughter, a cool looking gothgirl, a dude in a ninja outfit, and various others.

Now, I didn't approach these people in the first place. They approached me.

However: I've long believed that if you are going to get in the ring in the first place, then give your all to the fight. And here I am.

So I start talking to every person in a TV show or staff member T-shirt. I'm making contacts, cracking jokes, just being friendly, really.

Because if I'm in a contest at all, I want to win.

With no warning, I'm led into a room with my bags. There's a camera crew, a seat in the middle, and a panel of three people sat smiling helpfully. They ask me to take a seat. I take a seat.

The assault begins immediately.

"So: MENSA, eh?"

I nod.

"They'll let anyone in nowadays, eh?"

I smirk from ear to ear.

"Maybe so. Sorry, but are *you* in MENSA?"

The woman who asked me the question awkward-smiles and shuffles a bit.

"Er, no."

I smile more.

"Then I guess not."

And that's it. That's all it takes. I'm now in the zone and I will *not* be shifted. No matter what they do, I'm here on *my* terms.

I get *grilled* for ten minutes by these three about my music not being released yet, losing my club company, my family (no response, chickenwing, try elsewhere and leave them *out* of it...), about acting, about womanising, about being a male escort, the lot.

And I don't bat an eyelid. I just smack every question out the ballpark as sarcastically as I can.

I'm now having *fun.*

I'm then told the interview is over, and am led back out into the corridor to another room with the two Essex women who I swear to God, at *no* point stop talking.

In a smaller room, a member of staff pops out of an adjoining room to say:

"You three have all passed level one. You'll now be taken upstairs to level two."

I thank her personally, 'cause that's what my mum would have done. Essex Mom yells,

"Hey sweetart, can we grab yer for a second luv, need ta ask yar a few quesschunns...?"

I step out of the room before my soul ignites. Essex mom keeps me and Essex daughter outside for ten minutes. Essex daughter tells me she wants to be a model and a ton of other stuff, and seems way more normal without her mom around.

Essex mom comes out and we're herded back upstairs.

"So wot like yoo do, chuck?"

I explain I'm an actor and a rapper, and ask what she does.

"Oi'm not currintly emploiyed at the mowmint, burreye woz in iventz, loike: PR and markitinggg, and did big iventz for big cumpanies. Loike. Now oi'm here coz everywone said we'd mek a greaat duowowuh on *** *******."

I nod and remind myself at some point later to teach myself how to have an out-of-body-experience. We're led upstairs and into another room. I see yet more security and way, way more staff. Here is clearly where we get even more grilled.

So, on that note, bring on level two...

Level two starts off in a different room and now involves (I shit thee not) a thirty-one-page questionnaire that probes even more deeply.

We're talking shit like:

- *What's your most embarassing sexual experience?* Easy. Any time I couldn't get it up or was too masherooned to get a fucksock on. Or actually, once when I fell asleep going south of the border.

- *What are you most ashamed of?* Also easy. A lie I told once that shamed me to my core and hurt a ton of people, or a truth I told once that did the same thing.

- *Are you more introvert or extrovert?* I think I'm a tiny bit more of a PERvert. What kind of fucking question is this?

- *How do you get on with your closest three family members?* Long as we're stoned, we have a BALL.

- *Do you ever get drunk? If so what are you like?* Yes. Drunk.

- *Have you ever been in love?* Damn skimpy I have. That's what best mate's mothers are for...

- *Have you ever done something you were ashamed of?* Yeah, I once walked in to this reality TV audition and got asked questions that were so stupid the fucking paper they were written on was blushing...

- *What's been your wildest ever experience?* An 8-some on a yacht in Texas.

- *What do you wish you could have done for a living?* What I am doing. Although if not that, an astronaut. Or wait! Maybe a dinosaur hunter...

After a while as you can see I get a bit hacked off with all this, and just start answering in the most *me* way possible.

You want to know about my family? And my friends? Fuck that.

You're auditioning me. Period. Leave them *alone*.

I bomb through all the pages and hand my sheet in. I stop on the way out to give my number to a staggeringly beautiful girl by the door, and as I do, I hear Essex daughter ask Essex mom:

"Ay Mom! It sez here am yow an intravert or extraverted? Worrare they?"

To which, wonderfully, I hear, "Babe, intravert's like all in on yamself, and bad, and ay cool n' shit, and extravert's like... yoo nowe... *not*."

I leave the room with a smile.

We head to the first group exercise. There are two hosts in the middle behind a table, and a semi-circle of chairs out in front.

Three people are sat near the table. I walk to the apex of the circle, grab a chair, and pull it right in the middle.

You wanna see who I am? Then here we *go*, homenugget.

We're debating prostitution, apparently. And as you'd imagine, the crew so far is split. We have some attractive women sat about, and others coming in.

There's military wheelchair guy, who in my view has his head screwed on. There's gothgirl, strongly opinionated yet relaxed at the same time, which I've always found attractive. A ton of new people walk in, and you have to concede, it's the most amazing crew you'd ever see.

In fact I'm staggered they haven't released a behind-the-scenes of this show, cause believe you me, it'd be number one. For a start, I'd watch it, and I can't *stand* the actual programme.

"Number blahblah, what's your take on prostitution?"

My head swings round. That's my number. All eyes are on me as I pause to respond.

My French teacher Tim Swain taught me long ago when you give an assembly, your nerves and the awkwardness of silence will make you want to speak as fast as possible to strangle the silence.

This instinct is best kept in check, to allow everyone involved a moment to focus in on the speaker. It also screams confidence.

"I have no issue with prostitution so long as the people who work in it are protected and have some kind of insurance."

This doesn't go down well. People I don't know start shouting, "How can you say that?"

First goal, *done*.

"I used to go out with a female escort, and then she got me in the game. So it's a bit tricky for me to condemn it."

Silence.

Total silence. Silence like after someone broke wind at a funeral.

One of the hosts:

"Sorry, did you say you went out with an escort?"

Silence. The second host:

"And that you were one?"

I pause again.

"Yeah."

Everyone around me sounds like they're murmuring, but I'm staring so hard at host number two that I can't see them. I know the question that is coming, unless *everything* I learned so far in life is wrong...

"But why?"

I take a deep breath.

"We went out for six months. She danced at Strings. Halfway through she 'confesses' she's an escort. Which I don't care about because, well, it's kinda cool, and plus, who am I to judge? Figuring she told me to get it off her chest. Wrong. She informs me her agency is looking for guys to get involved, and that she thinks I'd be good at it. Which it turns out, I was. And having been there, I know that escorts, companions, prostitutes, whatever, actually provide a wanted, demanded service, and that in many cases, rather than breaking relationships or marriages up, it saves them."

"But didn't you mind her doing it?"

Knew that was coming too.

"You kidding? I loved it."

"Why? How? When there are other guys being with your woman?"

"Because they're paying £400 just to have her for an hour."

"And?"

"And I'm getting the whole lot for free."

Everyone laughs.

"Ask yourself: would you rather have a partner that no one wants, or one that's highly in demand?"

Suddenly the argument is flipped on its head. And I've managed, by simply telling the truth, to anchor the gravity right by my chair.

Next up is capital punishment.

Now, I used to be a bit of a Nazi on this. I wanted all murderers, rapists, paedophiles and war criminals to be executed. Preferably publicly. I was young and emotional.

And, as you'd imagine, this issue divides the room. It gets very intense and people are starting to argue. And, calamitously, Essex mom and daughter walk in.

Here's the reason they narc me. Essex has, as opposed to what you may have heard, the most successful women by income per capita in our country.

Yeah.

It's the truth.

Plus, they're fine as all *hell*.

Right now, this very second, I wanna send a shout out to all the ladies in Essex for your hard work and efforts. I love you all, ladies.

Plus, in case I didn't mention it, you're fine as all *hell*.

But these two misrepresented you *hideously*, girls. For truth.

And yet again, predictably, the question gets asked:

"Number blahblah, what do you think of capital punishment?"

Here's the thing: a lot of people are pro it, including a lot of my family and friends, and the old me.

In this room? Military guy and some other dudes I like are *extremely* pro it, to the extent where if you are *not* pro it, you better be ready to be on their wrong side.

And I'm prepared for more than that. It's just that it's more...

"Er, number blahblah?"

Sigh

"I'll be honest with you. In my heart of hearts I am absolutely, fundamentally all for capital punishment."

A mini cheer goes up. Now the liberals among us look at me like I just raped a baby wabbit.

"*However.*"

A mini 'eh?' goes up.

"Here's the thing. I don't see, in my mind, how a government we elect to represent us can outlaw murder and then murder people itself. It's hypocritical. And it's just less civilised than a ton of alternatives. And rock bottom, it's flawed. And flaws should not be able to send people to their death wrongly. And if it was my mum or nan in there wrongly accused, or my best friend, believe you me I'd dedicate the rest of my life to destroying that system. Stick people in a quarry if you have to. Imprison them. Do whatever. Because no matter what you do, if someone killed my most dearly loved, I wouldn't need or want the law. I'd fucking kill them myself."

Silence.

Then a roar of agreement, and unless my ears mistake me it's from both sides.

My anal nerve flutters in relief.

We're then given a group exercise, and mercy be, it's one I've had before at school. It's one of these "If you were stuck on a desert island, which ten items would you take out of these twenty?" questions. The twenty items are drawn on a whiteboard before us.

As you'd expect, the room erupts.

People are shouting their opinions, forcing their personalities up out amid the clamour. I'm actually taken aback. It's fucking impressive to see. And, also impressive, Essex mom and daughter have zero qualms about jumping into the breach. A voice next to me:

"We're never going to do this unless someone goes up by the poster."

The items are drawn on the whiteboard in front of us. The gent to my right is suggesting I go up there. I'm pretty sure that's suicide - an open, physical movement that screams 'look at me'. I have another idea. Leadership is sometimes finding the right detour needed to get back on the right path.

But I digress.

I get up and approach the host table.

"Can I borrow pen and paper please?"

The hosts both look at each other, then at me. I can feel the entire circle's eyes at my back.

"Er, yeah. Sure."

I take pen and paper and sit back down. I tell the two people next to me that I know the first answer. We take the mirror first (I know because I made the mistake of choosing water first when I was at school). That's so you can signal people.

The body apparently can live up to three days with no water. But water's more necessary than food. And getting the hell off the island is more important than anything.

I start writing. We're up to about five items when karma repays my risk.

"Hey, number blah, you wanna come up here?"

I look up. Thass me, ladies and bents. So up I get and stand next to the board. At this point, I can have done no more, far as I can tell.

I'm almost pleas...

"Ay. Hangonaminnit. Who da fuck ilected *you* tha leadah?"

My spider sense tingled the whole way I was headed to the board. I knew Essex duo couldn't let it slip. Now it's down to fate.

Military Man and the hosts leap to my defence, principally because I didn't *ask* to be here, and 'cause we needed someone to do *something* in order to actually *get* somewhere.

The Essex duo backs off. And now we're on. We discuss the list, and on we go.

Eventually I'm tapped on the shoulder, and someone whispers into my ear "you're headed downstairs. Level Three."

I see the host briefly in the stairs.

He smiles at me.

"That was exactly what you needed to do."

I smile back and thank him, because I couldn't have done it without him.

"Where am I headed next?" I ask.

He looks at me.

"You're going to the ***** room. To meet *** *******."

I walk back into the hallway with all the doors in it.

It reminds me of that film I saw as a kid that left such an impression on me. Matthew Povey introduced me to it, as he did so many things: "Red Dwarf", big dogs, and a functional home with tough, hard-working parents.

What the hell was it called, that film...?

Ah yes.

"Labyrinth."

The hallway now seems less imposing. I am getting used to it all. I check my watch.

That simply *cannot* be the time. I have apparently been here almost six hours.

I look around the hallway. I know that these are the most interesting people they could find, and I wonder what they all do.

Has no one considered getting them all together to do a project? Stick all these people together and Christ, even Yours Truly could make or sell something worthwhile.

It's wasted Talent, you see, and I hate that.

I genuinely loathe it. I want to scoop up all these people and get them into some kind of magnum opus. But before my mind can think of something appropriate, my name is called, and I'm walking into the room.

I sit in a chair. I place my bags down. I turn and look directly into a camera. And sure as the sky is blue, I hear the words:

"Hello Stephen. This is * ******* talking."**

I look into the camera.

The voice, you gotta admit, is impressive.

"Or should I call you... *Talent*?"

I keep looking into the camera.

"Well, my mum calls me Steve. My friends call me Ste or Brock. So you better call me Talent."

We talk for a while, and *** ******* has no qualms about attacking me about everything.

"You were a male escort?"

"Yes."

"Tell *** ******* about it."

"I escorted women for a year."

"For money."

"Yes."

"You were a prostitute."

"No. An escort."

"Prostitute."

"However you wish to think of it."

"And you were a soldier."

"For a very short time, and in the TA, but yes."

"Think we're a bit hard, do we?"

"No, it's just the way my jeans are cut."

"Hmm. And you're an 'Actor'."

"Yes."

"Been in anything *** ******* would have seen?"

"No. Not yet."

"So you're shit at it?"

"Possibly."

"And your relationship with your mother is important?"

"We're not going to talk about that."

"Stephen, *** ******* can ask anything it wants..."

"I said we're *not* going to talk about that."

"Who is Parimosita?"

I pause here and grit my teeth so hard I can feel my brain pulse.

"She's the love of my life, and the life of my love."

"Who is she?"

"None of your business."

Silence.

"Tell me about your music. Is that why you're wearing that shitty shirt?"

I laugh at this.

"Excuse me, this shirt and jacket are part of my stage gear."

"They're shit. It looks like something Peter Andre would wear."

I laugh again at this.

Getting a rise out of me is not that easy. Just like with everyone else, it's my choice as and when I rise to anything.

"Stephen... *** ******* is now going to tell you its opinion about you."

"I'm all ears."

Silence.

"*** ******* thinks this is all a front."

I'm confused.

"Eh?"

"*** ******* thinks the calm front, the cool exterior, is all a front, a character you have created and that basically, Stephen, you are full of *shit*."

I smile at this.

Had I been here a few years ago that would have resulted in a broken camera and an arrested me. Whoever is behind there is giving it a good go at getting a rise out of me. Unfortunately, this is not their day.

It's mine.

"Well, out of everyone, when it comes to being full of shit, *** ******* ought to know."

Silence.

"So you're a rapper?"

"Yes."

More silence.

"You don't look like a rapper."

"You don't look like a talking camera. Yet here we are."

Silence.

"And I'm an *award-nominated* rapper. For the record."

More silence.

"Go on then. Give us a freestyle. You've got 20 seconds."

I take a deep breath...

I leave Wembley Arena and head back home.

There are several missed calls and messages on my phone. I cannot believe what I have just gone through. And yet, of course, I can.

I have no idea how it went, except that I wouldn't change a word of it.

You'll have to accept that my recollection of it is after quite a while has passed, so some of it was paraphrased as close as I can recall.

But the essence of it is unchanged.

And, I have to concede, it was a hell of a lot of fun.

My issue now of course is, that I almost *want* to be on this show. *Almost*.

In 2009 I was lucky enough to be nominated for my first ever music award.

There's a fantastic company called the Exposure Music Awards that looks after and promotes unsigned talent.

They put on shows in London and elsewhere for bands to showcase their skills, and then they host an awards night at which they present awards to the winners in each category.

I was nominated for "Best Artist" in the out-of-area category.

Laughably, later in the same year, I got nominated again for the same one. I won neither, and losing at the awards ceremony was no walk in the park; but I went from being "an artist" to "an award-nominated artist."

And that's the game: one rung up at a time.

Just a brief aside - my boy Metis got nominated for three awards, but walked away with *four*.

Now, it takes a certain level of bad-assedness to win all your awards, but to win *more* awards than you were nominated for in the first place takes fucking *skills*.

Metis: in case I never made a big enough deal of it at the time (which I'm fairly sure I did) then let me reiterate just how savageliciously ninje (ninja) you really are.

Anyway. I'd said I'd do a show for them the year after and I don't break my word; so a show I'm going to do.

Now, I have to pick the right tag partners, so I decide I'm going to perform onstage in Shoreditch with:

- Popus, French rapper and art designer from "Morning Tea"
- Zuz, a rapper who works with Lord Fargas
- Ender, my fellow rock singer and artist from BTX HQ

So I have to make sure I book rehearsals and get us on point.

Performing onstage is one of the greatest feelings in the world.

I have only ever performed my own material, and that's the way it stays. I don't do covers. And when I'm onstage I like to *fucking rock it*. It's like taking all the crap in your system and battering it out by giving vent to what is inside you.

It is very healing.

Very cathartic.

People ask me a lot "Which do you prefer - music or film?"

To which my response (this is as close as I get to sitting on the fence) is always "They are both the same thing". This is usually met with derision and laughter.

However, that's normally from people who don't *do* film or music.

They are both media used to entertain and inspire, involving performance and control of the voice and the body.

Both are either done live (live show / theatre) or recorded (music video / film and TV).

Films need scores and soundtracks. Music requires physical performance. One requires lyrics, the other a script; unless one is "improvised" or the other "freestyled."

Either way, both require some kind of scaffold around which we tie the performance. They are both the same; they're just different dialects or accents of the same language, or different branches of the same tree.

So I find myself, for example, in my studio making the score for "Morning Tea" with Blaqmale. We've made an entire score (based on my melody, remember?) in about three days.

I have no idea if the director will like it, but it serves to show how closely united music and film are.

This I reflect in my made-up word "cinemusic," which I think states it nicely.

Blaqmale and I are a unique blend. He's black, I'm white. He's religious, I'm an agnostic. He's a producer, I'm a vocalist.

We've made about ten tracks together, but there's a slight hitch.

We bash heads like no one else I've ever worked with. Half the time I try my utmost to solve the problem. The other half I get aggravated that there even *is* a problem and react without thinking, making the issue worse.

Regardless, he's one of the most talented musicians I've ever had the pleasure of meeting, and I am fortunate to number him among my producers and more importantly my friends.

And to be fair, his criticisms have made me raise my own bar to levels I'd not have thought possible, even if they do cut me to the bone.

When Milan eventually comes in to see the music, I can see from his reaction we have differing views on it.

This is to be expected in cinemusic. For two people to have the same vision is both rare and difficult. Did we waste our three days composing? Hell no. There is no such thing as wasted experience, unless you fail to learn from it.

I still walk from the studio deflated though, as I hoped for both myself and Blaqmale we'd have our music in the film.

Next time, big man.

My mood is lifted when my next text message comes through.

I've just won an audition for what I think will be the best short film I've ever had chance to be in, entitled (to my delight) "War of the Sexes."

And yet again, Yours Truly is auditioning for the lead.

Mike 'Drews is a curious man.

For a director he is very laid back, quite softly spoken, and almost totally devoid of stress or angst. When I meet him he is cordial, friendly, and warm to the point it's disarming.

I've looked at the script and the idea just captures me. It's brilliantly conceived and brilliantly simple.

Cap (the role I'm going for and the lead) is the head honcho of a group of friends. He leads his friends into battle to wage war, in so far as victory is achieved via the seducing and taking home of women.

He has three friends he leads in such adventures, and they use military lingo, military tactics, and have a mate named "Comms" (in charge of communications) who is in charge of eavesdropping on the targets and relaying things they say back to the crew.

The whole thing operates off army metaphors. So the guys don't just get shot down - they fall to the ground and you hear a gunshot go off, and there's a totally over-the-top "Apocalypse Now" style death sequence.

I'm an ideas man. And I know off the bat that this is inspired thinking.

I also think the idea's good enough that were I Mike 'Drews, I'd be looking to shop this as a TV pilot.

I go to meet him after a long day when I'm tired and just have had enough.

I summon the reserves to meet and greet, and am introduced to his co-producer Sethster, who himself is a bit of a legend. By which I mean he's also cool as a fan, and allegedly fell into the sea smashed out of his gourd with his camera in his hands at the Cannes film festival.

Fortunately neither he nor the camera nor any animals were harmed during said event.

I meet potential other cast members, and do a pretty good read.

It's good enough that at some point even though I didn't knock it out the park, we're talking dates and availability, which is always a good sign.

I also see an absolute first.

Now, I'm not sexist.

Well, I take that back. I am sexist.

I believe women are by far the superior species. And fellas, if you're honest for five seconds, you'll not argue. Yes we're stronger. Yes we can drink more. Yes we can give directions without causing the listener to have a hernia. But firstly, women just look a trillion, billion, million, wonkadonkillion times better.

Secondly, we've had rule of the roost for a fair while on this planet (though mercifully, this is changing and has been for a while) and fucked it up pretty badly in lots of ways.

And thirdly, only a woman may give birth unto any child of the race of Man.

Rock bottom? It takes a woman to *make* a man.

Men might be the seed, but the woman provides the tree. It's no contest. If aliens came down and had to choose one gender only to preserve, be honest, they'd pick women.

However, there are a few areas in which my beloved females have yet to gain a universal level of mastery. One is in giving directions; another, according to one of my parents, is driving (cue booing and hissing - I know, my mum is actually a ruthlessly excellent driver); and another is in comedy.

Outside of Victoria Wood, I can't name you one female comedian I can think of that I rate massively.

Now to be fair, I'm not an encyclopaedia of female stand-ups.

Yet still I think there's some kind of drought for female comedy.

There is no female Jim Carrey, for instance. There's no she-version of Jasper Carrott, or of Robin Williams.

However at the audition for WOTS I see a woman whose comic timing and characterisation is so good, so honed, and so sharp that I'm genuinely and pleasantly surprised.

I can't help but watch her in the audition. She steals the show and does so unintentionally and without ego. She's not even my type, but I can feel myself becoming more attracted to her. I make a mental note to work with this girl again, and leave thanking the universe for being so generous with me.

If I get the part, "War of the Sexes" will be my best short film.

We have yet more issues with the electric companies and internet service.

I'm starting to think they're actually all just a cover for some kind of undercover organisation that tries to make you top yourself while measuring how long it takes. While I'm ranting on the phone I check my StarNow.

I apparently have an audition for a new feature. "Radio London" sounds like it's right up my street.

It's described as "a political thriller" based on real events, dealing with terrorism, culture and race in London. The audition is about half an hour East from me, and is for the role of a radio jockey who spouts racist vitriol on his programme.

Sounds like it *is* my street, because that's what we call a *character*.

I slam the phone down on some inane musical "do you mind holding?" crap, and pay a bit more attention.

I've also apparently just got a text off someone called Rozar about a short film called "The Debt Collectors", in which he wants me to play an Irish thug called Kent Mansey. Nice - another chance to showcase an accent and play a totally different character.

I've done one short and one feature previously; this could be my chance to double up and take my CV from *Beginner* status to *Winner* status.

Or at least to start the journey.

We'll see.

I get the usual requests for Valentine's Day.

I respond politely but in essence I have no inclination to focus on them.

If I'm not in a 100% serious relationship or one that is meaningful enough for her to be called my "girl" then Valentine's Day is simply another day.

Don't get me wrong - I'm as romantic as it gets and I prize women above all things.

Until I meet Miss Right, however, I am married to my work. I have to be. As a good friend of mine once said: first you earn the life you want, and then you find the woman that matches it.

'Nuff said.

The "Radio London" audition approaches quicker than Speedy Gonzales.

It's apparently in Ilford, so I head to Stratford bus station to visit the place for the first time.

When I finally step from the bus, I'm under-my-breath cursing all people who hold auditions that are not in Central London.

I walk across the road and see the location I am to compete in.

It's some kind of salesroom - like an estate agent's office. And screw me sideways; it's what we call a 'cattle call.'

There's about fifty people here and they're as diverse as at the *** ******* audition.

We're all asked to wait in the main room, and I see from people's expressions that we're all in the same boat; they want this film *badly*.

Unfortunately for them, I woke up on the right side of bed this morning and this role is going to *me*.

I speak to a few of the applicants and we chat for a while. There's a real nervousness in the air.

Then several are taken upstairs to audition for the radio jockey role. I'm asked to join them.

The room upstairs is an office with about ten desks in it. There's me and about five guys, all of whom are older, around forty-five to fifty by my guess. I'm instantly thinking I'm in trouble, cause this indicates they want an older guy.

There are several ex-military people, and I make a mental note that perhaps they're also looking for people with mil. experience for the film, which makes sense, and which puts me back in the running.

The age thing is still an issue, however.

We all do a script-read of a section for the radio jockey that again makes it clear that this is very much a film about racism and prejudice. I read a couple of times and am introduced to producer Raydolph Amponsah. Ray is a lovely guy and watches us read quietly and considerately.

I still get the feeling that we're talking an older guy here.

Hmmm. I need to do something to rock the boat a bit.

We head back downstairs and I see a guy who's been walking around, moving people into place, head outside to have a smoke.

I decide against leaving after my audition and head out to join him.

His name is Bahzad and he's one of the crew for the film; and also is fairly high up the food chain.

We start chatting after I borrow his light, and it turns out he is Islamic and very enthusiastic about the project.

He tells me the director's name is Rehan and points to a glass-walled office inside on the ground floor saying that Rehan's in there.

"So what makes you interested in this project?" Bahz asks.

I take my chance.

I tell Bahz about my Parachute Regiment experience and how strongly I feel about religion and politics.

I explain that while I am intensely proud of and in love with my country, I see a lot of issues here that the film might address.

I tell him about "Morning Tea" and playing Milan, and how keen I am on roles that others might find unpalatable or disturbing. I tell him I have written 120,000 words on my own belief system.

"Really?" he asks.

I tell him I refused to remain in the Paras after they asked for volunteers to ship out to Iraq and Afghanistan.

When one of my best friends was half-Iraqi and when you have the views I have, invading someone else's country is an absolute no-no.

Don't met wree gong - if my own country is invaded and my people are jeopardised then I'll pick up any weapon you like and repel borders till the cows come home.

Failing that, violence is an outlaw.

Bahz now looks at me differently.

"You serious?"

I nod.

And yes, in case you were wondering, I am serious as *hell*.

"You better come with me," he says, and heads back inside to the glass-fronted office, beckoning me to follow.

I'm stood in the middle of the glass-fronted office.

All the other actors who've turned up to audition have now clocked something is going on and are staring through the window.

This is a good sign. If the production staff pick someone out of a group of thirty and take them for a separate chat, you better hope that someone is you.

Bahz introduces me to Ray and then to Rehan. We shake hands.

He asks me about my experience and what I have done.

I tell him as flat as possible who I am and what I have done.

He asks why I want to be in the film, and do I mind being recorded?

I'm sat opposite all three across a conference room table.

"No I don't mind. Record whatever you like. I want in on this film because I think, from what I have read and heard, this film sounds important. There are things that need saying and addressing in our country and not many people have the sand to talk about them."

Rehan: "Sand?"

Me: "Guts. Intestinal fortitude. Bollocks."

He nods in agreement and pushes a script over the table.

"Have a look at the speech by Abdullah. The big one."

I do as told.

I read.

Holy. *Shit*.

I'm pretty extreme in most things I do. And there's not much that bothers me. But tug me off with a nailgun, this is hard-*core*.

Abdullah's speech consists of a full-page rant against the British Government and the West in general. It's about as anti-Capitalist as you can get, with added snakebile thrown in.

"But I don't look Arabic or Indian...?"

Rehan smiles gently.

"He's a revert."

"Hmm?"

"A re-vert. He was a normal British citizen until he converted to Islam."

"Hmmm. What's he do?"

"He's a drug-dealer turned street preacher. And he protects his community like they're his family."

"Hmmm."

I think I'm starting to get it.

The main character, Tariq, is a moderate British Muslim, a good man, a good father and husband, and a professor at a university. He's a decent man, and represents the 'good' in the British Muslim community. He is an innocent wrongly accused of crimes he did not commit.

Abdullah seems like the counterpoint to this: while he is still non-violent, his speech is laced with violent anti-Western vitriol of the most repugnant kind. He represents perhaps the "negative" or "troublesome" aspect in the British Islamic community. And the speech, whilst (Jesus *Christ* am I going to have to say *that*??? Dad is going to *kill* me...) full of bile, makes some salient points and has intelligence to it.

"What would he look like?"

They all look at each other.

"He'd wear a simple robe, have a full beard, and ideally have long hair, down to his shoulders."

"Hmmmmmm."

I have short hair, am clean-shaven, and haven't worn a robe in my life except very occasionally for some rather experimental encounters in the bedroom.

"Is he intelligent?"

Again they look at each other.

"Very."

I sigh to myself. I don't even know why I'm acting like I'm considering it. I want it now more than ever.

"Would you read for us? If you could stand up and deliver it straight at the camera, that would be great."

I take a deep breath. This is about to get real. I'm going to have to find some place I really, really don't like being in. I need a memory... something painful as fuck...to access the deeper, darker bits of my mind... ah *yes*...

I'm in Malta... the year is… 1992...?

I'm swimming around the hotel pool to my heart's delight. I think I'm about eleven years old, and I'm on holiday in Malta with my parents.

My mum and dad taught me to swim at a very young age, so I can swim my ass off. I like swimming. Dad said not to come out here without sunblock, but who needs it? I'm in a swimming pool and I'm cool as ice. There's even girls here I like to look at. Hopefully they'll see me diving and swimming, and I can start this "becoming an adult" thing Dad keeps talking about.

I see a beautiful girl across the pool. Maybe I can talk to her later.

I swim to the side to get out for a dive. I put my hands on the side and yank myself out the water.

That's weird: as I pull myself out, my legs aren't moving how I tell them to. I scrabble for a handhold to pull myself out, and look down. A woman screams really loud. Everyone at the pool freezes dead still.

There's blood all over the tiles around the swimming pool. It looks wrong in the sunshine and against the blue of the pool. Where is it coming from?

The screaming woman points at my back. I reach around and feel for what she is looking at. And then fire burns my spine.

I've been sunburned so bad my back has actually *bubbled.*

Blood is running down my sides and the pain is so bad I'm starting to cry my eyes out. I need mum and dad. Now. People go running from me around the pool.

I pull myself across the tiles, sobbing like a girl. Inch by inch I try to get to the lobby. People are now actually walking round me to avoid me. I must look really horrible.

The women start crying when they see me. I look like some kind of horror movie victim.

My back feels like it's been ripped apart by an alien. I can feel it.

The words "scorch" and "burn" and "cinder" keep running through my head. I can't stop thinking them. I try to spell them correctly in my head to take my mind off the pain. I manage to get across the lobby floor to the lift. Blood trails behind me. I weep so bad I can't breathe.

The lift button's really high. I have to dig my fingers into the wall ledges and use my arms and hands to raise myself up. I manage to hit the button and fall back to the marble floor. That hurt. Marble's hard.

I crawl into the lift and have to do it again to get up to the right button for the right floor and fall back to the lift floor again. I'm getting dizzy, it hurts so bad.

We get to the sixth floor and I see one thing you do *not* want to see when you're crawling about with sunburn. I start sobbing worse.

Carpet.

Bobbly, friction, rough; *carpet.* I start pulling myself along the floor and the carpet is like razor wire on my skin. A lady and her daughter speed up to get past me quicker. The daughter starts crying as soon as she sees me.

My legs still won't work.

It's like someone cut my control wires, and then poured petrol on my back and dropped lit matches on it.

I finally, eventually get to our door. I knock on it hard, like a crazy person.

"Mom! Dad! Please!! I'm burned really bad!"

I wonder what a pathetic sight I must look. And all because I wouldn't put sun cream on. What an idiot! Idiot *idiot* **idiot**!

I keep smacking on the door and I think I hear my mum crying. I knock harder, yelling louder. The door is still not open.

And then, with the finality of a tomb door closing, I hear a sentence behind the door:

"He has to *learn*."

I realise the door will not be opening.

I crawl back to the lift, my whole world aflame. I crawl-climb back up the wall, hit the button, fall down, crawl in the lift, back up the side, hit the button, fall back down.

I'm panting and wheezing due to the effort.

My rage is so sharp and so intense I think I'd kill someone if it would get rid of the pain. It's agony. I've never been so mad. Why wouldn't they let me *in*?

I arrive at the top floor and crawl out. Bloody *carpet*.

I reach the Holy Grail: the TV room. Back then, remember, hotel rooms didn't come with TV as standard. There was a TV room where us kids went to watch TV together.

I arrive there. I yank myself up onto a set of chairs and lie in what I think they call the foetal position, tears running down my face and blood along my side.

I'll pass out soon man it hurts the cartoons aren't working can't think straight what is happening to me...?

Heh. You learned something that day, didn't you, maggotfilth?

Jesus. It's got so dark in here that someone let Dr. Schadenfreude in.

*Oh yes they did. And I'm gonna run around and play a bit now, **freak**. You want dark? I'll give you black hole dark, I'll give you pre-Big Bang dark; I'll give you freaking **antimatter-meets-trapped-in-a-mineshaft dark**.*

Not sure this is a good idea. It may not be, y'know, 'safe'...

Safe? Safe's for pussies. You want to smash this room to bits and tear the building apart.

They'll give you their film role then, you spineless, self-hating, insectile bag of cu...

I stand up in the conference room.
The red mist has come down.
The camera is on.
I look down the barrel.

My voice when it comes sounds like someone else's. The words sear my mouth as they pass my lips. I rant and foam and spit and rage. I leave no Banner inside; I am only Hulk.

And I say to the camera or any other poor bastard watching:

"You can forget the French, shacked up with their gap-toothed goat-cheese-smelling no-talent model wannabe playthings, stuck up in their harems up on the Champs-Elysees, photo-opping insecure Cuban-heeled midgets, telling us the hijab is threatening the gates of Vienna like Suleiman the great.

"And you can forget day-time TV presenters feeding morsels off some silicon-enhanced model to some slack-jawed chav strung out on brown sugar.

"We're represented by Osama! They're represented by the O-bomber, thousands of feet high... forget live aid, live 8: band aid ain't going to patch up the severed hands, piled high on Leopold's beach.

"Forget onward Christian soldiers shot up on Pat Robertson's diecide: Blacks, Aboriginals, Jews, Iraqis; a perpetual boot to the face, under white man's insane hunger to plunder. Forget rebuilding the nation. We put up two bricks and it's a training camp; three bricks and the tanks arrive.

"Forget imported elections and sloganeering, and woman's rights and democracy; when our benign are bounced out by the blood-thirsty; bloodlines of lounging retards to watch over us. We're booted and rebooted, jacked and re-jacked, till we don't know which way is *up*...

"The only path to vigour - is a return to the original, purity of the message - reject all Bid'ah -this love for the Western spell.

"That's when the pain will end."

I'm panting. My body is trembling. I blink myself back into myself.

Rehan, Ray and Bahz stand there a second. They look at each other.

They look at me. Then:

"Can you do that again?"

I leave the showroom fully believing I have the part, but I want it so bad I am assuming as of now that I do not have it.

Assume the worse, hope for the best.

It takes me nearly an hour to calm down.

When the Doc rears his ugly head, he can be very difficult to get rid of. He's absolutely the most evil entity I have ever encountered.

And tragically, he lives in me. Or rather, as part of me.

I check my phone and see that I have an audition for another feature coming up, for a picture called "Cock Tales". Sounds interesting.

What's even more interesting is our upcoming house party.

I've been talking to Rooster and Chow Bella and we've got our first proper house party coming up sooner than I was aware of.

The flat is big enough to accommodate about seventy to a hundred people, and we could have a proper night in.

Should be a blast.

I head to the shoot for "Debt Collectors."

I call Metis as soon as I get there. Partly to calm my nerves and partly to check my accent works.

We chat on the phone and we're both laughing at the ridiculousness of our lives: his year is going to be every bit as manic as mine.

Nice to have a yin to your yang. If you know not of what I speak, I understand and I sympathise.

I get to the shoot location and meet Rozar and his crew.

They're all nice, and have picked the location at the bottom of a pub in a cellar. It's pretty dank, but perfect for the premise: two bumbling gangsters who kidnap a kid and threaten him with guns.

I've put on a touch of bulk for this over two weeks and have listened to Dara O'Briain non-stoppo to make sure the accent is nailed.

When I get there, the first thing everyone does when I meet them is look slightly shocked and go "I didn't know you actually *were* Irish...!"

Heh. That's called putting your money where your mouth is.

We get as much shot as we can, but we drop several scenes. The issue with short films is this: they often don't get completed. And I can see this one going the same way.

I keep the accent all day until my father calls. I can't bring myself to keep it up while we're on the phone so we have a normal chat.

The producer himself shoots me a mad look and mouths, "What the f... I thought you *were* Irish...?"

Heh. That's *right*, hombre.

"Loveblind" is taking shape nicely.

It's the first short I've ever written and I'm fairly impressed.

Course, I have to sell it to everybody else at some point. That's the tricky bit.

It's based on actual events I went through as an escort, with a touch of a 'Steve' twist on it.

The escort thing? Yeah I know.

More on that later, bellsmith.

Much later...

Back to the gameplan: and now we're pavement pounding.

See, there's two ways to gain height on the gameladder: first up, networking and ascending via contacts.

This, my boy Metis is doing beautifully. So: no need for both of us to carve the same path. In firearms terms, this is sniperwork. Pick your target, cock the weapon, release a round and bullseye it.

I like this method for its simplicity. I dislike it for its reliance on other people. And while I have all the faith in the world in some other people (you know who you are), I wouldn't trust the vast majority to make me a sandwich.

And I realise many of them have zero faith in me.

Shame, isn't it? Yet if you ask them who has supported them all the way through, been there through thick and thin, if my name isn't in the top three, the lie they are telling you is in the top one.

So I run the gauntlet of pavement pounding, which, firearms-wise, is machine-gunnery. It's line 'em up and blow 'em all away. It's blastering off a million rounds and then watching the wreckage.

It's an acknowledgement of the fact that Life is a numbers game.

Wanna take a beautiful woman home? Talk to ten.

Wanna have a hit single? Make a whole album.

Wanna have a hit film? Be in twenty.

And so on. Because the odds on getting it right first time are limited. Extremely limited. So back yourself up. Protect what you care about. Take a million shots and one will pay off.

I grab the actor's handbook again and see about three or four hundred agents, of which maybe two hundred and change are semi-appropriate to appropriate and are based in London.

So that's my target list. 200+.

So between my BTX co-founder and me we will have both angles covered. Sniperism and blitznukery. One way or another, to those at the top of the ladder, we're comin' for ya.

And to all those people who hated, doubted, semi-supported, weren't there, let us down, didn't show, talked trash, broke their word, took the piss, didn't repay, stole our time, didn't honour their commitments, coveted our work ethic, envied our advances, demanded much but gave nothing, borrowed without repaying, took without thanking, and criticised out of ego rather than genuine opinion, to you flagrantly disrespectful cowards, to you wannabe-"friends" with no notion of the word 'balance' or 'dues' or 'gratitude' or 'justice': to you people who deserve zero mercy and total disregard...

... I forgive you.

And I forget you.

Unless...

...well. You already know where that sentence goes.

The two (actually three) hardest phrases in the English language *or* in Earthspeak (any dialect):

"I'm sorry."

And

"I was wrong."

And actually, third:

"How did England do in the World Cup, again?"

It's critical I remain physically fit this year.

I hit the gym three to four times a week still. I burn 550 to 1100 calories running and add on thirty to sixty minutes of weights.

I'm not trying to get huge. No use being the size of the Hulk when you're an actor. I just need to be resilient as hell.

Moviemaking and music can be testing industries. So I need to be ready to be tested. Even the guys at the gym are like "You might wanna calm it down a bit."

Heh. Not in this lifetime.

The more my body and mind can tolerate, the more I'll be able to take on. I didn't ask for an easy ride. So I need to be able to handle a yearlong roller coaster.

Fair enough. Then so be it. What we have to do, we have to do. Bitching and moaning about our tasks will not change them. Only action has the power to alter circumstance.

So ACTion it is.

And with almost no warning at all, our first house party is upon us.

What a great way to end a month. The flat has been cleaned. Drinks have been purchased. Extra-curricular provisions have beed procured. Food is all over the shop.

We reckon we'll have about fifty people over.

So it's a tad of a surprise when almost a hundred people descend upon our abode.

Lady Harb, one of the loves of my life, walks in with her new man and a bottle of whisky. She wants me to like her new guy; this much I know. And one way to make sure I like someone is to get me drinking a whisky with them.

Lady Harb is the first female I ever shared a stage with on one emotional night at 24 Club. We've since performed at more venues than you can shake a tree at. She's also the main female contributor on my album, and one of my closest, most trusted crew.

Grace shows up and sees me bartending. She heads over and tries not to let everyone know she likes me. We've loved each other for nearly a decade. She's a stunning girl and a cracking actress.

Luckiya rocks up first with about eleven girls. I'm sat in my flat with Chow Bella, Lady Harb and fella, Grace, Luckiya and her eleven girls, and then Chow Bella's friends who walk in en masse.

It's me, a dude bearing gifts, and about twenty women. I'm so happy to bartend that it's unbelievable. Only one problem; and luckily it's not mine.

Rooster's been working on a massive project for quite some time.

He's got a massive dance project he's doing in Birmingham - some kind of TV series about ballet. When he first tells me I'm laughing so hard I nearly cough up my own colon.

He's been gone for five to six days out of seven for the last two months.

And right now when I call him to tell him it's me, el hombrero here, and twenty women, he informs me he's stuck on the motorway in traffic.

I try to restrain my laughter, but to no avail. He's less than amused.

My studio crew show up: Blaqmale, Mr Khryzzz, Alpha Omega, Prince Ade, and Stylah. Metis shows up with Junia. Ateezy rocks in solo as usual. LL rocks up with Merlin and Sahota. More of Chow Bella's friends rock in.

People bring wine, food, vodka, whisky, beer, rose, and tequila, the whole works. Couples walk off to rooms to have a play around. I continue bartending and spinning tunes.

I'm no DJ you understand (see, I actually *don't* want to do *everything*), I just like to hear what I like when I'm in my own home.

We've got some giant man with no hair who keeps asking me for straight vodka.

"Mate, you're going to be straight velocitwatted if you keep that up."

Luckiya dances her ass off and tells me she misses me. I miss her too. I miss tons of my friends I used to see daily and now, as Life gives us all new circumstances; I see them less and less frequently.

Some of them understand completely - my workload is not normal. So they come over and visit. Others?

Well.

Others do not.

And I mourn their presence.

A ton more people I don't know rock in.

MoneyBaby shows up along with Richie F, Smugz rocks in with Catherine, and Blaqmale tries and fails to ignore Giantman spanking his ass with a saucepan.

And no, I'm not kidding.

I hear reports of people doing blow, pot, shrooms, shots, each other, and Christ knows what else. It's a touch difficult to fully control a house party when you have over a hundred people in yer living room.

It feels, to me, all a good way of blowing off massively pent-up steam.

See, I don't really unload my stress or crap onto my friends. If anyone plays therapist, it's usually me. I know more about my crew than any man living, and usually if someone is tasked with holding it all together, it's Yours Truly.

This year that's been a little tough and is going to get tougher.

Hence the house parties. Myself, I don't really unload my emotional baggage. I come from a long line of tight-lippers. My own particular brand of therapy is very simple: women.

Best therapy on the planet.

The party kicks into high gear before Rooster shows up. He arrives just as everyone else is leaving. He's miffed, and understandably so.

Pretty much four-fifths of the crew has scarpered by the time he shows up. People are making out or asleep all over the shop. This is going to be a *nightmare* to clean up tomorrow...

I fall tipsily asleep and don't hear the beeping of my phone.

I wake up to a hangover from hell.

My alarms (plural) sound like a submarine alarum clanging on inside my head.

When I check my phone I'm thoroughly unprepared for what it tells me.

I've lost another film part, is the first bad news.

That I can *handle*.

The worse part is that the joint love of my life, guttingly, is getting *married*...

MARCH 2010:

"MARCH AS TO WAR (OF THE SEXES), AND A MAGIC MAN"

"And when you're lying next to me,
You bring out the best in me,
You're kind of like a test for me,
I think you are my destiny..."

- Talent -
"In Love With You"

- IMMORTALENTED 2013 -

March.

The end of Quarter One and the beginning of the new.

I start "pavement pounding" on a Tuesday and send out three agent applications, worded as well as I can make them and with all my relevant information.

I've an audition for a short film called "Magic Man," written and directed by a gentleman called Muzzy Ali. We meet in the city near where I used to work, have drinks, and talk.

Muzzy seems like a genuinely nice guy: he's considerate, generous, and both wrote the film and wants to direct it.

This we call ambition, or "drive." I know this from experience.

I have a shedload of it myself. Muzzy aims to make a feature the year after this one, and seems to have his shit together.

Rock bottom? I like him, and if he'll have me, I'm in.

The short is an office-based picture, giving me my first "normal" role since I started this whole shindig. It's also a bad guy role, so I can get my teeth into it a bit.

Note to all actors of the world: bad guys are simply way, *way* more fun to play than good guys.

James Bond may get all the girls, but Dr. Evil gets all the laughs and the best lines. So far I've played mostly bad guys, and I couldn't be happier.

Muzzy wants to make a film with a bit of a trick at the end for the audience, which is right up my street. I love the "Usual Suspects" and "Fight Clubs" of the world, so a trick movie has my name on it from the get-go. And it'll look good on my showreel.

But what I hope will look even better on my showreel, is the upcoming Rehan Malik picture "Radio London."

I'm set to meet Raydolph Amponsah in the City (after meeting Muzzy) to talk about the character of Abdullah.

I'm set to meet Ray, then Bahzad, and then Rehan to discuss this character, and I want to get it right.

See, the thing about film (and music) that make them so difficult are the actual industries themselves. You can have someone write a brilliant film. They can direct and shoot a cinematic masterpiece.

They can edit and cut something that would hypnotise Paul McKenna. And you'd think that'd be enough.

But it's not.

If you can't somehow distribute and market your film, or get it screened or into a festival, you're a bit fucked. This was the lesson of "Morning Tea;" no endgame.

I believe Rehan Malik and his film "Radio London" are not going to suffer the same problem.

I believe strongly that the film has legs, and ought to be shown at as many places as possible once it is done.

And with such thoughts in mind, I go to see Ray.

Ray is a gentle, kind-sounding man with a bearded face and glasses. He's well educated, and, like Bahz and Rehan, is a Muslim.

The film is also itself concerned with the issues facing Muslims living in Britain. So I have to be very respectful and very delicate in my dealings with this project, since I am myself agnostic / Selfist.

They've also landed me a highly controversial character in Abdullah, and one with which I have to tread carefully and respectfully.

So almost the whole of the first conversation we have is not so much about the character as it is about Islam.

And Islam, as it turns out, is quite impressive.

I was myself raised Protestant, but outside of that and the primary school I went to, I have zero religious affiliation. I am highly interested in the subject, but solely as an outsider looking in.

Islam, I am impressed to learn, does not categorise itself with Christianity, Daoism, or Hinduism. It does not see itself as a religion.

It more perceives itself to stand alongside Capitalism, Socialism, and Communism as an actual "social system."

It is also based on, or rather, finds its origin in, a combination of poetry and scientific enquiry.

The Moors, for example, were one of the most advanced races for their time in history, with an understanding of mathematics, astrology, and biology that far surpassed our own at the same period.

The current public perception of Islam is a little more harsh, and is obviously highly coloured by the global "War on Terrorism" and the historic events of 9/11.

The system also has a uniquely poetic flavour to it. When I ask Bahz about marriage in Islam, for example, he tells me the belief in an afterlife is so genuine that it is something a couple might have to discuss and deal with in *this* life in order to be prepared for the next one.

I discover, to my surprise, that there is quite a lot about Islam I like. But again, from an outsider's point of view.

See, the issue is, I was raised by a teacher and was generally taught I had the right to question everything.

This does *not* make me think I have all the answers. Not for a second.

But I certainly have a right to ask the questions.

And a friend of mine by the name of Merlin has spent many an hour educating me on the subject of physics and quantum mechanics.

I have found more universal truth, more spirituality, and more enlightenment in learning how the universe actually *works* than in the pages of any book on spirituality or religion.

I'm thinking all this on the way home to meet a gent by the name of Dave Warwick.

I am, as usual, knackered out of my mind, and could do with nothing as much as I could use sleep. But I have to get my showreel done to my satisfaction and Dave is the editor Rooster has suggested to do it.

Thankfully he is very easygoing and is a pleasure to work with.

While he hammers away at my showreel, I prepare for my mum arriving in London, and for my second short film shoot of the year: "Magic Man."

"Magic Man" is to take place at Ravensbourne Studios, which is about a trillion miles outside of London and a pain in the arse to get to.

But Muzzy studies there and their facilities are amazing, so I pony up and get prepped for a long couple of days.

"Dominic" is the most straightforward character I've ever been given. He's the office asshole who bullies his more competent, more moral, and more honest employee, Stuart.

Now even though he's not the hardest character to play, being a bad guy is always way more fun than being a goodie. You can go pretty OTT without fear of reprimand.

So all my rehearsing and line learning has involved me reading lines cynically, venomously, annoyingly, superciliously (yeah, that's a word, and if you don't know it, you should own a dictionary). Any way I can that's bothersome, I shoot for.

When I get to Ravensbourne College I'm hit with an absolute rarity: a moment of possigret (possible regret) [again, sorry for the Flowcabulary it's just how I am] {and obviously I'm not sorry, per se, just raised well enough to be polite}.

I think on whether I'd have preferred to study film at a film school than English Literature at UCL. Ravensbourne has TV studios, film edit suites, grading suites, high-end cameras, the works.

And I'd have loved to study at a film school, but I wouldn't change what I have and what I've done for anything.

I'm led through workshops and studios to Muzzy's green room (the Green Room is where all the actors and crew that aren't currently on set hang out).

I get changed and say hey to Alistair (playing Stuart) and the rest of the cast.

Filming is easygoing, and my concern begins to be if we will get what we need done done, but then, I'm not directing. I assist where I can, and the shoot goes pretty smoothly.

My mum comes to set on one day just so she can see what I do, and while I'm sure it wasn't the most incredible of days, she had some fun, I think.

And on that note, another note to all actors: when it comes to your scripts, here's a little trick to bear in mind.

Your script will look something like this:

INT: TRAIN - DAY

TALENT looks out the window and speaks to his imaginary audience.

TALENT

Hey guys. Waddup. And you guys who work for the HMRC? Fuck *off*.

Now.

When you get a script, write CHARACTER in big bold letters at the top right of the page, and write ACTION in big bold letters at the top left of the page.

As you go down the page, to the right of the text / dialogue / stage directions, write what you can about the character's actual character, his or her personality, what traits you realise are there in either the actual writing or the subtext.

So in the above example, as some nutter is talking to an imaginary audience, and rudely so, you might write:

- Rude
- Crazy
- Hallucinatory

And you now know three things about him you did not know before.

To the left of the text, you write what actions in your mind would accompany his speech or his action.

We're told off the bat he looks out the window. If we think he's actually visualising people in his mind, we might choose him an eye-level or a spot to look at.

As he's telling them to "fuck off," we might also make him flip people the bird.

So you'd write, to the left of the above text:

- Looks out the window
- Visualises listeners
- Flips the bird

And suddenly you know what he says, why he says it, and how he says it.

Your key after realising all this is, of course, practising it.

Why do we write it down?

Because it shows to both you and to *anyone else who reads your script* that you have done your homework. A written-on script is a well-understood and oft-studied one.

Trust me.

OK.

Our list is done. Our email is prepped. Time to smash these emails out. The gut-wrenchery of it is this: no matter how many I have to send out to get an agent, I'm going to have to do the *exact* same thing to get a music manager and a publisher and a booking agent and a literary agent.

So whatever number I hit, I have to quintuple in my head to have the team around me I need.

Sucks, innit?

However. We can jump off that bridge when we get to it. So I start, daily, sending out my emails.

This is going to take a *while*…

I post my *** ******* paperwork, including my passport, my bill documents, my proof of address, and so on.

It's taken me forever, but I've finally got it all. One of the things you have to get is the police-held information on your arrest-history.

I was, erm, how shall we say, a touch *nervous* about ordering that...

For those who want to know, I've spent the night behind bars three times, been arrested twice in this country and once in another.

And allegedly there is a warrant for my arrest in the state of Texas.

Allegedly.

Fortunately I was worried for no reason and there's nothing on my record. So off it goes in the post. We'll see how the whole thing goes.

I'm starting to think it wouldn't be as bad an idea as I originally thought. On TV, with heavy PR, it'd certainly be a step in the right direction for my profile. It might not for me as a person, however.

I speak to Loki about it. He, as usual, has a good way of framing things so I can make my decision easily.

"If you had to choose between your favourite feature film right now and the last series of *** *******, which would you choose?"

Oddly, part of me is pulled in the direction of *** *******, but I know my answer. I've started to care about "Radio London" a lot.

And I want that job.

Bad.

Music.

It took me almost a year just to *mix* my album, let alone record it.

Ricardo Fargas kindly worked with me for nigh on twelve months to get my music as close to exactly how I wanted it as possible. The album is one long story of pain.

I tell you what though, the next one will *not* be.

While Ricardo Fargas mixed it for / with me, the gentleman responsible for mastering it (both mixer and masterer have sons, interestingly) [fascinating story Richie told me about Fargas jr. - Richie is teaching the youngster only two things <OK not only two, but you smell what I'm cooking...> and those two things are music and football. Richie says he plays all the music he works on to his son, and that Reiss, if he finds something wrong with the music, will dance and rave and point and motion at the computer. If he finds the music satisfactory, he will gradually fall asleep to it. This I call the "Lullabye effect:" as in, it lullabies you so much you go bye-bye. And my music passes the Fargas jr. lullabye test, people. Try that for a game of soldiers...] is a man by the name of Guy Buss.

Guy and I have known each other probably close on ten months.

I have travelled to his home in Homerton on numerous occasions and sat with him to talk my music through.

Thankfully to all that is holy he seems to think I am on a decent path, musically speaking. That's the nice thing about working with folks like Fargas and Bussman. You get honesty.

If they say your music has merit, then it has merit. People who operate a no-bullshit-policy tend to end up around me. People who don't, don't.

So I'm collating all my files and the latest mixes to make sure Guy has the least amount of work to do possible. It took me a year to make my album, a year to mix it, and a year to master it, by tale's end. Which as any musician will tell you, is about two years too long. However. It'll only be like this once, I promise you.

I know most of what I talk about is film in this diary, and that's just how my year is going, since I swore off live performance until my album is actually finished; but the fact is I'm actually from more of a musical background.

My mother taught dance and was every inch a musical performer. I grew up helping her choreograph routines for her kids, and she always had music on.

I learned to play the piano as a child and was in the choir the whole way through my primary school.

My secondary school music teacher was a touch scary for my liking, (think Worzel Gummage crossed with Voldemort) so the choir was out.

But I kept writing lyrics and poetry the whole way through. My father sings very well and my mum also plays the piano.

Music is in our blood.

Therefore music is in my *blood*. I am actually more accredited a musician than I am anything else:

- Two-time EMA 'Best Artist - Out of Area' nominee
- Three-time UK Unsigned (UKU) finalist
- Host vocalist and freestyler for 'Respect The Mic' show, London
- I appear on several tracks by Metis, and an album by the Left Step Band, as well as my own
- I've done scorework for two shorts, one feature, and one TV pilot
- and done more live shows than I can remember

I love film, but performing live music is just the greatest feeling you can have with your clothes on.

So I prep my material for Guy Buss, and I pray he adds the finishing touches so my album will finally be complete.

The "Magic Man" shoot goes well, but leaves us needing pickups.

Only one thing doesn't go well, but it's nothing to do with the shoot.

A word on responsibility - and this is the ultimate Law of the Universe - **Action and Consequence**.

There is no escaping it. It is to be embraced, even when it causes us pain, because even when it hurts it is the only way things can be and we must learn this.

I discover through one means or t'other that something I wrote a long time ago as an exercise has come to light.

Ordinarily this would be no issue. I am not, as a rule, an irresponsible writer. This particular piece of writing, however, is going to be so badly misinterpreted that it may have serious and long-term consequences for me and for several members of my family.

I discover, idiotically, that it is my fault it has come to light.

Worse still - by which I mean *far* worse still - the contents are causing pain to someone I love very much and have loved my whole life, and who has been nothing but kindness and love for the whole of that duration.

No amount of explanation will change the result.

No amount of apology will undo the hurt.

No amount of wishing will build me a time machine and let me take it back.

No amount of "it was an exercise" will reduce the pain.

No amount of hoping will make my loved one feel better.

I rectify the situation as fast as I can and make amends in what piddling, shitty way I am able. There is almost no feeling I hate as much as that of guilt combined with remorse and regret.

I'm on set for Muzzy and his crew, and let me tell you something - I'm a *fucking* passionate actor.

This day I am literally burning with anger. I am so utterly disgusted with myself that I am staggered I can actually get any work done. I'm shocked I'm not burrowing into the brickwork with my fingernails or ripping out my own hair.

Responsibility.

Take the consequences of your own actions. If there are consequences you don't want to take, don't do the action.

If you have screwed up, take your life by the hair and face up to those consequences; swallow your pride along with a big slab of humble pie, and apologise.

Be a man about it.

I feel a sickness in my gut that is unmistakeable. It is the feeling of being utterly disgusted with oneself.

And it is not the only time I have had this feeling.

I am going to have it again, I am sure.

And I'll deal with it then, too.

I don't just make the music, my friend.

I *face* it.

I took Mum to the "Magic Man" shoot just so she could see what I do. I reckon for a lot of it she was bored out of her skull, which is A-grade understandable.

127

If you're not a film buff or working yourself, film sets look like places where not much happens save very infrequently, at which point it's more manic than anywhere you've ever been (unless you happen to like clubbing to Happy Hardcore, in which case you have bigger problems than I can help you with...). It can be mind-itchingly boring.

Hell, even if you are *working* on a film set it can still be mind-itchingly boring.

Still, she came to watch because she's the greatest mother I've ever known and wants to see her son do his job.

It's a nice experience and I'd recommend it.

So it's nearly month end and I'm looking at a finished showreel.

And it's not too shabby, if I don't say so myself. I spend a whole night uploading it everywhere and I'm feeling like this is a start.

I send another email off to Backstreet Merchandise (who do Dizzee Rascal's clothing and many other pop stars) and we're into designing preliminary T-shirts.

We're on for having 5 or 6 products done by year-end, and I'm hoping we keep on course the rest of the year.

I also get another email from the guys at *** *******.

It says nothing interesting, but the phone call I get *next* from them is like something out of MI5.

Apparently I've got through rounds one, two, three, and four, and am now going back in to have a crack at stage five.

I'm given passwords. I'm told to say nothing about this. I'm told eagles are landing, the package is to be delivered, and a dog is barking.

It's like something out of the A-Team. Except with shitter music.

Interesting. We'll have to see how this goes.

I meet Rehan to talk about the Abdullah character at my studio before we kick off with filming.

I've spent quite a lot of time prepping this character and it all hangs on my meeting with Rehan the director.

Now, I know Abdullah is not a likeable guy. A lot of what he says is absolutely repugnant, and he looks a bit like Jesus. He's highly inflammatory and basically, my father would take one look at him in the film and be inclined to spit all over it.

And yet I don't need him to be likeable. Even though, as an actor, this is a risk.

See, not many actors have the sand to be completely despicable.

And I'd like him to be as despicable as possible but even more so that he is as *challenging* as possible. He needs to represent an argument, not a conclusion.

Rehan's film is too good, the idea too clever, the intent too benevolent for me to make him an easily discardable lunatic.

So I've written an entire backstory to this character that includes:

- A fascination with quantum physics and a deep care for the universe
- An incredibly caring but detached family man - a lost soul, if you like
- A person who deliberately looked at every religion and chose, consciously, his call to Islam, as opposed to a family-inducted child or a brainwashee
- A profound, MENSA level intelligence that makes him highly eloquent - his IQ is higher than mine, a decent 179 (you ever tried to act like someone *smarter* than you? It's fucking *hard*...) [thirty points higher than mine, FYI, and why? It's the year of *Trinities*, remember...?]
- A passion so intense he captivates his speakers with the ease of a rock star
- A history of drug abuse and violence, meaning his intellect and his faith actually saved him from a gruesome ending, giving his faith an actual *power*
- A desire to never run from trouble, meaning like me he faces the music, and that ironically this *will* result in a gruesome ending... he will be punished for *my* sins
- And crucially, he is absolutely completely and utterly one hundred per cent pacifist

129

The question Abdullah is designed to bring to your attention is this:

How tolerant are you *really*? How much do you *really* defend free speech?

Especially if all of that free speech is from a worldview diametrically opposed to your own? Especially if it's everything you despise being said and it's in your living room? How then do you feel about a notion that, in America, is defended by the actual constitution of the country?

You may not agree with any of what he says, but Abdullah is physically hurting *no one*.

Will you want to condemn him, or will you look beyond his poisonous vitriol and agree that people can agree to disagree?

The lead, Tarik, is a moderate and 'good' British Muslim. He's a wronged innocent party. Abdullah needs to be the counterpoint to this; an extremist, an unaccused but guilty inflamer of hate, but one who never raises his fists in anger. And hopefully the combination of both Tarek and Abdullah will bring out the anger, the prejudice, the thought, and the consideration of the majority of the audience.

Watch the gifted actor who plays Tarek.

He's the *exact* counterpoint to Abdullah. He's quiet, calm, keeps himself to himself, and has an air of peace to him. The combination of the two is magnetic.

This is called "Working as a Team."

I sit, after explaining all this, watching Rehan, nervous as fuck, to see what he might say.

I am absolutely convinced that this was not what he was expecting. I may have talked myself out of a job...

Rehan, miraculously, incredibly, *staggeringly*, has 'no issue' with any of the things I have said. I'm so humbled and grateful that it's unbelievable.

"You sure?" I ask, hesitantly.

"I can't believe how much we agree on this character. You've clearly put a lot of time, a, a lot of effort into this character, and, to be honest, you know, it's like, Abdullah could become a real show-stealer, and, you know, I, I love what you've done, the science, the religion, the way he's into quantum physics, I mean, maybe, you know, we can present him in such a way that people can't just write him off as a headcase, you know?"

We embrace and depart from the studio. I have the role in "Radio London."

And this film, I can smell it, has a chance.
I'm over the moon.

OK.

So: I'm headed to Hammersmith to experience *** ******* the final stage.

And I'm torn. As in, extraordinarily so.

I don't know whether I want to do this or not. Either way, I want to get the fucking audition, as a matter of principle.

It's been like a military operation. We've got codewords and have to meet people that are only identifiable by their purple jackets and red umbrellas; the works.

A group of us are collected at the tube and then taken to a meeting point. The building we are moved to is not a million miles away from what I imagine a secret society headquarters would look like. I'm staggered I haven't had a retinal scan and some dude pulling on latex gloves grinning at my backside.

In total about ten of us are taken into a room with a mirrored wall. Behind that mirrored wall, I know, sits *** *******. I look.

Whether they look back or not, I have no idea.

We were all asked to bring in a personal item, something important to us. I brought in my graduation ring and a jacket I bought off a flatmate years ago.

There are about five women and five guys in this room. I know none of their names and I shall find out none of them. We are under strict instructions to give away as few details as humanly possible.

The idea is that information here is unimportant. Personality should shine through. I have no issue with that. What I do have an issue with is that I feel like I am off my game.

Something here isn't clicking.

"Guys, so you understand, this is an *unpopularity contest*: and this is your last chance. Win here and you get through to a show that may be watched by a million to twelve million viewers, according to our track record. So here's your chance. No point coming up to us at the end saying 'oh I'm actually a really interesting person, I just didn't get a chance to speak.' You're gonna have to make your chance to speak."

I look at the host who has just spoken. You want me to try to be more *popular* than these freaks? Are you crazy?

And then suddenly we're all introducing ourselves.

The guys are:

- BlondeHair - a truly cool-looking kid dressed all in black, with a haircut reminiscent of Dragon Ball Z or Guile from Street Fighter II
- Geezoire - an Essex lad with a cheek to his grin and who freely admits he's in severe need of an imminent shag
- WiffWaff - the most effeminate man I have ever seen; very well-mannered, polite, dressed in pink and blue, and if he's not gay, he needs to be
- NiceGuy - a slim, friendly young man who seems extremely nervous but is so likeable that you'd have a pint with him in five minutes flat
- And of course, Yours Truly

The women are:

- Norkia - an ebony black girl with beautiful skin and the most ample pectoral region I've seen since Baywatch was commissioned
- Elfin - an Asian girl who freely admits an addiction to shoes, and who is elegantly dressed, but quite quiet despite the glamorous outfit
- TomGirl - a rock-chick looking young woman, very cool in her appearance and blunt in her speech
- LadyBaba - a truly, *truly* unique hippy-dressed girl who brings in her magic carpet which she claims accompanies her all over the world (I'm not kidding…)

I scan the room to see if there's a 'Field Marshal' character type I'll have to compete with, but as a stroke of luck, there's none.

We go through Round One, where we introduce ourselves and explain our personal item.

Round Two is where we sit in pairs opposite each other and conduct interviews.

Round Three is a group game where we get split into threes and play improv games.

And Round Four is where we debate topics the panel give us.

And no matter what I do, I'm not really here. Something in me is revolting against the entire situation.

I study my opponents. BlondeStrike is a real find - a young man with so much gravitas he'd make a fine actor. Norkia is honest to the point of comic brutality and exactly my kind of person. The rest all seem cool enough, and they deserve my best.

But I'm just not in the ring.

This doesn't seem like a fight I want to have. Nor one I am going to win.

The competition is described as an unpopularity contest, and the two 'judges' in the room tell us again and again that this is the last chance to impress.

To impress?

Motherfucker, you called *me*.

I didn't call you or your fuckwit show that shows my people in their worst light, and that makes voyeurism a new fad for couch-dwelling potato crisp-devouring soap addicts.

Whoa. Hang on. Where did *that* come from??? That sounded like the Doc infused with Abdullah.

Fuck.

Concentrate.

I step in the ring briefly and have a few swings. I'm more than able to cope, but I'm just not here. And despite the fact my watch tells me this has taken three hours or more, before you know it, we're done.

We shake hands with people.

We say our goodbyes.

We leave.

I walk from the building in a haze of peaceful confusion. I know that sounds contradictory, but I don't care. It's how I feel.

Either I just smashed it and my radar is off, or I totally fucked it up and my radar is *still* off.

I've no idea what just happened.

QUARTER TWO - SPRINGSUMMER

"MAGIC MAN" 2010

"THE DEBT COLLECTORS" 2010

"WAR OF THE SEXES" 2010

APRIL 2010:

"THE AGE OF THE FOOL"

"Now Dog Dirt McGraw thinks he's the law
But he ain't never vexed BTX before,
It's high noon time for a fly tune rhyme,
We are bona fide, alone we ride!"

- Talent -
"Dog Dirt McGraw"

- IMMORTALENTED 2013 -

Rooster tells me there's a role going.

It's to play a Jehovah's Witness on a feature film called "The Ham and the Piper" by a director called Mark Norfolk.

"Do you wanna play it?" says he.

Schnig, do cows sleep standing up?

Hell *yes* I do. Plus, I *know* some people on this gig.

There's Smugz Malone, who's one of the funniest hustlermen I ever met, and a true character. Rooster is ADing (assistant directing), Twiggers is PAing (production assisting), Bartholomew the Schenk is DPing (directing photography), along with a whole host of new people who have very, very impressive credits. Pips, for example, has worked a ton of major features in the last year, including "Clash of the Titans." She's also so down to earth I wonder if she's got roots. Ed's doing locations, the little Hispanic bandit, and the director is one of the most chilled out cats you'll ever meet.

I suddenly see that not every director has to be a maniac on the verge of cardiac arrest.

So I'm dressed in a cheesy suit, I still have my "Radio London" beard and long hair, and am raring to go. It's only a few small scenes, but what do I care? It's cinemusic, and that's all I care about.

And women.

And my family.

Natch.

As I'm only on it for two days, I spend a lot of my time focusing on the wrap party.

I sort it at a local place down the road (we're in a massive mansion-esque house in Notting Hill, one of the trendier "rich areas" of central London), and after several days filming and numerous dramas featuring Smugz, we all head down for drinks.

Now, Twiggers and I have something of a chequered past. She's stayed in my room on more than one occasion, and we like each other.

She's a beautiful, tall, slender young woman, lovely as roses, and any man'd be nuts to turn her down.

However, guess who's a lunatic.

Yeah.

For a variety of reasons at this point, she's not my biggest fan. In general I think of it as being professional to avoid, erm, plundering the help, so to speak. However, I play this one badly and I suffer the consequences.

That's fair enough.

I can be as much of an asshole as anyone, and given I do what I do, I deserve as tough a rap as anyone else, if not tougher.

The first wrap party is at the local, where we're all intent on getting absolutely macarooned. Until, that is, a table of three strikingly attractive women appears in my vision.

One oriental-looking one is pretty but not my type, a pale-skinned delicate looker of a girl is again nice to look at, but not my brand of vodka either, and then there's a tanned, bronzed skin, Native-American-meets-African-meets-Egyptian-looking one that has my name written all over it. And she's dressed to *kill.*

Except I'm not a *complete* twunt. I know there are limits.

So I avoid going over, due to the presence of Twiggers and my own friends. No need to rub things in other people's faces. Play nice, I'm thinking.

Smugz, as usual, has other ideas.

"Why don't you go over, man? Show us old folk how the young 'uns do it. One of them's superfly!"

Yeah, I know that, Smugz, thanks.

And now, so does everyone else. Naturally, the more I try to steer the conversation away from the trio of hotness, the more the conversation stays exactly there. Except now it starts turning into a matter of male pride.

"Dude, if I was your age I'd be over there now. What's your excuse, Rooster? They're money, man. Go do the thing."

Smugz is now playing with fire; because, while I am aware I am being provoked and that makes it easier to leave it alone, my sense of maleness demands immediate action upon a whim or desire I believe to be reasonable.

The same sense of maleness also believes some people need telling, and Smugz, on occasion, needs telling. Shackling either instinct irks me and makes me borderline *loath* myself.

So: it's action stations.

I send a lingering, smiling, "Hi" of a look over to our big-haired, stylishly-dressed, beauty of unknown origin. She smiles back. I then grab my phone and walk out the pub dialling a number.

OK, the number happens to be my own answerphone, but then they don't know that. And it's a genuine call, meaning I am neither dissembling nor lying.

I repeat the look, and nod to her, saying "Hey" as I walk out.

She smiles and gives me a "Hey" in a voice so sexy my feet vibrate and my eyeballs itch.

Game theory states that, after making a minor connection with a woman, and then after repeating that connection, you cement the original one.

It also states that if I've left whilst on the phone, they'll know instinctively I'll return *off* the phone.

It states too that if they've seen me in a large group of people, of whom some are women who are laughing and joking, that they'll find that more than somewhat attractive and my status will rise.

I've made a gentle but clear opening gambit, and can either approach their table later or see if they step up and make a move.

I'm aware this might be construed as somewhat indelicate in front of Twiggers, and for that I feel my own self-rage, but no man living calls my friends or me a pussy unless it's deserved. And certainly not Rooster, who has nuts of steel even at the worst of times and trust me, is *no* pussy.

I walk back in the pub, calculating every possible outcome I can conceive of.

"Hey."

The oriental one greets me, and asks me to sit. See? Nice things *do* happen.

So I sit.

Now I feel every pair of eyes at the "Ham and the Piper" table boring into my back like drills.

The oriental one is friendly and amicable, and tells me that I'm "hot," and that I should have a drink with them. The whisky and coke I'd ordered before leaving the table and walking out on the phone arrives (as luck occasionally will have it) about two seconds later, making me look a tad James Bond. Or a tad raging alkie.

The paler one turns out to be French, and my spider-sense already tells me I'm being teed up for something. TribalBeauty still has yet to speak. The first two introduce themselves, and the oriental informs me that her delicately tanned friend on the end is single.

Jackpot.

Her name is Louise, and *oh... my... God...*

She looks like Lebanese royalty wrapped up in Coco Chanel multiplied by Mel B's hair, which had never occurred to me as being sexy until I actually *saw* it.

She was formerly a model and now works in fashion and part-time for charity. And lives around the corner.

Erm.

As the Preditors would say: "Mine."

"And pay."

We swap numbers, and are just in the process of making a date when we're interrupted.

Twiggers, understandably pissed at my somewhat inconsiderate actions, has struck for women everywhere and comes over. She confidently puts her arms round me, says (*superbly*) "Sorry to interrupt..." and then quieter, in my ear: "Outside. *Now.*"

I go outside. And before I do, Louise goes: "That your girlfriend?"

Volcanic with all kinds of oxblood boiling-over-how-*dare*-Twiggers-do-that fury, I try, as calmly as I can, to respond "No."

"But she'd like to be?" Tribalqueen asks.

"Right now, I'm guessing probably not," Englishtwat answers.

He leaves to go outside.

The conversation outside turns into (I don't know how, so don't ask) a kiss, and then a longer kiss, and then a near-argument.

The night ends with me booking a date with TribeQueen and watching Twiggers walk off extraordinarily irate with Yours Truly.

Part of me thinks: this could be funny in the morning. The other part of me thinks: keep this up and you won't *get* many more mornings. And that no, it's not funny.

C'est la vie.

"That was pretty fly, man. You get her number?"

I nod to Smugz and Rooster.

"That's gonna be fun..." says Smugz.

I sigh.

Louise and I set a date, and I'm more than a little excited.

She's my favourite kind of age, see, and also does charity work, and is hotter than a chilli-pepper factory on Mercury.

The age thing is important.

I used to be a massive fan of girls: now, not so much. Women are the new black. And don't get your crosses wired, I've felt like that for yonks, but it's worth stating.

See, there's all kinds of what I call "egotisn't" with girls ("honey, the reason you're saying that is because of your ego..." - "T'isn't!") [Geddit?].

With women, this is less often the case.

Louise doesn't have an ounce of bullshit in her body. Nor of fat, which kind of helps.

We have a very civil dinner with some nice wine, all the time talking about pleasant things, no hint of mischief or underlying tension. Which means, as any expert or PUA will tell you, that there's tons of it, and that your opponent is just good enough to play along.

We sit in the living room and talk. For a bit. And then, well, we go elsewhere and don't talk. This is the other benefit of women as opposed to girls - they cut the bullshit. And they also tend to have a better idea of what they're doing.

Again, don't wret me gong, if a twenty-year-old international playmate with the body of Venus and the face of Amora comes running, then I'm there.

Been there, done that. And I'm happy for rematches. But for Christ's sake, give me something with as much substance and shit to actually *say* as possible.

Louise and I collapse in a heap of sweat. She then comes out with one of the single greatest sentences I have ever heard.

Ever.

"You just made me... I mean... I just... I think… I just came so hard I *cried...*"

OK so we're on 121 agents.

So far, so good.

I've had bites from several; two smaller agencies being the first two credible ones. I'd like to get in off the bat with the big boys, but truth to tell I have no issue with starting at the bottom.

I never have.

In fact in many ways, I prefer it.

A one year contract: say three months to get up and running, and three months to fine tune it, we should be off and running by month seven.

We'll see. I've heard a lot of talk from a lot of people, but delivery I've seen from very few.

This is why the BTX are my crew. They are *doers.*

They get shit *done.*

Most people you meet do not grasp this simple, basic concept. Metis, with his music; Merlin with his company; LL with his new agency; Shanghai as a teacher-in-training; they all *get* it.

I take care of some stuff for my mum on Ebay and then get back on with sending out more invites and emails for my groups.

A message comes in on CastingCall Pro saying I'm under consideration for a lead in a new feature.

"Cock Tales" is an emotional drama-comedy.

It's about a guy who loses everything, becomes a drag queen, and has an emotionally charged relationship with another man - a quite physical and romantic relationship, to boot.

141

I immediately want the part.

I've got to make sure I don't get stereotyped, and so far I've managed to avoid it. This would be a good (although nerve-wracking) step in the right direction: it's going to be pretty hard to stereotype me if my first roles in features are Milan the Slovakian manic-depressive, the asshole man in Solito, a Jehovah's Witness, and a drag queen in this.

So I send the best email I can.

See, half of the trick is being polite enough to impress to the parents, but rude enough to impress the daughter.

So the email reads something like:

"Dear Izzy,

I am extraordinarily interested in this.

To the extent that I'd beg, steal, or possibly stage a one-man invasion of China to get an audition.

OK so maybe not, but you get the idea.
Best Regards, as always

Stephen,"

I have nothing against the Chinese, incidentally. It just seemed funnier, given the larger population.

And, more to the point, it got me the audition.

It's at times after I get an audition that I feel particularly good.

Reminds me that I have a yet bigger challenge to dance and dice with.

So it seems a fitting time to tell you the truth.

My apologies; it seems like a fitting time to tell you the *Truth*.

I was actually born Stephanie Cloisters Brocklehurst.

Yes, I know. Just hold your horses a second...

I knew when I was as young as (happens all the time to transsexuals, trust me) eight that I was born with the wrong body.

Film and music were to be my calling, but before that we'd have a larger problem to surmount: gender.

See, here is the thing. As a very young girl my mother's friends would often remark, "Your son is so handsome."

It fucking *gutted* me. She'd have to reply, "Actually, she's my daughter."

Hated.

It.

Plus, us ladies are not supposed to swear so much. And as you can probably tell, I fucking *love* swearing. "Bastard" is perhaps the most satisfying word to say in the world. After the words "fuck" and "c*nt," obviously.

Anyway.

It was difficult.

And not only did I know I was meant to be a man; *other people* could see it too. Hence the above comments. I wasn't imagining it. It was really true.

You would not believe how thankful I was to hear that.

It changed the course of my whole life.

Anyway.

Gender-alterational cosmetic surgery was not so common back then. In fact only one place on the planet existed (at the time) that could genuinely provide what I sought.

So a trip to the U.S. was organised. The problem was, how do you go for long enough and stay for recuperational therapy without raising suspicion amongst family and friends before you go?

Lightening struck - you go for a "year abroad," and tell everyone that you're "studying" for one annum, and then return, literally, a different person.

I was terrified of my family knowing.

Genuinely.

I could see Pop kicking my ass *big time*.

And how would they understand? Would Kev or any of the others ever accept me as a man? Several of them had been attracted to me. That I knew. I'd even been attracted to them, once upon a time.

It was only when I got back, and Kev asked me what the fuck had just happened, that I said...

...April Fool's.
...Beeeeyatch.
Had you going for a second...
(...didn't I...?)

;)

So I head to the middle of buttfuck nowhere to see my first agent. *Man* that's a depressing experience.

In every industry or craft there are strata, or rungs on the ladder, or as the woman of my world calls them, "echelons." I've never met anyone who is happy to admit his or her life's ambition is to be on the bottom one.

In acting, the bottom rungs are either called "Panto" (think some clown dressed like a farmer, about ten imbeciles in a dinosaur suit and 100 nutsacks yelling "He's behiiiiiind yooouuuu") or "light entertainment" (think being onboard a cruise to Vanuatu and some chump onstage knocking one out and crooning out hits by Sinatra).

This particular agent tells me firstly that I'm dressed like a bag of shit, and secondly that their clients are mostly in both the above.

I'm seething. I'm fairly shaking with anger.

Did these people not read my email? Do I look like I want to be in some stagefreak show called "The Phantom of Les Mis 2: He's Actually More to the Left of You?"

I leave a very disgruntled man.

And you know what *else* I hate? Agencies who "won't take you" without you *paying money* for the privilege of their representation and for "their photographer" (blatantly nailing them) to do your headshots.

You know what?

Grow up. Be an *adult*. If you are so bad at your job you have to charge your own actors to make ends meet, either admit it and seek help or admit it and fuck off.

In my parents' generation, professional competence was a matter of a small thing called *pride*.

There was none of this "I'm sueing you cause I was looking at *your* shop whilst plummeting to my death after I lobbed myself off the top of St Paul's" shit.

You either handled your business or it handled you.

I see another agent in the city. This one is marginally better, but is slightly marred by the fact one of the people interviewing me brought their fucking *dog* along for the experience.

You ever tried doing your monologue while a canine is giving your wingnuts a good sniffing? It's no vacation, take it from me.

I'm stunned these people actually made it through puberty.

Genuinely.

And the more I see it the more I believe it the job of parents to instil a little something in kids that we call *character*. Oh, and also integrity. It's not, you see, that I don't *trust* these people to represent me.

It's much, *much* worse. I wouldn't trust these people to make me a fucking *sandwich*.

"If you have to hesitate, don't do it" - A. Brocklehurst - 1998

So I leave.

And I'm massively disgruntled. I go to an audition for a modelling agency (*fuck* knows why) [actually off that, I know exactly why. It's all about shots in the chamber, lords and ladies: the more shots you take, the greater your chance of hitting the target] {"off that" is brokerspeak for "pull my bid or offer"} and it's at least better.

The guy running it is a nice guy. He's clearly not running Storm or Elite Models else I wouldn't be in here. He explains he's looking for actors too and he'd like to give it a go.

It's all very reasonable.

Now, on a professional level I figure I have little to gain here except being a "represented model" (typically I hate models, unless they are in my bed) [Christ this chapter's all *over* the shop...] {Good,

145

innit?} <Shut *up*, Tahira...> except the man before me is taking a risk by being honest with me.

A lot of people would "punish his naivety" by walking out.

Fuck that.

I'm a karma soldier. So I sign up.

We shake hands. I leave.

Now he's never gotten me anything. Nor has he called me. Not once. But he was straight with me, and I rewarded his honesty in whatever humble way I could.

Because I believed it the right thing to do.

I have another audition. This one I actually *want*.

This is for a music producer who is looking to take on new artists. Now far as that goes, I already *have* producers. I'll see your whomever and raise you one Blaqmale and one Ricardo Fargas.

When you're done crying after that come see me and I'll introduce you to 'em.

Anyway. I don't want a new producer. What I *do* want is the team behind the advert I saw that made me apply in the first place.

So I get to the middle of buttfuck nowhere, and here's how the shizzy goes dizzown.

(I'm a twat, I know, and as for the above, I can only apologise... I *really* have *no* idea...)

So I head out again to futtbuck nowhere. Takes me hours.

I fill out forms at the office we get to.

I wait for half an hour.

I finally get in front of three people and we talk music. My gut tells me this isn't happening, but, screw it. I'm here.

I perform my "Lost Tribe" track, having told the woman she needs to turn my track up more.

I cane it.

The woman concedes she should have turned my track up more. I leave, knowing in my heart I won't get a callback.

I get home to see an email from people I've never heard of: "The Casting Collective." They want to put me forward for some film called "Frostbite."

My first question is: how the Christ did these people get my details? But hey, it's a feature film, and that's my game. I email back saying I'm in for a penny, and in for a pound.

I'm told to head to Notting Hill on date blah at time blah.

I send my confirmation, expecting nothing.

I walk out of the tube station groggy and disoriented.

I'm not high or anything; it's just the morning. Which I hate.

I once put a slice of bread in my jacket pocket and tried to toast my leather gloves.

I follow my Google map to a building hidden from view. Slap me with a saucepan and call me Sally, the queue coming out the building is *huge*. As in, *mahoosive*.

It's *ridic*.

There's like 500 people coming out of this bastard. Erm. What kind of film are we talking about here? I stand in line for what would have been forever, had it not been for the marvellous invention of the iPod.

"Steves", for your information, get a rough time. In film or in music we get pretty beat up. Good guys aren't called Steve. Bad guys aren't even called Steve. Usually it's the absolute "who-the-hell-cares-about-*you*?" character who is called Steve. You know, the mate of the lead Character who spends his time watching "Star Trek Voyager," drinking decafe and toking on blunts.

Pisses me *right* off.

Not, however, with Steve Jobs.

This man is legit. He's the real deal. And his products are just 100% Hakuna Matata. Other famous Steves include:

- Stephen Dorff (actor)
- Steve Martin (actor / comedian)
- Steven Hendry (World snooker champion)
- Steven Spielberg (World's greatest director)
- Stephen Brocklehurst (soon, schniglin, soon...)

Anyway.

So I queue for about two hours (see, not all glitz and glam, this acting lark...) waiting patiently in the sun with hundreds of other men. (Sounds like the premise for a mass-orgy porno flick... entitled "The Queue", or something...) We get into the building and there's more paperwork and crap.

Until a woman comes out and asks if we all know why we're here. We murmur a "no."

"Ah," she says, "right. You're here to audition for the new Hollywood Major Motion Picture version of "Captain America: the First Avenger"."

I stare at her blankly for a moment.

"Anyone have any questions before we begin briefing you?" she says.

What leaves my mouth was intended to remain in my head.

"Captain America? Fuck. *Me...*"

MAY 2010:

"ANGELMOTHER, AND A MOVIE IN THE CANNES"

"It was the 5th of July in 1980,
The Gift of a Life was Given a Baby,
Mom got Miffed and Started to Slate Me,
She Missed the Tennis Finals, It was one of the Greats,
See...?"

- Talent -
"Lady Luck"

- IMMORTALENTED 2013 -

The beginning of May is always nice for me.

First of all it's Mayday, which sounds like a submarine red alert.

Secondly, that particular day is the day of my mother's birth, and this is something for which I am particularly grateful.

I don't have enough time here to explain just how professional a parent or majestic a person she is, and I don't think she'd want me to anyway.

I see my nan while I'm home with family and this has its usual effect. It calms me.

It brings me something I ache for yet rarely have: peace.

My nan's house is also the only other building on the planet in which I can sleep peacefully (along with my Home-home).

Everywhere else I'm practically an insomniac. I've never gotten to the bottom of this, although I have my theories.

Could be a case of guilty conscience, and though that doesn't sound like me, Lord knows I've done enough shit that it's a possibility I can't rule out. I'm inclined to think it may be a result of overactive imagination syndrome, or the fact I'm usually juggling a hundred things at once.

149

It could be a whole host of things. I'm not sure. Answers on a postcard, people.

My mum's birthday goes well. She is going to be seventy next year and come rain, shine, thunder or hail, we're going to party like it's 1999.

I realise I haven't spoken to my Parimosita in a while, and get that feeling in my gut again that she's about to be lost to me forever.

It's a weird feeling; mostly because I despise the idea, despite not wanting to change it. Which seems ludicrous, primarily because it *is* ludicrous.

Kid Ant's the solution to take my mind off things.

I met him through Hops from the Ibiza trip, and to be frank Ant is a lovely young man. He's looking to make a career change - to get into the world of broking, which he rightly sees as a game-changer.

Fortune, fame, and success, all just waiting for him there like gifts under the tree.

The reason he and I speak is that he wants my experience having been there to get him in the game.

Now, this is not as easy as you might think. The City has only recently been rocked by a small thing called the 'credit crunch.'

Getting a finance job without a degree in finance is not a walk in the park. On the contrary, it's more like ice-skating uphill.

And while I am not Mr City as I am no longer there, whatever advice I have to give and whatever help I may provide, he shall have.

So we have mentoring sessions wherein I work on his CV, and where we talk about tactically how best he might gain access to the City. We do the CV, and we speak at length about contacts and networking. All of which we do well, but the issue remains - he needs a client.

We're just going to have to try another route until I / we think of a better one, else it's off to uni for a finance degree.

I call my Parimosita.

We speak.

We are civil and kind to one another. She tells me she feels this may be the end of "our" era. This would be strange to most people since we have not been together for nearly six years. She says her family is well. I tell her I miss her. She says likewise.

We hang up.

I make certain I breathe deeply. In the selfsame year two of the loves of my life are to marry. I have a feeling in my gut about it.

And I'd change neither one, and I am happy for them both. But I have to hold fast to honesty - it still hurts.

Still, you grow up or you fuck off.

That applies to me too, if not even more so.

I'm still sending out applications like a madman, but the *one* piece of admin I wanted to take care of I have failed to do.

I wanted, the year I turned thirty, to cast my first vote.

My parents are very, very passionate about their voting, and whilst I admire this, and to a certain extent echo it, I do not replicate their actions. This is mostly because I am yet to be convinced that the system itself works.

I am intensely proud of my country, and I love Her dearly. The voting system here and the one in the U.S. (and yes I am aware there are significant differences betwixt the two) have the honourable monikers of being "democratic." I am not convinced I trust either of these systems to actually live up to that name.

There is something of the conspiracy theorist that lives within me and tells me that politics is really a grand circus that is being conducted for me and my countrymen to convince us of the illusion of choice.

I find a lot of truth in this notion.

However, as I have been told more than once, people fought and died for me to have the vote, so no matter how you look at it, my not voting is a form of disrespect to them.

And that I cannot abide.

So this year was to be the year. Except my voting application got sent back to me.

You ever tried registering on the day of the event?

It's a *madness*.

I travel from East London to Central London. I bus it, I cab, I walk. I ask, I plead, I beg. Nothing. Nada. Zip.

Bupkiss. The system has rejected me and is laughing at me.

And that *pisses* me off. I swear an oath to myself that this will never occur again whilst I live.

And then I accept defeat and sod off home.

Ayan Mitra is one of my oldest best friends in the world. He also turned 30 this year and the crew and I did not get to celebrate it with him.

Ayan like a Lion in Zion: we owe ourselves a parrrr-taaay...

It's the final audition for "Cock Tales" coming up.

And I've prepped my ass off.

I've been auditioning like a madman, for features including "How To Be a Criminal Mastermind," and "Identity," and "The Lost Men."

I've had callbacks for some and not for others. But the one I want is still "Cock Tales."

I head to the final audition in North East London; a nice pub with a lovely outdoors area. I read again, not for the main character but the second. There's a twisting feeling in my gut that tells me this is not to be.

Still, we'll see.

The next day I call Smugz and talk to Rooster about the Cannes Film Festival. This has become something of a paradox.

I can go, and I desperately want to go, but my lack of pass means I'd be there but I'd not be part of the actual Festival. I'd be an outsider looking in, not a VIP looking out.

This confuses me. I send Anita a birthday message and hit the sack. Sleep is still a commodity I don't get enough of.

Wonderfully my holiday time appears in the form of Marina's birthday, which we have at Monza in South Kensington.

Marina is unusual for a West London girl, in so far as she is more impressed by loyalty, honesty and friendship than she is by money, wealth, or extravagance.

She and I have known each other nearly a decade, and she is one of the inner circle. She was there for all the Parimosita and Anita sagas and has been there since. I have all the love in the world for her, and also for her partner in crime Halaya who is nuttier than a fruitbat but is a lovely, attractive lass who'd do anything for those she cares for.

Dinner at Monza is almost surreal.

I'm not running around, I'm not trying to catch my breath. It's just a nice evening with food and drinks. Loki and I catch up and he tells me all about his new girlfriend Angela, who I'll meet later on.

So moved am I by my time at Monza, on Saturday I decide to take a day off and go see Louise. This young woman has become more than a little important to me. She makes me remember there are other things to life than work and warfare.

And one of those things, is the 2010 Cannes Film Festival.

I leave to the airport with no idea of what is going to happen.

I'm also aware that I've not been abroad for quite some time, and while I'm excited as a man can be when he's nearly thirty, I'm also a bag of nerves.

The Cannes Film Festival - one of the major annual events in the global cinematic calendar. And I have never been.

As the good book says, there's a first time for everything.

I ensure I have spending money, passport, clothes, iPod and all the usual travel essentials for the journey. The flight is only a couple of hours long, so we should be there in no time. Rooster and MoneyBaby are already out there with Twiggers, who, it must be said, is taking to the film business like a duck to plum sauce.

I, naturally, have no pass for the festival. Which means I have no access to the tents or the actual festival. "So why go then, Talentino Slim?" I hear you ask.

Because. First off, I need a fucking vacation. And secondly, I just want to *see* the whole event: the yachts, the red carpet, the film hall, everything. So I can see just how hard I actually think it is going to be to crack this thing wide open. To watch and learn, and to see how possible it is to get from this side of the rope to that one.

I walk in the airport like a kid in a candy store.

I can't *wait* to be on holiday in Filmsville. I'm so worked up I barely register an absolutely gorgeous young woman walking into WH Smith's in the airport. She's got brownish blonde hair and looks, well, like a dessert ought to look to your appetite.

My immediate thought is to leave well alone.

We're in an *airport*, for God's sake.

Then Talent kicks in and demands to know why I am judging the possibility of something rather than just wading in.

Good question.

Never presume your own failure - it simply increases the odds of that outcome.

I hold fort near a pillar at the outside of Smiths and see our young Amazonian leave the store with a book in hand.

"What you reading?" says I.

She looks at me with that immediate-suspicion-of-stranger that this city somehow fosters. I'm not a fan of immediate cynicism. To her credit, she answers me. It's one of Obama's books.

Interesting.

We chat for a while, and it turns out she's a successful painter, selling her work out of a store in Milan. She's Italian. Now I'm interested.

We talk food for a minute, and then before I know it we're swapping numbers and booking a date to try out Spanish cuisine.

Also before I know it, we're doing something so not-permitted-in-an-airport that we get kicked out of a certain area. I'd give you the full breakdown, but that ain't what gentlemen do. Not that I'm a gent, you understand, but I'm trying.

I get on the plane to Cannes with new fire in my belly.

If you can pick up a girl in an airport (previously also had some success on a bus, a train, and oddly, once, on a horse) then who the hell am I to say what is and is not possible?

Day One at Cannes Film Festival 2010:

I land in Cannes excited as hell about seeing the place and about meeting up with Rooster and MoneyBaby.

My only reservation is that I've been to Cannes before with the love of my life and had a somewhat embarrassing incident there.

Actually, it was two incidents, now I think about it.

(You might be thinking I take the piss out of myself a lot, or am pretty self-deprecating. This is true, because it keeps you grounded. Also in this day and age where political correctness seems to have become so omnipresent as to be socially incorrect, it's the only safe way to go, comedy-wise. I can say what the hell I like about myself, knowing full well I may be the only person I *can* do that to who won't get offended…)

[much]

Last time I was in Cannes, my girlfriend attempted to teach me to rollerblade.

Now, I love the look of this sport. I absolutely do. Except despite the fact I have kickboxed, Thai-boxed, played tennis, hockey, American football, powerlifted, and been a dance instructor, I absolutely *cannot* skate, ski, rollerskate or rollerblade. Period.

And I don't mean 'I'm OK at it and just being humble;' I mean, 'if you place any value on your own safety, do not be near me on a slope or ice rink.'

Seriously. I've met corpses who were better.

My dear girl tried her very best to teach me over two days.

She encouraged, cajoled, advised, supported, did everything you'd want your woman to do. Her patience was astounding. Her success?

Not so much.

The upshot? I managed to fall over more than a dozen times on concrete; I knocked over two perfectly innocent young children; I went face-first into an ice-cream van, and lastly ended up cartoon-on-the-spot-skate-running in the middle of traffic at traffic lights on a main road in the centre of Cannes during rush hour.

I was working harder than I'd ever worked in my entire life only to fail to actually move. I was actually *sweating*. My beauty, laughing so hard she was actually shedding tears, eventually came to my aid and saved me from the situation.

Later that evening, my ego completely battered and my mood darker than an eclipse, we headed out to dinner.

Cannes has a range of stunning places on the sea front, and we picked one where we could sit outdoors.

Determined to regain my James Bond-hood, I offered to go get the first drinks (we were dressed to the nines… you shoulda *seen* her…) and rose from the table like a mighty phoenix.

My lady had often accused me of having a kind of 'cool mode,' insinuating that I acted differently depending on whom I was around.

I, naturally, objected to this strenuously, as my character needs no stone to hide beneath.

However, on this occasion I flared like a peacock. I arose from the table. I turned like a dancer.

I didn't just walk to the door of the bar, dear reader. Oh no. I *strode* to it. A waitress walked in ahead of me. A full restaurant was about to see young Talent at his very best. I think I may have been glowing a little. I could hear emotive rock music in the distance. I was about to reveal my holy presence.

And then, something a tad unfortunate happened.

My foot, as I was 'striding,' jammed right into a lip on the floor beneath the sliding doors by which you entered the restaurant.

I was moving with such deliberate precision and such ridiculous man-ness that my momentum jerked my body forward so that my torso ended up actually parallel to the floor.

My other unjammed leg had risen behind me so high my foot was a good two feet higher than my head, and in full panic mode, thinking *ohcrapshit fuckthisisgoing toruinmeforever...*! I did what any man would.

I reached out blindly to steady myself on anything I could get my hands on, moan-yelling "Ohhhh *shhiiiiiiiiitttt*!!!"

Regrettably, the only thing within grabbing distance was the back of the diminutive waitress's shirt. She, carrying a tray full of empty glasses and bottles, screamed so loud the activity and noise in the whole restaurant actually stopped, and then she nearly reverse face-pancaked backwards on the floor.

Glass shattered everywhere.

The tray fell.

The waitress turned on me with such immediate shame and hatred in her eyes that my whimper of a garbled apology could only have made it worse.

I went so red I could feel immediate perspiration.

I stood there with a whole restaurant looking at me, and the only thing I could hear after my own exhortation (a long list of such immaculate swearing that even *I'll* not repeat it here) was the united thought of every person within twenty feet of me.

That thought being "*what* a twat."

I didn't walk: I stalked from the restaurant; my only prayer being that the woman I loved had somehow not seen the galactic thunderfuck I had just committed, and that my ego would remain intact.

When I reached the table, she was literally quaking with the effort she was making to restrain and hide her laughter.

"Hey," I said.

"Nnrghhflmlm..." she replied.

A beat.

"Did you... see... the... I...?" asks I.

"Hhmmnnngrr... see... ha... hrr... see what, baby? Hmmn... hmhmhm..."

I look at her straight-as-a-die face. She holds my look.

The laughter she bursts into is so pure, so amused, and so honest, that by some miracle my self-rage (ask any of the crew how angry I get at myself. I have inflicted wounds upon myself far more terrible than those I have inflicted upon others. And I have done awful, *awful* things...) is instantly melted.

It makes me recall a passage I read in "Druss the Legend" (wicked book) about a similar instance. Any other day with almost any other person, I'd have been so darkly evil with myself that that tripfall would have ruined my whole day, and possibly my whole week.

Having her there changed all that. It made me laugh out loud. The more she laughed, the more I laughed. And vice versa.

Such a gift is to be treasured.

In a nutshell, I fucking *love* Cannes.

But that was then, and this is now.

So I land in Cannes and hop skip to the centre to meet my crew. Rooster, MoneyBaby and Twiggers are all looking immaculate.

We drop our bags off at the Villa (twenty minutes outside Cannes but I'm not complaining), which I can't really see or appreciate properly as it's dark, and then head out for drinks.

I've been working solid since Christmas and this is to be my catharsis.

And, as any one of the BTX will tell you, when I'm on a mission, chaos is never far behind...

Day 2 Cannes Film Festival:

I wake up absolutely mongeesed.

I've no idea where I was last night, nor who I was with. I just about recollect Smugz rocking up at cock o'clock, and then us going out and hitting the town.

Apparently we hit it so hard that it stayed hit.

Today is Friday, and my intentions are foul.

I want disorder, chaos, and carnage left in our wake. And I also want Roostinho and MoneyBaby to have a blast and talk to some women.

What's the point of being on holiday if you can't savour God's finest gifts?

I wake up to realise I'm in the villa, and I haven't even explored it properly. I find Smugz asleep upstairs.

He and I are apparently sharing a villa. I mosey over to Rooster and MoneyBaby's place and before I get there, I'm struck by lightening: it's been a long, long time since I've been on a beach or beneath the sun.

And I love both of them. Sun and sea added to a film festival and stick a fork in me: I'm done.

I say hi to Rooster and MoneyBaby, and when Smugz arrives we recount the events from the night before. We're laughing and joking like old friends, despite this being the first time we've ever gone abroad together.

Smugz also has useful information: "There's girls by the pool..."

I'm off.

We're at the pool swimming and chatting to three gorgeous and topless young women within two minutes of Smugz's sentence.

They tell me they're from Italy. I reckon I'm hung over, cause no matter how many times I hear it; I still think they're Russian. I start talking to one called Viara who tells me they're staying right next door to us.

"Erm. What?"

Smugz is on his game.

"She said they live right next..."

I've left before he finishes the sentence.

Sure enough, next door at a two-storey villa the same as ours, it appears there are two more brunettes and one blonde laughing and joking in their smalls in their living room.

Now when it comes to the fairer sex I'm not known for fucking around. I point the girls out to Rooster, and he's seeing what I'm seeing: potential.

"How do we get in? We can't just walk in..."

But I've already gone. Autopilot has kicked in.

This man is on vacation, people. This happens maybe once a year if I'm lucky. And an autopilot that ignores your Fear and makes you do what you want to do is really an *Oughtopilot*.

And I'm flying.

I introduce myself to the three girls, all of whom are quite pleasant and seemly to the eye. I place my boy with the two brunettes and start talking to the blonde. I'm clearly hung over since no matter how many times they tell me they are Italian, I am *still* convinced they are Russian.

Viara walks in and I strike up conversation with her again, which is not easy since she speaks no English and my Italian is limited to quasi-Spanish Italian.

Somehow we still end up in a separate room and, well, I do my bit to improve international relations. Although we do somehow break a ton of furniture and a potted plant in the process.

I stalk back out feeling a little better, and after MoneyBaby tells me Rooster's gone for lunch, I figure I'll join him cause food sounds like a good idea.

Now, Rooster's the kind of guy who likes a bit of a drink. Not mad with it, you realise, but understand - the man is a *film* producer.

At his tender age, he's been doing film for nearly ten years, has made his own feature films, has produced tens of features for other people, done over fifty shorts, and more music videos than you can shake a stick at. He's won or been nominated for awards, and you'd never know it just to look at him.

Producing is also a job with more stress than you can shake a whole pile of sticks at. So, far as I'm concerned, having a drink at lunch while on holiday is totally reasonable.

When my exhausted ass arrives, he's ordered a carafe of wine and decides he doesn't want it. Me on the other hand, well, let's just say I have no such reservations. One carafe disappears. We order another. Viara appears and sits by my side. We have drinks and attempt to talk. Neither of us can really understand each other but we don't care.

At some point she kindly informs me "You are a beautiful boy," and I make a note to make a note of her, and for God's sake to stay in touch.

She disappears at some point, and it's only then that I realise carafe two has also vanished.

"Where the fuck did that go?" I ask.

Rooster's smiling. That means trouble.

"You drank it," he says, "and your bird."

Ah. *Shat*.

That spells even more trouble.

I'm probably sounding like a bit of a maniac here, and truth be told sometimes I can be. But understand, I've been working more or less every day since fecking Christmas. I have a lot of shit to get out my system.

Rooster and MoneyBaby head into town to see a bit of the festival. I send some messages off my phone and sleep a while and then we're headed back into town for dinner.

Somehow Viara is with us again at dinner, which I am more than a little glad about. I buy her dinner and we small talk. I can't tell if I'm still hungover, and I'm still convinced she's from Russia, and she's still not.

We have dinner and she says she has to go catch her train.

I offer to escort her to the station and the cab ride there is more than somewhat entertaining. We kiss, and more, and she tells me she'll look me up on Facebook and come see me in London.

I swear by all that is holy or unholy that God's greatest work is that of Woman.

I rejoin the crew and we get ready for the evening. I don a shirt that is ripped all over the shop and has actual *chains* attached to it.

Rooster laughs as soon as he sees it.

"You actually going out in that? You look like a rock star..."

Hmm. I suppose there are worse things to look like.

We head into town. We pass a restaurant near the beach and somehow, I'm on fire. I meet two Spanish girls and we swap numbers. I see a bar with some American girls in and I get them to join us for a drink.

A crew of three stunning young girls is sat at a table outdoors at a restaurant. I mosey over and sit down, introducing myself.

Five minutes later and our crew is at a table with these three Moroccan angels, two of who are sisters, and we're having the time of our lives. Rooster and MoneyBaby are convinced I'm a man possessed.

I laugh when I see Rooster engaged in conversation with a girl who only speaks French, and he looks at me blankly, like "What the fuck do I do?" I laugh again and nod at her, replying, "Just keep talking. It doesn't really matter what you say as long as you slow it down and stay real friendly."

He does.

She responds kindly and they keep chatting. I bring two more girls over and even Smugz is now looking at me differently - half "how the hell are you doing this?" and half "are you crazy??"

We relocate to a cocktail bar that Rooster knows and when we walk in, the whole place stops. It's the second time I've walked in and stopped a place dead in Cannes.

Thankfully, this time, it's for the right reasons.

I'm opening groups of people, single people, couples, staff, and sticking them all at our table. I meet an older photographer, a lovely dude who says he'd like to get into directing. I introduce him to MoneyBaby (a director himself) who is highly unamused.

"Er, no dude. You're not leaving me with *this* guy..."

I wink at him and two seconds later a tray of cocktails arrives.

We're sat outside at the Cannes Film Festival with about seven girls and I could be no happier. My friends' biggest problem is they are stuck for which girl to talk to.

It's a thing of beauty.

Twiggers and her friend join us later and are somewhat stunned to see our new group. I think I would be too.

I make a less-than-amicable greeting to Twigger's friend and make the wrong impression.

I ought to be more controlled, but by this point I'm in my zone and have no cares in the world. The Moroccan girls tell us we're headed to an afterparty on a yacht, which sounds ideal to me but also is *blatantly* pushing it.

We're pretty in the zone by the time we get to the yacht, and no matter what tricks we try; we're not getting in. I could blag this, but I can't be bothered. I figure I've done my duty for the evening, so I don't really care.

Apparently we're going to another bar.

It's at some point here, to quote Smugz, that most of us lose audio and visual.

You might be wondering why I'm going into such detail on this.

That'd be a good question.

And the answer is simple.

Look at any of the people who work the highest pressured jobs: soldiers, doctors, armed police, investment bankers who are responsible for billions of dollars of other people's money, or superstar directors who have to make a 250 million dollar movie a success.

Look at how they blow off steam compared to people who work minimum stress jobs. It's *different*.

My work costs me a great deal. And I very rarely get time off. So when I do, things happen.

I recently had this exact argument with a guy who left broking to become a recruitment consultant. He left the former environment because "it was too stressful." We were debating the different pressures of different jobs and how it affected people.

He summed it up beautifully, so I've tried to summarise what he said below.

"Steve it's like this: suppose you take a tube of toothpaste and you put something fairly light on it. Something like a stone. The toothpaste, under very little pressure, will come out very slowly, and it will take a long time."

I agree with him.

He likens this to any low-stress job, and says there are major benefits to this. Such as the reduced odds of heart failure or cardiac arrest. I have to agree again.

"Then suppose you put something heavier on it. Like a housebrick. What happens?"

I reply the toothpaste comes out much quicker.

He nods, explaining this is higher impact / pressure / stress jobs.

"Now consider you drop something entirely different onto our tube of toothpaste. Something significant. Like, say, an airport. Now what happens?"

I laugh, and state the obvious – the whole tube erupts because of the massive pressure exerted.

"Precisely, Lord Talent. *Precisely*."

Day Three Cannes Film Festival:

I wake up a total shambles.

My skull feels worse than it has in quite some time.

This is not helped by the fact that I wake up outdoors. Is this the fucking villa *garden*...? What the *wilderbeast* am I doing out here...?

Mother of *Jesus*, my head hurts...

I feel like I've been hit in the head with a spade. Twice. And then piledrived off the top rope onto a metal chair.

Cars are driving past me honking their horns. Jesus Mother of *God* this is intolerable...

What the fuck happened to me???

Smugz provides me the intel.

"You fell off the couch bed skull-first onto the floor."

Erm. The fucking tiled floor? The one you could crack a *plant pot* on?

"Yeah brother. The crack was so loud I came running downstairs to check you were all right..."

Ah. Thanks, Smugz.

"...but then..."

Fuck.

"...you were on the floor holding your head, swearing like a trooper, and I thought I could either help you out or get you some meds."

Ah. Ok. Cheers, Smugz.

"But then..."

You *utter*...

"...I thought it would be funnier to take out my phone and just film ya. And weyhey! So I take out my phone, and you're just crawlin' round the floor like a fuckshot, man! Like a fuckshot you're just crawlin' round the floor. You're in so much pain you can't find your feet, so you're on the floor, and you get to the door, and you're tryin' a get out the front, but you can't understand that the glass door is actually made of fucking glass, but you're tryin', and I'm like, *heh heh, get the fuck outta here.* So you manage to pull yourself up, like, with one hand and shit, and I'm still filmin' ya, and you get to your feet, fuck only knows how you don't hurl, and man, you've just lost audio and visual man, you're just done. So I'm still filmin' ya, and you turn to me with the camera, and you're just lookin'. Heh. I mean you're just staring down the barrel dude like a fuckin' zombie. And you just wait for a second second, and then you go *fuck you, Smugz*, and give me the finger. At this point, I'm still laughin' at ya; and you try to get out the door, but you're in so much pain you can't even function. I mean that's one of the funniest things I've seen in my life. I felt for ya, but hey-ho. We live in hope. In the van."

...

......

I can barely talk; I'm in so much pain. But what I can say, is:

"And... you have this... nnghrrm... fucking footage... nnnrghgg... on your... fuck *me* this hurts... on your smegging phone...?"

Smugz shrugs as if to say 'and?'

"What the fuck? I'm a filmmaker, dude."

I can't even summon the energy to have a proper go at him.

I stagger out to the pool, thinking that it may help.

Yeah, 'cause that's what I need - to cook in the blazing heat and then immerse myself in water.

The looks on Rooster and MoneyBaby's faces are so amused up that I figure we must have had a blast.

I don't care. I just want the pain to stop.

I ask a passing waitress by the pool if she can get me some painkillers, by which I mean about a thousand. She kindly informs me they have none.

Smugz, to make my life easier, helpfully shoves me into the pool without warning, and then cracks up laughing.

I'm about to go psychotic.

There are women at the pool and I can't even lie straight. I haven't cried from pain in years but this is unbearable. I'm thinking I may have a concussion. Or maybe several.

Apparently according to the crew, there's a live music stage and a scaffold outside the hotel lobby.

Allegedly, a man resembling yours truly was seen performing on stage and then climbing this structure the night previous whilst being egged on by several people staying at the villas and whilst being threatened with being kicked out by the actual folks who run the joint.

I can't remember it for shit, and my head is on the verge of exploding.

It takes hours for my head to feel human.

Fortunately by the time we get into Cannes, and after about four painkillers, I'm re-approaching the human race.

Smugz and I have had to visit about ten different locations to get passes for Cannes. We're not going to be allowed in the tents, but to be fair I don't really care.

And then, *finally*, I see what we are here for, or rather what I am here for.

I take a long, hard look out to sea at the boats and the yachts.

They're close enough you can make out all kinds of detail on them, and see some of the people partying on board.

I also, more importantly, see the Cannes red carpet; the one the stars walk down when they arrive here. I take a long hard look at it.

The five of us, Twigs, MoneyBaby, Smugz, Rooster and myself all take a seat on the red carpet and I know instantly the trip has become what it was meant to be.

When we eventually arrive at a cafe, I see the most significant thing I have seen perhaps all year. We sit at a coffee shop and Rooster shows me a programme for the 2010 Cannes Film Festival.

Inside is a one-pager on "Morning Tea," and beneath that is a list of cast and crew, and beneath that, to my sheer joy, to my feral triumph, to my eternal roar, is the name *Stephen Brocklehurst*.

An exhalation comes from me that releases months of stress and crap.

The smile on my face is one of justice being done.

I'm in a kind of daze for the rest of the evening.

We all head to a bar in the centre of town, and we party on.

Rooster starts chatting to groups of women, Smugz is making me laugh so much that my feet hurt, and MoneyBaby is dressed so much like a director I think he should wear this outfit all the time.

I manage to offend Twiggers *yet* again, making me think that fucking up is the only purpose I serve on this trip, although to be fair I do somehow manage to kiss another woman, and then get food on the way home.

I no longer want a drink.

I've seen what I needed to see. The pressure on my shoulders has, for once, abated.

We get back to the villa, and once more, exhausted, but for once, finally, with a smile on my face, I manage to sleep.

Day 4 Cannes Film Festival:

I wake up in a state of exhaustion.

Several days of no sleep, womanising, drinking and partying takes its toll. I realise it's about two in the morning and my plane is at eleven. I don't trust myself to wake up at the right time due to my prehistoric state first thing in the mornings.

I assemble all my things and chuck them in my bag. I'm deffo still tired and feel tipsy from the day before.

I head to reception, pay for mine and Smugz's room and order a cab. The lobby guys are, it's safe to say, a tad happy to see the back of me.

I take cash out at a cashpoint and realise we are driving in absolute darkness. It's about five in the morning (God knows how) when I get to the airport. I'm in my same clothes from the night before, and I stagger into the airport and collapse on a chair. I pass out.

An hour later I'm woken up by extremely pissed off security who inform me I cannot sleep in the airport.

Are you *kidding*? All you see in airports is people queueing or asleep. I walk outside and realise I have about five or six hours to kill, and that Smugz is meant to be on my plane.

I see a beautiful young woman walk into the airport. I follow. We start chatting at the desk, and exchange numbers. I make a joke and she turns out to have a beautiful laugh. We exchange numbers and all is going well, until I get a tap on my shoulder. It's the security guard who booted me out earlier.

"Look," I explain, "I'm not asleep. Give a man a break."

He looks at me like he is going to kill me.

"I'm not here for that," he says.

I sigh. Now what?

"So what are you here for?"

He maintains his soon-an-icepick-will-be-entering-your-left-eyeball-courtesy-of-moi look.

"I'm here because it looks like you were trying to flirt with my wife."

I'm stunned. *Speechless*. I nearly start laughing.

"Your... wife? Ta femme? Are you crazy? Mate, you're so wrong on this one it hurts. I was talking to *her*."

I say this indicating the woman behind me. Deathstare continues.

"Oui, I know. That's my *wife*."

I start to say something.

I stop.

I look at him.

I turn and look at her.

There's no point. I lower my head and walk from the airport to the outside, which is starting to heat up and is very, very warm already. I realise I'm likely to be sat in the Cannes heat for the next six hours, but only if I can keep myself out of hospital (should this guy decide that he and his security buddies want to make my day a lot worse).

I sit down.

I'm dehydrated, ill, have a headache, and am sat beneath the Cannes sun for almost six hours.

I try to sleep and not to drench my clothes in sweat.

I pray to all kind of forces for cooler weather, a light breeze, or a quick monsoon.

Nothing works.

Karma is a bitch.

Smugz, of course, is late, and is looking like he'll miss the flight.

Rooster and MoneyBaby are having drinks in Cannes, while Twigger's friend is probably (and quite fairly) making a voodoo doll of me somewhere to chuck into a blender.

And what am I doing?

Pickling.

That's what I'm fecking doing.

I stagger into the departure lounge looking like something the cat dragged in: dehydrated, sunburned, exhausted, and just woken up from sleeping six hours on a pavement outside an airport.

I resemble a vaguely rockstar-esque homeless person who's spent the last four days injecting ethanol and spending the nights in a microwave.

So it's Sod's Law that in the departure lounge there is a stunning, *stunning* young woman who I see. I laugh to myself, now thinking that I'm delirious.

I'm probably in the least presentable state of my life. I must reek to high heaven. I could be in a takeaway restaurant trashcan and I'd look better. Any woman who wants to hear from me right now needs her head looking at.

Plus, I'm just *done*.

Moving each leg for every step feels like a titanic battle of willpower versus nature. I'm running on my very, very last reserves.

So I put my bag down and think "Nah, forget it. Give yourself a moment off. You'll have a heart attack at this rate."

And then I look over. This is no *girl* we are talking about; she's a *woman*. She's dressed all in black which tells me whilst she is stylish she doesn't feel a constant need to be overly ostentatious.

She's also reading a book, and women who read (take note, girls of the world) are infinitely preferable to women who don't.

Reading indicates a better vocabulary, patience, and a possible strength in terms of education. Her jewellery is classy but understated, which I like as it speaks of refinement, and her look tells me she is about thirty-something - which, given we're in Cannes, means she does something associated with entertainment somehow, and that she is likely to be well-travelled, giving her a fuller, more rounded view on things than most women.

She's also running solo (on her own), meaning she's either single and travelling alone, or with partner and *still* travelling alone, both of which indicate confidence and sense of independence.

Both of which I like a great deal.

She's also headed from the Cannes film festival to London, which are two 'event' locations, meaning she spends her time in all likelihood in 'event' circles. And when it comes to a choice between the Great and the Small, I choose the Great each and every time.

Lastly, her face is just mesmerising - it's like looking at a sculpture.

And the eyes, when I smile at her and she smiles back, are knowledgeable, but have a twinkle to them. Her physical form, her body, looks like she eats well and goes to the gym regularly, which makes her smart in another sense and also indicates dedication and discipline.

It also means she looks deliciously, delciously attractive.

"Stephen, leave it alone," comes the thought.

Smugz has even (how does he do it?) arrived, which should be more incentive to just stay sat down and have a hot chocolate.

But again, I'm already moving.

See, it's not easy being a Lifeaholic sometimes.

What my body needs is sleep and rest, and what I am doing instead is trying not to let this radiant woman know I feel like a swamp.

By some miracle, the young lady permits me to sit, and we begin talking.

Most of what she says confirms much of what I thought, and where it doesn't it actually exceeds it. This is a never-*ever*-happens event. I've seen pretty much the top of the female tree, and I'm rarely, *rarely* impressed.

This one's smart, and also highly driven, to boot; running her own company in vehicular design. She's got strong opinions and has no bones about saying what she thinks. And she's not overly eager to give out her number or email, which makes me think she places a high value on herself.

This is a very, *very* attractive quality.

It's so attractive a quality that once we're on the plane, I spend, literally, the entire trip sat in front of her talking to her.

She tells me about her family and her work, and I tell her about the films and the music. We joke and take the piss out of each other, and I find myself wondering why God doesn't just build factories to make women like this full-time.

Notice how much more time I've spent talking about this girl than any of the others. That's because this one, from the get-go, was simply more impressive and had more human gravity than any of the rest. I have a sixth sense for other people's Talent and success level, and this woman gives out a code green for All-Systems-Are-Go.

She's also got no bullshit to her.

She's not trying to impress me.

She also gives me the impression that her life has not been a walk in the park. People who are this strong didn't usually get this way from sheer DNA. They've normally been through acres of crap that has strengthened them beyond the levels most people reach at that age.

To stick it in a nutshell, I like this woman enough that I'd like to see her again.

I've spent almost two hours talking to this girl, who's part Italian, and not once have I been bored. This in itself is very rare.

Usually I can tell in minutes just how far a 'thing' with a woman could go, and this, I can only say, has potential.

I'm sure she, like me, has innumerate members of the opposite sex hunting for her time. She strikes me as hard work in some ways, and a bit of a pain in the arse; this is not necessarily a bad thing, as I'm pretty much the same way.

We agree to go out for food or a drink at some point, and before you know it, we've landed back in my beautiful city.

I'm glad to be home, but my God, I could have had that conversation *forever*...

I get back to London and before I know it, I am on a music video shoot.

It's literally an hour since I came back from Cannes, and all I am fit for is the rubbish heap, and yet here I am on a music shoot with Smugz, who, credit where credit is due, is an absolute workhorse when he so chooses to be.

I just about hold it together for a couple of hours, and then my bed is summoning me like a demon.

I depart and head home for my own sanity. Cannes has beaten me soundly. I can handle that. I saw the carpet and I saw the yachts.

I know now the challenge that lies before me, and before every creative in my business who wishes to succeed, or moreover just *survive*, in this thing we call the business of entertainment.

Homeward bound I am.

Finally.

I'm offered a directing job on a documentary called "Art For All," which is a concept propounded by a woman by the name of Lady Brass.

Lady Brass is a fascinating woman, a creative spirit who has decided to put her art to work.

She intends on making a film called "Art For All," a documentary showing her working with Special Needs individuals and teaching them to express themselves through sculpture and paint.

When we meet the Lady, I'm struck by the sheer force of her character, and especially by her drive to be a positive force for people who are in dire need of other people's assistance.

I sign on for it immediately.

See, this is the motive force behind everything I do. It is the underpinning ethos that binds my work together. I take part in projects that I think will benefit or inspire people.

Or at least, that's the aim.

I write a director's outline, I plan the shoot, I put together a shot list, and Rooster and I work it all over in our minds.

This all ends up being fruitless, as the project ends up in the hands of another group of people due to creative differences between different people on the production.

This is a common enough thing in the film business, but, as it's the first time it's happened to me, it hurts more than somewhat.

Lady Brass and I remain friends and stay in touch, which teaches me several things.

You can fall out with people over a certain subject, you can fire people, you can argue till you're blue in the face, but in the end, the wisest course is to keep your bridges intact and not burn them.

I appreciated that lesson.

It was one of many I was to learn.

Because next up, I had to die on the streets of London.

171

JUNE 2010:

"THE FIRST TIME I DIED"

"He's quiet but boisterous, though it isn't a choice,
And though he's everyone at school, he ain't nobody's
fool,
He knows the rules, if you smart you ain't cool,
Without the necessary tools to outdo all of these fools..."

- Talent -
"Only Son"

- IMMORTALENTED 2013 -

My name is Abdulllah, and I am dying.

I am lying on a pavement in North West London, looking up to see one solitary star in the sky.

The evening is cool, and there is blood all over my thobe.

I have been stabbed by a man called Marcus, and now I see buses and cars passing as I lie upon the street. My breath is slowing, coming in rasps, and there are smatterings of blood on my face.

I have deserved it, to be honest. I have not lived a good life. Allah knows all things, and he knows I am reaping what I sew.

Little Mariam is going to miss her father. My wife is going to shed tears at my passing.

My friends and brothers from the streets are going to have to cope without my words and prayers. I look down and see blood on my hands. I know it is mine, but given what I have done, it feels like the blood of many others.

It reminds me of Macbeth.

I am not afraid. I can see the heavens above Mother Earth.

The sky is dark, and getting darker, suddenly. I know I am going to a better place. The pain is subsiding now.

I am going to be home, soon...

The annoying thing at the minute is that, to be honest about it, I have a beard.

Not just "a beard", but "*a beard*."

I keep on getting told I look like Tom Cruise out of "The Last Samurai" (semi-flattering), the guy out of the film version of "Shogun" (less flattering), and Jesus (at which point you can fuck *off*).

I've never had a fondness for facial hair, and I never intended to grow a beard (Pari freaking *loves* it though - *typical*), and yet here I am.

Usually, I'm fairly down to earth.

I don't frequent posh restaurants, for example. Unless I'm breaking up with someone. I don't require nice suits or clothing to survive. I eat normal shit you buy in Tesco's.

So I'm not what you might call "pretentious." There isn't much Hyacinth in my Bucket, so to speak.

However, the beard changes all this.

As a rule, when asked a simple question (such as "what is the time?" or "what is your name?"), we answer the question directly.

We give the response pretty much immediately.

Only in the event of being asked a nutcracker of a question do we adopt the "Thinking Man" position (chin in hand, elbow on knee, usually uttering some kind of as-if-thinking-profoundly humming noise "*hmmm...*").

And by nutcracker of a question, I mean "Why are you here?" or "Is there a God?" or "Why is it there are tons of buses when you don't need one, but not a fucking *one* when it's you at the stop?"

And so on, and so forth.

Not.

    With.

       A.

         Beard.

Now, every fruitcake that stops me in the street to ask me directions is confronted by a half-Last-Samurai half-Jesus-Our-

Lord-And-Saviour imbecile scratching at his jaw like he is consulting some kind of mind's-eye-view Google map; a man on the verge not of saying "yeah mate, down there and left," but rather "continue in an easterly direction at 73 degrees to the tropic of idiocy, and do so with haste to avoid the impending light shower, my good fellow."

Like I said.

The beard is *pissing* me off.

So why don't I shave it, I hear you ask.

Well, here's the thing.

It's not, technically, *my* beard. It's Abdullah's.

Yes, I know. *Abdullah's.*

My now-good-friend Rehan Malik is making his full-length feature film on the subject of culture, terrorism, race, and tensions of this ilk in the modern day United Kingdom.

Which, in case you didn't know, is currently beset by complex issues of culture, terrorism, and race.

The film ("Radio London") is well written, carefully thought out, and is being shot in that gritty, in-your-face handheld style that I like. It's going to be, in a nutshell, the bog's dollocks.

And yours truly, as we have established, is in it.

And I play a guy who *was* called Roger, is *now* called Abdullah, converted to Islam, became a loving husband, became a loving Father, but now absolutely *despises* the British Government (some of the dialogue is so pointed and vitriolic that I actually had to have a whisky whilst reading it) [not that I need an excuse, you understand] {but whilst reading it, I mean, I'm known for doing some strange shit, but *fuck me...*} <and sorry about all the different brackets, you're just going to have to try to keep up...> and then gets brutally stabbed to death in the street.

Yeah. That's right, people. I got the role.

So. The beard isn't really mine.

It's Abdullah's.

And since I can't get rid of it until I get rid of him, which is only at the end of filming, I'm a bit fucked.

Because my new agent (Nic Knight, lovely guy, direct, honest, and sounds like a new lead for "Knight Rider") for film and TV is saying it needs to go. And moreover, my escort agent (new, the last one moved to Australia) isn't overly chuffed about it either. Since women don't tend to call in too frequently looking for companions who resemble a pint-sized, Katie Holmes-marrying scientologist, nor saying they need a date that looks like the Son of Man.

Plus I've got Louise now saying she *likes* the freaking thing, while my family is saying to get rid of it.

Kev's response is the usual: "Brock. You know *you*, yeah? Well, you're *bent*."

Now, I'm not saying the beard is a big issue (which I'll be selling soon, if finance continues at this rate...), but it just goes to show, that in the world of film, music, and financially procurable physical entertainment, things that are normally a small thing, can spiral into a whole new *ball game...*

So.

Just to recap: where exactly *are* we and who are we?

Well, we're still in London.

It's now June of the year of Trinities, 2010, and I'm still writing my diary: tentatively entitled "ImmorTalented."

Though I'm also playing with "The Deal" as a title. I quite like it.

As in, "So like, what the fuck is *the deal*, homie?" (in bad, overly strong American accent). [Though after a first re-reading I'm thinking "Lifeaholic" is actually the most accurate title].

In the last 6 months, as we have established, I have:

- Gained representation as an actor with Nic Knight management
- Played the lead in two feature films, "Morning Tea" and "Radio London"
- Been bricking it about turning the big 3-0 this year (fifth of July, Cancerian, which my flatmate believes is "appropriate")
- Had two of my album tracks picked up for another feature film (called "Solito", about a guy who's addicted to

175

masturbation, which my other flatmate believes is "even more appropriate")
- Trained as a PUA (PickUp Artist)
- Placed my first album (all mixed and edited) into the final mastering process so it gets ready for signing this year
- Started dating Frank LeBeouf's ex. Apparently he played for Chelsea and France. And I'm crazy about his ex.

It's been, to be fair, a bit nerve-racking. And it still is.

It's all the cumulation of a weird and wonderful lifetime of trying to get into the film and music business, and of trying to move from Willenhall, Wolverhampton, West Midlands, to the capital and cosmopolitan nexus we call "London."

That's of course after a year in Brownsboro in Texas, when I was supposed to be headed to sunny California. And that's after seven years at Queen Mary's Grammar School, in a town called Walsall.

It's all been, to be fair, a bit of a mish (mission).

And if I'm honest, I question my own sanity. This is ironic as, as my friends would tell you, I'm normally the guy with all the answers.

But see, I don't *have* all the answers. I don't even have *most* of the answers.

I tend to have actually near enough *none* of the answers.

I can only claim to be bravestupid enough to try to ask the *questions…*

So I'm sat here writing this and there are three immediate problems.

First, I'm having whisky. Not good, when you are writing.

Second - and take a second to understand this - second: *England*.

Yes, England.

Ing-er-lund.

I've just sat here and watched our game against Slovenia in the World Cup, and praise be to every deity that has ever existed (over 2,500 according to the Oxford Book of Gods), we won.

Problem is, we only won 1-0 and it should have been 2-0 or 3-0.

England.

176

My home.

My birthplace.

The "green and pleasant land" that ruled the waves and reigned over three-quarters of the Earth's surface.

And who invented football.

The issue, you see, is psychological.

And, obviously, that we are, well, fairly shit at football.

Shit at playing international football, when we are fucking amazing at playing premiere league football.

Watch Tim Henman or Andy Murray play tennis.

Watch us play football.

There is a lack of belief and a *tension* that is not such a problem with say, the Brazilians or the USA.

They just *play a game*, where we put ourselves into a work environment.

They have *no problem* admitting their own greatness.

We do.

I do.

And third, which is a bit of a fucker, is that I'm basically broke.

Tomorrow, for example, is itself a bit of an issue.

Enough to be fourth on a list of three.

I'll explain.

I'm sat here, writing my memoirs, after watching my nation go through to the last sixteen, after wrapping up a feature film yesterday, about to audition tomorrow for a major, *major* Hollywood film.

If I get it, it's about forty days of filming at £200 a day.

That's eight grand.

Enough to take me through the year and afford my rent and council tax next year.

Sounds good, right?

Except I need to care so little about tomorrow that I walk in swaggering like a rap star.

Which of course, I am.

But, being English (hence the above tirade), my mind *revolts* against this.

"Have some English stiff upper lip, son. We don't admit to *caring* about things..."

Well you know what?

Fuck. That.

I do care about tomorrow.

I *want. To get. **That job**.*

I was stabbed to death yesterday as Abdullah.

I have been going to the gym for six months straight and I was in the parachute regiment.

I *own this role.*

If someone else wants it, they have to take it away from me.

And if I don't get it, then I'm going to keep going *anyfuckingway.*

I will.

> *Not.*
>> Be.
>>> *Stopped.*

End of story.

So.

On to the next thing you are going to take issue with.

So here goes.

I *love the United States.*

(Ouch. I can hear my countrymen and other people across the globe sharpening knives as we speak...)

I know a lot of people hate the U.S.

I even know why.

You wanna know why?

Because England used to *be* the United States.

Whoever is number one, is hated.

Pete Sampras. The U.S. Mike Tyson. Maradonna.

And to all you people who refer to their supporters as "glory hunters", this is why you hate people who are number one.

Because you are (a) jealous, and (b) pissed off that your team is *not* number one.

I empathise.

I wish my country essentially ruled the world as do the United States.

But I have *lived* there.

My best friend is American.

And I can tell you *with authority* they are some of the kindest, most welcoming, polite, open people on planet Earth.

And they have some of the (literally) *finest* women in the world.

And they can kick a football.

The moral?

Don't hate on the people who are best at their job.

Love them. Emulate them. *Learn* from them.

And then beat them into the dust at their own game, by making it *your* own game.

Or die trying.

Incidentally, I'm about to take a shower, and shave off the beard.

Oddly, I'm kind of sad.

Reminds me of Abdullah dying.

(And for the record, watching yourself die from a stab wound on a London street while you are dressed like Jesus is *not* the easiest thing to watch. It's *heavy*.)

Both my flatmates are coming home, and are about to see me looking like a twelve-year-old.

And you know what's even *weirder*, is that it makes me miss Pari, and Louise, and Dana, and Rosie, and Anita, and Jade, and Louise, and Pauline, and Mandy, and Emma, and Natalie, and Fi, and Nicola and Lucy, and Samandra, and Emily, and others.

Still.

I have work to do tomorrow. And tonight. And now.

And the beard…

…has to *go*.

The male escort thing?

Ah.

I see.

"How can a man who kneels at the altar of morality and integrity condone financially procurable intimate companionship with the opposite sex?"

The actual answer is, it's none of your fucking *business*.

But, I run a 100% open book policy.

So, I'll answer that question.

All in good time.

"Did you enjoy being a male escort?"

Schniglin, is the Pope *white*?

Before I forget...

Mum, Nan, Dad, all the family: Helen of Troy, Gina Joy, Alison the Wise, Christmas Carol (best Boxing Day food you ever had), Hilliam Wale, Rosie the Red, Wonderland Alice, Big Ed, Special K, Neil, Aaron, Uncle Alan and Alison, Uncle Rog, Auntie Val (My godmother, to whom I owe more than I can say), Uncle Geoff, Kimbo Cop, Aunt Yvonne, James the lawman, Emma, Simon "Wilscot" (never forget those drawings, your Talent was on show from the moment you were born), Ang the Angelic, Dan the Man, Rosco Bosco (*still* the toughest kid in town), Matt, Glen, Nige, Uncle Derek, all my grandparents (rest in peace, and better yet, know you are *stil* loved and missed), this is for you.

And also, before I forget: Jedi, Kev, LL, Shanghai, Merlin, Ris, Blaqmale, Ricardo Fargas, Chris the Grinnerman, Christo my dearest, Jamie and Dani, Fatsalot, J, Christopher, Margherita, Trystan, Tom (I *will* shag you one day), Sharvitsu (you *will* shag me, one day), Marcus, Moe, Vadim, Ateezy, Mialicious, Ayan the Lion (SNES *was better than the Mega Drive*), Catherine, Stuart of the Sharp, Dani, Dunc the Monk, Big Gay Al, this is also for you.

Mike Fibbens, His Lordship, Peanut, Foremania, Toby G, Milady Papadakis, Kat, Liz, Mr Rix, Rehan, Rooster, Flowgirl, Smugz, Val, this is also for you.

And. Last but not least. *Never* least...

Pari.

To you.

AML. Jade. Anita. Sandy. Ashley Allen. Monica and Julie. Louisa. Kim (*still* love your pictures). Dana. Johari. Lucy. Jose.

Samandra. Louise. Gemma. The girl at Law Academy. Pauline. Jill. Ashley. Kate, more than any other. And to all the others, this is also for you.

I love you all beyond sanity and I would be lost without you.

I would be nothing.

But above all, beyond anyone else, beyond any gift I have ever been given, beyond anything that makes sense, beyond any reasonable motive a God might have to bestow gifts upon a mere mortal: I thank you above all for my mother.

She is the greatest teacher I have seen.

She is the reason I am here.

And to you also, dear reader, I send my love.

This is my only purpose.

I hope someday to meet you, and that we might share a word or two.

I love you.

All.

Would you believe, I am still sat here?

Haven't shaved the beard yet.

I am loath, apparently, to say goodbye to it.

A grown man, scared to shave his facial hair, afraid to see his own face.

Makes me laugh.

The longest match in Wimbledon history is taking place before my eyes, and I am afraid to set foot into the waters of the shower, and to take a razorblade to my own face.

Coward.

You fucking child.

You fucking CHILD.

Roll your fucking sleeves up, you utter waste of flesh.

Ah.

Sorry.

That's Dr. Schadenfreude again.

I don't recommend you meet him too often.

Partly because he's the worst that lives in me.

And partly because, well, you'll start to think I'm losing the plot a bit...

Takes two to tango, fuckstick...

Wow.

So the beard has gone.

I look like I'm about 12.

Now the fucking hair has to go as well because, in better news, I just got an audition for a small role in my first ever major Hollywood feature.

Hell.

Yes.

On the other manus, England just got their asses handed to them by a good-but-not-unbeatable Germany.

4-1.

And it could have been way worse than that.

Although Frank Lampard's goal being disallowed was a travesty, and *could* in all fairness have altered the course of the match.

But that ain't the story.

The story is, we scored three goals in four games and won once.

Come *home*, gents, and have a long hard think about your selves.

Is this really the performance of people on over £100,000 a week?

What's the lesson?

English.

Psychology.

People afraid of their own greatness, and whose egos get in the way.

I love my country and my football, but my *God* that was disappointing.

And of course now it'll be post-mortem time. "Where did it all go wrong?" "Should Capello go?" "Did someone clone Wayne Rooney and implant his surrogate with the tactical brain of an aardvark before putting it onfield?" "If so, where's the *real* Wayne Rooney, and has his missus noticed anything yet...?"

And so on.

Still. The beard has still gone.

(Jesus. Is *that* what I actually *look* like??)

Worse is yet to come.

I have my first audition for a Hollywood feature soon.

And that means all the hair has to go.

And that means I'll look like I'm twelve years old.

And *that* means, I may have to wait till I'm forty before I actually lie with a woman again...

(*Who the sweet Moses are you fucking kidding? You are. A slag.*)

Gee, thanks Doc.

Appreciate the pep talk…

Praise be to Allah and God and Zeus and Buddha and all that jazz, cause I've GOT THE FRICKIN' JOB AND AM ABOUT TO BE IN A **HOLLYWOOD PICTURE**, ladies and germs!

And about feckin' time too.

Soon as I found out, I came home to see my family.

I say my family, but it's actually a lot more complicated than that.

A *lot. More. Complicated.*

But that'll come later.

I'm still convinced the only reason I got the gig is because I was in the military when I was at uni.

More on that later, too.

The reason I bring this up is the following.

When I got the dates for filming, and for when it all kicks off, the very first date fell on a somewhat important date for me.

The fifth of July.

Which is of course, my birthday.

The fifth of July 1980, to be accurate.

Why is that significant?

It's significant because, for every year I have been alive, since I was born, have been upon the face of the Earth, I have shared this day with my nearest and dearest, those for whom I have the most love.

Namely, my mum, my nan, and my closest of close friends.

No matter where I've been, or what I've done; I have shared this day with my inner circle. My family, both bloodline and extended.

So at first I was a bit hacked off that this film business was about to break my tradition.

Put a spanner in the works.

Fuck with my Wa, so to speak.

And then, in a flash of genius, my flatmate enlightened me.

(*Note* - to enlighten someone: to supply them with knowledge? Sure. To increase their wisdom? Fine. To augment their awareness of certain facts? Without doubt. *But also* - to liberate them from the *weight* of bignorance [big time ignorance] by shining *light* onto the darkness in their minds.)

{You're welcome}.

"So you're a bit pissed about this film gig wrecking your chances of seeing your family?"

"Yeah."

"Miffed that you can't be sat at home with your loved ones, on the day of your birth?"

"What did I just say? *Yes*."

"Cause, like, if you *were* going to break that tradition, you'd wanna do it for something *big*, something record-breaking, something so *huge*, that it might even set a *new* tradition, and would make up for the family-time you are losing?"

"Rooster, what did I just fucking say? Y-E-S. Get to the point."

"Something, say, like on the very day of your thirtieth birthday, being onset on a Hollywood feature, in what will likely be the biggest release of the year, with proper stars, hundred of people in the absolute *mix* in the industry you love above all, doing what you love most, in the fineness of this beautiful British summer, after the World Cup and Wimbledon, the day you turn thirty years old...?"

"Ah."

At which point, I shut the hell up.

Had he been female, at this point, I'd have done intimate and improper hings to him.

Life, Ladies and Gents.

The great thing about Lady Luck is that she's female. So while she can be an absolute *bitch* at times, she's also absolutely and utterly fucking wonderful.

The moral of the tale?

Stop. Fucking. *Moaning*.

You hang on in there long enough, you chip away hard enough for enough time, you refuse to give in *no matter* what, and at some point, the game will begin to show cracks and chips.

And then, reinvigorated, you swing *harder*.

Success = talent + persistence x time.

Remember this.

A word of warning:

My album is almost done.

My first Hollywood feature is about to kick off.

My book and my belief system are almost finished.

My site is up and running.

My TV show is about to start.

And we have a new feature of our own in the works.

So:

Once my crew and I are in this little thing we call the 'talent business,' a few people are likely to *rue the day* you ever heard of us.

This is *not* how an industry so simple should work.

Mark.

    My.

        Words.

I'm not bitter, by the way.

;)

I totally get it.

The people *in* the industry are loath to let newcomers in.

Days gone by, all you needed was Talent.

Then all you needed was Talent, and a "look."

Then you didn't even need Talent, you just needed a "look."

(Don't believe me? *Orlando Bloom.* I rest my case…)

[I'm not hating on the guy, you understand. He's done amazingly. But to stick someone onscreen with Geoffrey Rush and Johnny Depp at their finest? Wasn't even *fair*.]

Now every dickhead on the planet wants into the Big Brother House, onto TV, or into a film.

Without earning the right.

So the people on the *inside* look at people on the *outside* and make it pretty fucking hard to get in.

Now you need a following: Facebook friends, Myspace adds, a website, a merchandise machine, a brand, a story, and a million other things.

Well, my crew and I are *getting* all that or have it *already*.

But still, I get it.

However.

Once we're in, we're changing all that.

And there is one, obvious, glowing, can't-believe-no-one's-done-it-already way to change it.

"And what's that, Talent?"

Heh.

Yeah.

Like I'm *that* stupid.

And to all of you who'd call me a slag, know this:

(Don't get me wrong, like; I am a *bit* of a slag.)

There was a knockout blonde in my bed only two nights ago.

Did anything happen?

Did it *fuck*.

So *there*.

The film and music industry, as you may know, have taken a bit of a knock.

As have most industries.

Due, in no small part, to this small thing we've called the "credit crunch."

Personally speaking, I would have named it better than that.

"Credit crunch" sounds less like a financial disaster and more like an Oil Trader's healthy high-fibre, low-calorie breakfast, as far as I'm concerned, but then there you go.

And, speaking of said current affair, I owe you a minor apology.

See, there's been tons of debate over what caused the credit crunch.

Unstable markets, banks without sufficient regulations, the fact the Chinese own *everything*, and so on.

But the real cause, the actual root at the tree of the financial fallout, I'm sorry to say - truly so, in fact - is me.

("Sorry, come again...?")

Yeah. I know.

I'll explain.

As every Englishman born prior to the millenium knows, you do not fuck with Fate.

You don't tempt it; you don't ask for trouble, you don't stare gift horses in the mouth.

Now, back in '08, a friend of mine offered to help me into the world of finance.

He needed a man he could trust, and I needed money for my website, music video, and album.

Seemed to make sense.

So.

I went through three rounds of interviews with three different companies (no prior experience, no particular care for the Finance business [which, in case you are wondering, while reported to be glamorous and glitzier than Pamela Anderson's buttocks, is actually roughly as exciting as a do-it-yourself lobotomy] and no real interest in it whatsoever except for the money) and got offers from all three of them.

Hmmm. Could this be exceptional interview skills?

Or was it the fact that I knew a ton of people in finance?

Our survey *says...*

Is the City nepotistic?

Did George W Bush shave his teeth and brush his face?

You're damn *skimpy* he did.

So.

187

I get into the world of broking.

Broking, by the way, is simply the art of middle manning.

Which is to say that there is no reason for it to exist.

Most brokers I met knew more or less as much about their financial products as I do about the economic climate for SMEs in Vanuatu.

Degrees in finance? Fuck. *Off.*

But could they broker you into a deal?

They could've sold vuvuzelas to the Safricans. (Safrican = South African.)

So.

I get my first finance job.

And what does my colleague at my prior-to-the-City-job job say in exuberant celebration?

Now.

Before I tell you what he said, let's go back a second.

As every Englishman born prior to the millenium knows, you do not fuck with Fate.

Every person in this country born before 2000 should be familiar with a word.

And that word, striking terror into the hearts of all and sundry, is "Jinx."

This particular term is used in two instances.

The first, my favourite, is when two people say the same word at the exact same time.

So, if I hear my friend order a grande venti-coffee-frappucino-light-double-blend with sugar-free hazelnut syrup and extra man-froth, and the guy behind the counter says *at the exact same time I do* the word "knob," then one of us might say "Jinx," to avoid "Jinxing" the moment.

(*Note* - to Jinx something = to imbue it with bad luck.)

If we *both* say "Jinx" at the same time, then one of us must go "Double Jinx," or the Jinx is doubled in its intensity.

If we *both* say "Double Jinx" at the same time, we double the already-doubled jinxedness, and chances are a small rhinoceros with chronic diarrhoea is about to land on his or my head from a plane overhead carrying precious London Zoo cargo over from Cameroon.

In other words, if *that* shit happens, you *bail* like a rape convict.

The *other* usage of the word "Jinx" is its simple and original meaning, which is to "Jinx" something.

So.

If I say out loud "Andy Murray is going to beat the *tapas* out of Rafa Nadal on Friday," then I may in fact be jinxing young Murray's chances.

So.

My colleague, laughing, looks at me in the office of my prior-to-cityjob job and goes, with absolutely no idea of the immutable curse he is about to place upon both the entire globe and me:

"Ha. Haha. So, Machine, you rock up into the fookin' city, and any money says, in three months flat, haha, literally, haha, the whole fookin' world'll go into financial meltdown. Haha. Ha. Hm."

I literally froze.

I turned slowly and looked him in the face.

I checked my surroundings to see if there was a sharp implement I might kindly introduce to his left eyeball.

There wasn't.

I'm not sure if lightning struck or if thunder rolled (if it did, a *tenner* says it rolled snake eyes... *again*...), but I knew there and then, disaster was en route.

And what happened when I arrived in the City?

In a nutshell:

Other than nearly getting arrested for a drunken quadbiking accident in Switzerland, nearly being fired for being a "rent boy" [not a rent boy, fuckers, the word is *escort...FFS*...], and sleeping with three female colleagues, which *again* was a sackable offence, my arrival resulted two months later in an aggressive, prosperous marketplace tumbling into the catastrophic shitstorm we now know as the credit crunch.

Cheers, Mac.

You fucked up the world.

Or rather, you made *me* fuck up the world.

To all those affected, I humbly offer my sincerest apologies.

Genuinely. It's my bad.

See, I was never really *sure* about all that "Jinx" shit.

Seemed a bit, well, *juvenile*.

But if you see me in the street, Broseph, and we say the same shit simultaneously, you better keep that "Double Jinx" shit to yourself while I say it.

Else I may have to go all *Harvey Keitel* on your ass...

To be fair, the City was and is an amazing place.

And the current rollicking bankers are getting at the minute is a bit OTT.

For instance: to be an actor or a rapper requires zero training.

You just pick up a mic and get on with it.

To get into finance (unless you are connected) you need:

- A-levels like Einstein.
- A degree in business, economics, or finance.
- A CV that looks like *I* wrote it.
- Good interview skills.
- Years of training.

The fucking *works*.

And once you're in, what do you get?

A twelve-hour day with no lunch break sat at the same desk on the same phone in front of the same computer.

It.

Sucks.

So why do people do it?

Why is it seen as the pinnacle of paid employment?

(Other than sports commentary, people who run Laserquest centres, and, frankly speaking, directing pornography...)

Well, in a word, *money*.

Wanna be rich?

Then get studying, son, and get prepped to work your knackers off.

You're headed to the Square Mile.

To every banker, broker, analyst, VP or such on the planet: I respect the buttnuggets out of you.

You work hard, you play hard.

I know you've been landed with this credit crunch shit, but let's be honest: unless you are one of about a hundred twats in twat-suits in a twatmobile on a twatphone with a twatbelt making stupid decision about world governance, it wasn't really your fault.

You work like wage-slaves and you earn like kings.

Do. Your fucking. *Thing*.

I've been there.
I *know*.

Headline:
ACTOR / RAPPER / WRITER / ESCORT IN "I APPROVE OF
THE CITY" SCANDAL.
Yeah?
Fuck. *Off.*
If it wasn't for the City, this country would be selling turdcakes
to the Orient.
Which we practically are anyway.
So:
Leave.
The financiers.
Alone.
Send your kids to school, to uni, and then to the City, and you
know what?
This time next year, they'll be millionaires.

You ever worked a twelve-hour day with no lunch break?
And then had to take clients out you didn't even know or
necessarily like at the close of play?
For five days a week, and two evenings on top?
With only twenty days holiday?
With the responsibility of trading millions of dollars of shit you
don't understand?
Then shut your fucking mouth.
These are professional soldiers.
Or rather, they are soldiers of profession.
I'd trust them to run the country before the mongeese we have in
power now.
Believe that.
To all my boys at you-know-where, I love ya and miss ya.

And no, I do *not* look like fucking *Wicksy*...

"Has it been an easy ride?" the blonde in my bed asks me.

Always play sentences like this carefully, lads.

The temptation to reply, "well, at first you were a bit uncomfortable, but the vodka and rohyp certainly loosened you up..." will probably get you dropkicked off the bed.

Trust me.

So I tell her my LowMo.

A LowMo is your lowest moment.

That instant where you really think that Life hates you, and that Lady Luck is cheating on you with pretty much every and anyone else.

Mine I call the "£1.79" moment.

I'm sat on the floor in my flat in King's Cross (*still* my favourite area of London), and I'm staring up at the side in my kitchen.

I'm broke.

I have no money.

On the side in my kitchen is a bag of pasta.

On that bag of pasta it reads £1.79.

I realise that I cannot afford food for another two weeks until payday.

I am almost tempted to eat my own elbows, I am that hungry.

Fortunately, I can walk to work.

Unfortunately, that means I have to make that bag of pasta last two *weeks*.

Fortunately, I have friends who are willing to help me out.

Unfortunately, I am not going to ask them. Been there, done that. Lost the T-shirt.

Fortunately, no one at work needs to know.

Unfortunately, I have no fucking pasta sauce.

Fortunately, I have balsamic and olive oil.

Unfortunately, both have nearly run out.

(All I can hear at this moment is the galactic song of my own failure, and it sounds like a chant... *£1.79... £1.79... £1.79...*)

Fortunately, I have survived everything life has thrown at me, and I'll probably survive this.

Unfortunately, once I calculate the calorie count of a bag of pasta over two weeks, I am not certain I will survive this.

Fortunately, I am going to try, which brings me hope.

Unfortunately, I may fail, which brings me tears, and despair, and a desperate longing to be home, and to be free of this unceasing desire for my own vocation.

Fortunately, I am onstage later this very evening, at the Troy Bar in Old Street.

Unfortunately, I barely have the energy to walk out my flat, or get changed, or do anything. Let alone fucking *inspire* people…

Fortunately, my friends and family are such that they will forgive such mammoth failures.

Unfortunately, I am not, and I will not, and I do not, and I can not.

(£1.79… £1.79… £1.79… I told you, you fucking endless sack of ceaseless screwups… you are not going to get anywhere NEAR what you want… NEVER… not so long as I exist…)

Fortunately, I can hack Dr. Invictus Schadenfreude's insane rants, as a rule.

Unfortunately, this is not a normal situation: I have failed, I am failing, and all my rules lie broken…

"Has it been an easy ride?"

Silence.

Then:

"No, my platinum-haired, lusciously formed, superbly put-together pinnacle-of-existence. It has not."

Silence again.

Then:

"So why didn't you jack it in? How comes you didn't give up?"

* *Sigh* *…

There is a rule.

It is not my rule.

It is not your rule.

It is simply a universal constant.

It is one our current climate dislikes *greatly*.

It is a constant nevertheless.

It cares nothing for what we think of it.

It exists whether we accept it or not.

Whether we accept it or not, we must accept it.

It is mathematically true, and inescapable.

It is what you might call truth.

It is perhaps even more appropriate to call it Truth.

It is applying to you and I now, and to every being on the planet as we speak.

It is the equivalent of God, were God sexier and *way* more simple.

It is a law.

It is a law with no possible transgressions.

Attempt it by all means.

See how far you get.

The rule is simple:

Action and Consequence.

In human terms we often call this "Responsibility."

In physics it is stated, "For Every Action, There is an Equal and Opposite Reaction."

For every action you undertake, there is a consequence.

Failure to accept said consequence results in failure.

Blame your divorce on your wife?

Think your school let you down?

Think your boss is holding you back?

Believe God is to blame for all your woes?

Feel like your kids meant you couldn't live the life you wanted?

Blame your boyfriend for cheating on you?

Blame your girlfriend for sleeping with your brother?

Feel like you should have won that hand at poker?

Fuck.

You.

You take the action, you take the fucking consequences.

Like a man.

Or woman.

194

So then, the response:

"I didn't give up because I believe I have a responsibility. To my family, to my race, to my children who are not yet born, to every woman I ever loved, to my friends, to the future, to my work, and most of all, to myself.

"To be the best I can be; to set the best example, to soar as high as possible, so that others might see the flight path, and themselves feel a need to fly.

"To follow the Song of Armstrong, and deny that the sky be the limit. To seek to set my footprint upon the surface of the moon. To set new standards. To improve everything I see however I can.

"To make my children proud of their father. To make my wife proud of her husband, and my mother proud of her son.

"To ensure that my every day counted for *something*. Whether that be in the eyes of a stranger, or God, or whoever the fuck, I know not. But to be able above all things to look myself in the eye in the mirror in the morning and say: you do all right, man. You do all right.

"We're given life. We're the luckiest people in the history of history. We have to *do* something with it.

"To be able to live. With myself."

Because living with yourself is *hard*.

I'm nearly thirty years old.

Which, to be fair, is nothing.

And everything.

It's young.

It's *old*.

And I just saw one of my parents for my birthday.

Dinner, drinks, the usual.

And I fucked it up.

I wasn't really there.

Dinner was pleasant, drinks were nice, the whole thing was; well, nice.

And as any woman will tell you, describing something as nice is not going to cut it.

You are *born* alone. And you will *die* alone.

This is not something to fear, or cry over, or regret.

It is the ultimate sign of simultaneous independence and connectedness.

No man is an island?

Utter bollocks.

Every man is an island.

However. All islands are linked by the sea, and are just differently located extremities of the same land mass.

Every man is *the* island.

QUARTER THREE – AUTUMN

ABDULLAH THE PREACHER 2010

THE HOTHOUSE CREW 2010

IBIZA JULY 2010

- THE KMN-ID TOUR - FIRST BLOOD

JULY 2010:

"THE "KILL ME NOW...I'M *DONE*..." TOUR"

"They lashed me, crashed me, smashed me down to my knees, 'n' said,
'Talent Leave' n' said, 'We want you to beg and plead', I said...
"Motherfucker, please; as long as I breathe 'n' believe in freedom I won't leave,
This is my joy, this is my toy, this is the gift I live for my girl and my boy...""

- Talent and Ender -
"Will I Rise"

- IMMORTALENTED 2013 -

So I'm literally three hours away from turning thirty.
And I have been, chick-like, crying.
Wow. That sounds sexist, huh?
OK, I'll rephrase.
I have shed tears.
Multiple.
It always, *always* fucks me up leaving Wolverhampton.
Not that leaving Wolverhampton is to be mourned. On the contrary, if you had to leave anywhere, it might not be the worst place to leave.
But my *family* is there.
My *history* is there.
My *life*, my *story*, my *everything* originates there.
And leaving my parent(s) always cuts me deep.
They outdid themselves, my family.

Ruined me.

Got me a mic, a mic stand, books, DVDs, cards that had Shakespearean poetry of life written within their pages, and a scrapbook of my life.

And *of course*, single malt whisky.

And one of my boys rode his bike from Birmingham to Wolvo just to be there.

(Had to nag him, mind, but then he forgets that I love him like a sibling. Forgets he *is* my sibling. But then of all people, I can't complain about the Alzheimers of others....)

Ended up wrecking me.

How can we feel both connected and yet utterly alone?

How can we feel the intensity of unity and yet also the sharpness of singularity?

I don't pretend to have all the answers. Only to have the idiocy / balls / nous to ask the fecking questions.

And *yes*, I swear a lot.

But while we're on that particular subject, if you don't like it, you know what you can do?

You guessed it.

Fuck.

Off.

Because we *do* swear.

A *lot*.

My generation, that is.

Let alone the military.

Let alone the younger generations.

Who I see *immense* potential in, by the way.

As well as immense - fucking - *waste*.

You have no *idea* how easy you have it.

Not compared with my generation.

We had it easy too.

I mean in comparison with my mother's generation and my grandfather's generation before that.

You have no.

Fucking.

Idea.

So you don't like the swearing?

Cool. Fuck off.

Don't buy the book.

Because I don't *need* you.

And you don't *need* me.

If you're there, reading this, hearing these words at all, it's not because of me, or because of my language, or because of my fondness for fucking formulaic use of allite-fucking-ration.

It's because you've been *waiting*.

Waiting.

Waiting... for someone... *anyone*... to have the nuts to stand up and tell the truth.

Or rather, the *Truth*.

The Truth.

If that be the case, then *hombre*, you came to the right bar...

It's not just you. I'm equally as guilty.

I knew I was afraid of the truth on two occasions.

The first was this:

TA Parachute Regiment, 2003.

London.

With my best friend at the time, whose suggestion it was in the first place.

Stupidest thing I've ever done, other than getting a chick I barely knew knocked up (Lord forgive me, I *beg* of you...) and studying Mediaeval Italian Literature when I didn't speak *modern* fucking Italian...

OK, along with... actually... you know what? That could take a *while*...

So:

The log race.

100 men lie facedown upon the grass and stone.

They are wearing military uniforms.

They are terribly, *terribly* afraid.

A man on the ground is so afraid that he urinates himself.

The wind carries the fetid smell into our nostrils.

Usually this would instigate a round of piss-taking *so* severe, he would walk off the base *immediately*.

Not now.

Not here.

Not at the log race.

To get into the Parachute Regiment of the British Army, there are seven tests you must pass, called "Pegasus Company", or "P-Company".

(Coolest name in the world, no?)

Seven tests.

(1) The Trainasium - an aerial assault course consisting of ropes, jumps, ladders, and all other manner of shit most ten-year-olds run across but most twenty-year-olds wet themselves at.

(2) The Two miler - a two mile sprint carrying a twenty-five pound loaded weapon and a fifty-five pound stuffed-like-Barrymore backpack called a "Bergen".

(3) The Ten miler - same as above, basically, but ten miles.

(4) Milling - hand to hand combat, with no dodging allowed, where you attempt to knock another man's teeth out. He's likely to be your friend.

(5) The Stretcher Race - a five-and-a-half mile run with eight men, four of whom carry a solid steel stretcher while the other four run behind. This, as they say, is a bitch.

(6) The Steeplechase - a one-and-a-half mile run cross-country, followed by a Krypton Factor style assault course, in wet, soggy clothing that drags you down like an anchor.

(7) The *log race*.

I don't really know what to tell you. Except that Nightmares are *real*.

The log race is so terrifying that you hear of it *day one* of training.

"Yo, you heard about the log race?"

"No."

"Dude."

"What?"

"*Dude.* I heard a guy got dragged on the concrete on his face for over a mile and ended up in hospital like, forever."

"Erm. What?"

So: more than a hundred men lie upon the ground.

One of our cadre has wet himself.

I thank every God in existence, *there and **then***, that it was not me.

I look for my friend. I cannot see him. I pray that he is less scared than I.

My manhood is on the line.

My word to my parents as a *son* is on the line.

Whatever Pari does or does not think of me is on the line.

My reflection in the mirror, is on, the fucking, line.

Each log is a telegraph pole.

Each log has eight nooses around it.

The idea is, you leg it up to the log once the gun goes off, stick your wrist in the noose (four either side, better *pray* you get the right side if you're a righty or a lefty) and then, basically, you sprint.

You sprint for a mile and a half, carrying a telegraph pole with seven other men, up hill and down valley, through stream and over brook, in webbing, boots, helmet, combats, and army T-shirt.

You may choose to fall off the log, but then you fail.

And are regarded, quite rightly, as a pussy.

And if you *fuck up* falling off the log, you may end up tripping over and being dragged on your face on the concrete by seven men who *do not wish* to appear to be pussies for somewhere up to a mile and a half.

And then you may require more than a little plastic surgery.

As I say.

I was *shitting* it.

I knew I was not fit enough.

For the first time in my whole life, I believed that I was going to fail something.

Fail the Parachute Regiment.

Which wasn't even my fucking *idea*.

But my dad had been military.

So had my grandfather.

And now I'd chucked my hat in the ring.

I was private number fifteen.

I had, covertly, been on the phone to my mum and to Pari at night, under the covers, just to hear a sane voice, to hear a voice tell me:

"Do *not* give up. You can *do* this. You have *trained* for this for four months. Just give yourself a *chance*."

You are NOT going to do this, you shrivel of a man. You are going to FAIL.

First time for everything, hotshot.

And NOW is the time.

You are NOTHING.

(How do I give myself a chance...?)

Ah.

I know.

I'll memorise something.

A poem. A song.

Just *one* thing, that when the going gets tough (as it will do, very soon) I can *cling* on to and hold tight to with everything I have, and then all I have to do becomes simplicity itself.

Just.

    Hang.

        On.

So I memorised this thing the Paras gave us. Like a motto, except longer.

"So," I think to myself, "if I can just remember this one thing..."

BANG.

No.

Surely that can't have been it? The starting gun?

And yet it *was*.

Men are now sprinting towards the logs.

I give it all I have, and end up with my right hand hovering over a log to my right.

I am elated.

Until some Egyptian dude shoulders me off that log and nicks the noose I had my eyes on.

That just leaves me the log to my left, and means I have to sprint a mile and a half attached by my *left hand* (with which I have *no* co-ordination [played tennis, no football, my left-sided co-ordination is roughly as proficient as the daytime vision of a bat who's had its eyes plucked out with a spoon]) to a fucking telegraph pole.

I am, to put it mildly, unamused.

I look back and see seven other men on the log.

I breathe a deep breath.

So does the lance corporal.

"RAHN, YOU FAHCKING CAAAAAHHHHNTTTSSSS!!!"

I start running.

I realise after roughly sixty seconds that I am not fit enough.

I realise *also* after a further thirty seconds that my webbing is too high on my body, and is holding my chest and my lungs in a grip that restricts my breathing.

Get halfway...if you need to start reciting that shit halfway through, then fair enough. But at least get HALFWAY.

My head is pounding. We are leaping through streams, running uphill, sprinting for all we are worth, and the corporals and PTs (physical trainers) are running alongside us and helpfully informing us that we are all cunts, and useless, and worth nothing.

We run.

My lungs are pounding.

I have never felt such pain. I've felt more for short periods but *fuck* me this is *constant*.

I have been knocked unconscious, drunker than Dionysius, had a cyst in my ear, and been more humiliated than you can *possibly* imagine, and yet I'd swap it *all* for this shit...

I am in *agony*.

I can hear the guy behind me sucking air.

"FACKING RAHN NUMBER FIFTEEN YOU FAHCKING *CAAAAHNT*!"

I keep running.

We turn a corner.

My whole body is revolting against me.

It's a physical mutiny.

I am close to begging for my life.

I'd rather be beaten into oblivion than face this.

My stomach is full of battery acid.

My mouth is dryer than the Sahara.

My head pounds and pounds and pounds and pounds and pounds and pounds and pounds and pounds.

Do *not* start reciting that shit yet. You can *do* this...

I think of my mother. I think of my girlfriend. I think of my friends, who have followed my journey throughout this ordeal and who have faith in me.

I think they ought to reconsider their bets.

I think I would bribe Mother Theresa to get out of this.

I keep running.

I think for a split second that I am coping, we *must* have been running a couple of minutes, maybe even three or four (a couple is two, people, a few is three plus) and that perhaps I can survive. I daydream of hearing my father's voice tell me he is proud of his son.

And of my girlfriend looking at me with adoring eyes.

And of my nan smiling at me, knowing her faith has not been in vain.

And of my mother, laughing, knowing her son is too stubborn to be beatable.

And *above all*, of me seeing my reflection and not having to look away in shame.

I begin to control my breath, and almost, for a moment, to smile.

And then the log dips.

At first I do not comprehend what has happened, as I am at the front of the log on the right.

My wrist feels like a dog is chewing at it.

Which is odd, since I did not notice any pain in my wrist before.

I risk a glance back...

"WHAAT THE **FACK** ARE YOU LOOKING AT, YOU *CAAAAAHNT*?!?!"

...and see that not one, not two, but *three* men have fallen off our log.

We are now five men carrying what should be transported by eight.

My vision begins to blur, and my eyes begin to water.

I begin (to my eternal shame) to pray to a God, any God, that he might give me more strength.

The gods are apparently unavailable right now. And will I please leave a message.

I cannot believe the weight and pressure on my body to quit.

I am losing.

I am dying.

I am gone.

I realise that I am about to think of ways to submit without looking like a pussy.

My brain no longer works coherently.

I feel that this is what it is to be tortured.

I hope Pari will forgive me.

I hope I will forgive myself.

And then a corporal begins running alongside me.

I am bleeding from the nose, apparently. The taste is fucking horrible.

My lungs are *still* being squeezed by my webbing.

I would like to cry, were I man enough to do so.

"CAHM ON NUMBAH FIFTEEN, YOUSE KNOW YOUSE IN THE LEEAD, *DON'TCHA*?"

At first I don't get what he's saying.

At first, I just want him to fuck off.

Or shoot me, and put me out of my misery.

Then my brain processes what he has just said.

We're winning? We're the fastest log? We're at the front? Surely that's *impossible*...

I look back again, earning more swearing and spittle on my brow from the lance corporal next to the corporal.

But sure enough: two logs have quit, and there are four or five logs running behind us, and more behind them.

Holy fucking Godsack... my brain feebly realises... **We're *winning*...**

Charlie, a solid and fit-as-fuck recruit is shouting encouragement, and the lance corporal joins him.

They know I'm not fit enough.

But I'm not giving in.

Except I *am*.

As soon as I can work out how to.

My mind is occupied with this, when I realise that, exactly as the Sgt Major said only days ago, my mind is likely to give out before my body.

Hold on... my mind is likely to give out *before* my body...?

So what, like I *choose* to chicken out, or I *pass* out...?

And then, something strange, not like determination, or guts, or courage, but more like sheer stubborn fuck-you-ness sets in.

If that be the case, then go on, fucking *pass out*...

But... says I...

But how do we cope with the pain?

Since, let's be honest here, Doc, it's fucking *agonising*...?

At which point, I begin reciting, mantra-like, the piece I had memorised.

The pain is so great I realise I have been "thinking-to-myself" for over five minutes, have no idea where I am, and I am pretty sure I am dying, or tht I'm about to shit myself.

I cannot look back, nor move, for fear of falling.

And if I fall, I am done. I've seen guys fall on the log and get dragged for miles on their faces on the dirt and stones...

I can taste blood in my mouth. I think it is from my nose, which started bleeding a while back, but I can't be sure.

My brain, traitor-like, begins to think of my Grandparents looking down on me, and begs them for help and for mercy.

I hold to my mantra.

If my body falls, then it falls.

All I need to is to *hold fast*, and then I may keep my chin raised in pride.

Suddenly, my mind, realising what I am up to, begins traitoring me left, right and centre.

You are a fucking coward.

Think of your Mum, your Dad, your Nan, look at the pain you are in you FUCKING INSECT...

I keep chanting my mantra in my head.

I get the feeling, if this works; I'll be doing it a *lot*...

I feel something go in my left leg, and look down to see my wrist.

All I can see is a sharp red-pinkish colour.

I am now limping.

My breath comes in rasps, making me sound like I have asthma.

I thank God I do not have asthma.

I curse myself that I smoke.

The lance corporal is running next to me and is (is this possible?) shouting encouragement.

The sweat covers the whole of my body. I have a wedgie that I'd love to fix but if I move a *muscle* my concentration will go and I will be dragged uphill on my face and be disfigured like a mongrel and Jesus my saviour why dost thou punish thy children in such ways am I going insane oh Jesus I'm hitting some kind of wall insane fuck fuck *fuck*...

Hold the phone.

Uphill?

My vision clears for a brief second, and we are now running *uphill*.

Sprinting.

Uphill.

Attached to a telegraph pole.

I start laughing involuntarily and nearly choke on my own tongue.

"YOU THINK THIS IS FAHCKING *FUNNY YOU CAHHNTT*?!?!?!?!!?!?!?"

I see at the top of the hill - **Dear God let it be so** - what looks like, no, can it be...?

A finish line.

A fucking *finish* line.

We keep running.

I chant harder and harder and harder and harder and suddenly we are there, before I even realise it.

We are at the top of the hill and I am being shouted at and STAND TO ATTENTION YOU *CAAAHNTS* and dropping the log and my webbing was too tight, sir, and falling and sky and clouds and falling and grass and still and falling and blackness and oblivion and darkness and *gone...*

I wake up in the med bay, only because the constant beeping fucks me *off*.

My body feels like I have had to fight my way through West Ham.

Some dude in a white coat stands there looking at me, shocked.

"What happened?" says I. My mouth is dry.

He begins telling me I need to rest and lie down.

I grab him by the fuff (fucking scruff) of the neck and go "What. *Happened?*"

"?"

He looks at me, terrified, as if staring into the maw of a beast.

Which at that precise second, unless I receive a response, he *is*.

"You came in, Private."

That's. Not. *Good enough.*

"What...fucking...happened...?" says I again. "On the fucking *log* race...?"

The dude in the white coat looks at me like a rabid animal.

Which, to be fair, I am.

"Private, you completed the log race. Your log came in first. You won."

And you'd think that'd be it.

You'd think the Fear of the Truth had suddenly been conquered.

You'd think, to be fair, I'd be *happy*.

But Life hadn't done with me yet.

I made it through the ten-miler.

The two-miler.

The milling.

The steeplechase.

The stretcher race.

The Trainasium.

And got to the "passing out parade."

We are all lined up on the parade ground with maroon berets on our heads.

If we pass, we get to keep them.

If not, then, well, *not*.

This is all for a piece of clothing you can buy at a military or army navy store for about a fiver.

A maroon beret.

Except it is, clearly, nothing to do with that. The beret is a symbol.

This is about manhood.

Being a *man*.

And my boy (whose idea this all was) and I are about to face the music.

To be fair, I reckon I'm failing.

Which means a *very* long ride back to London with my boy having passed and me having failed and us not being able to speak for days.

Since, basically, I *fucking despise* failure.

My mate Dave (no joke) is up in the bleachers opposite, having failed the ten-miler. Bless him; he had a heart of gold. What he needed was more fitness.

"Number One: FAIL."

What they do is call your number out, and simply say pass or fail.

"Number Two: FAIL."

You stand to attention when they call your number, and then if they call "Pass" you stand as you are, or if they call "Fail", you get the *fuck* off their parade ground.

"Number Three: FAIL."

"Number Four: PASS."

Fuck me, I think, **has only one person in** *four* **passed so far...??? Well fuck it, maybe it was just an unlucky start and we're onto the positive streak hereon in...**

"Number Five: FAIL."

 Or not...

"Number Six: FAIL."

Suddenly my mind races... **what fucking number am I?**

"Number Seven: FAIL."

OK fuck, thank God, I'm number fifteen.

"Number Eight: FAIL."

Hold on, number fifteen, right? What number is my boy though? Dave, up in the bleachers, starts chewing his nails.

"Number Nine: FAIL."

Fuck me sideways; has *anyone* **else passed this shit?**

"Number Ten: PASS."

Thank *fuck*...

"Number Eleven: FAIL."

Bollocks...

"Number Twelve: FAIL."

Please God please God...

"Number Thirteen: FAIL."

Shocker. Bad pick, guy...

"Number Fourteen: FAIL."

Please forgive me shit my beret's *not* **getting taken off me I** *like* **this shit...**

"Number Fifteen: PASS."

Holy hell what number is my boy, OK I have to leave the Parade Ground and... hold up...waitaminnit...*WHAT DID HE SAY...?*

"Number Sixteen: FAIL."

Did he just fucking say PASS?????????? Is *that* **why Dave is waving at me like a maniac?**

"Number Seventeen: PASS."

SHEEYIT. *SHIT.* **Is** *that* **my boy's number? FUCK ME RUNNING did I pass???**

"Number Eighteen: FAIL."

FUCK. ME. WHAT FUCKING NUMBER IS HE GOD*FUCKIT please let him pass*...

"Number Nineteen:..."

Ah. That's him.

"...FAIL."

Oh.

Fuck.

The coach journey back was long.

My boy was inconsolable.

As you would be.

Not cry-your-eyes out inconsolable but do-not-fucking-speak-to-me inconsolable.

I called my parents.

One of who said "well done," and that was more or less it.

The other of whom put the phone down, got in the car, and drove 120 miles to London to say *congratulations* to my fucking *face*.

Take note, parents of the world.

We get back to halls of residence at uni and our friends are waiting, at the edge of their seats.

They see me come in with a maroon beret.

They go fucking *apeshit*.

My boy walks into his room and shuts the door.

The door-shut says, "Do not disturb. Fuck off, in fact. For quite some time."

Our friends look at me questioningly.

"Only one of us got in," says I.

And from the coach journey and the imbalance of justice I realised there and then, not only had I been afraid of the Truth of the Log (which was that I knew fear, and that fear was rational, and that that rationale was that I was *not* fit enough, and that therefore I probably *should* fail), but also I was afraid of the Truth of the Door.

And the Truth of the Door is a tough nut to crack; that sometimes *my* happy endings are not *our* happy endings and while I preferred infinitely the idea of *our* happy ending, I'd rather have *my own* happy ending than *not* have it, and if *that* meant only *one* of us could have a happy ending then I wanted *my* happy ending and while I *mourned like a mofo* my boy's sorrows, it was infinitely better than *me* mourning *my* sorrows.

And as soon as I realised both fears of both differing Truths, the fear, as usual, evaporated.

Because I had conquered the first on my *own*.

And because my boy would survive the second.

And, moreover, because, were he to have known at that moment that I had *pitied* him, he would have felt a greater, more acerbic pain than any lack of a maroon-coloured beret might ever have afflicted him with.

Anyway.

Bit of a sideroad.

So it's 2:19am in the morning, and I'm thirty years old.

And in no more no less than three hours I need to leave the flat and be on set at major studios outside London to start training for a primo Hollywood film.

And to be fair, I'm going to be exhausted.

Knackered.

Sleep-deprived.

And you know what?

I could care *less*.

I'm thirty.

Bring.

It.

On.

Oh.

Oh wow.

As in, *oh*. And then: *wow*.

I'm not sure I have ever felt like this.

And I thought other moments would be difficult to describe.

This, however, is going to be a mission.

As in, *mission*.

Because I have actually never felt this feeling before.

A war has just been won; a war has just been lost. Thirty years are done, and thirty years are lost. I sit atop a mountaintop in the Capitol, kept company by the moon. I have just broken many laws, and have just made many laws anew, with the greatest Sunslingers the Western world has ever known. Many friends have fallen; all of them rose again. Love was made between two strangers from two different many shores.

And I have just been soundly beaten. Defeated. Resoundingly, completely, and *utterly* broken.

And of all things on earth that have been hated by any man, I hate, venomously, the concept of defeat. But this time, this one time, I have been defeated roundly and soundly by my own flesh and blood. My own family have taken me and thrown me from my own home, my own country, and beaten me.

I know. I'm talking absolute shit.

I'd better explain…

THE MISSION: - "KILL ME NOW… I'M DONE."

For the following mission debrief:

All units shall be referred to by their FieldName to avoid public disclosure of their identities and thereby jeopardise their public field activities.

This unit shall be referred to as "Birthday Boy" due to his recently updated birthstatus as a tri-decenarian. Which is a word that probably doesn't exist. But you know what?

Fuck *it*.

DAY ONE – "KIDNAPPED AGAINST MY WILL, AND IBIZA LANDING..."

TUESDAY 06/07/2010 - 08:30am - 09:00am next day

All I was told is when it was all supposed to happen.

I didn't know who was going, and I didn't know *where* we were going. I basically knew *fuck all*. So it was pretty much business as usual.

I'd had word on the grapevine of who wasn't going, but that didn't matter. What mattered was, who *was* going.

I received a message from both the Wizard and the White Knight prior to going, warning me they were not going to be there.

To be frank, I was *pissed*. Not at them, mind, but just that I'd miss the shit out of them.

Cunning bastards.

Cunning. *Bastards.*

So I arrived at Liverpool Street and saw: the Moreganiser (legend, this being mostly his efforts and work), the Wizard (cunning bastard), Vinaigrette (thank *God*, couldn't have survived without her), and *fuck me running* is that *Blitzshorty*???

Heh. This trip is going to be *interesting...*

Vinaigrette tells me on the sly "It's OK, I can tell you, we're headed to China..."

Erm. *China?*

You *sure?*

That's a fair way away for... oh hold on... these are my *friends...* you can't trust a *word* they say if it's in your best interest. So uh-huh, sure, China.

After this, li'l Vinaigrette proceeded to almost let slip about fifteen major secret details of the trip. Kept it secret for two months and now couldn't keep it under wraps for two hours. Typical.

It's only after getting *through* check-in, to the gate, that I see the immortal word: *Ibiza.*

I immediately BBM White Knight: *Ibiza? With me? Jesus. That's brave...*

We get to Ibiza, and the hotel is *sick.* Just stupidly sick: pool, full menu, we're 10 minutes from the beach, people, and no *that's impossible* there before my very eyes are TnT (*Jesus* haven't seen

215

you in *ages*...!) and Brings The Pressure BTP, at which point I nearly lose it. *Nearly.*

She then of course kicks off abusing me and my hair, which to be fair, I expected.

We head first to Space nightclub, and Moreganiser shows us all the venue, which is *massive*.

It's a riotous laserlight show of *immense* proportions. It's got men in robot suits walking round and ice showers and music and drinks and it's just too much.

TnT introduces her friends BlondeGrass, FrenchChick and GreetingCard, who subsequently asks TnT "is this him?"

TnT nods, and GreetingCard proceeds to walk up to Birthday Boy and, without uttering a word, lapdances him on the terrace of Space, the night Carl Cox is playing.

Vinaigrette buys Birthday Boy a T-shirt from Space, and the night kicks on in style.

The whole crew dances while BTP kindly offers medical assistance, which the crew accepts gracefully, before partying it off until six am in the morning.

We see that Moreganiser has this planned to a "T," and that Blitzshorty intends to basically not stop dancing until the break of, well, everything.

The Wizard, also a first-timer to Ibiza, remarks on several occasions to Birthday Boy, "how much. Is this. The fucking nizzuts...?"

This, Ladies and Germs, is how my friends decided to throw me a thirtieth Birthday Party...

MVP - Vinaigretta

DAY TWO – "SPACE, SNOOPS PETRELLI, AND TABLE TENNIS GONE BATTY..."

WEDNESDAY 07/07/2010 - 05:30am - 05:00am

We watched the sun come up from the waves of the ocean at Bora Bora beach.

After being harassed by two Italian chicks, three Coventry girls and one tramp, Birthday Boy proceeded to lose all his jewellery in the sea after being bodytackled by the Moreganiser.

Wednesday.

Day two.

We're out by the pool. And *Jesus* Christ... were the BTX shattered from the night before. Blitzshorty was gone. As in, *gone*.

Never in my life have I see a man so gone he had passed out and was nearly in a coma, but who, when the music came on, was still capable of dancing. *Unconscious* dancing...

Immediate MVP status conferred.

Blitzshorty, BTP and Birthday Boy headed out to Bora Bora beach for a day party.

After a jug of sangria and yet more medical assistance from BringsThe Pressure, the day was full of promise, until a 6'3'' guy with a skintight sky-blue shirt and same coloured shorts decided to approach and chat up Blitzshorty for fifteen minutes.

Birthday Boy, like all other onlookers, assumed this was a client or friend. Subsequently, Shorty turns to Birthday Boy to reveal "I have no fucking idea who that was."

After Bora Bora the crew reunited and headed out to Ushuara, where the waitresses are so magma hot that the sand turns to glass.

Moreganiser's eagle eyes quickly spotted the single, solitary perfect arse on the tour, stuck to the back of a blonde girl.

Snoops arrived and was immediately force-fed his "catchup" drink, which consisted of: *one* shot tequila, *one* shot sambuca, and *two* Jaegerbombs. At which point Snoops Petrelli began to regret going to Ibiza.

The Wizard then got in round two (same as above) and poured it all into one pint glass. He turned to Snoops.

"Down it. *Bitch*."

Snoops, in true BTX style, downed it like a man. And then took off running.

By the time he had got to Space, he had only one thing on his mind - partying. He was showing signs of developing the higher state of consciousness he would epitomise later in the trip. After a long night dancing and downing more shots of sambuca, Birthday Boy and Snoops were seen stumbling around the pool playing the world's worst and most inept game of table tennis, drunk-mumbling a long overdue catchup chat.

"You get the ball. I'm too fucked."

"You get the fucking ball. I can't...oh *fuck* it..."

MVP - BlitzShorty

DAY THREE – "PACHA, DAVID GUETTA, THE GREATEST TABLE IN HISTORY, AND BTX OWNS THE NIGHT..."

MVP? The *Wizard*...

THURSDAY 08/07/2010 - 05:30am - 08:00am next day

The day began with issues. Pacha's booking woman was dicking around with Moreganiser, who, basically, had had enough of her shit.

We figured we'd maybe have to book elsewhere, and were looking for Plan B's.

Moreganiser: "What's Plan B, Snoops?"

Snoops: "Plan B is to do Plan A better."

Quote of the Century.

God I love my friends. Birthday Boy was knocked for six when White Knight showed up, and of course at this moment, all problems seemed to disappear. We were set.

Pacha. David Guetta. A table. VIP.

Heh. You *must* be kidding. Us? *Pacha*? Goodbye sweet world. Was nice knowing ya...

We had dinner beforehand. Snoops, Birthday Boy, Blitzshorty (still going... fucking *animal*...) and Vinaigretta ate *way* too much and figured vom was on the way.

Pacha VIP'd us in all the way - entered in through the kitchen, no queueing, it was the *nuts*.

Moreganiser and the crew had sorted out a table which was basically a massive altar in the middle of the dancefloor, raised like lookout mountain from "The Lion King," and in the heart of all the action with front-row views of the DJ booth, dance floor and podiums.

It was also covered, by which I mean *covered*, in alcohol. Grey Goose, Whisky, Champagne, mixers, juices; you name it, we gamed it.

BTP provided medical support as ever, to which the Knight warned: "Dogg, BTP says these are *strong*."

This is the equivalent of Oliver Reed passing you a quadruple JD and coke and adding the warning "watch out, chum, that bevvy's got a bit of a *kick*..."

BTP had sufficient meds that her first half hour was spent mesmerised in her phone. Blondie, Frenchchick and Greeting Card were absolutely lovely, and in fantastic moods.

BlondeGrass summed it up perfectly:

"How much do you feel like the luckiest man in the World right now?"

At which point, Birthday Boy lost it and had to walk off to have a bit of a quiet moment.

Hops was the one-legged dance wonder of the evening, dancing like a demon and loving every second of it.

BTP gave Birthday Boy *constant* abuse about him cracking up on the night, referring to him as a "pussy" and a "boyband member."

White Knight received constant accolades for (a) at no point cracking so much as a smile, due to sheer coolness, and (b) doing his part for international relations and keeping the BTX in favour with the EU.

Blitzshorty, I swear to God, *still* didn't stop. At all. Ever. Dancing and partying like this was his blueprint.

Vinaigrette danced and partied away, pouring drinks and managing to lower the Sarson's level for the evening; and also looking stunning in a new Native-American style headdress thing that Hops gave her.

The Moreganiser danced and laughed and as ever, hosted the table like he was born to do so.

Everyone got in problem free, the table was served beautifully, and the night went *off*. (My thanks to you, Sir.)

Guetta came on to *thunderous* reception - his set proving every bit as good as anticipated. More meds were passed out, an ocean of cameraphones clicked off at the Spaniard, and the finest women you have *ever seen* danced pole while Guetta spun.

Wizard reached a new level. With new tag partner Snoops Petrelli, he held court and danced and joked and flirted and drank with TnT and her friends, and decided "no inhibitions. Not tonight."

To behold such a thing happening, one's nearest and dearest, on a foreign shore, dancing to David Guetta, drinking, making merry, at the best club in the world, is something that will stay with me for a very, very long time...

So the night blasted *off*.

One member of the BTX gave a perfect demonstration of pickup - no words needed, no fancy shit, just a simple head movement and job *done*.

Another BTX member was seen making out with a girl on the *floor* of the VIP table.

Yet another BTX member vanished off round the club having to come down after receiving BTP's medical assistance.

The podium dancers poured liquid chocolate over themselves and then fashioned rudimentary chocolate underwear from it.

Birthday Boy's shades got nicked, but such was the night that he didn't care. Guetta played the set of his life and set the tone.

Snoops got in trouble for playing with someone's armpit hair (previously, BTP had tried to ignite Shorty's armpit hair during his Doritos coma) without permission.

Frenchchick turned to Wizard and asked, "you know what they say about Ibiza, right?"

Wizard: "No. What?

French: "What happens in Ibiza, stays in Ibiza..."

At which point, so overcome with emotion, so high on life (lifehigh) was he, so perfect a night was it, that he was heard turning to White Knight and uttering the immortal words:

"Dude. Kill Me Now.... I'm *done*..."

Of course, what none of us yet knew, was the price we were going to pay the *next* day. Snoops and Birthday Boy had yet to crash, and crash *big*...

MVP - The Wizard

DAY 4 – "SALINAS BEACH, CRASH CRASH, AND AMNESIAC DAKOTA..."

FRIDAY 09/07/2010 - 08:30am - 09:00am next day

It was crash city.

After a Subway and some light refreshment, Birthday Boy confessed to feeling slightly more human. However by the time they hit Salinas Beach, he could no longer walk or talk coherently.

The Wizard observed, "Dude. We're in the Ocean. It's fucking boiling out here, and you're shivering. Are you *dribbling*...?"

"I CAN'T DO THIS. I NEED, LIKE, WATER. AND SHADE. AND SOMEWHERE TO SIT DOWN. AND WHERE'S MY FUCKING NECKLACE GONE...?" – Birthday Boy

Dinner was lovely. A chilled out 'evening by the beach' affair, where White Knight explained his craft and his music to Moreganiser, and where Vin regained some of her spiritual strength.

The boys and BTP decided the trip for the night (Going out? After Pacha? Hahahaha, stop… haha...no, really, *stop*...) was going to be Amnesia.

At which point Wizard and Birthday Boy began crying, and White Knight ran for the bleachers. Vinaigrette faked a mild seizure and excused herself from proceedings. Wizard lost control…

"Dogg. You gotta help me. I'm going, man. Going, going, gone..."

The Wizard was not in good shape.

BTP, Snoops and Morg were all itching for a rumbustifying night out. Wizard was close to tears. But, we'd said we'd go, after some platinum sales work by Snoops and Morg, so go we did. Shorty saw a work colleague, and toddled off to say hello.

Amnesia was off the *heezy*, and Snoops observed how they had danced till the morning light and the Sun came up through the windows.

All before, as they say, *that* afterparty...

DAY FIVE – "NONSENSE, DAKOTA REDUX, AND OCEAN BLUE MARLIN"

SATURDAY 10/07/2010 - 08:30am - 09:00am next day

06:30am - Dakota Club

After crash city, the day began at Dakota. BTP, Snoops Petrelli, and the Moreganiser (Shorty too, of course, *still* going...is the man *immortal*...?) were all partying it up at Dakota.

The Wizard had crashed, but Birthday Boy was headed to Dakota.

Moreganiser was about to crash after a legendary performance, and the four guys from Gay Pride Argentina who kept pinching his ass did *not* help.

Snoops went home to crash as well, for the second time in the trip. Shorty, BTP and Birthday Boy stayed for drinks, one allegedly facilitating a medical trade for a group of Spaniards and a group of Frenchmen.

221

The initial plan was to hit Zoo Project, which got shelved as its location in San Antonio meant possible fraternising with the enemy.

Not.

Happening.

So it was off to Blue Marlin and Jemanga. Where, to be frank, the food was the *nuts*. Drinks all round, food all round, it was operation *recovery* before the final trip home.

Vin got Birthday Boy *another* T-shirt (generosity itself, see?). Wizard and White Knight had a long overdue chat about quantum mechanics, life, the universe and everything. BTP was on self-medication, everyone jumped in the ocean.

It rocked.

Back at the hotel, White Knight got his present for Birthday Boy, who subsequently lost control of his shit and started, allegedly, so they say, rumours unconfirmed, crying.

To be fair, it had been the best trip of his *life* featuring the best *night* of his life.

To top it all off, they found out that one BTX member, having crashed horrendously after a legendary performance, had gotten so ill that he had attempted to Ruth down the toilet, only to find himself losing bowel control and thunderdumping at the same time.

This was so legendarily comic, that all BTX members lost their shit at the same time. I was, literally, crying with laughter.

And thus was born the term "shomitting."

At which point, negotiations began between BTP, Wizard, and Birthday Boy, about whether they might stay one more day, to be in Spain the day the Spanish had the chance, for the first time ever, to win the World Cup...

DAY SIX – "SUNDAY – LEAVING AGAINST MY WILL – *AGAIN...*"

SUNDAY 11/07/2010 - 08:30am - Lift Off

And there we were.

Do we stay or do we go now...?

Brings The Pressure was *not* going to let it go.

"Why aren't you staying though?"

It had been too much: the gifts, the friends, the Pacha night, the perfect, perfect trip. Something just clicked and said this was not the right thing to do.

222

But the Wizard said he was in, so I was in, too.

Until, that is, we checked the times and availability and it was *not* happening. For a moment I was over the moon about staying another day to see the World Cup finals, and as it turned out (never, *ever* argue with Brings The Pressure....) it was a *monstrosity* of a day.

But, we left at eight am to get our ten am flights. And we did so with heavy heart.

We had the slowest Burger King in the world at the airport, and we had a quiet journey back where Wizard and Birthday Boy laughed a lot and relived the whole trip, moment by moment, in order to make this particular part of the story accurate.

White Knight, Moreganiser, and Shorty caught some Zs on the way home, and a teary-eyed farewell was bid at the airport.

And Brings The Pressure's next BBM, predictably, wonderfully, *gloriously*, just read:

"Dude. Spain just won the World Cup. Ibiza's about to go *off...*"

MVP? Brings The Pressure. *Natch.*

That was the celebration my friends decided to provide me for my thirthieth birthday.

To Moreganiser, Vinaigretta, Hops, BTP, TnT, Blitzshorty, White Knight, the Wizard, Snoops Petrelli, and the Natski girls, I love you all ridiculously.

As in, window-licker-icious all-sorts love you.

You rock the world.

The greatest gift I was born with was my mother, and then my own Self.

The greatest gift I have been given *since* birth, was you lot.

So. Like I said above: I've been beaten.

I make it my business to get those I love the greatest gifts I can.

And of all the gifts I've ever got *anyone*, that trip just knocked the socks off it.

Beaten. By all of you.

And especially the Moreganiser.

You lot of vicious, rebellious, troublemaking, wondrous, uber-gifted Sunslingers.

Let's.

Do that.

Again...

AUGUST 2010:

"THE HOLLYWOOD SIGN"

"I went on a journey, to try to uncover the
Truth about myself and made a profound discovery;
The soul is not just one solitary individual
Not a fish, but a shoal, a collective indivisible;
I am the son, the friend and the father,
The lover and a poet and a ladycharmer;
And I had difficulty trying to comprehend this never-
ending coalition,
So I bring it on stage to spoken-word my definition..."

- Talent -
"Everyman"

- IMMORTALENTED 2013 -

My name is Clint Felgate.
I am at Camp Lehigh, and we march onward.
I am absolutely exhausted.
I was up for work at 0430 hours, and have been on the go for fifteen hours since. I did the same yesterday.
I didn't so much as fall asleep as pass out.
The Sun batters down, and men are passing out from heat exhaustion.
A chopper grunts overhead and flings the baked soil through the hazy air.
A man has just yelled "grenade," and my brothers scatter.
I hit the dirt just in time to see a man leap through the air to land upon the grenade, shielding his compadres with his own body, courageously, and likely to result in him being blown to pieces in front of men he calls his friends...

There are hundreds of men in uniform around me.

The medics run to and fro while Military Police command the scene.

Jeeps and trucks whip up the dirt, which is blown, sandstorm-like, across the field.

The day is baking hot, and I feel my sweat trickle down my spine.

The grenade was apparently a dud, and has left me in the most ridiculous position you can be in without inserting something into your tradesman's.

Gunfire rings out and batters my ears, while grown men hobble and limp across the field, having marched and worked and ran and walked and fought for over fourteen hours running.

I am, of course, on set. And utterly elated.

This is the first scene to be filmed on my first ever Hollywood feature.

I cannot believe my eyes.

I have had no sleep.

My eyes do not know how to stay open.

My feet ache with such ferocity that all my skills as an actor are being used to conceal the difficulty I now have with walking, for fear I am made to leave the set or get fired.

I have to remember to conserve what little I can for the actual *filming*.

The guy in charge of military extras and core soldier group: "You OK son? Want to see the nurse?"

Me: "Nah, I'm fine. Hold up... is she fit?"

Him: "Er, not sure. She's like, sixty."

Me: "Ah. Then perhaps not."

I have only one pair of socks on and no orthotics.

(My TA Parachute Regiment training taught me that in military boots you *always* wear two pairs of socks [so they rub against each other, instead of your feet rubbing on leather boots])

(And as I found out in my teens, I am [fucking infuriatingly] flat-footed. So I wear insoles called 'orthotics.' I need these to walk properly and support my feet and my spine. I currently have none, and am walking on concrete, gravel, and stones, for between thirteen to fifteen hours at a time.)

I have been in full military uniform for two days, for over fourteen hours each day, with only four hours sleep in the middle, and have been beneath the scorching sun marching and walking and running and pressups and star jumps and standing. For hours.

I am on the verge of tears, but not because of the pain.

I am stood on set, in what looks like a military training camp, for what will be one of the biggest blockbuster movies of all time.

It is a film about a comic book hero I grew up reading about.

And it stars some major Hollywood talent.

And now it stars one major London Talent.

The tears, if they existed, would stream down my face because I have dreamt of this moment for over two decades.

I have fought for every single inch I have gained in my life, and I dreamed and dreamed and dreamed and fought and fought and slaved and fought and battled and encouraged and dreamed and suffered and clawed and punched and dreamed and hit and sworn and wrote and acted and sung and rapped and fucked and loved and lost and hated and hurt and ached and battled and fucking *warred* for precisely *this* moment.

I am now a feature film actor onset at one of the UK's biggest film studios, in soon-to-be the year's biggest Hollywood feature, about one of my childhood idol super-heroes, on the same screen as a whole handful of my movie idols, such as:

- Tommy Lee Jones (The Bad Guy – "Under Siege")
- Samuel L Jackson (Nick Fury – "Iron Man 2")
- Hayley Atwell ("The Sweeney")
- Chris Evans (The Human Torch – "Fantastic Four")
- Stanley Tucci ("The Devil Wears Prada")
- Hugo Weaving (Agent Smith – "The Matrix")

I can barely take it. It is all too much.

And yet, of course, I can take it.

Although I cannot believe they are actually *paying* me for it.

I will get to go to the cinema and watch a Hollywood box office smash that I am actually *in*.

And I have been doing this full-time for six months.

The victory roar I can feel coming is *huge*. It is *feral*. It is that of the hunter who foolishly decided he would hunt the Tyrannosaur, and after years of study and training, and many injuries, setbacks, and near-deaths, finally sees the Tyrannosaur caught in his trap, and screams his exultation to the stars.

I know I will not be able to walk tomorrow.

I am meant to be directing a music promo for my friend.

If I am physically able to do so, then I will.
If not, the day will still be a resounding success.
I *swear* it.

OK. Things have just taken a turn for the surreal.

So I leave on the train to Surrey at about five in the morning, highly unamused.

I hate mornings.

I'm a night person.

All the best things happen at night.

Sex, for example. Clubbing. Drinking. Sleep. And so on.

Anyway, I'm headed out to Surrey in a semi-vegetative state.

And it's a fitting day for the Hollywood feature.

Or so I think...

Film studios, major ones, are like massive plots of land covered by aircraft hangars. They are *huge*. People run to and fro carrying props and costumes and all manner of weirdness. A tank just went past me. It's a bit manic.

I get to the studios and it's all weird. The people are talking about this movie but it isn't quite right.

The costumes are different, for example. And from different time periods.

And the drill is different.

And the ADs (Assistant Directors) are different.

I turn to a guy and comment on how this seems weird for the movie, and that you'd think the organisation on something like "Captain America: The First Avenger" would be better than this.

He looks me in the face.

"This isn't Captain America: The First Avenger."

I look at him.

"OK. Um. So what is it?"

"It's "War Horse.""

I look at him some more.

"It's *what*?"

"It's "War Horse". The new Steven Spielberg movie."

I look at him a *lot* more.

"No... *shit*...?"

My feral Tyrannosaur hunter's roar is going to be louder than I thought.

My brain can no longer cope with this.

I'm in a Steven Spielberg feature. As well as one starring Tommy Lee Jones.

Life can't get much better than that.

I don't know what I did in a previous life, but whatever it was, I am blessed beyond measure.

My name is Klaus Von SchauMauser.

I am ein German infantryman in France. It is ze year 1914, and ze world is at war. I am in camp mit mein squad, and ze smell of ze mess tent has been delicately teasing mein nasal passages all of ze morning. I am ravenous. And regrettably, I am now awake.

That was until ze trumpets sounded, and my friends and brotherz began yelling "Alarm! Alarm!"

I run from ze tent, palming ze tent-flap aside and groggily wiping mein eyes, as I had only just up woken.

The sound of thunder assaults mein senses. I look down because my feet seem to be hallucinating: ze ground feels like it is trembling.

I look up and see ze impossible: almost ein hundred men on horseback are thundering towards our kamp, swords drawn und raised, and battle-madness foaming on zeir faces.

"Nein! Schnell! Schnell!" goes ze cry.

Two of meinen Bruder rocket past me at breakneck schpeed.

Ze smell of a scoff fire fills mein nose. A pan of water spillsch onto ze fire and douses its flamesch.

I grab mein rifle, mein trusted Mauser, and conschider letting a few rounds off. Ze wall of thunder-sound changes my mind.

Mein legsch move of zeir own volition. I begin running. Over a hundred und fifty men are careening towards ze tree line.

Ze tree line is not close. It is at least 200 metres away. I hear screamsch behind me as swords rip into German flesh, and as ze stuttersnort of ze horses echoes around ze fields.

I run.

Mein lungs pound furiously, und I dare not look back. Ve have machine gun emplacementsch at ze trees: if ve can just reach zem, ve can get to schafety. Ze quaking sound lumbers nearer still, and ze next fatal yell I hear is much closer.

I run for mein very life.

Mein uniform and webbing weigh me down, und mein weapon feels heavier zan it is. English cavalrymen are renowned for zeir prowess with ze blade, and I do not vish to meet my maker at ze end of such a weapon.

Acid scheems to in my lungs burnen, and I hear a man cut down right behind me.

Somezing wet schmatters my face. I know what it is: ze last earthly signature a brother of mein vould make. By some miracle I am nearly at ze trees when I make my first and only error: I see safety near and schpin to bring ze Mauser to bear on diese Englander.

A hoof swings through ze air beneath the shadow of a beast und cannons me backward.

I feel as if I have been hit by a steam engine. I land mit ein flump, and touching my brow, discover my own blood now signs my visage.

I scrabble in ze soil and grassblades for my Mauser. It has gone AWOL.

I see ze beast rear before me, und believe I am at ze end of all things.

Zis is when ze forced stutter-shots of our machine gun emplacements roar to life, Gruss Gott, und a hailstorm of hot lead cuts like a blade across ze ocean of cavalry.

Ze beast disappears in ein crimson cloud, und ze sky turns red as ash, blood, and pieces of English cavalrymen and zeir steeds fly off into the rural air.

Mein breathing isch maddened, und my heartbeat hammering.

I will calm. Until ze Englishman who had sat atop ze beast who kicked me appears lying on ze emerald plain, mein Mauser in his handsch und ein vicked glint in his eye.

I hear mein countrymen shout cries of victory.

Ze plains are littered with Her Majesty's children. My body moves too schlow, as if zrough water. I do not wish to drown. Not at ze hands of diese *schwein*.

Ze criesch continue, but I hear only one thing more before I disappear into ze night...

***Click*...**

My name is actually still Stephen Brocklehurst.

I am onset at the biggest scene of the biggest movie I have ever been in which is being helmed by the biggest director in the World.

This is, quite literally, a childhood dream come true.

Had I a different, bigger role on this film, I would be the happiest man alive.

I am close to that already.

I cannot believe where I am.

The movie is a film adaptation of a play that has recently been shown in London's West End. It is of course, "War Horse."

London feels pretty far away right now.

I am with 150 extras or "supporting artists," over fifty crew, eighty-plus men on horseback, and one world-famous director of whom you would know and by whom you have in all probability not seen "a film" but "many films."

To top it off, he and I share a name. Kind of.

He brought us someone who had to go home, a legendary whip-cracking adventurer, and numerous movies featuring sharks.

To those who wish to work in the film business, understand this: it is not all glitz and glamour, and even to be here in this lowly role (though I care not, have *you* ever been in a Hollywood feature?) requires very hard work.

You wake up at 0345 hours to leave at 0400 hours to Euston station.

Bear in mind you worked the same hours the day before, all week in the countryside, marching and running for fourteen-hour stints beneath the English Sun.

You get on a coach at 0500. If you are wise, you sleep the hour and a half it takes to get to location. Which in this case, is Reading.

You arrive on location, exhausted, at 0630. You have breakfast, as much as you can, to last till lunch.

Food on film sets is the *nuts*, by the way. So, you stock up on a bowl of cereal, some fruit juice, and a fry-up so you have carbs and energy for the rest of the day.

It feels goooooooooood...

This, you will soon realise, despite feeling 'gooooood,' is what we in the business call "a schoolboy" (as in, 'Schoolboy Error').

You'll see why later.

You then go to costume and wardrobe while the ADs (assistant directors) yell at you. Understandable, as they have an army of people to organise on a daily basis.

So, you and the other hundred and fifty men get changed, painstakingly, into a 1914 German military uniform.

For the record, these outfits are heavy, cumbersome, stuffy, and make movements of any kind pretty awkward.

Get used to it. You'll be in this five to six days a week, with webbing, rifle, backpack and helmet, in the blazing Sun, for four weeks in August and four weeks in October. I had to put on:

- One German T-shirt, long sleeved
- One pair of fuzzy, stupidly warm, right-up-your-ass-crack German trousers
- One pair of German braces, ridiculously tight and pulling your fuzz-trousers *further* up your ass-crack (bear in mind, folks, the next week is all about *running* away from *cavalry*...)
- One large German overshirt
- One massively large German winter fuzzy overcoat, stupidly warm and making me sweat already
- One pair German one-size-fits-no-one boots, over two pair German "ha-ha-ha-I-could-build-a-house-out-of-these" socks
- One set of webbing
- A gas mask
- One utterly pointless German helmet (they weren't bulletproof, or even flyproof, by my judgement) [interesting insight into humanity: apparently headshot deaths went *up* after the invention of protective headgear, because troops figured they could, for the first time, have a ganders over the trench parapet and see what was going on... and of

course what was going on was a bullet was flying directly at their boat race... go *figure*...]
- One set of "putties" which translates to ludicrously cumbersome long bits of material that you wrap around your lower legs, from ankle to knee

When I walk out of costume (I say "walk," the word "creak" or "amble" is probably more appropriate) I am almost perspiring, and am fervently wishing I had had just a glass of milk for breakfast.

You then go to hair and makeup where (God willing) you get left alone.

Usually, you don't.

Hair department: got a beard? Shave it. We're giving you "clean-cut with a tache."

Clean-cut? We're gluing a beard to your face.

Bald? Hope you like wigs.

Have long hair? Not now you don't. Now you have your Dad's hair. When he was young.

Now, off to makeup.

Makeup are fucking cool; principally because they are all women, and are usually very amicable.

I'm usually very at home in the makeup department, because of the sheer ratio if nothing else. It looks to me a little like a firing range.

Here however, their job is to apply sufficient mud to my face to make me look like an early-last-century trenches soldier. So you sit there as they apply mud to your face out of a paint-pot, and use brushes to dab and squelch this onto your face, and into your ears.

If someone did this to you in the street, you'd release the Kraken.

The interesting thing is this: if you get in there first thing before anyone else you have one experience, and if you get in there last you have entirely another.

If you're first in and there's loads of time you get a Picasso of a make-up artist, delicately applying blobs of dirt with a brush, artistically dabbing your face with their oily mixtures and paints.

If you're last in and they're pushed for time, you get them WWE-style slamming your head into a bucket of mud and then going "you're done."

Then it's off to the armoury for your rifle, where men (usually ex-military) explain how dangerous the weapons are, how they must *never* be left alone, and how you need to give us your ID, your mother's maiden name, and a urine sample before the weapon can be released to you.

Of course these happen to be fucking *rubber* weapons, and I am not fooled.

This is all to ensure we don't act like twats and run around doing combat rolls down hills and end up losing their fake guns.

Then you are herded, en masse, towards the coaches.

By this time, guaranteed, 95% of the time every day, you will feel the impending tremble of needing a dump.

However: you will *not* go for a shit.

You will calculate, like an imbecile, how soon you will actually be able to last without bursting blood vessels. Or losing an eye.

Since the vans take you to location, you must be on the van. Or *else*.

So you do not wish to be caught last man standing, van warm and revving to go, while you've spent thirty minutes in the bog de-robing through five layers of clothing and sweat, only to hear the pap of a horn and have to start rush-wiping prior to rush-dressing prior to rush-arriving at the van like some red-faced wank addict who just *had* to knock one out prior to going onset.

Plus: one hundred and fifty extras (male) [and some days we had over 500] added to eighty cavalrymen (male) added to over fifty crew (male) all use how many toilets?

Oh two.

Two.

Two *portaloos.*

Right.

Gotcha.

I'll be clear: you *never* want to go in here unless absolutely necessary. Ever.

Then it's on the vans and off to set: the reason we are all here - *moviemaking...*

I am now sat here having a deliberate epiphany moment.

We call these "deliphanies."

I have learned through the course of my life that we can in fact choose, at times, when and where we have them.

And I'm having one now. Partly because I am *exactly* where I wish to be, and partly also because I am hardly ever in the countryside.

And my oh my, God, if you exist, I can only utter with complete humility: Thank You.

This planet, this country even, are the work of a master. Those trees were designed precisely to be painted with *that* green. Which indicates to me that infinity must exist because I am looking at its definition in colour form. There is an endless variety of that colour.

The sky on its own dwarfs everything beneath it. It is a masterwork.

It is all splashes of warm gold laughing through a creamy cloudscape, itself a loving decoration on that silky blue backdrop.

The breeze amid the Sun's rays is almost pornographic.

It feels as though I truly am in a military camp. I hear four men speaking German next to me. Someone's just said the magic word ("cut") and someone else just said the others: "there's tea over there." And since I've needed to drop my guts and slash like an animal for the last three hours, I'm off...

See, this is why you have a *small* breakfast.

It took me almost twenty minutes just to get undressed enough to even *use* a toilet. Then it took another twenty minutes for, well, bombs away.

Christ that felt better.

I'm now after a cup of tea, and wouldn't you know it, that too is an absolute mish. After walking about a kilometre to the fecking tea table, I now find it occupied by a platoon of wasps, 'cause some joker put a bin right next to the fecking table.

The guy currently trying desperately to make himself tea looks like he's doing fucking Riverdance on hot coals with no shoes on just to avoid getting stung.

The comedian who just managed a tea for himself informs me: "if you just stay still, you'll be fine". Oh. Oh *good*. Stay still? What do I look like, a fucking *beekeeper*?

Like I said, you wanna be in this business? *Earn* it.

While I'm onset, between takes, I am:

- Messaging my website designer to send me my logos
- Texting the cast of our upcoming TV show
- Messaging the mixmaster of my album about how best to package it for sending it all out to agents
- And writing this…

Get *used* to hard work. The name of this game is to rely on no one else.

D.I.Y. is the way forward.

I stand in the middle of a battleground, and there are bodies all around me.

Man and horse lie riddled with bullet wounds under a blanket of battlesmoke fuming through the air. There are more bodies than I have seen in my life.

The machine guns cut through the cavalry like butter, and the ruins of the English horsemen lie before me. The spectre of Death is near...

And so here we are. I'm on the coach back again, and the sky is an insolently beautiful mixture of golds and blues.

I hear my fellow supporting artists / extras talking around me about what it is like to work with "this director," and discussing others they would and "would not" like to work with.

- James Cameron: "surely that's the ultimate", one says
- Tarantino: "apparently he's a megalomaniac" says one
- Robert Rodriguez: "would be cool"
- Oliver Stone: "the *best* movies"
- Michael Mann: "God how *sick* do his pictures look?"

As usual, this kind of talk makes me smile.

I sit apart from the others. I am not anti-social, as such. I was a nightclub promoter, for God's sake. I simply enjoy being alone sometimes; to gather my thoughts, to consider the day, and soon, to write lyrics for my mix-tape on the journey home.

Am I exhausted? Yes.

Have I been up since four this morning? Sure.

Did I work a fifteen-hour day on four hours sleep? No doubt.

Did we run uphill cross-country in full army gear for six hours in the sun away from cavalry? Definitely.

But I was in a Spielberg movie. I don't give a *fuck* about yer bitchin'. And now, suitably inspired, I have to plan for a weekend of more work (cast meeting, crew meeting, various bits of admin, record a track, the usual) and then Monday it is back to our feature film.

Am I a workaholic?

I suppose that is a fair accusation. My father did me the honour of hammering two words into my head as I grew up.

"Work. Ethic."

And the Parachute Regiment taught me what can be achieved simply when you hang on in there.

So in a sense, yes, I am a workaholic. But only in so far as I see my life as my work, and my work therefore as my life.

I am one hundred per cent a Lifeaholic.

I am addicted to this life, as are we all save for those who decide upon taking their own lives. I dreamchase because I see no other logical alternative.

I am not being stubborn. Trust me. I could have jacked all this in years ago. And believe me, at times I have wanted to.

But I haven't. And I won't. Ever.

I watched the master of moviemaking at work today. On the one hand, he is just a human being. This is incontestably true.

On the other, he is a living legend, a master of his craft, giving direction to over 200 people on a field in the middle of summer, and forging works of genius from his pure imagination.

This is as close as it currently gets to beholding magic.

Something that exists only in a man's mind becomes tangible, real, manifest.

I feel privileged. I feel honoured. I also feel like my legs are going to seize up and that I need to shower for about a week to get all the dirt, soil and sweat off me.

Two other things of note occurred.

First, a catering girl I had half-recognised previously came up to me at the end of the day when my legs felt like they were made of eggshell.

"Hi. Do I know you?"

I look at her. Something clicks, but I can't tell what.

"I think so. But I'm not sure from where."

"Do you do music?"

I smile. She continues.

"You do huh? What's your name?"

I look at her. Beautiful ebony skin.

"Here my name is Stephen. But onstage or in the booth my name is Talent."

"Ahhhhh..."

She nods affirmatively. She smiles and looks at me.

"You hosted Respect The Mic. The freestyler, right? Working with Celecia Smith?"

I nod. I now recognise her.

Still the same lovely, infectious smile. (Isn't it incredible how we can be REmind-ed of something? Had no fucking idea *who* she was a moment prior, but some ember, some shadow in my head said: I know her. And as soon as she provided the missing link, the memory chain healed itself and I knew exactly who she was and from where. *Amazing…*)

I look at her, shake her hand, and kiss her on both cheeks.

"Lovely to see you again," I say.

It is not often I am recognised. If I don't know the other person I tend to get a bit awkward. But here, now, it feels like a blessing: which, of course, it is.

Second thing: I sat in the back of the people-wagon coming back (a trailer attached to the back of a jeep, with no roof, similar to the landing boats in "Saving Private Ryan"). The rain was coming down thick.

It was the end of the day. I was shattered.

I looked up.

The sight was of the kaleidoscopic forest, of the endless greens and trees towering above us as the raindrops fell upon my face. I was covered in mud and dirt, head to toe: hair filthy and disgusting, face like I'd dived mouth first into a puddle of filth, body like I'd gone twelve rounds.

But I didn't care. The chatter of people around me disappeared.

We drove from the set, the camp we had just fought on burning, sending plumes of smoke up into the sky like signals of defeat.

But they felt like signals of victory.

In the woods it felt like being in "The Thin Red Line," or "Platoon," or "Saving Private Ryan." It was beautifully tranquil.

Tranquility. You would not think, given how I live, that I could love this notion, this feeling so much.

But I do.

Victory.
One of my favourite words.

I'm almost in hysterics. Merlin and his beloved young ladyfriend have just moved in to their new place.

Their new place happens to be a split-level duplex penthouse apartment on the East Side of London next to the Olympic site.

Sound familiar? Cause it should.

He's just moved in *next door*.

The BTX now shares two-thirds of the top two Penthouse floors of a building.

It's like having the Batcave as your house, except with your best mate next door, and cooler.

My weeks right now are nuts. They look like this:

Monday to Friday - The new Spielberg movie, from 0400 to 2200.

Saturday to Sunday - "HOTHouse" and my album development, from 1000 to 1900.

This is not the life I had in mind when I started the year.

But you know what? I care not. If I have to slave twenty-four-seven right now, then so be it.

Wouldn't you?

Earn the life you want, and then you have all the time in the World.

SEPTEMBER 2010:

"HOTHOUSE, BABY"

"The doc says, "Talent, it is nearly time"
Don't worry Doc, I am feeling fine,
There's no more worry or fear 'n fright,
And I ain't that scared, cause I did all right;
Just leave me a picture of my Mom,
And ideally, my Lost Tribe song,
And the letters from my Nan she'd always write me,
And a Blaqmale track if that's all right..."

- Talent -
"Last Rights"

- IMMORTALENTED 2013 -

Huzzah.

Last day of filming till October. On the feature, I mean. And the Sun is out in all its glory.

It's cracksweatingly hot, and the sky is that sacred blue colour that almost hurts to look at. What a beautiful day, and a great way to start a month.

And this month is special, Ladies and Gents, since it is el month de "HOTHouse."

And what, pray tell, is "HOTHouse?"

"HOTHouse" is a new six-part TV sitcom series that Rooster and I are producing. And it came about like this:

Rooster went to a meeting to interview for a new TV show. Or rather for a new series of a TV show.

240

It was for the new series of, for argument's sake, "Blue Short Person." That's not the name, you understand, it's the name I'm giving it to avoid getting sued.

Change the colour, change the term, and you'll get what I am talking about.

Suffice to say it was a cult classic and everyone loves the show.

He went in to try to get the job of line-producing the new series. The new series that they were going to make for rather a lot of money.

This kind of job we call a "game-changer," as in it changes your whole game and takes you up a level.

They offered him the job, and he presumably got an immediate semi, and prepared to celebrate like it was 1999.

That is, until, they looked at his paperwork and realised they couldn't legally hire him for reasons beyond his control.

So they offered him the job. And then they were forced to take it away.

This is a bit like an actor being offered the lead role in the new "Batman" film, only to have it taken away because one of your ears has below standard hearing and has done since birth.

Not your fault, but it is your problem.

So.

One of the founders of 'Blue Short Person' takes our young Rooster aside, and tells him that he's got the contacts, he's got the knowledge, he's got the know-how, why doesn't he do what a certain 'Blue Short Person' actor did and film his own TV show?

This particular actor (we'll call him Bob Llanfydd for sake of argument) found himself a little in acting limbo after 'Blue Short Person' was taken off the air.

He did odd bits and bobs for ten years.

So, he then went and made his own TV show, got an online following, put it on iTunes, sold a shitload of copies, and then sold the concept to the BBC, making a fortune in the process.

Now, when the founder of an International hit TV show suggests you do something, you fucking *listen*.

So: Rooster comes home half-depressed and half-inspired, and says to Yours Truly, "you feel like coming up with an idea for a TV show?"

241

He tells me the story, and while my heart bleeds for him getting and then losing the job, I am of course moved to see him take it on the chin and look to make the best of a bad situation.

So we sit, and for three days, over five bottles of whisky and about a million smokes and arguments, we hammer out the best idea we can.

And here's my thinking, explained as best I can in written format.

"OK, so, the most popular, zeitgeist-y shows on at the moment are:

1. REALITY TV-ESQUE FACT / FICTION BLENDS i.e. like "the Hills."

2. SEXY YOUNG PEOPLE IN CINEMUSIC SHOWS i.e. like "Entourage."

Hmm.

Now I can make a show on the back of either in no time; but neither of the above really has enough meat on the bones as an idea.

Plus whatever we do has to be cheap and easily shootable, i.e. in less than a week.

Aha!

OK, try this: a group of sexy young people trying to make it in the media businesses, who live at an amazing location, never-before-seen, and who are actually real people trying to make it in the real media business - i.e. like me and Rooster living at Studio 107, which is a duplex penthouse on the East Side built on the line of time.

Hmmm.

And howzabout this group of people is joined by a former glamour model turned photographer, and live in a flat that is *also* a film studio, a music studio, a photography set, and, once a week, a nightclub?

And howzabout they run the club and their group like a member's club / secret society? With laws and rules that they live by, to always excel and constantly help each other ascend the ladder?"

Rooster points out that we can't just make a sexy show, or even a sexy show based on real life - we need to have cutting-edge dialogue.

He has a point.

ADD IN - smart, choppy dialogue i.e. like "The Thick of It"

ADD IN - smart, quick, fast interplay i.e. like "Studio 60."

ADD IN – a sense of nobility and purpose i.e. like "Fight Club."

Now we're talking...

And so was born: "HOTHouse"...

So in a little under a week I'm directing rehearsals for a week with a cast of about twenty of the finest individuals you could possibly ask for.

We then, the week after, shoot episode one.

I wrote the first episode (first, second, third, fourth, fifth, and sixth to twelfth drafts), am cast in the first episode playing "Lox," am co-producing the show (a first for me), and am directing both the shoot and the edit.

To be honest, I'm being a bit of a twat.

That's a lot of work for anyone to take on.

Plus I have to help sort catering, travel, and raise enough finance to do it. *And* I have to actually *perform* in it, whilst making sure everyone else does too while under my direction.

Additionally I have to source and direct the music / score so we are protected on that front and also obviously so we have good (by which I mean award-nominated) music.

On top of that I have to crack the whip at my agent to get me more work, at my masterer to finish my album, and at various other people to get their shit together.

Not easy, eh?

No problem. I never asked for it to be.

Like I said - get used to working hard. Make it your new religion.

And this month's prayer is music: I'm sending out 225 applications to music managers and labels.

My album is almost finished and to be honest with you I am *sick* of waiting on other people.

D.I.Y. is the name of the game.
Hold on a second, lyrics coming through...

D.I.Y. Till the D.A.Y. that I D.I.E. Or I F.L.Y.
Sky high lie die
Free I fly
I.D.
Re-a-lise

So.
225 is the figure. Taking my overall applications this year to 450.

Then guess what, *this very book* goes out to another 50-150 publishing agents, which will give us another nice round figure of 500 or 600 applications in one year.

And there's more to come...

If you want something, you fucking *go* for it like a madman.

Non-stop. And you tell everyone else to wait while you do it.

And here's why:

Realspeak: okay, listen up; this is no longer Stephen Brocklehurst speaking, this is Talent on the mic, so pay a little fucking *attention*.

You (as in you) have (statistically speaking and no matter what you believe) *one* life on planet earth as the person you are.

There may be no and there is thus far evidence of no heaven, no afterlife, no reincarnation, and even if there *is*, that does not change the following: you are born alone and you will die alone.

The only things that will mean shit to you in-between are your family and your achievements, along with what joy you have experienced and what positive difference you have made.

Lastly, the Familiends (family-level friends) you have chancemet and the laughs you have had that have almost made you cry.

So don't fuck about. Make the best use of your time possible to get what *you* want done, done.

And to be the person you wish to be.

Talent *out*.

OK I'm back.

So I'm sat here at a new feature with Rosemania.

It's for some film called "The Weekender." The good news is, it's paid. The bad news is, it's only £30, it's seven in the morning, I've been up for an hour, and I fucking *hate* the mornings.

And whilst he *is* one of the funniest people I've ever met, Rosemania is not what you might call "chilled out."

He's playing one of the lead characters in "HOTHouse," and depending on whom you ask, he's either called "Gary Barflow" (his version) or "Take-It-Up-The-Gary Gary" (my version).

And he's not happy about it. At *all*.

Here's the skinny - our show is a touch controversial, and in episode one our dear Gary gets, well, taken. Up the gary. Hence the name.

And Gary is a straight white male. The person who takes him is Julian Vernon. Julian is a gay black man who's all of about 5'5".

One critic has called this act "a twisted revenge on slavery." I call it good TV.

Anyway. He's not best pleased with me atm (at the moment).

Still.

You can't please everyone.

The Spielberg feature combined with all the "HOTHouse" work has made going to the gym nigh on impossible for two months.

Which I'm not happy about, since I was down to a decent thirteen stone and only had another half stone or stone to go.

Thanks to zero gym time for two months, I'm back up to thirteen stone seven. Irritating. However, it is of no matter. I hit the gym today for a good hour and a half. Unfortunately the gym hit back and whupped my ass.

For "HOTHouse" I have now:

-   Completed the final script (with Trent Devlin's assistance)
-   Met the DP (Director of Photography) and clarified the shotlist

- Met with Art Department and discussed how I want it to look (the set)
- Set up a meet with Ricardo Fargas (legend) to discuss music / score
- Sent out a first rehearsal schedule
- Recorded six segments of live, unrehearsed footage (I'm all about the freestyle)
- Written a synopsis for episodes two to six
- Raised 400 squids in financing
- And just initiated a deal with a nightclub to let us go there once a month and begin our marketing strategy with them

Would you believe in with all that I have still managed the laundry, the washing up, getting my room sorted and rewiring my entire home studio (without killing myself).

Only twenty-four hours in a day? Pah. That's plenty.

But do not think for a second my optimism (hip-hoptimism to those in the know) makes me naïve.

And don't get me wrong: my boy Metis'd tell you I actually *am* naïve, but only in a *when-someone-says-"that's impossible"-I-look-at-them-"naively"-as-if-to-say-"what the fuck are you talking about?"* - naive.

That I'll cop to.

But no. I am not blind. I know what the most obvious and pertinent criticism of my methods is. I've heard it more than once.

"You take on too much."

"You spread yourself too thin."

"You'll be a Jack of All Trades and a Master of None."

I am not ignorant of such views. I simply find them inaccurate. I know what I am doing.

Trust me; I'm from *Willenhall*.

OK maybe scratch that last comment. I'm *fooked*.

I've never focused on something so hard in my life.

"HOTHouse" is literally the only reason I live and breathe right now.

How are rehearsals going?

Good question.

'Well,' is the even better answer. But my mind is a mish-mash of a thousand variables and problems that could occur.

I have a million alterations to the script to deal with, as well as having to get every actor out of twenty on the same page. Plus I can't sleep properly and I haven't eaten for two days.

Probably not the smartest tactics to ensure solid production. On the other hand we're well on schedule and I'd like to keep it that way.

So everything else takes a back seat.

Procuring twins for the opening shot is more of a mish (mission, remember?) than I had anticipated. I've still got to monitor my album progress and still also haven't been paid yet for any of my feature work.

Would-be-actors and musicians of the world take note - slaving and toiling to *get* the work is only stage one. Actually getting *paid* for what you have done and seeing to it that a finished product ends up being screened somewhere is entirely another skillset, and one you want to hone.

"You been in the military?" Liam asks me. "Or done any martial arts?"

I look at him for a moment. "Not being funny, just a guess," he says, diplomatically.

"Yeah," says I, "I was in the parachute regiment briefly and did kickboxing for quite some time."

I don't explain that both are still very much part of who I am: my military experience having been one of the most profound experiences of my life (limited though it was) and martial arts being part of my code so much so that one of my crew is (I shit you not) a ninja and another does more martial arts than Bruce Lee.

It makes me wonder why he asked.

"Well, you just seem really organised, and nothing seems to get to you, and no matter what gets chucked at you, you seem to handle it."

I look at him for a moment to see if he is mocking me. The urge to laugh hysterically is working its mischievous way up my gullet. I almost leap across the table at him to shake some sense into him.

But then, that is *my* insanity to deal with, and not his.

Filmmaking and music production are not easy. There are reasons why lots of people do not do it.

For a start, it's not easy to get in.

247

Second, the people who *are* in have no incentive to let you in in the first place unless you have something they want or need. And you don't.

Third, it's about as stressful and high-octane as you can get.

Today's been a Saturday. To give you an example of just how messed up it can get, check *this* out...

So you wake up at about eight am, mostly just to stretch and get the kinks out. And also because you sleep like a T-Rex and nothing short of some C4 going off next to your ears is going to wake you up.

You then proceed to the kitchen to make some tea to feel human.

You fail, not least because you're still so knackered you put the tea bag straight in the bin and poured milk in the sink. You then stuck your laundry in the waste disposal and three bags of refuse into the washing machine, before remembering you forgot to have a shower.

You then read through all your lines twice because you are also in the production. It's now nine am.

You then prep your room to be turned upside down by the art design people and for it to be turned from your room into a film set.

It's now ten am. On *Saturday*.

You rectify all this and down the tea. You then have four people show up to your house at ten am. You have to rehearse with one set from ten to twelve, another set from twelve to two pm, then lunch (never, *ever* going to happen); then another set three pm to five pm, then back upstairs to dress the set and redesign your entire apartment.

Then you have to correct the script all evening and check what you have missed or what else is outstanding.

You may get done by around ten pm.

You will want to kill someone, but will do *precisely* the same the next day.

On a *Sunday*.

Well, it's Wednesday morning, ten am, and I'm on the way to Waterloo to then head to Longcross for another "War Horse" fitting.

Tonight we finish dressing the set for "HOTHouse." Tomorrow we begin filming.

And, as per usual, I'm bricking it.

We've had over a week of rehearsals and gone over lines and checked costumes and altered makeup and recast people and everything else that has come up has been addressed as well as we could address it.

I am, to put a finger on it, knackered out of my mind. I'll not soon again work on a project where I produce, direct, write, and star in it.

It's like juggling, except with grenades and lit sticks of dynamite.

We have a young man onset by the name of Liam Heath. He's eighteen years young and a lovely young man. He's running our behind-the-scenes and our making-of.

I'm pretty sure he's fairly scared out of his wits at the prospect.

What impresses me greatly is that despite this, he's cracking on with it.

Courage, ladies and germs, is not the absence of fear. It takes no great fortitude to do something of which you have no fear. It takes a helluva lot more to step inside a ring of which you are utterly petrified.

I'm never inclined to take on complete beginners. It tends to slow things down and it results in problems.

However, as Rooster said, we've all been given chances in life, so giving an opportunity to the new generation makes a lot of sense to me, karmically speaking.

While I contemplate his courage and the colossal test we all face over the next four days of filming, I see in the papers that Rafa Nadal has won the US Open (little surprise there - Spain are proving to be the World's athletic elite this year, due to hard work and beauty of play, while my own country's teams and players, love them as I do, wallow around in defeat and scandal - take *note*, people...) and also that France has just outlawed the Burqa.

This strikes me as a particularly brave move.

Did you know incidentally that in a host of the World's travel magazines France often comes up as the 'Best Place to Live on the Planet'?

(Usually this is measured via indices including but not limited to: Standard of Living, Education, Economic Prosperity, Climate, Healthcare, and Liberty [the last of which the French have ever been renowned for]).

Now in today's climate you'd think banning the Burqa is next to suicidal: politically incorrect, and, on the face of it, liberally inhibiting, what with Al Qaeda having made numerous threats to wreak "terrible revenge" on the French were the ban ever to be carried out.

And now it has.

It's not very fashionable to be an Englishman who commends other European countries. It's a bit against the tide, so to speak.

However, I've never given a rat's ass what people think about a lot of shit, so I'm hardly going to start now.

My sincerest commendations go to Spain and La France for their immaculate success and their recent actions this year. I hope in both cases it continues.

Not that I have anything against Burqas, mind.

Totally the opposite. I don't. I have nothing against Bibles, Burqas, Churches, Mosques, Crosses, Zeus, Lightening, Paganism, Druidry (is that the noun?), Satanism, Ra, the Pope, Prophets, Sons of Man, Gods (to reiterate: 2,500 + according to the Oxford Encyclopaedia of gods), Saints, Virgins (maternal or otherwise), Priests, Martyrs, or any of that kind of thing.

In fact, religion as a whole tends to fascinate me.

No, I have nothing against any of the above. I don't advocate them either.

If you choose one particular creed over another, that's your business. However, do *not* attempt to make it mine.

If I wish to run my own home by the laws of Torunga the Snail Goddess, then that's *my* business. And it's none of yours. Unless you set foot in my house, at which point you can bow down before Her slime-covered Holiness or you can get the fuck *out*.

My house, my rules.

And if you happen to believe in the Holy Scunthorpian Pantheon of Cookie Dough Deities, then that's fine and dandy. Just don't bring that shit into *my* house.

On the other hand, if I want to come stay at *your* house, odds are I better get used to the idea of chocolate chips and a lot of involuntary sweating…

Translation: if the French people voted to get rid of the Burqa, fine. That's up to them. It's *not* up to anyone else.

Threatening people who do not behave the way you want them to says nothing about them other than that they have principles and that they have courage. It reveals more about you as the threatener.

Mahatma Ghandi and Martin Luther King got what they wanted and what the world wanted and needed via peaceful means. If you and your crew can't? Then you're in the wrong game.

Take up the gun and you'll lose everyone's attention. Put the gun down and suddenly I'm listening.

See, Torunga the Snail Goddess is my own invention. It's man-made. But then so, so I'm told, are the rest of them.

The issue occurs only when I come *out* my house in "the name of peace," only to then declare war on you and yours for "worshipping false idols," unless ye bow before Torunga and be saved.

Which of course makes you leave your abode, machine-gun in hand, to battle for victory in the name of the Scunthorpian Pantheon of Cookie Dough deities.

So we go to war.

Whoever wins expands their domain and enslaves more followers and gains greater market share of fairy-tale followers. It's probably the best business model I've ever heard of.

People not buying your product? Lop a few heads off. That'll bring 'em round.

I'm currently so France-friendly that I'm practically speeding up the growth of my own armpit hair by force of will alone. France *rules*.

This entire line of thought (while I am on the train - never stop working towards what you want) somehow brings me to an image of my Beloved, which attacks me so suddenly and so viciously that I actually have to put the phone down to regain my composure.

She'd probably not believe she still has this effect on me. But then, she never did.

I succeed. I have an entire show to film. In four days. And we begin tomorrow. And I'm already exhausted before we begin.

Time for a train nap, methinks.

Please God do not let me miss my stop.

I suppose the other question is: what's the Plan?

Why work this hard?

Why do this in the first place?

Why drive yourself to near lunacy for anything?

What is so important that one must live like this?

All fair questions.

All *good* questions.

And good questions deserve good answers.

So here's my stab at it.

I'm in the process of making or have made:

- An album, "ImmorTalented"
- TV pilots, "The HOTHouse" and "Going Commando"
- A book, "Lifeaholic"
- A music video, "Everyman"
- A documentary, "Talent 2009"
- A clothing line for our "BTX"
- A Feature Film "Morning Tea" and another, "Radio London"
- And a belief system called "Selfism"

Fashion, film, music, literature.

This type of Magnum Opus is called a "360 degree" project, due to its multi-faceted nature. The idea being that each product is interlinked in some way and will therefore be to the benefit of every other project.

Multiplicity in Unity.

We aim to take the show to various networks, the book to various publishers, the album to every manager on planet Earth, and so on and so forth.

Because I'm an egomaniac?

Because I'm obsessed with "fame and fortune"?

Because I need to see my name in lights?

Yeah, good one. I wish. That'd be a million times simpler.

No, ladies and gents, that ain't naffin' to do widdit.

I'm basically the guy who you see lying on the beach at night looking up at the stars in a daze, so moved by what he sees that he begins scribbling furiously on paper.

Then he has to move to grab an instrument or microphone, and then a camera and a cast and a set and a crew; predominantly to take what he has just seen and pass it on to as many people as possible.

Especially women.

It sounds nuts, I know.

But those who desire to inspire, educate, and entertain are not *all* egomaniacs.

Some of us just love our fellow human beings enough to dedicate our lives to the firing of their imagination, to take them to that higher place.

That higher place we sometimes call "OtherWhere."

It is an act of love.

Anyway.

That's that.

The escort thing? Again?

I told you, schniggles, all in good time.

We're nearing filming with every hour that goes by, and the house / flat is completely transformed.

We have artwork, banners, skulls, paintings, prints, urns, helms, a Hall of Fame, DJ decks, lights, drinks, globes, gun-shaped ashtrays, the works. There's even a banner across the wall that reads simply "The HOThouse."

Manuel Nashi and his Lairdship Jim Hatton Brown have done us proud. They finish the job today.

If you ever need a set designing or props and artwork, call these guys asap. Although in all likelihood and if at all possible, I'll be employing 'em. Heh.

And as we near the Moment of Truth (interesting turn of phrase, that one) people are getting more into character and working harder at their lines.

And the tension is rising. By which I mean a group of the cast and crew were up drinking and talking until 5 in the morning the other night (one had jury duty next day, bless her) and a pairing of cast and crew allegedly may have perhaps been seen dabbling in procreative acts outside our actual building next to a Thai restaurant, a bus stop and a dustbin.

Maybe.

Certain actors are fighting hard to perfect their work. One particular member of cast is more a model than anything else (and a beautiful one at that) but is digging his heels in, determined to shine as much as he can.

Another is still ragingly pissed at me because of his character development but is showing the fortitude necessary to soldier on, trusting my judgement.

It's impressive to watch.

And it is very moving. Because this is no nine to five operation.

There's no medical or dental, and you often work hard and receive absolutely zero pay. And yet *still* people do it.

This is called *Love for the Game*.

I frickin' *love* movie studios.

I love the vehicles, the aircraft hangars filled with costumes, the props and fake weapons, the works.

I've just walked out from my fitting and my hair is recut and I look better. And, better yet, I got *paid* for it.

Gaffers and sparks move and recut scenery and fake walls. SFX and pyro crews test various explosives and fire-trickery. Makeup and hair have lines of people all waiting to be made up into better looking versions of themselves.

"Why is this status thing important?" Liam asked us last night.

Our dear behind-the-scenes director has had a deep and meaningful with Rooster, and much of it has related to women.

I'd been explaining that much of Life (job interviews, sarging, one's appearance) is about raising one's status. This had somewhat confused our young Romeo.

"So like you're bragging all the time? Or boasting?"

I sigh. Not at him, you understand. At my own lack of eloquence.

"No. Not at all. It's really just about being the best you can be, as often as you can."

"But, like, after you've bagged the girl, when can you forget all that and just relax?"

I look at him.

"You can't. Until you are off-duty. And even then, you remain vigilant. You just ask yourself the question 'do I want to be the best son I can be? The best man I can be? The best boyfriend, filmmaker, and person I can be? Or do I want to be anything else?'"

"Of course I do. Yeah."

"Then that's the end of it."

The "HOThouse" shoot."

This shoot was set for the 16th, 17th, 18th and 19th of September 2010.

The first time I have ever filmed my own TV pilot.

And it went a little something like this:

DAY ONE - THURSDAY

It's day one of filming on "The HOTHouse" and I'm extremely aware of my own failings, fear, and mortality.

Still, no time for that shit, we have to get this right.

The good news is we seem to have struck gold with the camera.

Rooster and I are now apparently shooting our little project on the ALEXA camera, and we are one of only ten crews in the country using this particular piece of technological wonderment.

The only other two people I know in the country using this camera are Steven Spielberg and Martin Scorsese.

I rest my case.

We start off with Alex Rendall's scenes. Best to get as many exteriors out the way as humanly possible. So we get Alex Rendall in and start shooting.

Alex Rendall is an unusual actor. In the character Ben Sharon I first saw Simon Wegrzyn playing the role; the actor I worked with on "War Of the Sexes." He's got the perfect look, the right kind of loveable gentleness, and is a highly gifted actor. I shit you not, he's the business. Plus he has a shock of red hair that gives him a really unique look.

He couldn't make rehearsals or filming, so we auditioned over fifty people for the role.

And we found no one who was "right" enough with the script balanced as it was. But hiring any one of these immensely gifted individuals would mean re-writing and re-casting at least two, maybe three characters.

No and *Way* was the response.

Until Alex Rendall walked in as a late option. And he was so good in rehearsal that we asked him back in immediately.

He read on the evening when he only came *in* on the morning and was just wonderful. He is a committed actor and a talented performer, is highly method and made his own character's Facebook page without being required to.

He has the look of a CK Model and can do both chic and geek. He's memorised his lines, altered some out of his own readings, rehearsed over and over, and offered genuine contributions on every question he's posed.

This, ladies and germs, is called dedication. And he worked through the whole of rehearsals and filming with one arm in a cast.

Alex is so cool he not only is an actor but also works in a bar making cocktails. He's my kinda guy. He cut his hand in a bartending accident and probably should have been nowhere near a film set.

Alex, I salute you.

Thom Wright comes in to DP (Director of Photography) for us, and I am glad to have him on board.

He's got a good sense of humour, is a very likeable guy, and basically does not fuck around. I met him on Metis's video shoot and Holy God, the man is good. Mostly because he *gets what the director is talking about*. And since I'm both director *and* writer I know the work inside out, and I need the DP to get what I am talking about. And he does.

So our first shots are off the balcony to get a panoramic wide shot of Ben. And I have to confess, the shot looks beautiful.

I've got a ton of people around me and I need to make sure I don't fuck this up, because there's a lot of people depending on me.

And this is our first shot. I've got sound, camera, and the team on standby, and Rooster is ADing for me.

We get some fantastic shots.

We head next to the corridor outside to shoot the "Ben entering the HOTHouse for the first time" shot. And for that we need "Blowy Chloe", otherwise known as Chloe Heaver.

Chloe is a gem of a girl.

First off she's teeth-gnashingly attractive, and looks about as 'Chelsea Girl' as anyone I've ever met. Except Chloe has a good sense of humour and is entirely dedicated to her work. She's a horse-rider (Cavalrywoman?) and is very good at constructing character with her voice.

She's lovely to work with and very honest with you if you are directing. She also never complains and is, in my opinion, the epitome of class.

In their scene, Ben comes round the corner to finally enter "the HOTHouse." He sees "Blowy Chloe" leaving "the HOTHouse" in a state of near-ecstasy. She walks up to him, kisses him passionately, and then waltzes off.

If you ever got greeted like this outside a building, you'd cease going anywhere else.

Chloe's on point.

She's rehearsed this and we've talked about it extensively. We do maybe five takes and I'm loving what I am seeing.

Alex Rendall (playing Ben) is fully dedicated to the character, willingly allowing Chloe to kiss him repeatedly until I get my perfect shots.

Acting can be such a tough gig...

Watch Chloe when she walks from the door. She doesn't even *speak*, and yet you want to know more about her. This is called "natural gravitas," and is so rare you can't *buy* it. You can only be lucky or good enough to *find* it.

And luckily, I'm lucky. Sometimes.

Rooster tells me we're then headed downstairs for the next setup.

So we head back to ground floor to film the concierge scenes.

I realise I'm really, *really* tired after rehearsing and writing and not eating for a couple of days. But I feel good enough as long as the footage is good.

We hadn't been able to cast The Concierge either, until on my feature I found the perfect actor. You know those guys who talk like they just do *not* give a shit? I don't mean in that cowboy, maverick, and "I'm the nuts" kind of way. That's how I talk. I mean in that Onslo from "Keeping Up Appearances" kind of way that's just built-in comedy.

So I found my guy on the feature. But then he couldn't make rehearsals or shooting either, bless him.

Claire Yellowlees provided us with the solution.

Claire is herself also a highly formidable woman. See, this is the issue being a director-writer-actor blah blah, whatever: were I not filming and directing these people, I'd be in love with half of them if not more in about five seconds flat. She's been a model and is an actress, and has no ego-issues with her work.

She'll get her job done with minimum fuss, and is drop-dead gorgeous to boot.

She's had the nous and discipline to come to all our meetings, and has had patience with me even when we weren't sure she'd appear in the actual episode.

She's been to all the photo shoots, and to my humble knowledge at least two members of the crew have something of a thing for her.

She tells me she has a possible solution to the Concierge issue.

She shows me her suggestion on her phone. I almost gag from my own surprise.

I *know* the guy.

I met the man in the photo before me by complete accident.

I was with friends on Wardour Street and we'd had a bad night "trying out bars" in Central London encountering asshole security who had no love for anyone (Note to readers: do *not* go out in London without hookups; it's like turning up to Chechnya armed only with a sharp tongue and a *really* posh vocabulary).

We end up at Floridita, which I love for many reasons, and encounter a truly pleasant doorman.

He's so pleasant we start talking, and he turns out to be an actor by the name of Aidan Feore. I ask him what he's been in and when he tells me I nearly drop all thought of going out in favour of just listening to him tell stories.

You ever seen "The Dark Knight"?

You remember that bit in the prison where the Joker is about to blow the jail to shit? And there's a guy in a cell having stomach pains? He passes out and we see a phone sewn into his gut. It turns out to be a phone bomb and blows the jail to shit.

That's Aidan Feore.

And he's whom Claire's suggested.

I immediately say yes, I want him.

And when we move inside to film the Concierge bit, he's learning his lines and prepping his performance.

God, I love real actors. He's one of a rare breed - Americans who can "do" English accents (you think that's easy? Tell me how many films Johnny Depp did before getting it "right" in Pirates of the Caribbean. Three? Four?).

So we need the Ben scene (Ben first entering the building) with the Concierge, and then the Chloe scene with the Concierge (it's good visual comedy, so I won't spoil it for you). The Ben and Concierge scene goes swimmingly. Alex / Ben is well rehearsed, and Aidan / Concierge, despite *no* rehearsals, delivers it as an American perfectly.

See, the Concierge has to be *good*, 'cause were I to sign this programme, I'd want to make best use of relatively "normal" minor characters for additional colour and comment. Think Gunther in "Friends" (not in general, mind, just for this example).

And he smashes it.

Alex / Ben gets just the right balance of nerves and lovability, and has added a walk to his character that reminds me so much of an old friend from my secondary school that I feel thankful to have such gifted people working with me (Iain Coleman, I'm still your boy, wherever you are).

We then put Chloe in to do her bit (not a million miles away from her previous scene, repetition comedy) and having had zero rehearsal, she smashes it again.

Chloe, I'm a fan.

That's all you need to know.

OK, on to the next setup.

These are the shots of Ben leaving the station, walking over the bridge, entering and also leaving the building. That's the building we don't have permission to shoot in, in which we've set up a green room, a basic HQ, costume, wardrobe, and set up lights, kinos, an Alexa Camera, and over ten crew and over ten cast.

If anyone finds this out I'm probably (a) fired and (b) kicked out of my building and therefore (c) homeless.

Again.

We get our first bit of bad news in the only way we can: droplets of rain begin falling from the sky and I begin wanting to curse like a madman. Droplets turn into a downpour and we have lunch watching this meteorological crap-storm.

Now, there's many things I can do, including write and direct and be in and score a pilot or feature; I can run a 10 miler, fight a man to a standstill, write a novel, and make a really mean *fusilli arrabiata*.

However I *still* haven't learned how to get the Almighty on the phone and tell him I *really* don't need him pissing it down on us at that precise moment.

I start begging every force I can think of to get rid of the rain. I leg it up to the balcony to look at the sky. I realise surely it cannot be my job to look at the sky to see where the clouds are. And yet it is.

I feel massively grateful but realise I haven't got time for this shit. I think I see what's going on in the distance, but I'm no fucking weatherman; if I call this wrong, then we waste the entire rest of the day losing all our shots and that's my call.

I *cannot* let these people down. But there's no one else to ask.

No, that's not true. There's no one else to blame. That's the truth.

I make my call. We head outside.

We manage to shoot Ben leaving the station, and get some good shots. I have a secret plan for this programme, and one of them is interacting with and fucking with the audience as much as possible.

My boy Ricki Naqvi is who I'm using for this.

He's also an unusual man.

He's good-looking enough to have been a finalist in the Mr UK competition (or something similar), and is a good actor with a strong variety of voices. His look is irreplaceable and he gives pretty much his all to everything I've seen him in.

He's my ace-in-the-hole.

There's a momentary scare as we have several police walking around us. This is a scare because, as usual, we have zero permission to shoot this.

We cover the station bit, the bridge bit, and the exteriors, again using Ricki as an ace-in-the-hole. We also realise we have no radio mics, which is a problem I could do without.

Sound design is a *bitch*.

We then, *finally*, get around to shooting the Sid and Margherita scene, which features our beloved Clair Yellowlees and an actor by the name of Tomasz Aleksander.

Tomasz plays Sid Richards, the best friend of our lead character Ben Sharon.

I initially hadn't planned for the audience to actually see Sid Richards. We'd see him as a character maybe in the second episode.

I'd done that because I knew he'd be hard to cast.

Sid Richards is based on a friend of mine called Adam Moore.

He's similar to Ben in some ways, except he's cooler. He's tall, a little wiry, plays the guitar, smokes up, and loves surfing. He's kind of a modern man, except he doesn't fight; predominantly because he doesn't *need* to, because *everyone* who knows him loves him.

This is who I based Sid Richards on. And figured I'd not be able to find him, because Adam Moore is so particular a person.

Tomasz Aleksander comes into our auditions to play Ben Sharon.

I see immediately that we could cast him for that but that we'd have to do a lot of rebalancing everywhere else in the script. Ben has to be more clean-cut. I then realise immediately that Tom is *perfect* for Sid Richards.

If he's willing to consider it.

Tom's an actor's actor. He fights for his work and cares a hell of a lot about it. His acting comes first, second *and* third.

He's basically very fucking good. He's also got that unique "thing" about him that makes him both very "ahhhh" for the ladies and yet watchable for the guys in the audience.

He was the very *first* person to come up to me at the end of the shoot and say "Now the hard work begins, mate... make sure you get this somewhere."

Had this been *anybody* else on the shoot, I'd have lost it with them.

(For the records, my beloved Sistrothers {Sisters and Brothers} I didn't lose it *once* on the shoot, not even when Smugz was on the phone on my balcony and I could hear him fucking a take up. I came close a couple of times and very, very close on the second day, but I held it together and didn't scream at anyone. Actually I also came close on the last day, but at that point I'd had next to zero sleep and was more than a little tired.)

Anyway: we shoot the Sid and Margherita scene and I realise they are perfect.

The plan is we'd create a possible love triangle situation in the future between Sid, Margherita and Ben. Margherita, for the record, is based on a Spanish ex of mine who I was very much in love with.

She was never my girlfriend per se but my God, was she a character.

And Claire is doing very well, even coming in for a meeting purely based on character so we could discuss it at length. Her appearance fits perfectly, her hair and makeup also making the character complete.

Day One comes to a close and I stop moving at a thousand miles per hour.

See, we scheduled the whole first day so I would *not* be in filming, so I could have one day to get used to directing on its own and then jump into directing and acting on day two (this we call Diracting).

I thank everyone for coming and shake as many hands as I can, including Rooster and all the crew.

I get into my flat and collapse on the couch.

I can't believe how tired I am and I haven't even yet been in a single scene.

This is when Rooster comes up and tells me authoritatively that, 100%, no doubt, we only missed one scene, and yes it was a good day's work, but we now have a *serious* problem.

I sip my tea and couldn't care less. We got through day one, and how bad can it really be?

Rooster looks at me, fidgeting. Now I get a bit nervous, cause he's relaxed as water as a rule.

"What is it?" I ask.

"I don't want you to get pissed off," he says "but something has happened."

"Yeah I get that, Roostinho."

"And you might lose it a bit. It's kind of, erm, serious," he adds.

"What is it Rooster?"

He sighs. "You know the super-extremo-mega-camera we have?"

"Yeah."

"The one we booked for our four day shoot?"

"Yeah."

"We just lost it ten minutes ago. Someone else just booked it out. For like a week."

"Ah. Does that mean we don't have a camera?"

"That's right."

"At all?"

"No. And we also just lost a member of cast."

"Ah. *Fuck.*"

DAY TWO - FRIDAY

I wake up knackered.

262

I'm so knackered and fed up of being knackered that I'm just tired of being tired. (Note to self, good lyric, "Tired of Being Tired").

I'm struck by the notion that I haven't spoken to my mother enough in the last few weeks because of all "the HOTHouse" work. And that makes me sad. I don't recommend being sad and tired on the opening of your day whilst diracting film.

I'm so tired that I barely register a BBM (BlackBerry Messenger message) that comes through first thing as I wake up.

I shower and get ready, prepping my costume as I do.

While I'm showering I realise what my eyes just saw but my brain didn't realise.

It was from the joint love of my life who is currently living in Colombia, and who I have loved since the moment we met.

And here's what it reads.

HER MESSAGE: I have news.

MY MESSAGE: OK. Am listening.

HER MESSAGE: I am engaged. And apart from my mother you are the first to know.

This takes a while to sink in. Then, tears threaten to come. Then:

MY MESSAGE: My sincerest congratulations to both you, your fiancé who is indeed a fortunate man, and to all of your family on this blessed day. All my love to you both. And thank you for telling me, from the bottom of my heart, to the top of forever. I love you now and always, and am never anywhere but here for you, no matter where I am.

HER MESSAGE: I love you very much. You are forever my Englishman. Thank you for your wishes. You are in my heart and you belong there.

My fist is clenched so hard in the shower that I can feel body tremors threaten to unsettle me entirely.

We do not *have time for this shit*. Get it together, Stephen.

I get upstairs trying to conceal the wound.

I fail.

My eyes are straining against the tears. Everyone starts asking me what is wrong, for which I am grateful but we just don't have the time.

Rosemania shows up, thank Jesus, and I no longer worry for my sanity. He's very good at keeping me sane, but he asks immediately, "Mate, what's wrong?"

No time for that. Keep *moving*.

We start the day having to fix the camera problem. Our budget is as limited as Gordon Brown's leadership skills, but we have no choice but to cough up £400 for a RED camera or it's curtains for the project.

Curtains for the project?

On *my* watch?

No, schnig, that ain't how we roll in Stratford. We book the camera. Now we just have that casting problem, as one of our actors for the interview just dropped out.

"How we going to fix this?" Rooster asked the day before, reasonably.

"Can I use a member of crew, create a new character, write a new segment, and get it filmed from scratch?"

Rooster looks at me weirdly.

"In... like... how? Before we shoot?" he asks.

"Yeah."

"Er, yeah. Sure." He thought I was a maniac, I'm sure.

Now, here, today, he looks at me weird again.

"You OK?" he asks.

I look at him. I want to tell him.

He's my boy, and my co-producer, and my flatmate. But if I tell him now and assign it its correct importance then he'll then be worried about me, and he's got more than enough on his plate. So I simply tell him I'll explain later.

We start off getting the RED camera in and set up.

I have a special fondness for the RED as "Morning Tea" was shot on it, and that was my first ever lead in my first ever feature.

That was almost now nine months ago. And that on its own seems impossible.

While I'm thinking about setting up I'm looking at our runners.

There's Sebastian, an American guy in a hat who likes to talk but doesn't complain when he's given tasks. There's a young girl I haven't seen much of who seems to be running a good ship downstairs. There's Jamie, who I think I'm going to get in a scene later, because he has a unique look and hasn't complained once. He's also got a really nice demeanour and I need that right now.

Theo walks in who's doing sound for us and who I've worked with on several occasions. I love Theo because not only does he do sound, he's also a producer (music) and from what I've heard and seen, he's good. He's come to stand in for Rodney who did sound the day before.

Rodney had a good eye for detail and has apparently offered to do our grading for us. Then Matthew walks upstairs.

Matthew hasn't bitched or moaned once in the whole time he's been here. He's also constantly on the go. (A note to all runners of the World: *do not stop moving.* A runner who isn't moving isn't working, unless he / she is fixing some kind of equipment. It's called "running" for a reason.)

We had a chat previously the night before about if he'd be willing to play a character to cover for our lack of an 'interview character.' I had a minor major idea.

If he was willing to be in the show, and I had no idea how good or bad an actor he'd make.

"HOTHouse" is somewhat about playing with stereotypes.

Except it's about complicating or sophisticating stereotypes in a London fashion. Now, my fashion sense (or lack of it) has been remarked upon more than once. I happen to own a hoodie that is covered in comic book images.

Hey, I use it for round the house.

Soon as I looked at Matt, I saw him in that top, and as long as he could do some kind of voice, we could have him play a comic-book-convention-esque nerd type of thing.

Thing is, he can't just play "a nerd" because that ain't "HOTHouse." Nerds are officially now cool, as far as "HOTHouse" is concerned. So he needs to be a *playboy* nerd who attends comic and Star Trek conventions to pick up attractive women who like the same stuff he does.

I told him the night before and despite no major acting experience he was more than willing.

We did a quick run of the voice and it seems workable. The hoodie also works, and he even says himself that he has Transformer wristbands, which would be perfect.

He now walks in, and I realise how close I am coming to gambling on this one. If it fucks up, it's my fault. I am considering praying. Or sacrificing something to some God who might care.

We move to shoot the scene of Ris (Rooster's character) waking up.

Manuel Nashi and Jim Hatton Brown in Art Design have outdone themselves yet again. His room looks perfect, and we stick a teddy bear into the bed next to him to add to his slobby character.

This whole thing is not easy for Rooster. He's not, in his head, an actor.

You wouldn't know that if you'd seen him rehearse.

He knows his lines, he has his wardrobe, we know his makeup, and he's got all his blocking. Plus his nerves at acting are not hiding his true character, so we have a good shot at making him a real standout. A couple of takes later and we're moving on.

We're moving on to the scene of Tahira Taylor waking up, who is played in our production by Emily Clark.

Emily Clark is bit of a paradox. She has been an actress, a girl band member, a glamour model, a model, has worked on "Cage Rage," has been in music videos, can sing, rap, dance, write, and is now studying psychology and playing the lead in our TV pilot.

And she's trouser-threateningly attractive.

I'll be honest with you: it's risky casting.

But then I knew that from day one. She's extremely low maintenance in that she picks up direction easily, is fluid with her lines and can change or adapt them at will, has outperformed all my expectations in improvisation and is easily one of the most talented people I have ever met in my life.

She's also argued with me every day about her makeup, never gives in when I tell her what she can and cannot wear, and to say "she likes to chat" between takes is like saying Keith Richards "occasionally liked to dabble" with substances that were not technically legal.

We see her wake up and pull some of the funniest faces imaginable.

It's beauty with humour.

On to the next setup.

It's the Lox character waking up, and that's me for the first time.

I'm already in costume; I'm ready, except I've had no makeup and probably look like shit. Which thankfully, playing Lox, is fine.

Again when I see the room I am moved by Jim Hatton Brown and Manuel Nashi's attention to detail. There are posters and pictures on the wall that simply blow me away. Red posters reading "screw me like a dog;" a beautiful handdrawn picture of a Fallen Angel (*perfect*!), and a load of prints JHB did which almost shame my own work.

We do a couple of takes and we move on.

What we move on to is almost so good that I nearly feel a twinge of the sin we call pride.

We set our interview segment up in the living room. The living room setup is just genius. There are posters, an entire cutout man and woman. There's rules on the wall, there's empty bottles, there's DJ decks; I mean our entire flat has actually become a club. It's just humbling.

And then interview candidate one walks in: Pablo the Mexican wank addict, played by Tom Reid.

Tom came in to play Ben Sharon, and we knew we couldn't have him for that due to age and height restrictions. But let me tell you this: Tom Reid is not afraid of taking risks.

He came into our first audition with one of the oddest outfits I'd ever seen and a joke so cringeworthy that Rooster was nearly in tears of laughter.

He's gutsy, and a good-looking kid, so I thought there was no sense in not having him in. So we got him in as an interview candidate (for this segment think: the housemate segments in between episode-sections of "Friends").

It's in this section that Chow Bella's costume and wardrobe ability shines to its brightest.

Now, one might say I'm biased as she is my flatmate, but let me just say this: Chow Bella has worked on feature films with the likes of Danny Dyer and is no newbie to what she does. She's not only a costume and wardrobe Head Of Department (H.O.D.) on my pilot but she's also an artist and has had *hours* of talks with me about "HOTHouse."

She understands colour palette and character creation. So when Pablo walks in, he looks so funny I nearly start laughing out loud.

During his speech, the whole crew is trying hard as they can not to burst out laughing. This continues throughout the next two interviews.

This is what we call a "good sign" when we are making comedy.

Alistair Reith comes in as Father McLeish, and knocks it out the ballpark.

By "knock it out the ballpark" I mean I have three near-perfect takes with him. This is not easy for an actor when he is playing not one but *two* roles in your project.

Alistair has survived as an actor for over a decade, which is not easy either. He's also the only person I know whom Steven Spielberg has personally directed. He is 100% in the top three character actors I know.

When he leaves, before Matt comes in, I prep the whole crew.

"When Matt comes upstairs, I want no-one to show nerves about him not "being" an actor. Give him a bit of a cheer and a load of encouragement like no matter what he does, he's going to slam it. And then, ***trust me on this***, he will."

Everyone nods. They're good, this crew.

And then Matt walks in as Cecil Burke.

Everyone has to stop themselves from laughing off the bat and they all shout encouragement.

We shoot the first take and I shit you not, everyone starts laughing and cheering at the top of his or her lungs, not because I said to do so, but because the take, after the welcome he got, was perfect.

I know we got the shot because I see it on the monitor. We do one more for safety and I'm happy as Larry.

This, people, is called courage. To Matt, aka Cecil Burke, I tip my hat to you. That was some badass, one-take-wonder performing.

And after that, we're supposed to film the biggest scene of the whole show and this is where it all goes wrong. We're behind time and we get nowhere *near* the footage we need.

So we cut to our photoshoot segment.

At which point we bring in Soraya Radford and Jenny Harper.

I have to make special mention to both these two young ladies for several reasons.

Reason One - the patience they displayed for waiting almost all day for one scene; my sincerest thanks for that.

Reason Two - Jenny Harper has the character and smile to make any man fall in love almost immediately, and Soraya Radford has one of the most strikingly beautiful faces you've ever seen.

We shoot the photo shoot segment and every guy in the room is trying hard *not* to stare like a windowlicker.

I explain to both Soraya and Jenny the look I am trying to get in the shoot - it's that of the "nearly kiss" event between two females, a moment of beauty shot like a postcard between two women sent to the male race to explain beauty and understanding, and how wrong homophobia, or any other kind of phobia, actually is.

Thankfully they get the premise, and we get the shot. I also get credits here for not cracking up laughing at just how good a job directing can be.

How anyone can not enjoy doing this is beyond me.

The end of the day comes and I collapse yet again.

And I need to talk to Rosemania.

Rosemania is an actor in the making and is one of my oldest and closest friends in London.

He's got a scene tomorrow and I think he's going to smash it.

He's also ADing for us (Assistant Directing) and has never done it before. He's making me proud with every second that he works. I tell him about the message I received in the morning, and he looks at me stunned.

"You been carrying that around all day?" he asks, incredulously, "While you were *working*?"

I nod, exhausted. It's about all I can do.

I need sleep and either *I* or *we* fucked up today. This is going to necessitate reshooting and that is *precisely* what I wanted to avoid.

Plus the love of my life is now marrying another man, and I just cannot handle any more bad news.

Rooster comes up and looks at me, and we both know this is going to take reshoots. He adds in one more piece of information that almost, for the first time, makes me lose it like a madman.

And me losing it is not good.

I have legendary self-control precisely because of this reason, that reason being that when I'm drunk but more so when I am genuinely out of control, everything around me gets turned into a *war zone*.

"What?" I ask.

"I've just been called into a meeting tomorrow I cannot avoid. I'm going to be offset for about three hours, and there's nothing I can do about it."

"Ah," I say.

It's not his fault, by any means.

This is just God upstairs laughing at me after he sent us rain and tried to nick our camera and sent us a ton of our equipment late, and has me running round like a madman, and Rooster headed to meetings when he'd rather be here watching over our baby: "the HOTHouse."

He's more gutted than I am.

And I'm *gutted*, cause he's the Daniel Tripp to my Matt Albie. Or maybe he's the Matt Albie to my Daniel Tripp...?

"Anything I can do tonight to make tomorrow easier?"

I think for a second.

"Yeah," I reply, "Whisky and coke'd be a good start..."

DAY THREE - SATURDAY

At this point you can guess how I wake up.

I had two drinks last night and I can feel them already. I read somewhere once that if you get only four hours sleep two nights running then you are legally drunk.

In which case, I must be a-goner.

The day kicks off with our scene of Lox, Tahira and Ris on the couch. We do a lot of freestyle shooting and it goes relatively well.

The scene we shoot next, to my mind, steals the show.

We see Tahira and Gary (Emily and Alex) in "The Break-Up Scene."

Tahira is dumping Gary, and not in an angry way, or a hurt way, or in a he's-cheated-on-her way, but in a she-sees-other-people-and-he-knows-it-and-is-dumping-him-because-he's-not-stepped-up-to-the-plate, kind of way.

Emily and Rosemania have rehearsed this plenty; in terms of their physical blocking, their vocals, their tender moments, everything. We do about six takes and I'm over the moon.

This may be the single best scene in the whole thing.

We then do the Ris and Tuff Kooki scene on the balcony, and are absolutely cluster-shagged by the wind. To be fair, this is the single biggest directorial mistake I made during the whole shoot.

It should have been shot inside the house as it was rehearsed. But I caved to a suggestion from a crewmember, partly because I wanted to shoot the balcony because the view is just so beautiful, and partly because I figured a crewmember winning one was a bit overdue.

However. A wiser man than me would have known the wind would've made it impossible.

I'll not make that mistake again.

Not ever.

The annoying thing being that Rooster and TK were on point and knew exactly what looks to give. To be fair, this may all be solvable in ADR (Additional Dialogue Recording... when your dialogue screws up, then you go to the studio to re-record to avoid having to re-shoot the footage).

We'll see. I haven't yet seen the takes.

Fingers crossed.

At which point Rooster has to bugger off to a meeting that he cannot avoid. No one could.

And he's *still* more gutted than I am.

I now realise that Rosemania and I have to AD and manage the whole rest of the day without him. I get goosebumps at the thought of doing this without him around, because he's got, to be fair, acres of experience doing this, where, as far as ADing goes, I have zillimetres.

We then move outside to shoot Bella and Goins MacFarlane's scene.

Bella Young is played by our very own Kelly Schembri.

Kelly is yet another (I don't know how we find these people) young, extremely talented girl who sings, dances, pretty much manages her own girl band, is *in* her own girl band, models, runs her own agency, and a whole host of other shit.

She's got a strong heart, and for her pains I give her a lot of flak.

Her stage name is Kelly Stelfox, and for this of course I call her "Smellfox." Partly because I want our banter to make her as comfortable as possible when filming, because we have issues we've worked on with her voice.

Yet again, if you see this woman onstage or performing, you better do so without your woman around, or she'll get antsy. Kelly, as all of us, has had work issues.

Fortunately, we've got around a lot of them and her work has paid off. She knows her lines and is always punctual. I recommend her work highly.

In her scene we see a walking conversation between her and Goins "The Loins" MacFarlane, played again by Alistair Reith.

The whole scene is a deathtrap - we're outdoors, we're on a street, we're walking backwards and sidewards, having to avoid cars and people and Christ knows what else. Jamie the runner gets into the scene (you'll see him standing by a lamppost) and Theo outdoes himself on sound, dodging cars and lampposts like a pro.

Alistair makes me laugh before he's said anything. I give full, 100% no-holds-barred ups to Chow Bella, Amanda and Alistair for his costume. It was pretty much as iconic as you'll get.

His hair is orange and spiky, he is wearing makeup, and he has a pierced everything. He's all in black and my God, I wish I'd written the whole thing just about him.

We shoot about five takes and we're done. For this scene Ali and Kelly improv'd a lot, and the scene works very well.

My hat is tipped to you both for your work on that.

Then it's another walking scene, and this time we're in the Park.

Thom the DP suggests we go to Victoria Park. I suggest a nearby alleyway. We have to get a cab, a van, and a pushbike to the park.

Thom's suggestion was better. The Park is beautiful. Hence, sometimes you let crew win, and if your judgement is sound, you *still* win.

And here we see our first scenes with Jerome Prince and Coralie Robinson.

Jerome Prince is a true find. He's got just about the perfect face, for a start. He's been a supermodel for years and has appeared in several British feature films. He's committed to his work and wants the best performance he can get.

He's been unsure about having red lipstick in his scenes, but while contesting my view has also made it clear he is willing to do it. Plus he's had to play a homosexual character and has to kiss another man when he is not homosexual.

You think this isn't a big deal? Go find your nearest straight guy and ask him, stone cold sober, to pull a man.

Then tell me how off he tells you to fuck.

Jerome's motto:

"Don't let Fear make you its Bitch."

We've rehearsed his scenes over and over and he's worked very hard.

In these scenes we have also our dear Coralie Robinson, who is a real gem of a person. And again, one look at her and you'll be howling at the moon. She's a lingerie model, actress, sex columnist, and pet owner of extraordinary personality.

She's had a very challenging time in the press, but has no malice in her soul.

On the contrary, she possesses a kindness and gentleness that is best reflected in the love she has for her dog, Kingston.

Coralie is the first person of the whole cast and crew who has been kind (or crazy?) enough to turn round and offer to cook dinner (nah, crazy...) for Rooster and myself just to say thank you for our hard work. I'm not saying we deserve that dinner, mind, but fuck me sideways I'm happy to accept the offer.

Always nice to have your work appreciated.

We hit the park, and Coralie and Jerome are in outfits that have me chortling already. No one in the park can avert his or her eyes.

The view is spectacular, with a fountain in the background, greenery everywhere, and the sun shining down.

Thom had warned me about this - had we not shot the footage fast enough, we might lose the Sunshine and that changes *all* the lighting in the park.

And now the Sun God Ra is torturing me. The sun comes out. The sun disappears. The sun comes out. It fucks off again.

I'm about to start crying.

Fuck it.

I get about six takes to cover my ass and then we're off. I know Jerome and Coralie, and as long as they don't fuck their dialogue up, we're happy. Because you'll be too busy looking at them to notice anything. And they don't fuck it up anyway.

I'm in love with both of them.

We move back to HQ to film our last scene of the day.

Last scene is our Ace-in-the-Hole chasing our lead Alex Rendall who is running away from a cop shop.

Minor issue: Alex Rendall has to be carrying two blow-up sex dolls and wear a jacket made of condoms. And the guy chasing him is dressed like a *copper*.

You ever tried pulling this off in the street whilst remaining inconspicuous?

Nah. Me neither.

So we go out into the street getting muchos weird looks, and we get a wide shot and a few closer ones.

We get our stills wunderkind, young Will Coddington (my best friend's brother), to step inside our HQ and take a set of stills we can use to cheat a few scenes in the pilot.

To be fair, after seeing the shots, I no longer consider them cheating. They're wicked.

We wrap the day up and head inside.

Rooster and I then sit upstairs and try to get rid of the shakes.

Before we get to bed, Liam and Tuff Kooki want to show us the music they have prepared for tomorrow.

To be honest, I feel like anyone who mentions "HOTHouse" right now ought to have their gullet slit. But that's not the attitude we need, so I force myself to sit still and listen.

It ain't right, because, Liam tells me, he's using a trumpet instead of a guitar.

Fine, says we, *then grab the booing guitar.*

So he does.

And then, of course, magic happens.

Sound. I no longer need to worry about music.

Just the last day to worry about.

Which is another monster day of shooting.

I check the clock. It's one in the morning.

And after watching the rushes, everyone is now getting really excited, especially about the Rosemania and Emily scene, after which it appears Rooster has had a brand new idea.

At this point, I'm drinking whisky and coke (a Rockschool, people), and as long as it doesn't involve more work, I don't care.

"Let's shoot a short film involving Emily and Rosemania tomorrow before we start - something involving domestic violence and a good beating and some other shit. We'll just call all the crew in early, and then get Rosemania and Emily to improv it. What do you think?"

I look at him as God might behold Satan, were the Horned One to arrive at the Pearly Gates with a trillion sinners following Him, suggesting helpfully:

"I've had an idea, yeah Big Man? We take all of Hell, and we take all of Heaven, and then we start a new gaff called Injingo Mongo, and then we stick the two together, and then you and me's can split the owning and split the take? What you say, geezwoir?"

I sigh as though the weight of the world had just been replaced on my shoulders.

"Rooster, I'm going to kill you. But fuck it... tell me your idea..."

DAY FOUR - SUNDAY

I can barely stand up straight.

I remember reading the Knightfall saga with Batman getting his ass handed to him by all of his enemies and then by Bane, and that's close to how I feel.

You know what though?

I don't *give a shit*. It's our last day of filming and I'm over the moon we got this far. Cause so far, from what I can see, nothing has gone wrong that isn't fixable in minimal time.

I know we start the day with two nice scenes: DJ Ricardo Fargas and Tuff Kooki entering "the HOTHouse."

DJ Ricardo Fargas is one of my closest friends and is a DJ to die for.

He produces, mixes, and DJs music of the absolute highest level, and specialises in an art form known as "Fidget House" which to my mind is *the* new sound that everyone is going for.

He's also a good-looking dude who's going to look the *nuts* on camera.

Tuff Kooki (playing herself) is also a top class singer and absolute "HOTHouse" soldier who has given her all for "HOTHouse." My only regret with her is that she doesn't have more scenes, but I can deal with that in the rest of the series.

She's had a tough set of circumstances thrown her way and fights for every inch she ascends.

She's been in talks with a major record label to sign her as a singer-songwriter, and my God she deserves it. She's also, *yet again*, so much of a looker that my dad'd push me out the way, if he were given half a chance.

Chow Bella has again outdone herself with their outfits. TK looks like a new Quentin Tarantino girl, and Richie's looking like Kanye West would if he had a better face.

We shoot the scene of them entering and follow it up with the scene of him setting up his decks.

The living room is still looking like a club and is just perfect.

The style of the piece is very much "The Thick of It" (if you haven't seen it, *watch* it).

It's all handheld documentary style, chiefly because we're half making fiction and half making a documentary. If I haven't made it clear before, I'll make it clear now: "the HOTHouse" is a real place.

I live there. Lox, Ris, Tahira and Ben are all real characters, just with different names.

Tuff Kooki and Richie are real *people*, with their real names.

I'll leave it to you to work out why we did it like that.

We move to the hallway to shoot the scene where we have a queue outside "the HOTHouse," with Shanghai working the door and Trent Devlin trying to get in.

Shanghai is my little sister and has been my best female friend for a decade. She's about to become a teacher, and has been everything from a nightclub promoter to a PR girl to a saleswoman.

She's the best friend you could ask for.

She can also be the most vinegary woman in the world, but with such dryness that it can't help but make you laugh. She's been a dancer, a singer, and has many other skills to boot. She's also completely insane, but then you kind of have to be to be one of my best friends. Ask Metis, Merlin or LL; they'll tell ya.

Trent Devlin (not kidding, that's actually his name) and I have also known each other a long time.

He used to manage a club I used to run (I ran a nightclub business, remember?) and that's where I started out in London.

He's since become a fitness instructor (built like he could carry a carthorse in each hand) and writer (has representation and is very, *very* good) and has made many literary contributions to our script.

We've butted heads over it more than once, but nothing we couldn't handle.

And he's now also working at the bar of the frickin' hall of residence I went to when I went to uni.

International Hall, I'm yer boy still...

The scene sees Trent Devlin, a footballer, trying to gain access to the club of dreams. Shanghai, our gatekeeper, keeps bouncing him out with pretty much no mercy.

This is not fiction. I have seen this *exact* scene before my eyes a hundred times at CC Club.

CC, I miss you like none other. In many ways in my London life I was born at CC.

They play the scene fine despite the fact that we took ages setting up. We have ten people in the queue and I know costume and makeup must be having a *nightmare* with this many people.

We get our shots.

We move back upstairs into the actual house to shoot the "Welcome" scene.

Rooster, bless his cotton socks, is rehearsing and rehearsing his lines over and over to make sure he is comfortable. The scene sees Ris, Lox, and Tahira welcome everyone to "HOTHouse."

We've had to wait about an hour just to *get* everyone up here. And this is the first time I see Kid Ant and Lady King arrive on set.

Kid Ant is a real character - he's our new, modern day Del Boy, and he's just like it in real life.

He wants to be a broker and is working hard to get there. He's got a heart of gold and looks more like a Calvin Klein model than any man I have ever seen. He's dressed to kill and ready to go.

Lady King is both in our show and in real life Kid Ant's missus.

She's a professional dancer and can't walk into a room without turning so many heads that groups of grown men end up in casualty.

She's also dressed to kill and looks the part. We shoot the welcome scene and Rooster's rehearsals have paid off perfectly - he nails it pretty much every time except one.

We then shoot one of my favourite scenes in the whole piece.

Gary Barflow and Lox face off in the living room. Gary loses it after being dumped by Tahira and rants at both her and Ris. We shoot that, and then Lox enters and puts Gary in his place. I realise dimly that I'm Lox, *and oh God please don't let me collapse or fuck it up please God please God now I'm on set and oh fuck if this goes wrong we unbalance everything Jesus please...*

I come back around to the sound of applause and someone grasping my hand.

The room applauds and apparently that's because of Rosemania / Gary's performance and mine / Lox's. I'm either the luckiest man on Earth or there's something here that's working.

Rooster and Rosemania had almost entirely improvised their scene and it seemed to work like a charm.

We then do a "Hills" style subtitle shot of Lox and Bella Young, with nowhere near enough time, and then Alex Rendall falls into the room with two sex dolls and a jacket made of condoms.

We do his scene up to our little face-off, another good one, and then the General makes his big entrance.

Jamie Thompson plays our General.

He's got the look (yet again) of a catwalk model, the sound and presence of a Shakespearean actor, and the voice of one too. He's made several script suggestions, and pointed out early doors that "and not just because I want more screen time, but actually because it's true, we *need* to see more of the General."

You wanna know something?

It takes guts to say that. And more importantly, it takes both guts *and* nous to say that and to be right. And he was right. Trent Devlin'll verify it.

He also writes his own plays and screenplays, and is something of a musician to boot.

He is the General, the man who started off the cult / tradition / game / group known as "the HOTHouse," and began the rules which run the crew.

Those rules being:

1) Earn Your Place
2) Invite Only
3) Women Reign
4) Realspeak Only
5) Violence is an Outlaw
6) No Single Men
7) Choose Your Poison
8) Bear Gifts
9) Not For You? Leave.
10) ** CONFIDENTIAL - Crew Access Only **

The General faces Lox down and then encourages something that made my day a tad more difficult.

Lox, one of the leads, a straight guy - and played by me, is then forced into kissing Julian Vernon - our in-house superstar.

So, for I think three takes in a row, on camera, in front of all of my cast and crew and friends on set, I end up lip-locking Jerome Prince, our guy who plays Julian Vernon.

To say the house of people cheered would be an understatement.

Rosemania is practically urinating in his Y-fronts seeing me do this.

Smellfox informs me the whole project was worth it just to see me kiss a man.

I begin considering ejector-seating myself off the balcony.

We then see the scene between Gary Barflow and Julian Vernon, and here time just starts kicking my ass, but we do get some very nice footage of Blowy Chloe lighting a cigarette beforehand.

And, credit to him, after weeks of arguing back and forth, we have no arguments from Rosemania as he is chatted up and seduced by a gay black man.

We then kick into the party scene, and fuck me running, I can't *actually* stop.

I'm a film addict with a camera getting all the footage he can before he runs out of time. We get final shots of Chloe and the Twins doing their speech.

The Collings twins play our Shipwrecked Twins, and were initially loath to enter "the HOTHouse." I had to leave the flat to audition them in a pub personally.

They've done reality TV, comedy sketches, film, TV, photo shoots, the lot.

They kindly and generously spent about an hour teaching me some of the challenges they face, being identical twins.

I tell you what, as non-twin people we just have *no* idea.

Imagine waking up and seeing your own reflection, except on someone else's face, on someone else's body, with someone else's opinions. And *God help me* but they have previously fallen for the same man.

Can you imagine? They've also been dancers before, and are hotter than a chilli on the surface of the sun.

So the twins are made up to look very, very similar but *slightly* different. Which is where Amanda White came in.

I met Amanda on "Morning Tea" and man, can she do makeup.

279

She's very good with the cast, chatty but not to the point it slows her down, is very knowledgable about makeup but not as if that's all there is in the world, and entirely committed to what she does.

She's made up everyone on set (except Yours Truly) and done an exceptional job, especially with the twins, with Jerome, and with Emily Clark.

She has always been candid with me about matters that don't directly have any benefit to her; we've discussed script, character, the "look" of the film, and I am fortunate indeed to consider her a colleague and a friend.

So the twins look stunning and deliver their speech line-by-line one of them after the other.

They're so good they require no direction.

Chloe delivers a last line, and then we see the band come in.

The band is Tuff Kooki and our very own Behind-The-Scenes youngster Liam Heath, who's had more than his fair share of crap to deal with on our shoot.

Liam plays guitar, and TK sings a song she has written herself and adapted to "HOTHouse."

The whole house is mesmerised, partly at Liam's playing, partly at TK's singing which is just note-perfect, and partly at the occasion.

We do three or four takes, and at the end of every single one the house goes mental.

Finally we see Clair Yellowlees aka Margherita and Tom Aleksander aka Sid Richards walk in and do the "Caught Red-Handed" scene.

The look on Clair's face says it all, and Tom is so funny without saying anything that I'm borderline ecstatic. We get that, and one final between-the-legs shot I fucking *love*, and then before I know it, someone's voice is yelling "That's a wrap," and people are cheering, and then I realise the voice was mine.

Rooster asks people to cheer the crew. We cheer.

He congratulates the DP, we cheer; he congratulates the AD, and we cheer; and then I turn and instruct whoever is nearest me to locate alcohol absolutely ASA-fucking-P because I need a drink right this *second...*

So we have Rooster, Em, TK, Amanda, Chloe, the Twins, Claire Yellowlees, Tom Aleksander, Francesco, Richie, and Yours Truly at the wrap party mark I.

Mark II when we do it for rizzeal will be the "proper" wrap party.

We have: about ten bottles of alcohol, five bags of extra-curricular, and a jacket made out of condoms along with two sex dolls; one of which, just to vent a bit, I punch off the nineteenth floor balcony.

Just as a little "tell the Grandkids" thing.

Now to be fair, at a house party, I'd usually know whom I'm going to bed and waking up with.

But I cannot do that.

Partly 'cause right now I wouldn't inflict myself (state I'm in? Are you *high*?) on any sane woman, and partly 'cause business is business: I'm the director.

Period.

And these people are under my watch. I just have to keep my eye on them, make sure they all get to bed or to sleep somewhere safe and sound, and then I can slump-sleep in a corner for about a year.

I know at least two couples are about to get it on, and so I try to make myself scarce. Thing is, at the wrap party, everyone wants to grab you for five minutes, which I completely understand, except one of my colleagues apparently does *not*.

He's been trying to get it on with an exquisite young lady for about an hour, and every time someone wants to talk to me and we walk away from the main action, I end up walking round the corner or down the stairs or into the room he is in with said girl, midway through getting his thing on.

"Dude, can you *please* fuck off?"

I try not to laugh, but I'm so tipsy-tired and shattered full stop that I can't even manage to hide it. Plus, every time he tries to crack on again he relocates, thinking that'll reduce the chances of me interrupting again.

Which is true.

However, I think the *exact same thing*, that if I relocate when talking to someone, then that'll reduce the chances of me interrupting.

Either one is true on their own. Both simultaneously actually increases the chances of me interrupting. Again.

"DUDE! I'm *not fucking kidding around*!!! Would you please - FUCK - *OFF*!!!"

I apologise profusely, and fuck off as instructed.

When Chloe and Francesco and Claire and Amanda are finally tired enough to pass out, I can almost taste blood in my mouth.

I'm so utterly bereft of energy, tipsy-tired and exhausted that I probably need a hospital bed. I figure the easiest way to sleep is three girls in the master bedroom, one elsewhere, and Francesco and me upstairs.

Easy.

I stagger downstairs to make sure one girl knows where she's headed, and find Francesco asleep on a futon in the masterroom.

Now, the whole three-girls-in-here-thing won't work with him in here. So I rouse him from slumber to relocate him, and usher girl one into bed for some well, well deserved kip.

She then mumbles something about me not getting in with her.

Honey, any time except for on this shoot you might be right.

Right now I'd swap a week with every Sports Illustrated cover girl for a comfy armchair, a woolly cardigan and a large mug of Horlicks.

I relocate Fran to Rooster's room briefly to re-order sleeping arrangements, and he gratefully slips into bed and back to sleep immediately.

Now here's the thing: while I'm doing this, our enraptured couple have gone for a shower, and allocated themselves this *very* room.

They've *already* checked Rooster's room and *found* Francesco *in* there. They've then relocated him *already* to the master room.

So I had just re-relocated him, but he was too comatose to properly explain.

So the happy couple takes a quick shower, and proceeds to their room, fully expecting an empty bed, an entertaining night, and a bit of peace and quiet.

So: imagine their inebriated and incredulous surprise when they discover the man they had *just* thrown out their bed into the masterroom had somehow teleported magically straight back into their bed, and was now sound asleep.

I'd gone back upstairs at this point to tactically re-plan, because all I craved was sleep.

The music Richie spun was amazing, and Claire and Amanda were there having a chat but I swear on all that is Holy, I just wanted sleep.

And that's when I hear, from downstairs:

"For *fuck's sake*, Fran, we *JUST MOVED YOU* - how the **FUCKING HELL** did YOU get back in fucking *HERE*??!?"

At which point I lose it.

I laugh so hard I think God must hear me.

I vaguely recall walking a woman downstairs while she tells me x and y and z, and then, "I'm also a Cancerian," which is the first time I truly look at her, which is dangerous, because I had never *really* looked at her.

I avoid that when working with people. It's all nuggets of information and brief convos, so it doesn't really happen.

"Yeah, I'm just the female *you*, right?"

We'd just had a fairly deep conversation, and believe me when I tell you that no woman *living* has ever said these words to me.

And had any woman said them to me, I'd laugh it off as being ridiculous.

Except I don't.

I suddenly see her again, as for the first time. My brain kicks in and says "Get away from her; just make sure she gets home safe. *Now*."

Confused at words beyond my shattered comprehension, I return to the lift and elevate myself within the building.

I stagger back inside and see the confusion of a highly groggy Fran, and a very unamused couple whose look they send over at me actually has teeth.

I laugh, give one last look round the flat to make sure everyone has either gone home safe or is located safely, and stagger into my room.

I collapse.

DAY FIVE - MONDAY - UNSCHEDULED - THE AFTER EFFECTS

I wake up in my room thinking I've been shot, raped by a herd of rhinoceri, or slipped rohypnol.

Possibly all three.

Four days straight I've been directing, acting, re-writing, not really eating much, drinking zero water, and I think I need to brush my face and shave my teeth.

I walk out of my room and remember I was very, very shattered last night.

To the point where I can see no sign of the woman I was meant to wake up with and a shitload of a woman I don't know, and a man I recognise as a crewmember.

And of course, the flat is a war zone. It looks like it's located in Basra. This is going to take *days* of cleaning.

And I'm going to take days of recovery. I manage (just about) to make a start on the cleaning, and realise I am getting very, very sick.

My immune system is so fucked it's now a *mune* system. One runner on the set excused himself due to being ill. I think as he walked out, his cold walked right back in.

About halfway through the day I collapse on the couch and see Facebook full of comments and my inbox full of mail.

I then realise I cannot handle this.

Sorry reader, but even I have limits.

I need to go fall over or sleep, or puke, or something.

DAY SIX - TUESDAY - UNSCHEDULED - THE AFTER EFFECTS MARK II

So essentially I'm on the couch and I've been here for a day and a half.

I can just about stand up and move from the bedroom to the couch.

And that's yer lot.

Anything else and I'm good for nothing. I'm on Lempsip, herbal tea, painkillers, and a lot more.

The shoot is now done, and months of my work have come to their conclusion. I'm shattered like almost never before. Because where for most other people that's yer lot, guess what Rooster and I now have to do.

We have to watch all the footage (we captured over twenty-six hours in four days) and look at all the stills to see what is usable and where.

We then have to make a basic arrangement of all the footage and see what we are missing and how long our reshoots and pickups need to be.

We have to cut, edit, and put the music to all the footage. Then we have to film whatever we are missing. Then there's the launch party, and then there's promoting it to all the channels and networks.

Then there's holding the actual screening for the cast and crew.

And *that*'s while Rooster has to run and find his next projects and I have to film the rest of the feature.

Alistair Reith, who *smashed* the performance of "Goins MacFarlane," said to me "You don't like an easy life, do you?"

I tried to find a smart line to respond with, but I was too knackered to think straight.

Plus, he was right.

So I'm watching "Studio 60," which if you haven't seen, you ought to see.

It's helping.

From what I can tell, I'm also no longer seeing a young lady who was instrumental in helping the show; partly in her contribution musically and partly in her performance, but mostly in doing a *load* of shit she didn't actually have to do, and also in managing my psycho ass self prior to the event.

TK, wherever you are, stay at it. You're good enough. Stay focused.

If you think my professional life is a mess, then my lovelife is a *car wreck*.

However, that's OK.

It's OK because my work comes first. I can't even think about this right now, because I'm sweating and shaking and ill and have a cold and just need rest.

I can't think about the message or the shoot or editing or anything until I'm back on my feet. I've almost decided to take a long weekend, or go home to see Mum, or something.

I'm still in pieces, taking Lemsip and painkillers and about to go to bed, when the phone rings. It's Rehan Malik, my director on "Radio London."

Were it anyone else, I'd have dropped the call.

"Hey Mr Brocklehurst, are you free tomorrow?"

You don't say 'no' to directors like Rehan.

Except I'm not sure I'm physically going to be in any condition to do anything tomorrow. Maybe he just wants a meeting or a catchup coffee or something.

"I was thinking we'd shoot your scene for a few hours where Abdullah is tortured, thrown in jail, and gets waterboarded. Just a bit, like. If you don't mind?"

I have to bite my own wrist to not collapse in immediate hysterics and / or tears.

The request couldn't have been worse timed if someone just asked me to go twelve rounds with Tyson after I'd just been run over by a stampeding herd of Wildebeest.

I'm literally crying with pent-up, barely concealed exhaustion-laughter.

"Nnghh... sure Rehan... send me a callsheet and I'll smgnnhfff... have a look..."

"Looking forward to seeing you tomorrow, Doctor B."

I put the phone down and laugh so hard that I nearly cough my lungs up.

With tears in my eyes and a body that really, *really* hates me, I go to bed.

DAY SEVEN - UNSCHEDULED - THE AFTER EFFECTS MARK III - BACK TO REALITY

Laughably, I'm on my way to get waterboarded.

Voluntarily.

For "Radio London."

I'm sweating, shaking a bit, and my voice is *FUBAR*.

I need my head looking at. I have a day full of work tomorrow and then am full steam on watching the rushes and finalising the list of what else we need for "HOTHouse."

Currently I feel like I'd lose a fight against a half-drunk armadillo.

C'est la vie.

Getting on the tube in this state is highly unadvisable for all kinds of reasons, but chiefly the heat and the proximity of other people.

I just can't take it.

My boy Metis BBMs me and says he's on holiday. Thank fuck. He works his ass off and could use a break. Had I the time and money, I'd be there with him.

The weather is *lovely*: I haven't even seen the sky properly for days.

Christ, I'm fucked up.

I should be in bed. Still, it's Rehan and it's "Radio London," so what do I care?

Mind you, I still need to drink about four oceans of water and have some food (yes I *know* oceans are saltwater, genius, I'm talking quantity, not quality...).

I eventually get to the station and am too busy writing this to actually think much of anything.

Two girls, Roshni Gandecha and another pick me up at the station and drive me to what looks like some kind of Western meat locker.

I struggle out the car and greet Rehan, who gentlemanly apologises for getting me out of the house when I feel like utter dogshit.

He looks at me and his face immediately changes. He says I look like I have a fever. He is concerned, I can tell.

I tell him not to worry, and I mean it. His film is going to be *sick*.

Proper sick, I mean; to the point where, if it doesn't win something somewhere, we simply haven't promoted it right.

I walk in the building and suddenly what I am about to do dawns on me fully.

There is a wiry black camper bed frame in the centre of a concrete floor. Atop this frame lies a wooden board.

At both ends, top and bottom, are bulky metal shackles. Next to the frame is a bucket of water, which looks about as warm as a polar bear's cock.

I'm about to come pretty much as close to being waterboarded as you can without being kidnapped by highly wired people in the outlying regions of Afghanistan.

I should have mentally prepped more on the train, schniggles.

There's an assistant on hand called Charlie, a lovely oriental kid who seems more than a little nervous at having to hold me down and restrain me.

Then there's Ronaldas Buozis who's DPing, calm as ice, with the RED One camera. Then there's Roshni Gandecha and the other girl.

All look a tad perturbed, but are smiling.

"Can you change into this, Lord Brocklehurst?" Rehan asks.

He holds aloft a white plain T, combat trousers, and an orange prison jump suit. I grasp all three and begin walking, slowly, up the creaky wooden stairs.

I'm gonna have to improv this like a mofo.

I get changed at a laughably slow pace.

See, when I am tired and have a monster of a cold, and need another day's sleep and a *lot* more medicine, I'm just no good.

But I'm trying.

I clump my way back downstairs, and Rehan starts to tell me how this is all going to work.

"OK, so, we have you lying this way on like, the board, yeah, and then Charlie's going to force you down and I'm going to, like, grab you, yeah, and then we shackle both your hands in chains, and we film that. Then we do close ups and pick up coverage, yeah, shackle your other hand, stick like a rag in your mouth and a cloth on your face, yeah, and then we pour water over your head and face, so it'll be just like they do when they actually waterboard someone, yeah, but if you're uncomfortable at any point then just say yeah and we'll stop..."

With a rag in my mouth, a cloth over my head, and water pouring down onto my face?

Yeah, I'll just say a safety word like "supercalifragilisticexpialidocious," shall I?

Rehan. Gotta love him. Both a director and a comedian.

He's a genuinely, inherently *decent* man. He's insistent on checking I'm OK, and makes sure I've a glass of water and a quick chat to recuperate after every shot.

He's also one of the very few directors I actively *like* working for. My day rate at time of press is £150 a day according to Equity.

I'd do his shit for expenses only.

That's how good he is.

We get a better idea. I'll hold a pair of scissors while I'm struggling, attempt not to puncture my own lungs, and then just drop them if I'm uncomfortable. That'll be our signal.

"Erm. Scissors?"

Roshni looks over.

"Hmm. That may be a bad idea. Give him the metal bowl."

That's what I like; a girl with common sense.

And so it begins.

And here's how it's meant to play.

Abdullah (me) is sat on the board, looks up, and Charlie punches him in the face. Charlie then slams him in the chest and pins him to the board. At this point, Abdullah is struggling so maniacally that I'm almost foaming at the mouth.

Rehan (as another security or heavy) grabs me from behind and lowers me down backwards.

I slam my head on the board for added effect. Regrettable, I discover, as the girls informed me earlier there are nails sticking out of the board, and to say it hurts is a bit, well, - let's just say it *hurts*.

I then try to semi-strangle Charlie to get him off me, while Rehan grips and shackles my first hand.

He then snatches my hand from off Charlie and double-handed forces it into the next shackle. My screams as this all happens are apparently becoming difficult for the girls to listen to.

Rehan then takes a wet rag and stuffs it in my mouth as I shunt my head from side to side; he takes a wet cloth, and grips it over my head, at which point I can neither speak nor see.

Now, here's the tricky bit: he then has to pour water over my face and have it come as close to my nose and mouth as possible, without *actually* waterboarding me.

He pours two, maybe three sets of water, and I scream and struggle as this is happening.

This all takes place over the course of maybe four hours, during which time we do maybe nine to eleven takes of the *same* thing.

My mind is all over the place. I want this to look as real as humanly possible because Rehan is my boy and I love his film.

So I force my mind down what I call my little cul-de-sac.

Cul-de-sac theory or CDS theory is this: your life has or is a main road.

It starts at birth and continues on to the end we know as death, at which point the road runs out.

I concede after that something else may happen involving some clouds, a male voice choir, and people with wings, but that doesn't change the fact the road stops there.

Now, your mind and your perception *are* your life.

So your focus and thoughts are kind of the road too. Now, while your life cannot have CDS's, it begins and travels and ends, the mind itself actually *can*.

It can meander off down whatever practical or impractical path it likes. Some, for example, we call Dreams. Others, we call nightmares.

So in order to get my movements, voice, looks, eye expressions, screams, gargles, chokes, and lack of hope right, I send my mind off into its own Bermuda Triangle.

This is the Parts Unknown in which lives our not-so-good Dr. Schadenfreude.

I'm sending my mind for a little sleepover at his house.

I force my attention to Pari getting married, to needing to shoot more on "HOTHouse," to how much less I see my friends, to the image of my mum in hospital (*not* good, I actually started screaming at this point), to the image of Anita getting married, to every time I fucked up, to my father, to my own guilt, to losing all the girls, to the sunburn day, to seeing less of my crew, to what I did to Mandy in the States, to my never having seen my grandfather's face, to my oath to enter Britain's Got Talent, to the log race, to how afraid I am of letting my family down, and to...

I warned you, maggot.

I told you you wouldn't be able to live without me.

And now what, you're here asking for my help, because you can't fucking deal with things?

What, cause you have a little sniffle?

Christ alive, I've met <u>wasps</u> harder than you.

OK then, fuckaroo, you want access to your worst thoughts and feelings and nightmares and hatred and hurt and blackness and shit?

Heh.

*Happy Hunting, you unmitigated and sloppy coward...try **this** on for size...*

I come to.

My eyes blink open. I lie in a pool of water on a board in a cellar.

I am Abdullah.

I cough up water and phlegm.

The man standing over me holds a cloth.

He is going to try to waterboard me and perhaps kill me. I shall try to bite his hands off.

Another man stands to my left, nearer my feet. He keeps hitting me, and restraining me on the board by placing his elbow at my larynx.

I shall try next time he is near enough to rip his throat out with my fingers.

They slam me to the board.

I scream and wrestle and contort my body like an animal. I rack and ram against the chains which hold me to the board.

Water pools around me. I can taste the copper of blood in my mouth.

The motherwhore above me tries to force a rag into my mouth. I gargle my defiance and try to gnash his fingers off.

I fail.

I kick out so hard I feel the chains crack against my ankle.

The man trying to restrain my legs is loosening his grip. If I can, I will break his bones.

A black cloth is lowered above my head.

I thrash and struggle harder: I know what that shadow means.

It is lowered onto my face and I scream loud as I see the face of my daughter in the shroud now upon my face.

I hear women nearby crying.

But I also hear the glug of water.

My wrestling pauses for a frosted second: *what the f...?*

Water trammels down onto my face, into the rag, and down my gullet.

Everything is black: I can see nothing.

I thrash and slam and wreak havoc against the steel but the chains are large, and my arms and shoulders are tired.

A nail stabs into my head and I feel dizzy.

I cannot breathe.

I am going to die.

I feel like I am being baptised, but in reverse. Like water is my normal air, and now I am being thrust face-first into a barrel of air and oxygen.

A moment's respite.

I try to relax.

To calm myself.

To centre myself against all the...

Water.

Water glug-funnels down onto me again and interrupts my thoughts. It is omnipresent. The element of life becomes my death.

I'd see the irony if I had time to think. I feel it splash against my hands and face. I hear a camera whirr somewhere near to me.

I scream and gargle and yell my rage and murder and hurt and pain and agony and bile and dirt and sore, but it changes nothing.

The rag and cloth are removed.

The chains are taken.

It matters not.

At some point, your body reaches ground zero, where it has nothing left.

I lie on the board in a pool of water. I have nothing. This is what they wanted me to understand.

I understand it now.

I am myself again.

Finally.

I feel shaky.

I walk from the building having thanked everyone. I am back in my own mind. I call my mum to tell her I have just been waterboarded, but that I feel better. The previous two days felt like a *coma*.

Now I am more awake than I have been for days. Somehow, a process designed for torture feels like it has cleansed my system and brought me back to myself. I get some food. I make a call. I go home. I write some more of this.

I thank whatever stars I was born beneath that I am feeling better.

I thank Rehan and the crew for baptising me back to life; for necromancing me in the cleansing waters.

Rehan thanks me for my performance. I ask him why. He tells me "Your screams were so bad the girls had to leave the set."

I am pleased.

I thank you too, Dear Reader, for whatever good measures you have taken, and hope the selfsame cleansing waters may stream a little in your direction.

My name is Robert Howsley Frankton.

I am a bomber in Her Majesty's Grenadier Corps.

I am in the worst place on Earth. I am in the worst place in the history of the planet.

I am about to die.

I am in a trench with my men, about to go over the top for my country in the era of the Great War.

I have never, ever been so scared. I pass the letter for my mother to Lance Corporal Jobbie, and pray it reaches her in one piece.

A whistle blows, and the world erupts around me.

Rounds zip overhead, leaving streaks in the sky. Smoke billows out across the trench. Shells clatterplode against our defences and walls, and screams go up with each explosion.

The Highlanders take the high ridge as Corporal Pete Russell hands me my grenades. I am a bomber, and my gear is likely to kill me. It slows me down too much.

I climb the ladder before me.

Our section, along with 10 others, is ensconced in a trench: man's war-cut in Mother Nature's hide.

I reach the top and the land before me is a scar-torn, mortar-blasted wasteland. Rounds zip past at greater speed. Men in front of me are tossed aside like rag dolls, or simply fall as though their wires had been cut.

I mutter "Jesus Christ," as I leap over in the single most frightening moment of my existence. I scarper like Hell past four Belgian Gates, their barbed wire inching past my face as I then throw myself forward into a bomb hole.

I send a round or two in Jerry's direction. Sweat and soil mix and stream into my eyes.

The noise is deafening; the precise opposite to what Nature intended in a place such as this.

I run to the next nearest cover, and am almost there when a shell hits at the same time as something else and the ground literally shakes. I'm jammed from my feet and land awkwardly.

I see George, Jimmy, Bill and Will go down in a hail of hot lead one after another, leaving little blood clouds as the rounds exit.

I see Jerry in the bunker before me as a horse collapses into the clay and mud beside me. The animal's eyes are fish eyes; dead and gone, nobody home.

The grenade I have unclasped is somehow de-pinned, and I hurl it with all my force and aim at the bunker. As it sails in and I hear "Schwein! Englisch schwein!"

I roar my laughter.

Except I've not reached cover. I motion forward and hear thup thup thup.

I've stopped.

I look down.

Crimson trails run from my chest.

I hear the bunker blast as I start to fall backwards. At least we did something, I think.

The last thing I see is the bunker, the sky, rolling down, and then brown muddy water, and then darkness...

I search my mind, as I look at the most mind-blowing film set I've ever been on to see if I've ever seen anything like this.

It's like actually *being* there.

I look long and hard at the trench.

I wonder if there can ever have been anything as courage demanding as this. You're talking about climbing a ladder into a war zone that makes Hell look inviting.

I have a whole newfound respect for my grandfather's generation and my nan's generation.

And to be fair, I had a pretty healthy respect for them beforehand.

But this is different level.

This was simply heroic. To my knowledge (which is very limited and may therefore be wrong) we have no modern equivalent. The kind of guts and fortitude it takes to do this under machine gun fire and mortaring seems dazzling to me.

Whether German, English, French, I care not: my thanks go to all our ancestors, in the sincerest way possible, for performing deeds of such extraordinary difficulty that they beggar description.

Whenever anyone asks me *ever* again whom I wish I could have gotten to meet, I shall answer "my grandfather." What a man that must have been.

I look around beneath the rain, my clothes soaked through and my mind awash with challenges: the album, "Radio London," "HOTHouse," and so on.

They all seem trivial and petty in comparison with what I see now.

And yet... and *yet*, it is the business I am *in* that lets me be here this precise second.

How else can a thirty year old in the 21st Century come anywhere *near* seeing what his or her Forefathers did for us? This place is like a wake-up call:

Remember, Stephen, to keep the noble in all you do. Do not produce to show off, but to make things better in whatever way you can.

And of course, this isn't just a good work ethic (thanks, Pop). It's a good ethic full stop. A life ethic.

So it's a Lifethic.

I'll not forget it. And now that I see it, the next four weeks of work are going to be *hard*. And I still am nowhere near 100% after "HOTHouse" and being ill. Which I still am.

I'm in deep shit...

295

I climb over the parapet after ascending the ladder.

I have to admit, despite knowing we are all actors and that this is not "real," we are all scared.

Pete Russell, the soundest kind of man alive, is leading our crew.

We're section five, and we're about to go over the top.

We've got:

- Pete Russell; a young-looking former soldier turned actor who you'd be happy to have leading your team. He's an actor and a good person, and a laugh to boot
- Alistair Reith; my tag partner on "War Horse" in that he keeps me sane, and "HOTHouse's" very own Goins MacFarlane
- Michael Coleman; an eccentric but lovely-hearted man who is devoted to his craft and has no malice in his soul. He loves cars and ought to have his own one-man show
- George; the most "officerish" looking guy you'll ever meet, with a wicked sense of humour and a strong educational background on top
- Steve Poulson; the epitome of a professional supporting artist, really an actor, and raising his daughter on his own (for which I could have no higher respect)
- Will; a young, nice looking lad who brings his book to set and has a keen eye for detail, as well as for the sheer lunacy of our situation
- Joe Crook; our weapons expert who loves his guns, and who volunteers for everything without complaint. He's previously been CCF and is more competent than many who claim to be ex-Mil
- Bill; a moustachioed young man, again with a good sense of humour and a good touch on our runs; he knows his way and stays out the way of others
- And a load of others I've yet to meet

We are all about to leave the trench and run the gauntlet of No Man's Land.

Frankly speaking, I'm more than a little unnerved by the whole situation. I climb the ladder next to Joe's while Ali holds it fast, both of us screaming our war cries.

I get over the top and watch, as Joe starts running our rehearsed path, which both of us know inside out.

We take off.

We run through Belgian Gates (spiky wooden shit plus barbed wire). And then, unexpectedly, the world explodes.

The SFX and pyro teams have rigged this 65,000 tonne set with explosives, charges, water hits, smoke machines, machine guns firing blanks, and all manner of hellshit.

This is beyond acting.

It's purer than that. This is REacting.

A huge blast goes off to my right, and water and debris fill the sky and rain down on us all.

Another *WHOOOMP* roars to my left, and splits the air with its force, nearly knocking me sideways. The mud is ankle deep, being constantly fed by bowsers of varying sizes.

A third *crack* goes up and water *chooooms* into the air as if geyser-sent, and then falls down on us like tropical rain.

We leg through slush and filth, and then take up firing positions against imaginary Germans.

The heat beneath the uniform makes you sweat almost instantly.

Men scream and yell and run until the airhorn blows, and we reset to do it all over again.

And again.

And *again*.

Joe and Joe Tache and I return from a lunch one day and see that the trench is being filmed and we shouldn't interrupt.

We pick a spot miles away from filming. We take a seat and recline. Joe takes a bite out of his apple, I roll a smoke, and Joe Tache does the same.

We're relaxed as kittens.

Until, with no warning, KABOOOM!!!

A massive blast kicks out from about ten feet away from us, sending a ton of muckshit about thirty feet up in the air. It's like a volcano going off.

Joe's apple is covered in wood chips and clay.

My and Joe Tache's rollups disappear in clouds of ash and crud.

We're all frozen stiff from the shock. We look at each other, all like woodchip / crap covered snowmen. We laugh our arses off, aware that serious injury was only feet away.

Later, Joe and I are given live (real) weapons with eight others.

We repeat the earlier scene, running across No Man's Land, this time cocking our weapons and firing blanks as we go. We have about a hundred safety warnings, since blanks will still cut through inches of cardboard (and skin) if you hit someone at close range.

We run the lines again, cocking and firing our weapons. Michael and I make a good team: we hold the line and yell to each other, constantly making each other aware of our positions. We kick the shiznit out of it.

If you can't get kicks from doing this kind of shit, you really need to go home.

The rain comes down and we watch the director command the field, along with his first AD for whom I now have immortal respect: he's literally leaping into the fray. Adam Sumner is *everywhere*.

He yells, he speaks, he megaphones it. He must be the best in his business.

It's moving to watch. I've never seen someone and heard the precise echo of my own manic energy before.

At the end of the day we're all knackered to oblivion, but we don't care. My feet are shot to shit and my legs feel like I've done the log race again.

But who cares?

This has easily been the most fun day of shooting and the closest you can get to WW1 without owning a tardis.

I get on the coach to go home after picking up my chit (chit sheet = the piece of paper that describes your pay) and I have no complaints other than my feet hurting.

One more month to go, and we're *done*, homies.

And it's all for the experience of working with the World's best, along with the money and the compadreship - and the teeth-grittingly hard toil that makes the planet's finest utter the eternal phrase:

"Good job guys. That's a fine day's work."

It's all going to plan. We even hear the Big S crack a funny, as, during the day's most torrential downpour, he megaphones to the first AD:

"Turn the rain off, please."

It rules. Until I get a message from Rooster that breaks my heart into a billion shards.

"HOTHouse" was shot over four days. We knew we needed a day, maybe a day and a half of pickups and dropped scenes. This message almost breaks my heart. I'm too knackered-vulnerable to hack this.

There was some kind of technical issue with the memory card for Day Four. Day Four being the day we shot a shitload, including the main party scene.

298

This technical problem is significant. It means we have lost *all* the footage for Day Four.

I have had an amazing day. And I was looking forward to a great sleep on the coach back.

Now we have to reshoot for three days, which is only one day shorter than the initial shoot.

I clench my teeth.

I ball my hands into fists.

I hear people celebrating around me.

I want to smash the bus to pieces.

I don't know how much more of this I can handle.

I wish to nuke the world and pour oil into the oceans.

I want to take the axe to every rainforest on earth.

I want to chew magma, I'm that angry.

"HOTHouse" is in trouble. And I have nothing left in the tank.

Which means we are in trouble.

Which means I am in trouble.

I eventually fall asleep on the coach, but I recall that my dreams that night were dark and cruel.

QUARTER FOUR
AUTUMN LEAVES – WINTER COMES

RIS, TAHIRA, AND LOX OF HOTHOUSE

**STEPHEN DIRECTS "GOINS 'THE LOINS'
MACFARLANE" AND "SMELLFOX"**

OCTOBER 2010:

"THE HORSE OF WAR"

"Walk in the spot and I timed it well,
Tell the door girl "Girl, I'm fine as Hell!"
And if you got no dough, and you hate being broke,
Raise up them glasses of H2O!"

- Talent -
"Klap"

- IMMORTALENTED 2013 -

October begins as September ended.

I do Friday on "War Horse" and am battered to the brink.

I have worked six days solid on this, plus a day on "HOTHouse," a rehearsal day on "War Horse," and prior to that, nineteen days straight on "HOTHouse."

The notion of a weekend off has me salivating.

Today is Friday.

The weather forecast is so bad the weathermen didn't even bother with multiple-word descriptions. Most came out yesterday, pointed at the map with "Friday" on it, and either just said "bollocks" or started making 'wank' signs in the air.

The day is brutal.

To start with, I almost miss the fecking bus, which doesn't help.

Then I don't get my hour sleep-catch-up on the bus. And then the sky opens.

The rain is constant. It varies between 'medium drizzle' and 'Bahamian Monsoon season on speed,' but it's constant.

The "War Horse" no-man's-land has become almost a square kilometre of pure shit.

Mud is mixed in with clay, soil, peat, filth, and massive pools of water. Shell-holes dot the landscape and huge plumes of smoke choke the sky.

302

All the eye takes in is a ceiling painted with a near infinite pallette of greys, and a floorspace of innumerate browns, mixed in with yellow clay scars and steel coloured pools of water.

Belgian gates stand guard in front of the trench, and upturned carts burn brazenly beneath the blanket of rain.

"Shitting hell. You know what time it is?" I ask Alistair.

"It's Cock O'Clock," he replies, grimly.

Fuck *yes* it is.

We're on set at eight after being awake four hours already.

Our schedule for the day is pretty simple. *See all that mud and shit, lads? Just leg through it and yer done. Piece of piss.*

I get soaked.

I get cold.

So much so that costume girls walk up and beg me to get myself a cup of tea.

I'm lying face down in the wet mud, playing dead.

Now I'm a "water-runner," legging it for take after take through nad-deep water to jump and land in shin-deep *shhhluurrpp* mud.

For those not on the in, *shhhluurrpp* mud is the kind you put your foot on and realise your leg has disappeared up to your thigh.

To retrieve your boot, your foot, or your dignity, you have to grab hold of something solid that's nearby (like a tree stump, or a small hotel) and *shhhluurrpp* your way out to the soundtrack of that bog-sucking sound we all remember from primary school trips to the middle of futtnuck bowhere.

I'm getting on better with the ADs and some other staff, minus the minor fall-flat-on-my-face-in-the-mud incident from the day prior.

In fact, today the weather can throw whatever shit it likes at me.

I've had a 'perspective moment' or epiphany of late, and it has brought me much calm and peace. It's more accurate actually to say a cluster of epiphanies, since there were several.

But we'll get to that.

When we wrap, I realise I am content.

Today has been a thoroughly demanding experience that has brought out some of my best, and is itself best termed "a good day's work."

I find immense satisfaction in that. I feel good.

The "War Horse" experience is teaching me a lot. And it's bringing me all kinds of new information.

On the way home Al and I talk a lot about family.

We speak of his parents and my parents. I realise I feel a little parentsick. I haven't seen them in what feels like an age.

I shall have to make sure we speak on the weekend.

"You ought to be in a mental institution with your background..." Ali says.

My body is shattered to shit, but my mind is sharp.

I can feel my form overcoming the bitch of a cold I picked up from "HOTHouse." I can handle whatever Spielberg throws at me. I'm close to having my own TV pilot and my own album, as well as my own book and T-shirt line.

I've got maybe one more year that I can survive like this. Maybe.

As always, I'm going to give it hell.

Oh yeah, the epiphanies.

Right. Sorry.

Nearly forgot.

The first:

So I'm onset, and I'm talking to AD Tom Edmonson. Tom is a rarity - he's an AD that doesn't feel the need to shout or yell much, due to his ability to command respect and obedience without doing so.

He and I talk for about half an hour about how he got in the business, what films he's done, and the industry in general.

I ask him what he did before, and am stunned to hear him say he worked in the City.

"So did I..." I respond quietly.

I ask him why he left, and his response sounds like someone else looking into my mind or chest and reading off what they saw there.

The phrases "good money" and "but I was just unhappy" and "felt I needed something more" are all unsurprisingly paramount in his description.

A penny drops in my head.

The interesting thing is, this penny's already dropped. It dropped years ago.

It's just now it is REdropping.

I have backups. I can do other shit. I can return to the City if I so need.

But truth be told, I'm not stupid enough to think that money is everything. And I'm not stupid enough to think it's nothing. It's just another 'something.'

And it's not as important as looking in the mirror and knowing whatever it is you need to know.

We have one life. I'll not waste mine doing anything I regard as a waste of it. I have, or will have, children to make proud. And that's not good enough for them.

I walked down the trench, pondering this repiphany.

"Cut."

"Reset."

I walk back down the trench and turn to Tom, thanking him for the time he's taken to explain these things to me in greater detail than I had them before.

As I finish my sentence, my boot catches on the wooden walkway, and I comedy-slo-mo – *oh Jesus no* –slowlyfirst – thenquickernext – face-pancake my ass into the wooden pallet and the wet, sodden, muddy floor.

I raise myself up, one big fleshy bag of simmering evil (entirely at myself), which is then broken by the sound of Ali laughing his hind legs off, and Cookie, Pete Russ, Declan and Mike applauding and giving me the judges' scores for twattishness.

I light a rollup.

"Fuck off."

This would be the perfect retort: simple, sharp, to the point.

Were it not for the fact that as I say it, the words send my rolled-four-seconds-ago-and-lit-even-more-recently rollup careening through the air into a gloop of wet mud.

The sound of laughter echoes down the trench as now every man within fifteen feet of me pisses themselves.

You're not gonna believe it. I actually have a day *off*.

And not one, in fact, but two.

It's like Christmas.

Rooster is trying to fix the technical hitch we now have with "HOTHouse," and I'm busy trying to recuperate enough to be in one piece for yet *another* week of filming on "War Horse."

I'm pretty sure I'm sailing close to the wind on this, and burning the candle at both ends whilst napalming the middle.

My nan would *not* be impressed. And rightly so.

As it is, I end up (on my frickin' day off) proofing "HOTHouse" stills, and making plans with Rooster about correcting this bitch of a technical hitch.

Merlin comes round with his sister Aicha and we have a beer and relax.

I'm so grateful for any time off I get that you wouldn't believe it.

I manage to spend most of the day on the couch, and am very grateful to do so.

Back to work in the morning.

Which means up at four.

Leave at four-twenty am.

Get the coach at five am.

Get to nuttbuck fowhere at six am.

Breakfast till six-thirty am.

Costume and wardrobe to change into ten layers of 1917 British military clothing at 06:30am until 07:00am.

Hair and makeup till 07:30 or 08:00am.

On set at about 08:30 am.

And then running, jumping, climbing, shooting, legging through mud and clay and shit and waist-deep water and take after take after take after take till about 20:00pm.

Sign your chit sheet.

On the coach around 20:30pm.

Back to Euston for about 21:30pm.

Tube.

Am nearly dying at this point.

Home in the door round 22:30 to 23:00pm.

Collapse.

God, I love this job.

;)

Rooster sends me a link to my IMDB page.

It's right there in front of me: revealing that I've been in "Morning Tea" the feature and "War of the Sexes" the short (soon to be a TV pilot).

My other films are going up there soon. It's like a final nail in the coffin of doubt.

Look me up on Reverbnation and it'll tell you I'm a rapper and singer.

Look me up on Myspace and it'll tell you I'm a creative and an artist.

Look me up on IMDB, schniggles, and it'll tell you I'm an actor.

Damn. *Right.*

I feel pride very rarely: mostly because, well, I'm too busy kicking my own ass for my mistakes to give myself pats on the back.

Still.

At this precise moment I feel a twinge that is something akin to pride.

When all my credits are on there it'll go a little something like this:

- "Thou Art Sick" - short (lead)
- "One Way Street" - short (lead)
- "Everyman" - music video (lead)
- "Chameleon" - music video
- "Talent 2008" - documentary (lead)
- "BTX "- rockumentary (lead)
- EMAs 2009 - documentary (lead)
- "Morning Tea" - feature (lead)
- "Solito" - feature
- "Debt Collectors" - short (lead)
- "War of the Sexes" - short (lead)
- "Radio London" - feature (lead)
- "War Horse" - feature
- "ImmorTalented" - album (lead)

- "HOTHouse" - TV (lead)
- Plus 9 commercials

And that to my mind, for eight months of work, ain't looking bad.

I'm building a decent foundation as an actor, writer, director and musician.

And this is all I seek.

By the end of this year I'll have survived one annum working in entertainment.

Again, I find no small measure of pride in this.

All in all, it could have been a *lot* worse.

And, as sure as rain, bad news plummets like a depth charge into my waters.

The technical issue on "HOTHouse" is not fixable.

We have to reshoot all of Day Four. That means that we now need a three-day shoot and I am just disembowelled.

It feels like the straw that broke the camel's back.

You can heave all the weight you want up a mountain, but when someone asks you to walk twenty steps back that you've already taken, it's almost too much.

I'd drop the whole fucking thing if I were a less responsible man.

But I can't.

Rooster and "HOTHouse" depend on us.

This. Is going.

To *kill* me.

I spend the day trudging through mud and shit, my body close to giving up on me, and my mind even closer.

I try to be a pillar of strength as much as I can, but right now I've had enough.

"HOTHouse" is in trouble.

Rooster needs another job, pronto. I'm physically exhausted. I haven't seen my family in forever, and things just feel as if they are slipping away from me. The day on the feature is soul draining. I have little in the way of fight left.

Fuck this. *Fuck* this.

Fuck this all the way home.

Heh. Feeling sorry for yourself, maggot? Good. Excellent.

Perfecto allstars.

While you're like this, have a think about Mandy, Jahira, Lulu, and all the women you have hurt.

Think on the pain you have caused those you love.

Think on the awards you failed to win.

Think on the chances you have missed.

Think on the money you have squandered.

Think on the lies you have told and think on your aborted children.

Think on your bullshit philosophy and think on those you could not help.

Think on your wasted time, your lack of wife and child.

Think on your crippled body, and your weakling mind.

Think on your nightmares made real.

Think on those you have betrayed and left.

Think on those who look up at you looking down at you in the gutter.

Think on your loved ones marrying other men; bearing their children, and the suffering you inflicted on them.

Think on your fear, you insufferable coward.

Think on it until it chokes you dry.

Think on the mountain still before you and think on how far you are from its peak.

Think on what it will cost you for every step, knowing I am here to drag you down.

Think on your sorrow, and wallow in it.

Think on the family you never met you God-cursed irretrievable mistake.

Think on the difference you could have made and the meaninglessness you now possess.

Think on all this.

As I rejoice and **revel** *in it...*

I'm in darkness.
I walk around the set like a zombie.
I'm a punch-drunk boxer in the 12th round, and I'm losing on points and am to be struck unconscious.
Lost.
The word is *lost…*

Self-love is not selfishness.

Selfishness has been made into a bad word.

It is now understood as "self-obsession to the point of neglecting others" or "over-self-prioritisation."

Self-love is one of the most important characteristics of successful, rounded, complete people.

It is critical for a healthy mindset. The only possible alternatives to self-love (in case you doubt these words) are self-indifference and self-hate.

Neither of which have any great merit.

Self-love is the love you have for your Self - as an individual and as a part of the Universal Entity.

It is as necessary as breathing and is like nourishment for the spirit.

Self-hate, self-loathing, self-detesting, self-disgust, however, of which I have plenty at time of press, are not.

It's our band of brothers on "War Horse" who bring me back to my senses.

I'm having a soul-destroying day, walking up and down the same hill over and over again.

My misery is a weight I cannot shift. I'm in pain, mindlessly bored, and overwhelmed by my own failure, along with the Doc's voice inside my mind.

It's Nicky "Trig" Tregenza, Corporal Adamski and D.I. Kev Crouch who start my rehabilitation.

I vaguely come to in the middle of a conversation they're having about what films they've been in.

I'm not sure, but I think I haven't actually spoken to a single human being in about three days.

Amazingly they rack up an astounding number of box-office smash pictures, including but not limited to, "The Dark Knight," "Batman Begins," "Elizabeth," "To Kill A King," and loads more.

Nicky T takes our names in the morning for the bus and is so cool that once, when Fate threatened to make me miss the coach to set, he was kind enough to delay it 5 minutes so that I had a chance to make it.

He now works in VFX and as an actor. Kev spent years in the Air Force before taking the daring step into full-time filmmaking.

I listen to them talk.

It feels rejuvenating.

I remember that I am not dying of poverty or hunger in any one of all the many countries that have such drastic, imperative problems to deal with.

My mind begins to emerge from the depths.

Kev "Water-Runner" Hudson shows me a letter he scribbled the day before.

He penned a fictional letter from a German man to the love of his life, a prostitute, telling her how he cannot wait to see her again.

It's intended to be both funny and emotive at the same time, and I am moved to see someone other than myself using his or her time between takes productively, and it also makes me laugh my ass off.

It goes like this:

KEV HUDSON LETTER ON "WAR HORSE"

"Letter to a Lover

Via: Frau Shiessehausse's Pleasure Emporium

My Dearest Fraulein Pumpernickel,

Oh, how I look forward to the day when this senseless war will be over and I can be in the warm submissiveness of your flabby arms once more.

I remember with fond anxiety how we'd visit that quiet little Dockside Tavern in Hamburg, and I would anoint my little schnitzel in the sticky, sweet juices of your opulent strudel.

Oh my divine one, I am becoming quite hardened... in my resolve to see this situation through to its inevitable and messy climax.

I cannot help but harken back to the first time I felt your warm tender lips upon my cheek on that summer's day when we picnicked by the lake.

How kind you were to suck out the poison from the bee sting on my taut rosy buttock. 'Twas sweet bliss, my feckless little mattress-bouncer.

Until we meet again,

Your devoted Hans Uberfiddler, France"

Later it is Alistair Reith, James Taylor and Benos Noble who manage to cheer my mood.

We've discussed on many occasions the idea of a comedy sketch show based around extras on a movie set, featuring scenes and ideas and characters we encounter every day at work.

Ali and Benos have come up with two new ones.

First up is the Shaolin AD (assistant director) - a film professional taught in Tibetan monasteries, where they study the holy arts of martial ADing in kung fu stances, using walkie talkies like katana swords, chucking chit sheets out like shuriken, chant-reciting "cut... reset... stand by..." monk-like, as in Ace Ventura in "Call of Nature."

Al has also come up with a diamond: 'slanking;' otherwise known as sleep-wanking.

This is like sleep walking except, well, you get the idea.

The idea is so funny I am bent double with laughter. I rise above the depths and come within sight of the surface.

I'm even able to cope with some piss taking about me being late the other day and having to pay a fucking £69.00 cab fare after I missed the bus.

I said *some*.

Later still I have a laugh and a joke with James Taylor.

He's a young actor full of promise, with a true salt-of-the-Earth sincerity to him.

He works as an actor and also runs his own furniture business whilst also raising his young son.

I know from experience that working three jobs is hard, and am again inspired by James's commitment and dedication.

There are many who consider the world of Cinemusic, and film especially, to be all glitz and glam, to be all wrapping and no present.

Many consider London herself to be the same: a bizarre circus in the South of the Country that only serves to confuse those in the Midlands or up North.

Hear the truth now from an industry insider - to people who share the above beliefs, you are *mistaken*.

The industry and the City herself are made up of men who deliver furniture, of stuntmen who have to be set alight or wrestle horses to the ground on a daily basis.

They're made up of former RAF airmen and TA soldiers, of ADs who previously worked in the city and found they hated it.

They're made up of barmen who have what are to them, greater aspirations, and of sixteen-year-old youngsters with asthma who are made to run uphill away from cavalry or through trenches for sixteen hours a day on as little as three hours sleep.

They're made up of policemen, firemen, writers, teachers, builders, brickies, and people who are not afraid of a hard day's graft. What you see is a global superstar in a movie directed by a global superstar.

What you *don't* see is the literally *hundreds* of people who woke up at three every morning and worked in the rain and the cold and the shit and the frost and the dark and the wet for longer hours than almost any other job, just to entertain the rest of us for two hours.

So.

Have a little respect.

And put things into perspective.

Stephen, that applies to you too, son.

Ok, so we have to shoot three more days on "HOTHouse."

Fair enough. Then that is what we shall do. I'll go into maniac detail on the storyboard and tighten the shoot up so much that it's even more airtight than it was before.

And no matter what - no matter how well or badly the rest of the year goes, I should remember my own advice.

Which is to bear in mind that I'll survive it. The world won't end if things go wrong.

Suddenly a ray of light creeps in through the clouds of my self-pity, and I realise I have spent enough time mourning.

Onward and upward, as the good book says.

So once again, it is my "War Horse" brethren who undrown me.

I'm having perhaps the easiest day's work I've ever had.

For some reason we have been called to set, gone to costume and wardrobe, gone to makeup, gone to the armoury, gone to set, been brought back from set to HQ, and been asked to sit in the sun for hours while we drink tea and eat food.

This kind of gig, I can *handle*.

I spend about two hours of my day listening to Benos Noble's story, which involves working his way up in retail, to relocating to Australia, to marrying a woman, to making his own movies, to martial arts, to returning to London, to working for his stuntman course.

I see a video; I shit you not, of him dressed as Batman, leaping out of a plane and diving through the air. I also see a video of his previous girl. She is dressed as Wonder Woman.

I nearly laugh from sheer love of life.

When I tell you the story is epic, I mean it is *epic*.

The man is thirty-three.

I spend the day in costume with a face full of mud and shit, relaxing in the sun.

This is entirely new ground for me. If I earn money but don't graft my nads off, something must be wrong. Yet it isn't.

The sun is shining brightly. The sky is a postcard pallette of blues and greys.

We have lunch.

We discuss all manner of things, whilst waiting for an AD to tell us we are needed on set.

I spend a good deal of time with Alex Gatehouse - a wonderfully English man with a 'tache the size of Peckham. He has some kind of gas cape he's been given by costume and we're all in stitches because he looks like a WW1 superhero.

He's also disarmingly polite - there's not a malicious bone in his body, and we discuss the nature of fidelity and single versus multiple relationships.

To my pleasant surprise, he is non-judgemental, and listens to my polyamorous views without condemnation.

The day snails by.

Eventually, sun-drenched and dehydrated, we all board the coach and get ready to head home.

I have somehow been nominated the designated war-mongerer for all extras and have to wage a minor war to ensure myself, Ali,

Kev and a few others are recompensed for the previous day's activities, which involved standing knee to waist deep in muckwater and shiquid (liquid made of, well, you can guess, can't you?) for over an hour and thereby having one's socks and boots filled with naturecrap.

When we finally arrive back in my City, we've all either snoozed or watched "Demolition Man" on the coach.

I am yet again reminded of the importance of this business. It is the land of dreams.

We've just all also received a text from our agent informing us we are not required for tomorrow.

I'm close to ecstasy.

A three-day weekend? Are you *shitting* me?

I'll take that with both hands.

Finally I find myself at a pub with Nicky T and Ali.

We're working our way through five pints apiece and really just decompressing from the week.

I listen to Ali talk about an idea he's had for a Shakespeare run during the Olympics. I listen to Nicky Trig talk of a fantastic job opportunity that may be coming his way after nearly a decade of hard graft.

I realise yet again how lucky I am just to be sat at this table.

I thank whatever stars I was born under for such an opportunity.

I mostly keep my mouth shut during the encounter. It is a pleasure just to listen. The sheer act revitalises me. It gives energy to my blood.

I behold two of my newest friends discussing such things that I would never have thought imaginable, and I consider myself a lottery winner.

If my life is to be made of such moments, I shall be thankful foreverafter.

Speaking of which, I've just cleaned the house and taken the trash out.

Cathartic, that.

And I'm now on the way after a day of shooting (a week of shooting, bellend... need *sleep*...) to my best friend's music video shoot.

Am I going because I want to be in it? No, I'd love to have been, but time wasn't going to allow that.

I'd rather go for five minutes than not at all.

Showing your support for your crew is no small thing. I'm not just a Lifeaholic, homenugget. I'm a flag-waving, card-carrying advocate of Lifeaholism *full stop*. And if my boy is at a nightclub filming his video and he wants me there, then I'm there, no matter *what*.

When I get home, we're back to room cleaning, storyboard drawing, and a workout. The body has to stay fit and supple despite the abuses we pile upon it. So it's a workout tonight, the gym tomorrow, and calorie counting.

The 'glamorous' life of a raptor (rapper and actor... minor issue... how do we incorporate 'director' and 'writer' and 'escort' into that word? Hmm. Answers on a postcard...)

Diwraptercort?

Nah. Too long-winded.

Raptorcort isn't bad though. But 'isn't bad' doesn't cut it in our World, schniggles.

Never has.

Never will.

I stare in sheer disbelief.

I cannot believe what I've just heard.

I'm leaving in thirty minutes back on the feature to head to slupduck gowhere and the news Rooster has just delivered has spinning-bird-kicked me into a cocked hat.

I may need a sit down. *Shit*. I'm already sat down.

Hammock, anyone?

"You've got two new features just come in, and Liam Heath (our Behind The Scenes guy on HH) is on "Pirates Four"? And you've got *who* for a day on your current film? For a grand? Are you *crazy*???"

My words are, on occasion, less than eloquent.

I don't idolise people, as a rule.

I mean my mum and my Nan are deified to me and have my full idolisation and worship.

But other people? Muggles?

Nah.

In the film world, however, I reserve the right not to be starstruck but to be as complimentary as I like.

And, if you've been in "Layer Cake," been a Shakespearean actor, been a Hollywood Star, *and* you've been knighted???

Then first up you're a bit of a ledge (legend) and second you're doing just fine, thank you very much.

Somehow, Rooster has procured or is in the process of procuring the services of one Sir Michael Gambon for his latest picture.

And for a very impressive sum indeed. I've never bribed anyone in my life - but I'm considering it now to meet the gangsterrific legend that is Sir Michael Gambon.

And what am I off to do? Run around in the mud and the shit for another week.

Sometimes life just ain't fair.

It's my first ever night shoot.

I'm back onset and the bad news is today we don't have a coach; we have two minibuses.

That's not cool.

Our hours are now bizarre city. We get on the coach for 14:30pm to leave for 14:45pm. We then get changed to get onset for 16:00pm to 16:30pm.

We're then working till about 04:00am in the morning.

We get home around six am or seven to sleep till about midday.

Then we're up to get the minibuses again.

On a positive note, we're headed this week to the hospital scene, where, rumour has it; we're lying in bed being attended to by nurses.

The idea alone brings a smile to my face.

I feel better after scripting new original storyboards for "HOTHouse."

We need a three-day shoot but my head is slowly coming round to the idea. Bottom line?

We have to do what we have to do.

End of story.

It's nice out here.

Nighttime in the trenches must have been more peaceful than the day.

At least, when they weren't being shelled to all hell it might have been.

It'd be better yet if I didn't feel a bit dodgy after lunch, breakfast *and* dinner.

And better still if I wasn't listening to Alistair Reith, Kev Hudson and Adam informing me of something so horrific I can barely believe my ears.

"I'm telling you," one begins, "they have to do it in "Joseph" the stage play."

I look at him. His gaze is inscrutable.

I look at him some more. This can *not* be right. He changes not a jot and worse still, continues.

"Right, they use a live donkey in the stage performance of Joseph. So they have to."

"Joseph as in And His Technicolor Dream Coat?" asks I.

"Yeah. They can't have the donkey walk out in front of the kids with a hard-on, so she tosses him off before he goes onstage."

I look at him. This is clearly deception of the foulest kind.

I inform him thus.

"No. Tellin' you. I *met* her."

I laugh this off as bollocks. Until Adam jumps in, telling me, "At a stud farm, they bring the lass in to get the stallions aroused, in the mood like, and they can't let all that sperm go tae waste, so someone has tae, y'know, masturbate them off tae climax."

I'm clusterboggled by this.

This is a Biblical revelation, and I refuse to believe it. Cause there's no *way* I'm believing that.

"You're telling me, around the country, and possibly the planet, there are people whose job it is, whose actual fucking *job* it is, to wank off a horse...?"

Alistair and Adam remain stony faced. Kev pipes up:

"Yeah," he grins. "Animal wankers."
I blink.
I start to speak.
I stop.
I leave.

Same day and I listen to Benos, James Taylor, and Norm having a discussion regarding their personal beliefs.

It's a nightshoot, so all our body clocks are off.

Despite this, I can't quite believe what I am hearing.

James Taylor believes in: aliens, black magic, God, the Devil, an afterlife, Heaven, Hell, Jesus of Nazareth, but not angels and not some other shit.

Benos believes in: an afterlife, immortality, ghosts, God (but not the biblical kind), angels, and the Bermuda Triangle, *and* the Double Slit Experiment. When defending his belief in ghosts, Benos informs us that he's closed a deal with his gran that if they do exist, she'll come let him know after clog-popping day.

James Taylor can't handle this information.

"Jesus Christ... how the fuck'd that come up? *Hey Gran, will you come visit us after you've passed? Oh and do us a favour, pass the brussel sprouts...*"

This has me literally crying with laughter. Sometimes it's just too much.

Norm believes in numerology, and that we're all off our loon. I'm inclined to agree, and enjoying the shit out of the conversation.

See, belief and knowledge are extremely important to me.

Knowledge isn't really arguable. Facts are facts, i.e. the capital of France is Paris.

And no I don't care if you want to argue the toss. The capital of England is London.

Now fuck *off.*

Belief, on the other hand, due to the in-built presence of doubt, is all too contestable.

"The world was created in seven days by a bloke with a beard."

"No, it was knocked out by Amun-Ra and his right hand, to which he was married."

"Heh. Both wrong... it was burped out by Flooglemump the Spaghetti Monster."

See, if the tools of "proof," "evidence" and "logic" are thrown out the window, then you can make up any claptrap you like.

Tell enough people, either by sharpness of tongue or blade, throw in some wine and a few virgins, and you got yourself a party.

Or the makings of a religion.

And I'm not anti-religion.

The belief systems of the world give people hope and sustenance, and do some of the best humanitarian and charity work on the planet.

I just think they've all got lazy. They've sat on their laurels, claiming their One book and their One Path is the Only True One and that all other sinful, evil, smarter alternatives lead you to an eternity of barbecue.

Yeah.

Right.

We know more now about the universe than we ever have.

Religion is not a tool designed to correct or impede science.

It is there as a method of reverence, thanks, worship, and reflection on subjects that fall beyond science's current reach.

The whole "What happened before the Big Bang?" question being an ideal example.

Science is the law of the universe.

Religion should be the interpretation and philosophy of those laws. Not some mythical set of characters designed to frighten children.

And above *all*, absolutely *above all*, having different religions divides people.

There is only one 'science.' Biology, chemistry, physics, quantum mechanics and cosmology are all sub-categories of science.

Scientists may disagree over particular facts, but they rarely declare war over it and they still tend to agree on the methods.

I'd like to see religions of the world do the same thing.

It is not offensive to state that there is more practically useful information and more information *period* on the internet (the Book of Man) than there is in the Bible (the Book of Man's God).

This is simply Truth.

And I'd also like to see those people who decry religious fanaticism (Dawkins) cease being quite so retardedly dismissive of the World's belief systems, and in such a fanatical way.

The lunacy of the definite statement "there is a God" is only matched by the lunacy in the definite statement "there is no God."

Common sense response: how the *fuck* do you know?

Honest reply: you don't.

End of story.

I'll deal with this at much greater length in my foundation work on a new belief system that is heavily based on scientific enquiry and quantum mechanics, a system called "Selfism."

However.

That's another story.

Suffice to say I revel in hearing the many weird and wonderful things people do and do not choose to believe in. I used to be a venomous critic of religious belief.

Now, when I hear James tell me he believes in both God and aliens, and that he worries this may technically be a touch hypocritical, we both laugh our asses off and I sympathise.

God bless my race.

(If He exists, like...)

My eyes snap open.

I'm on the catering bus.

My stomach growls.

I feel a bowel twitch.

My friends on set nod a "Mornin', soldier" at me.

I realise I have to go to the toilet this precise second.

Not in ten minutes, not in five minutes, but in about thirty seconds flat or I am going to have a serious issue.

Whatever the food issue was, it's just hit. Damn *sandwiches*.

Ali said they were dodgy. There are twenty guys around me. Oh Jesus *Lord* this is going to be bad.

I manage to get to my feet and start exiting the bus without shitting myself.

Mostly thanks to luck, not to me.

I manage to conceal the fact I am stagger-walking and just about, with gritted teeth, get step by painful step out to head to the portacabins.

Fucking *lunch*.

With every step I am praying to whatever Gods exist that I do not shit my own pants.

There are 200+ men on set. I do not wish to be the one poor sod known for soiling himself cause he can't handle his fucking *food*.

My anal nerve is tweaking so bad it's like when you're that drunk that vomitting isn't a matter of *if*, it's a matter of when, where, and how.

The involuntary spasms have already started; you're now just playing a game called 'beat the clock.'

In a nutshell, the toilets look fucking *miles* away.

I can already feel myself sweating. My body is pushing ill materials out by any means necessary. In seconds I'm sure I'll be crying and I'll probably have a nosebleed, the effort to hold the airlock shut is *that* immense.

It's my own fault, karma-wise.

What kind of madman invents a phrase like 'crumping', (which means 'crydumping,' which is when you are both crying from the effort of not shitting and yet shitting at the same time)? What kind of madman?

I thank you.

I manage to reach the toilet steps and am hearing those revolting, strangled, miniature-trumpet arse-sounds that are driving me insane.

The words 'wet' and 'strain' and 'tributary' keep protruding into my mind. I can no longer walk properly. My legs are tremble-spasming.

Both toilets are engaged.

Oh Mary Mother of God do not desert me now…

My knees begin trembling. The urge is now turning from an urge into an actual event.

By the power of prayer a tech guy exits cubicle two. He looks me in the eye, deadpan, with a slightly regret-filled and perhaps piteous look to him, and then passes me with an innocent-as-you-like, "Alright, mate."

"Nrrflmpp."

I lurch uncertainly into the cubicle, the moment of truth approaching at speed.

My gluteus muscles are quaking.

Before I'm even *in* the cubicle, a smell so powerful, an odour so pungent, a scent so overwhelmingly *unpalatable* molests my sense of smell like a polar bear sexually assaulting a squirrel. My eyes are now streaming and I am almost choking on someone else's plug-fumes.

I now understand the look on the tech-guy's face. It read: *good fucking luck.*

I retch whilst screwing my tradesman's so tight that a vein stands out on my head.

And as always, once you get near excretory facilities, the body kicks into autopilot.

The ejector button has been hit more forcefully and I am now near to weeping, whilst simultaneously trying not to due to the additional difficulty it adds to restraining my shitfactory.

Occasional bouts of laughter punctuate my torment as I imagine what the lads would think if they beheld my ludicrous position.

My teeth are almost chattering when a death-knell sounds. I actually shed a tear because of what I now see.

One of the costume and wardrobe people, in a vengefully cruel act, has tied my respirator bag all the way round my jacket and under my webbing and then quintuple knotted it.

Ordinarily, you'd just drop trou and all's good.

But my trousers have braces. The braces are under my jacket. The jacket is under my webbing. The webbing is under my respirator, which is motherfucking quintuple sailor soldier Boy Scout fuck-knotted around the rest of this clustermonging outfit...

"Oh Lord above pleasepleasepleaseplease..."

More butt-trumpetry. This time with a word that sends terror down my spine.

Wetness.

It's decision time, folks.

I'm now leant up against the sidewall of the cubicle and sweat is drenching me.

My mind calculates: which is worse? Shit yourself and have to clean your uniform, and have everyone else see and smell it? Fuck that.

Rip the uniform apart and have to explain later? Oh, Jesus, here we *go...*

I throw caution to the wind as I hear an assburp that means it's about to be game *over.*

I start gnashing through the knot with my teeth, slashing at it wildly with my nails, ripping and tearing at the bastard cause of my bastard pain.

A sudden, sharp knock at the door almost has me literally shit myself.

My speed quickens. By some divine miracle the knot releases.

Respirator bag *off.*

Please Lord.

Webbing clatters to the floor.

Knock knock.

FUCK.

OFF.

Jacket off.

Here it comes. Braces down. *Pleasepleaseplease.* I drop trou quicker than man has ever dropped trou.

Boxers down. Time to release the Kraken. I can't believe I am almost home.

It's man versus nature and the victory is...

SWEET JEEEEEEESUUUUUS!!!

I force-splattershit all over the shop.

The sheer intensity has me coughing and clutching at the wall, tears of premature joy running down my face. My spider sense tells me I've just covered the back wall with regurgitated whatever-I-had-for-lunch.

I turn, tentatively, to inspect the devastation.

"Nuh... no... please... not... the uniform... Lord I'll quit drink... women... I'll quit breathing... just help... me... *now*..."

Staggeringly, wonderfully, I've got about 70% in the bog. Give or take.

30 to 50% is now decorating the toilet and the back wall. None is on my uniform. I'm giddy with delight. The place could use air freshening, mind.

What.

The fuck.

Now?

I walk proudly from the cubicle, clean as a whistle and my head held high as a kite.

All in all, it took a little over an hour to let fly the bogs of war and then clean it.

That was an experience I'll not soon look to repeat. I then had to wash and redress myself, and make sure I looked like nothing happened.

I'm so paranoid and distrusting of my bowels that I am wary to even look at food.

Not that I'm embarrassed, you understand.

How ashamed can you be if you write it in a fucking book? No.

It's only that there and then at that precise time, well y'know, it was all a bit much to handle.

One of our lads, Cookie, is in the 501st "Vader's Fist" Stormtrooper Legion.

This is a costume club of 5000 people that is in the Guiness Book of Records for being the biggest costume club in the world.

For "Star Wars," no less.

It is the only one sanctioned by George Lucas himself. The primary member founded it in 1994/5 because his daughter had a brain tumour; it was started for her and turned into a costume group who do events on behalf of different charities across the board. It is entirely non-profit.

Cookie's been in this magnificent group for six years, and has been in the military for eighteen. In the last four years members who were in the military have been deployed on UN duties to Afghanistan.

They lost three members who are servicemen on operational duties overseas.

The names remain withheld out of respect to the families.

Declan, another of our military crew, teaches history and geography, and remains in the army reserves; he's a part-time extra.

He's led the piss-taking: the boys have been giving me a hard time about paying sixty-nine squids for that damned cab the other day.

The lads now give me a present on the day of boredom.

It's a torn out page from the Metro about people missing their transport and having to get tickets for... fuck *off*... *£69.00 to get to their original destination...*

I almost died from laughing today.

Our lad Tim tells me about the phenomenon of people who are headed home pissed from nights out shitting in the street, and advises a group of us how best to spot which turds are animal and which turds are human.

I'm clearly losing it cause I'm laughing so hard I nearly swallow my own tongue.

When he admits to having done it himself, and having wiped with an Argyle sock, I laugh so hard I almost have a heart attack.

Martin Brignall finishes me off describing his fear of getting tapeworm, and vividly recounts how he has heard you solve the problem: this is done by pulling the critters out your mouth, or, your... well, you get the picture.

We may have all become deranged doing this job, but strike me in the knackers and call me Moses, it's funny.

My name is Clifford Sarlock.

I was wounded in the early weeks of this, what they are now calling The Great War.

I am, in all likelihood, destined to meet my maker in due course.

It is fair. I have lived well enough.

The snow across the rooftops is a crisp blanket beneath the dark. The night air is cleansing, like a cool shower.

I lie in the med bay with blood running down my arm. I am bandaged and medicated; yet still I feel the pain.

A bandage round my head confirms what I feared; my ears and lobes have been blown off.

My hearing is unaffected, shockingly, but I look like an Egyptian mummy's nephew.

The snow falls like it is meant to. The white glitters in the night and the cobbled streets of the estate are wet underfoot, and as I walk from the med bay I feel the cold keenly.

A fire in an oil drum warms my shoulder as I pass it. My fellow warriors sit hunched beneath the doorframes and on crates. They have a worn, beaten look to them. The cold creeps beneath their uniforms and into their bones, as it does to mine.

Snow crunches underfoot.

The smell of brew draws me to a particular tent.

Inside I see a beautiful woman. She has blonde hair. She tells me her name is Nicola Matthews, and that she has heard I am a writer.

"Is it true? Are you?"

I nod, although with my arm out of action, it'll be some time before I write again. That's if I survive the impending gangrene.

She strokes the side of my head, looking at the place where hearing tools ought to be.

"Then I have an amazing story for you to write," she says. She has my attention. And not just because of her face. I look at her.

A good woman with a beautiful story? This can only go one way.

She looks at me as if to say, "Will you do it?"

I smirk. Partly because I always do it, and partly, well, because I just can't help myself.

"I'm all ears," says I.

Her laugh is all the payment I need.

Today is the day I worked on a film by the greatest director in the world and the day he walked past me and tapped me on the arm.

Here's to hoping (touch wood) some of the magic is passed on. It reminded me vaguely of the scene in Gladiator. Russell Crowe laughs at Oliver Reed, saying:

"You knew Marcus Aurelius?"

Oliver Reed snaps back.

"I did not say I knew him. I said he touched me on the arm once."

I don't know Steven Spielberg. He touched me on the arm once.

Right before he congratulated me and us for a good week's work.

I was, and am, and always will be, very proud of that.

We sit on the last night shoot.

We've had almost an entire week of doing nothing except hanging around onset. Am I pissed off? No, of course not. I love my job. I love my industry.

Bit by bit I am coming to terms with the fact that I love my life, despite the year's recent and gutsmashing losses.

But, like my father said, security is everything. If you love something, you must protect it. Make sure it has the power to last.

And that is the sixty million dollar question: how to make this a durable state of being.

I shall find a way.

Home.

Thank *God*.

A weekend to recover from a week of night shoots.

It is much needed and much appreciated.

I get in at about six in the morning on Saturday. I'm absolutely shattered.

I walk in the flat.

I chill for about fifteen minutes. I collapse.

I sleep till seven pm Saturday evening.

Man *alive* that feels good.

At some point Merlin and LL come in to try to wake me up, but it's no good. I'm in fuck-off-now-or-die mode, and am not moving.

We go out Saturday night to watch "The Social Network." It's a strong film directed by David Fincher and written by Aaron Sorkin, both of whose work I love.

"Studio 60" and "The West Wing" are both Sorkin's. Aside from being entertaining, "The Social Network" is inspirational - a twenty-six year old building something that comes to be worth twenty-five billion dollars, and that is available entirely free of charge to the entire world.

Genius.

Mark Zuckerberg is now added to the list of the ImmorTalented, along with Neil Armstrong and the rest. I'm sure he couldn't care less, but I could.

I get home after the movie and relax with a joint and a drink.

Merlin keeps me entertained a few hours and I hit the sack round two-ish.

And the rest of the weekend is looking all chill and lovely till I get a message at five am in the morning from BTP, who I didn't even realise was in town.

"I'm at Fabric. It's the tenth anniversary. Come down. *Now*."

Erm, I got news for ya. I'm at home. It's five in the morning. Not leaving.

Ever.

"Stephen..."

After twenty minutes of BTPishness I give up, get ready, and head out to Fabric.

I have no idea why except I want to see BTP and I rarely get the chance to do so. Haven't seen her since Ibiza and my birthday.

Plus, being frank, a week of nightshoots has left me itching for a bit of fun, and Fabric is nothing if not that.

After the week in Spain we messaged each other, and it seemed to both of us like we had unfinished business.

BTP and I kind of dated when I first went to uni.

We'd've been going out, I reckon, save we were both young and had a bit too much, well, playing the field to do.

Plus we both had trust issues; meaning I didn't trust her and she didn't trust me.

"You're a player," I'd be told.

"Pot? This is the kettle," I'd respond. "You're black."

So in a nutshell it never really happened. At least not properly.

To give you a bit more info on BTP: her face means she's a knockout, and she is absolute royalty as far as our crew is concerned.

She provided medicinal services on the KMN-ID tour, got Merlin roof-trollied more than I've ever seen him, and has made her way through Snoops Petrelli, LL, Tobias G, BlitzShorty and myself.

She's also best friends with Shanghai, who introduced me to her in the first place.

This is vitally important: my level of trust for Shanghai is second to none.

Don't get me wrong, the girl isn't flawless, but she'd do things for me and tell me truth when probably no one else living would. Her word is law.

BTP herself was also formerly a snowboarding instructor and loves the mountains and the snow; she has modelled and quit it due to it being 'too boring' (remind you of anyone?), has lived in more countries than I've even been to, is about to hit thirty, is on the verge of running her own business, is multi-lingual, is equally at home in a top class restaurant and a warehouse-turned underground house club, and is so loyal that once when a girl back at school was bullying our beloved Shanghai, she smacked her so hard in the face she broke her jaw and put her in hospital.

She was also instrumental in making my thirtiethth birthday what it was.

This, ladies and germs, is my kind of woman.

And what's my kind of woman?

Oh, you mean the wom*en*?

Oh.

OK.

I see.

Hmmm.

I think we'd better avoid overall numbers (for my sanity) [and reputation] {are you fucking *kidding*?} and the whole "they weren't around for long" contributors, and just focus on those who played lead roles in the madness of my life.

I was at primary school (Junior High) when I first 'went out' with someone.

I had two girlfriends simultaneously who were actually good friends with each other; Haley Ryan and Bethany Parr.

Of course, this was the young, actually-means-nothing kind of going out, but they are probably the first that ought to be entered into the books. They also handily display the kind of thinking I'd employ later.

The first of the real ones was Lucia (five months).

She was my first true foray into the world of women, and due to my lack of any real experience, I completely fucked it up.

It was not consummated, which I think was actually something that, given the circumstances, she'd be glad to reflect on. She was a good girl and was probably far too kind for me to be inflicted upon her at so young an age.

There was Silver (English - one year), a redhead beauty of a secondary school girlfriend who I was head over heels in love with. Lads of the world take note: first timers will do that to you. She broke my heart and tore me to shreds.

But then again, I deserved it, and it took the putty I was made of and cooked it into steel. I see her every now and again and we stay in touch.

There was Raquelle (English - six months), who was beautiful but didn't last long. I had not yet learned how to cope with women with attitude. For my sins I was punished, and again, this was a degree course in what not to do with women.

Then there was Rhiannon (American - six months), a beautiful dancer from the USA, and complete and utter beauty who I treated abominably and from whom I probably deserve eternal hatred.

In fact, no, from whom I *do* deserve eternal hatred.

There was Jill and Monique (American); sisters from the States who I spent a lot of time with and became good friends with. The issue was, the more we became friends, the more I found myself attracted to both of them. Rumour has it that events transpired which indicate the feeling was mutual, but then rumour can be a bitch.

They were about as loyal and as much fun as two people can be.

Then there was Katrine (English - one year), a tough-as-you-like London girl I met at University who took no shit but gave plenty. She and I remain in touch and have a date still that remains unfulfilled.

Then there was Giana (Greek - six months), a luscious and strong Greek girl who ships half the world to the other half. We fought each other verbally to establish supremacy and are now best friends.

Time will tell if business here remains unfinished.

Then there was Anna Mary (Colombian - three years), a bronze-skinned Latin American beauty with a figure blueprinted to distract your attention. She controls a multinational corporation, is bilingual and does martial arts. Our three years changed me from a teenager to a young man. She is the love of my life, and I would invade planets for her.

She remains my best friend, and is the closest to a female equal I have ever met.

Diana Finn (Turkish / Irish - six months) was a former Miss Turkey and TV star in her own country with the best body I've ever seen, and a true definition of the word "woman." I think I caused her a lot of pain, and I regret this hugely. She was what you call a catch.

She had previously been in a Jackie Chan film and dated a guy from "Black Hawk Down."

Last I heard, she was with Quentin Tarantino.

Katrine (Phillipino / English - six months) is a half-Filipino half-English sculpture of a woman with possibly the most attractive face I've ever seen, with whom I worked with for a while, but again from whom I probably deserve nothing but venom.

There was Marbella Girl (English / Spanish) who I only glimpsed on rare occasions but who nearly made me believe in love at first glance, and is, incontestably, *the* most beautiful woman I have ever seen.

This was my introduction to love at first sight. The phrase 'womanhood' conjures her up in my mind. Emma Mann was, I believe, the name.

There was Anina, (Spanish - one year), a stunning Spaniard girl with a fiery spirit and a gorgeous face. We were deeply in love, and she taught me things I did not even know I could know. I loved her very much. She despises me for the fact that she does not despise me, and recently sent me some pretty impressive hate mail.

I have hopes that we will be friends again. And I have never stopped loving her. Nor will I.

There was Becca Hay (English - six months), a Peppermint Hippo gentleman's club dancer who had been a singer on a popular TV talent show. She loved me more than I deserved, and was the perfect girlfriend.

There was Luckiya (Gibraltan / English - on and off - six months total), a half-Gibraltan girl who was even wilder than me. She's an absolute looker and a *lot* of fun when the sun went to bed. Even if she couldn't ever seem to remember us being together in the first place (that one made me laugh out loud... or perhaps I mean cry...?).

We remain best friends.

There was Rosie Court (English - four months), and you know what? They just do not build women like this as standard. A playboy model and regular lads' mag favourite, we had a very intense few months. She is stunningly beautiful and as down to Earth as a woman can be.

No woman I have met has been sexier.

There was Paula (French - six months): a French rapper, singer and art designer. We spent a very important few months together. I saw her perform live onstage and *still* remember how much it moved me.

She taught me letting go, and fights to this day for a mega-corporation to do the right thing by her.

There was Louise (Lebanese / Liberian - six months) - half-Liberian half-Lebanese model and charity worker, with the joint most beautiful face I've ever seen. She too taught me things I have yet to understand fully, including the art of chilling out sufficiently in order to locate that peace I find so lacking.

There was Natalya (English - six months) - a blonde English girl with a voice to rival Alicia Keys and the body to match. She and I fought a great deal when we were not otherwise engaged.

She was a soldier for the cause, and I am sure found me intensely frustrating.

Zahara (Omani – three months) was a half-Omani Princess who I dated and introduced to my family. She and I met when she wanted an 'acting coach', and ended up instead with a love affair. To this day, she is my flatmate's favourite.

But my Pari is the most important one. It is she who holds my heart.

And there are now others. But I'll not embarrass them here.

That's about the most important ones.

And yes, there have been others.

You don't work as a nightclub promoter, or be an Englishman in the United States, or be a male escort without going round the block once or twice.

You want the number?

Yeah, *good* one.

And I want a winning Euromillions ticket…

So anyway.

I head into Fabric and BTP and Hops are there with friends.

They're already on vodka red bull.

I get there at seven in the morning. Four hours of dancing, eight rounds of drinks and muchos extra curriculars later, it's all going swimmingly.

BTP and I get to talking, and we agree it's time we saw more of each other. Hops, as ever, is on immaculate form.

I say 'hi' to various people I am never going to remember and again stand amazed at just how massive a place Fabric actually is.

It's basically a militarised zone that got demilitarised and had about fifteen bars welded to it.

Eventually I say my goodbyes after buying one more round, whereupon the cute-as-flames waitress writes her number on the back of a receipt.

Clever. Clever, and *sexy*.

When I leave, it is light outside, and Merlin and LL are there picking me up for lunch.

No *way* I can face food. I have one pint and then my body puts me on red alert. Need.

To go.

Home.

LL is on crutches when I see him. If there's one thing I cannot stomach, if I have one Achilles' Heel, it is seeing my loved ones in pain (my mother noted this years ago and warned me it made me an easy target - few people have ever made use of this fact, save The Hulk this year who accuses me of not being supportive [probably true] and being a 'lying bastard' [not so true]).

And that has happened too much this year: my loved ones have suffered. One of my family and one of my best friends has been in hospital this year with serious injuries.

This is tough for me to swallow, because the sheer randomness of such things makes them seem crueller.

And LL of all people does not deserve such misfortune. He co-runs his own company along with South, another good friend of mine, and also along with Merlin. He and I have worked together longer than I have worked with anyone in my life.

We ran Mischief together. We ran clubs together. We picked up women together. We formed an army together.

At one point Merlin told me we had more than thirty-eight employees on the books. We ran thirteen nights a week at the height of our powers at venues that played host to the biggest celebs in the world and the most demanding clubbing audience in the country.

We came up with ideas that had not been done in the city before and we made them commonplace. In short, we were very good at it.

And LL and I started the whole thing.

He's also been my flatmate, my advisor, and my best friend for many, many years, getting on for a decade.

And he was working hard this year at getting into the gym and at getting into shape until this crap happened and sent his plans fruit-shaped.

Which let's you know one thing above all others - one thing that underpins everything we do and that occurs on this planet: we have finite capacity for damage, which really means we have finite Time.

Our bodies can only take finite punishment. We need to take care of what we have and to cherish our own selves.

Finity equals responsibility, whether we like it or not.

Our last week is here. And truth be told, I can't be arsed.

After yesterday's seventeen-hour hour marathon, I'm just losing the will to live.

I may call waitress girl today. That'll brighten my mood.

Three more days this week and then one next week and it's all over for me and Spielberg.

After that, it's back to "HOTHouse." And after that it's off for a break, for a retreat, for some me time.

So I can complete the book up to November and finish the album.

And then we'll see where we are after that.

Same day.

Still bored. Eight hours sat waiting in the cold.

Like I said: not all glamorous.

Plus, I'm pretty sure it's getting *so* cold I can no longer feel my own feet…

Can't handle it. Been working 17 hour dayys for 3 days in a row on 2 hrs to 3 hr s sleep a night. Body feels fkd. Isn'yt legal for us to work without 11 hrs resty between shooting days. And still been woreking on hothouse. Need more sleepm.

The following is an undercover field report from the production known as 'The Feature', codenamed: Dartmoor, regarding a field officer by the name of Um Bongo Sean 'Elbows' *schtthhhurrrp* McDixon. Codename 'Elbows' for short.

It is alleged by the supporting artistry of Dartmoor that such a phenomenon exists as 'shuttersluttery.'

This phenomenon is explained as an individual who will do anything, by which we mean absolutely *anything*, to get to the front of a shot to be closest to the camera.

In an effort to achieve this, shuttersluts will often: elbow their way through a crowd of hundreds, disrupt continuity for an entire feature film, sellotape themselves to the focus puller, and even feign immediate and sudden epileptic fits if asked to retire to a greater distance from the camera.

Um Bongo Sean 'Elbows' *schtthhhurrp* McDixon is charged with all the above, as well as employing Messrs Kev Hudson and Kev Crouch to act as his body doubles, allowing him to be in multiple places at the same time, and also to distribute his CV and headshot at multiple locations without the consent of those to whom they are distributed.

From the entire body of Supporting Artistry on Dartmoor, Um Bongo Sean 'Elbows' *schtthhhurrrp* McDixon, we salute you in all your efforts.

Now bore off, for fuck's sake. And let some of us have a go.

;)

(Only kiddin', Elbows. Don't go shutterslutting me on my wedding day.)

I call Waitress Girl when I get home and we talk for almost an hour and a half.

Fascinating woman. We organise to have a movie night in, which works fine for me since the weather has gone from chilly to nadshrinkingly freezing.

It makes me smile to have something to look forward to.

To have some *human* time to look forward to.

Thank you to the powers that be.

Alex Gatehouse also manages the same day to make me laugh so much my toes sweat. We have a running joke on set about Sean Connery (legend, incontestable legend) and his immaculate accent.

Alex has come up with the single greatest possible sentence for our beloved Sean to ever be caught saying in an interview.

(You have to understand that most of Lord Connery's 's' sounds are actually more like 'sh' sounds, for this. That, or buy a fucking movie…)

"We were sitting on this sleek slope on the Missisippi; my sexy guests consisted of Susan Sarandon and Sissy Spacek, and we were listening to Scissor Sisters and sizzling Soul Sessions. It was scintillating stuff."

Legend.

My name is Friedrich Schlumberhaus.

I sit beneath a sky so blue that only the divine Gott himself can have made it.

The sun caresses the field beneath it, and steam rises in waves from tents still frozen from the cold of the night. The plain undulates away before us and the woods enclose us as in a giant embrace.

Strange: there is peace even in wartime.

I hope Isabella remains my own, wheresoever across our world she may be.

I love her still.

Almost at the end of Dartmoor, a.k.a. "War Horse."

And we are at Boreham Wood, where they filmed "Gladiator," and "Robin Hood," and are now filming "Warhorse," "X-Men," and many more.

The place is legend.

It is my favourite set yet.

We were freezing like popsicles this morning after a four am start, but now we are warm and at ease beneath the sun.

I am fascinated now by all of this.

I wonder how my grandfather coped in such situations as the one we are now mimicking. I have rarely felt that I missed him, but now I miss him keenly.

I never met the man as he died before I was born.

I would dearly love now to sit and listen to his story, to hear him speak of the Great War and how things came to pass.

By all accounts, he was a fine man indeed.

My middle name is his first. Clifford is a very English name, and one I am coming to love more the older I get. As my father has often said, those who choose to ignore the mistakes of the Past are doomed to repeat them.

It is Truth.

Boreham Wood is stunning.

It felt alien, unwelcoming, and *unreal* early in the morning. But then I'd only slept four hours and my own skinsack feels alien when I'm that fucked.

Now it feels very much like a place I have neglected, or like a home you live in but have never taken the time to truly decorate or make your own.

When I was a boy my father would take me for long walks over Milfield Common, or to climb and boulder at Stanage Edge.

He took me swimming and diving in streams and rivers in the countryside, and to see Roman ruins and Olde Worlde English towns that I'd never have beheld had it not been for him.

It was a stroke of parenting genius. It taught me an immense amount.

My father has a miraculous memory for detail and for dates. By merely listening to him talk about history I became transported to other parts of the world, and to other times. It gave me an appreciation and a respect for that which has passed before, although my knowledge of it is as nothing compared to his.

I am conscious while we re-enact scenes from the early 20th Century here at Boreham of just what else has happened here.

Blood may well have been shed right beneath my feet. Vikings may have slain innocents running from their fury.

Normans might have charged down Saxons and cut them down like blades of grass. It strikes me as a poetic notion:

The present of our entire planet is soaked in the viciousness of our past.

Weird, isn't it?

You wait forever for a bus, a cab, good Mexican food in London, or a fine woman, and then ten show up at once.

If October is seeming long in this, that's because it is.

I've had so little time to date or, as Marco De Cristofaro puts it, 'nourish my soul,' that I'd almost forgotten how much fun it is.

Almost.

So I suddenly have several options on the table. First up is a playmate that messaged me on Facebook.

Second we have an actress who doesn't do dating.

Third is an underwear model who lives in the States (minor distance issue).

And lastly we have Tattgirl, the beautiful waitress from the club.

I'm home on Friday, battered and worn from "War Horse." The night and Saturday day seem to pass in a blur. I take care of a load of admin and try to rest as best I can.

Playmate messages me and says she wants to see me next week.

All cool.

Rooster's off for a night out with Lovechick, who he seems to be getting on well with. I can feel the onset of some kind of doom n' gloom mood, and no matter what I do, it's threatening to dig its heels in.

Until, that is, my phone goes and Tattgirl messages saying she's ill and could do with some company, even though I'm not meant to see her till Tuesday. Hmmm.

We make it so she comes over, and come over she does.

Now: the critical combination, to my mind, in a woman, is the following:

- So attractive they are other-men's-necks-breakingly beautiful
- Smart enough that it's noticeable
- A smile to die for
- A body to live for
- A good enough sense of humour that I can make her laugh but truly the ideal is that she can make me laugh (this is as rare as dinosaurshit)
- Some sense of the bigger picture and of 'important' things
- And, ideally, that combination of purer-than-the-driven-snow along with, erm, not so much

Tattgirl seems from our text conversations and a long phone chat to have a lot, if not all, of the above.

So we sit and talk and drink a while. Then we hook up. Then we head to bed. We hook up some more. Then, gloriously, we sleep.

We wake up. We hook up again. We talk. We hook up a lot. We go for a shower. We hook up more. We get out of the shower. We hook up like clotheshangers.

We sit on the couch.

Loki arrives with Wisdom and Rooster comes up to join us. We watch, in this order: "Hostel 2," "Kick-Ass," and then "Beverly Hills Cop 2."

We order Chinese food, we drinks wine, and we light a J. We relax on couches so welcoming that it's just untrue.

Loki leaves, and Rooster goes to bed.

Tattchick books a cab and departs.

And I am left with a strange feeling.

Marco De Cristofaro on "War Horse" talks a lot about following the Path that brings you the most "Spirit Nourishment" or "Nourishment of the Soul."

The feeling I am left with is imbecilic in its simplicity. Which is: that I enjoy making myself feel good. And that I spend very little time focusing on this.

I do it, don't get me wrong. I love my work. I love my vocation.

But there's enjoying that and there's enjoying lying on a hammock on a beach with a cocktail.

The difference?

The 'stress' we put our bodies under. This is of no small consequence. It is cited as the biggest killer in the world.

Therefore, the more stress you take on, the quicker you die. Unless you exercise, eat healthy, and chill out.

Tattchick brought me that ever-escaping peace I seek. And it felt strange because I had not felt it in quite some time.

That's not good; but the fact that she made me feel it, is.

I head to bed early (ish) to make sure I am in one piece for tomorrow's final push: the last day for me on Steven Spielberg's epic "War Horse."

It's the Last day of "War Horse."

The sun is out and the day is beautiful.

The sky is killer blue, and there's neither sight nor sound of clouds.

I'm relaxed and calm.

I handle these days much better than I used to.

I'm in plenty of time for the coach. I know how to navigate breakfast, costume, makeup and hair and in which order. I am pleased: I know now how to not only survive the set of a major Hollywood feature; I also know how to optimise the whole experience.

So, for all the budding extras of the world, here's the skinny:

-   Get there early: being late makes others irate.

-   Get to know your fellow SAs (Supporting Artists) and find the coolest ones you can so you enjoy the experience.

-   Volunteer for everything you can that will get you 'features': this will ensure the ADs (Assistant Directors) get to know you and you will be making an active contribution while the chavplums are still sleeping.

- *Learn* - make sure you are fluent in Cinespeak (the language of cinema). *And*, if you want to save face, keep the lower half closed.

- Know the rules: extra work is governed by specific rules and guidelines: have at least some knowledge of what does and doesn't make you extra money. Inclement weather, for example, nets you an extra twelve quid. Pissing and moaning because you're bored, does not.

- Bring alternative activity: I've written 100,000 words of this book between takes on a Steven Spielberg film on my *phone*. Have a DS, or an iPod, or something that means you are not coma-bored when shit isn't happening.

- Follow the action: know where the camera is and what shot is taking place so you are keyed up on what's actually going on.

- Play the part: always have an 'action' in the scene. "My character is asleep on this ammunition crate" is a good way to get yourself on the "sackable twat" list.

- Respect the ADs: these guys are going to yell at you a lot. This doesn't mean they hate you, or have childhood issues, or fell out of the womb onto hot coals. This is just how some people get large bodies of people to react as needed.

- Respect the runner: do not fuck with these people. They are likely to be ADs someday and have as hard a job as you do.

- Unite: make sure you have a large circle of friends amongst the extras.

- Record: take all the other extras and the ADs contact details and start a facebook page. It may never bring you anything, *or* it may preserve some of your favourite memories and get you your next job.

- Make an effort and be as friendly as possible with costume and makeup. You'll see these people every day, and while you don't get a call sheet, they do. They know what's going on and they are very clued in on what's happening.

- *Be. Fucking. Polite.* There's nothing more annoying than SAs who can't string a coherent sentence together and end up sounding like a commercial for contraception.

The day sees us mostly walking up and down what is now affectionately known as "Bastard Hill."

In Boreham Wood, where "Robin Hood" was shot, Ridley Scott had a castle built up on a hill.

Now, here, we have about a hundred extras, tens of horses, and a cannon the size of Wales all moving or being dragged up a hill that is roughly as steep as a brick wall. A tall one.

I talk a lot to Gary Comerford, who is a Gentleman's extra.

He's done all kinds of stuff and is the epitome of professionalism. He's also got a Mr Burns impression that in just one word has me laughing.

"Excellent..."

Benos is yet to do his presentation. He's got gifts for all the ADs and the top dogs themselves.

It's a classy move, and one that underlines just how focused Benos Noble can be. He's done an impeccable, exemplary job of showing how it should be done onset, and has gained a lot from the experience.

I am sad to miss tomorrow and the presentation ceremony. Gutted, in fact.

But needs must.

I talk also a lot to Hendrik Herodes, our young lad who inspires me a great deal. He's young as they come, and is eager to improve his discourse with the opposite sex.

He's no hesitation in admitting his own weaknesses, and wants to hear from this ageing and decrepit escort and PUA just how certain things should be done to make him a ladies' man. I'm happy to tell him what I know, purely because something in him tells me he may actually act on this and go all out to become a better man.

To give you an idea of why I am impressed: many of the other lads his age are either asleep in a fucking tent, trying to chav tobacco off people to put into rizlas they have yet to steal, chucking bits of soil or stone at each other, or telling each uvva mad tales of all da wimmin dey is bangin', innit blad?

Pisses. Me. *Off.*

I make sure all the hillwalkers have water, and talk about "HOTHouse" and my music video to Gary and Mike Archer, a lovely young man who has clearly been through the ringer but has a heart of solid gold.

We get lunch after every other fucker on set, at which point I'd have eaten my own shoes, given the chance.

And before we know it, we're back to HQ.

My last day is over on this epic piece of work.

And I am more gutted than ever to be missing the last day. Still, I am to see them at the wrap party.

And I'll not lose touch with the Core War Horsers, thanks to the modern technological wonderment of Facebook.

I get changed and say my goodbyes to more people than I'd have expected to come to care about on a set that has, itself, come to mean a lot to me.

I say adios to Michael "Are You Well?" Coleman, to Benos "My Dad thinks he's always right, and that can't be true, 'cause actually I am" Noble, to Richard "EppeMaster" Hall, to Pete "Sound as Music" Russell, to Declan "How Military Do I Look" Patch, to Gary "Eeexcellent" Comerford, to Mike "the Ghosthunter" Archer, to Andy "Let's chuck the chavs in the ditch" Phillips, to Nicky "Trig" Tregenza, to Carlo "Built like a shithouse? No, a shit*factory*" De Cristofaro, to Chris "The Accent" Bowen, to Alistair "The Manyman" Reith, to Sean "Elbows" McDixon, to Chas, to the ADs, to Kev "Sudoku" Hudson, to Ashwyn, to Catherine Heys, to Michael Stevenson the Living Legend, to Chris Judd, to Natasha Phelan, to Ollie, to as many as I can.

And something doesn't feel right. You know when you walk out the house, and you check, and yes you do have your bag, and your wallet, and your crack pipe (*kidding*, Nan) and yet you still feel like something is missing?

I sit down to fill out my chit. My pen won't write.

Eh?

This only happens when whatever I think I'm about to do gets SeanMcDixon'd out the way by some other, get-to-the-front-first idea.

I ask for a piece of paper.

The pen starts writing.

Oh. *Shit...*

345

Dear Chris Judd, Adam Sumner, Michael "The Legend" Stevenson, Tom Edmonson, Andy Madden, Celine Coulson, Natasha Phelan, Ollie Hazell, Kathy (misspelt, God I'm stupid), Christian Labarta, Michael Michael, and 'The Guv' (couldn't bring myself to actually write 'Mr Spielberg')

I can't tell you what it has meant to me to have this experience. Working with you all has been a dream come true for this humble actor and has been a complete and utter pleasure.

Since I was 12 years old I have dreamed of working on a film like this and with a crew like this, and it has been my absolute honour to do so.

I look forward to working with you in the future and am grateful for the time, the laughs, and the experiences we have shared.

I hope the film outdoes all expectations, and wish you all the very best for the future.

My sincerest, most heartfelt thanks.

SB

I look at what I've just written.

It's honest.

It looks OK.

But it could be wildly inappropriate.

This is my first proper rodeo as a supporting artist, and I don't really like the idea of being blacklisted from all future productions for being a production set fruitcake or some kind of filmset Smithers (stop *laughing*, Comerford).

Hmmm. How do I tell?

I look up. My chit's still unsigned. I fill it out. I walk over to the ADs chit-signing area.

A*ha*.

There are four ADs round one table, and if I ask one of them I have to ask all four of them.

Not good. And, as any PUA or AD will tell you, giving people a choice is sometimes a bad idea. Slows shit down.

Don't think. *Act*.

On the other table is AD Natasha P. She's been a diamond on this. She doesn't think shouting is always necessary, is cool as mint choc chip, and always has a smile on her face. Honestly.

Even at like, six in the morning, when I'm still trying to put my gloves on my feet and wondering why it's not happening.

"'Tash, I need your opinion on something. Can you have a look at this in a minute and tell me which of those (the four other ADs) I should give it to? If any?"

She gives me an *erm, ok, nutbar* look, momentarily. Then she reads it.

She smiles a bit.

She laughs.

"I'd definitely give it to [unnamed], and also to [unnamed]. And probably also to [unnamed]."

I explain I don't really want to wait while people read it. I don't want people uncomfortable or thanking me, see.

That ain't the point.

I want them to understand how much I appreciate their work and their time. As you can see from what I wrote, I'm proud as a futhermucker of this project, however small a contribution I may have made.

When she offers to show it round herself, I'm moved. When she tells me I can photocopy it, I'm off like a shot.

Fifteen copies later and I hand them all round. I thank Tash. I leave.

I get the minibus to the coach, and write all the way home.

Tattgirl messages me to say she's coming to see me, and Rooster has been beavering away on "HOThouse." I have tonight only to enjoy my memories of the last three months fully, and enjoy them I shall.

To all the lads and ladettes on "War Horse," I am honoured and privileged to have met and worked with you.

I look forward greatly to working with you again, hopefully in a greater capacity, but then the dice will fall where they may.

It seems impossible, but the end of October is finally nigh.

And somehow "HOTHouse" has been hit yet *again* by a massive blow to the head.

Two days before we are scheduled to undertake the reshoot, our DP pulls out with our camera.

I'm starting to think I am karmically cursed.

Rooster and I sit and chat about it over a glass of whisky. We think we have a new gameplan. While we're talking, I get a message from Benos saying the "War Horse" wrap party is tonight.

Thank God, something to distract me while I'm in this Earth-wrecker of a mood.

My agent then buzzes me and tells me he has an audition for me for a Maltesers commercial. I'm stunned. First one in 4 months.

Let's hope it's the start of something and not just a one-off. I then get calls saying I have appointments to get on the full-time books at Ray Knight (one of the best TV and background agencies in the world), Casting Collective (the guys who got me "War Horse") and Mad Dog Casting (the guys who currently have "Pirates Four").

Eh? What is going *on* here?

Maybe the Youniverse is showing a touch of clemency to yours truly.

See, here's what I'm thinking.

As an artist (actor or rapper or, in my case, both) getting unpaid or expenses only work is easy as. It's the whole making-it-my-survivable-living thing that's the trick.

So if I can generate enough paid work from features and TV, it'll then allow me to take on other projects where I play leads even if the pay is crap. Speculate to accumulate, 'n shit.

That'd give me three background agents (two for features and one for TV) and my own agent proper. If I can then get a manager and booking agent for music on top, I should be able to get more work than I can take on.

And that's how you get to raise your price.

Too much demand? Up the price.

Too little demand? Then you're struggling.

So the key is to overkill, as per usual.

We get the above four agents firing on all cylinders, then add a music manager and a booking agent. Then we add a book, a TV show, a film, and an album to market.

And then we see how they like *them* apples.

"War Horse" wrap party.

I'm en route. This could get messy.

And I'm supposed to be meeting a girl by the name of Ruby Sarland.

It's Heaven.

I've no shoot this weekend, no work at all, in fact. I have time *off*.

I can recuperate and see some people I care about.

The "War Horse" wrap party is immense. Tattgirl comes over and to give credit where it is certainly due, handles herself admirably. The lads find her charming, and I cannot help but respect her natural ability to put people at ease.

Helen Green from "HOTHouse" comes down with a friend, Ruby Sarland, and the lads all look at me funny.

"Steve, you the man, man!"

Eh?

"No one else brung wimmin' out. 'Cept Benos. And you brung three man! How'd you do it?"

I sigh. Some people should just have a "sterilise me" sticker on their foreheads.

Helen and Ruby are in their element, as two women surrounded by thirty men should be.

Men of the world take note: *spoil* your womenfolk.

It'll pay you back a hundredfold.

I'm headed home and feeling peachy.

The world is good and things, despite certain setbacks, are looking good.

I'm in an effervescent mood ("ooh, Matron, ooh, posh word, ooh, we say 'bubbly' at our 'ouse...") on the way home when my phone buzzes.

I see the message.

Unconsciously, I start running.

That kind of message only gets sent rarely. It's from Rooster and I'd rather have read just about anything else.

Chow Bella's in hospital. She's been in a car accident. A car smashed into the minibus she was in on set. She's in bed in the hospital now...

I bomb it into the tube station and head home like a rocket on speed.

And the month was going *so* well...

NOVEMBER 2010:

"NEW NINES"

"The truth is not subject to your or my opinion,
Like the mortality of this planet is to our dominion,
The truth is an eternal moment of a tear in the eye of the
creator,
No name, no book, no gimmick,
The truth is Native Americans said it best:
The land, the Earth, the one Uni-verse of a Great Spirit,
It's honest; it's true as the Devil's Promise,
It's true by day and it's true by night,
'Cause God is love, but get it in writing..."

- Talent -
"Veritasks"

- IMMORTALENTED 2013 -

November.
Novus means new.
Embers are that which remains after a fire has burnt down to ashes.
New embers.
Wonder if that could be the feeling that remains after "War Horse."
Film sets are like mini-worlds of their own. You forget anything else exists.
And I miss the lads. I miss them *terribly*.
But there are amazing photos of the lads with the Guv'nor himself. It's a life-changing event. It's a milestone in my life.
Anyways.
Back to business.
I go with Alexsh Gatehoushe to the Casting Collective meeting.

I've no idea if they'll take him on or not without him having a booked appointment. But there's only one way to find out.

We walk in, and unbelievably there's not even a question asked. There's like fifty people in the office waiting to sign up.

Like I said, a *lot* of people want to do this job.

We sign up.

I've got Ray Knight and Mad Dog to get through yet, but if all goes according to plan, then money should no longer be a worry.

Between the three, next year should become a profitable enterprise. This in itself seems like a minor miracle. I'm still not going to believe it until I see it.

And since my aim was to have that happen in two years, I'm a year ahead of schedule. This is very, very good news.

And I'm *still* not believing it until I see it.

What's better news is that Chow Bella is fine. It's taken a few days but she's recovering well.

Some twat ran his car into her van and put her into hospital.

If I see this minging, putrid self-loather of a scumbag then I'll do him the favour of putting *him* in hospital.

Twat.

What kind of scumbag does this to a woman?

Amazingly, it's the same story with Ray Knight as it was before.

To clarify: I've been trying to get with this agency for the whole of the year.

But you send an email and it gets bounced. They're very busy and they come very highly recommended.

They do a huge amount of TV work and that's an area in which I have next to zero experience. And that's a mistake I wish to correct.

Fortunately, James "The Legend" Taylor who I met and befriended on "War Horse" made a quick call to them and recommended me.

And now I've got a meeting with them.

I tell Alexsshh Gatehousshhe to meet me there and we walk in.

The office, to be frank, is *manic*.

We meet the photographer and the assistants and the bookers and the manager and *here's a seat sit down and let's get your pictures and why can I smell whisky? Oh you're hung over oh I see well let's get your details ta thanks a bunch and come we'll take your picture and now we'll walk around the streets and now come meet everyone and holy HELL...*

Gatehoussssssssshhhhhhe turns to me bemused.

"This... this is... this is like a French farce..."

I bust out laughing.

When I tell you Ray Knight work hard to earn their money, I mean they are *non-stop*.

It's an amazing sight to see.

And again, they sign up Al without any hesitation.

OK, two down, one to go.

Soon it'll be time to go see a man about a Mad Dog...

I leave the house with a new sense of calm.

I'm headed to an audition for a movie called "Love Tomorrow;" it's a tale of a happy couple who get torn asunder when the woman is told she has HIV.

She heads out into the night and runs into an extrovert Cuban dancer who shows her what life is like on the edge.

Their thirty-six-hour hedonism takes them on an unexpected journey, wherein they meet Cal and his civil partner Peter, both of whom run a dance company.

I'm about to read for the role of Peter J. Clements.

It feels good to be reading for a gay role after losing the part in "Cock Tales." I wanted that part. Bad.

Plus, I'm kind of on a roll, having just got on the books at Casting Collective and Ray Knight, and hopefully soon also at Mad Dog.

This sense of peace comes from two things.

Firstly I am starting to build conviction that I can actually make a living doing this. Those three agents and my own combined together should have me a constant influx of paid work.

My album, book, film and TV show remain the aces up my sleeve. If I can get a similar team together in music, then I'm laughing.

The second reason I'm chilled as a cucumber is that I am headed Home.

I need to see Kev for his birthday, Nan for hers, catch up with my dad, and spend some quality time with my mum.

The character I'm auditioning for in "Love Tomorrow" is Peter.

He's described as a suave, relaxed gay man. He is the calm, controlled foil to his more eccentric and flamboyant partner.

So I'm in a smart pink shirt, slimfit blue jeans, decent black shoes, and a nice suit jacket. I put on one ring and shave before I head out.

I'm as relaxed as I have ever been.

I get to Moorgate and breeze into the building a touch late due to tube strikes.

It doesn't matter. From the second I walk in and meet Chris Payne (lovely guy, easygoing, nice relaxed air to him) and Stephanie Moon (sweet look to her, charming air, gentle eyes), we're on easy street.

We get on, we chat. I talk about my work, the Parachute Regiment, and the image I've put together in my head of the character.

"Peter J. Clements is a calm, suave, confident man who runs the business side of Cal and his dance company. He's not limp-wristed and he's no queen. He's the kind of guy the girls in Sex and the City would approach in a bar, and who would charm the pants off them for an hour, before telling them all much to their dismay that he was waiting for his boyfriend."

This gets a laugh and seems to punctuate the meeting.

We shake hands and smile and say how good it's been to meet each other. I have a quick word with Rooster and then set off back to the flat.

I get to go *home* today. I get a few days to *relax*. It feels like a mini-holiday.

Praise be to the powers above.

I've a special place in my heart for Euston station.

Of all the stations in the whole world, this one is my favourite.

It is the gateway to my Home. It houses the vehicles that take me to that wondrous place where my loved ones live.

I read through most of what I have written while I await the magical carriage that will take me to my Home.

I have to admit; it's a decent read.

It's a true story and it makes me laugh to read it. It also serves to keep me grounded. I've still so much work to do that it's still nerve-wracking, but one step at a time, I'm getting my head around this business.

In fact, I realise as I read through I'm quite chuffed with progress so far.

My new agent Ray Knight has just called me with a couple days work for "Sherlock Holmes 2."

Couple that with the audition this morning and I have plenty of work coming up in November. Paid work. *Good* work. On films I'm proud to be in.

You can't get any bigger than "War Horse," "Captain America" or "Sherlock Holmes 2." And you can't get any better roles than the leads in movies like "Morning Tea" or "Radio London."

The trick, of course, is going to be combining the two to play the lead roles but in the massive features.

But, as my favourite woman on Earth says, one step at a time, Martin.

First off, get home, and remind yourself of who you are, and of *why* you are doing this.

I get home and collapse in the living room.

Within the first twenty-four hours I feel infinitely more human.

I also get Ray Knight on the phone telling me I have confirmed work on the new "Sherlock Holmes" film and on, wait for it, "Eastenders."

I nearly crack up laughing. My mum swears this is about the only thing that could convince her to actually *watch* an episode of the fricking programme.

Between that and "Love Tomorrow," I have a decent finale to the year lined up already.

This is much, *much* more like it; agents calling me with work only days after I've seen them.

See, ladies and germs, hard work *does* pay off.

My home is a humble place, but it is the single most sacred location on Earth to me.

It's a bungalow in the Black Country and is the only place my family has lived since I was born.

My cat Misty brightened the place too until she died recently.

My mum greets me like a long lost stranger, which I almost am.

I haven't been home in almost four months.

That's a long, *long* time for me. The reinvigoration I get from that hug would solve every issue on the planet if I could just work out how to bottle it and sell it.

It eases the war in my chest.

Walking in to my house and getting a cup of tea in the warm instantly relaxes and changes me. I'm a totally different human being at Home. Relaxed. Calm. Laid back.

I get time to nap, to lie on a couch, and shit like that.

It's basically my battery recharger. I come home for a change of oil, new tyres, and a bit of a rest.

It's my Lazarus pit and it is absolutely everything to me.

Kev comes over and we talk education, as always.

He's the head of modern languages at a school in Birmingham, and has been my best friend for nearly fifteen years.

He's also sharper than a tack with a ninja sword, and harder than nails on 'roids.

If you've never sat in a room with two near-geniuses like my mum and Kev and listened to them talk about the state of the country's youth, their education and the future, then I recommend it.

He informs me that a group of average twelve-year-olds at a secondary school he visited today cannot complete ten press-ups.

Nor can they correctly utilise English grammar, to the extent that at this age they are still incapable of using commas.

The horror. This strikes me as a blow to the yarbles.

My mother and Kev share the same trade. The first is an ex-teacher; the second is a teacher still.

I grieve for the high standards to which my beautiful country used to adhere whenever I hear them talk.

Their stories, both past and present, are of a mighty people, a decent people, let down by a spineless and profiteering 'government' whose thirst for power resulted in the fall in standards and the loss of excellence of a country once built upon the both.

You think I'm being melodramatic?

I wish that I were.

It saddens and angers me always. But it also stokes the fire of my will to do something about it.

Told ya: I'd be a teacher or a politician. But we've got the first one covered. And the second one, not so much. But you can do more good through film and music than any politician I've seen.

Don't believe me?

Which did more for gay rights, Gordon Brown's premiership, or "Brokeback Mountain?"

Thank you.

The defence rests.

The next day I head to Great Wyrley to see the second woman who raised me and taught me.

Seeing my nan is like having your spirit massaged.

The woman should be elected Ruler of the Universe as soon as possible. There is not one atom of malice in her body.

Her home is about the only location in which I can comfortably fall asleep without preoccupation. And no matter what food is or is not in the fridge, there's always an amazing, healthy, nutritious meal just waiting for you.

She is a natural healer. She rubs people's feet when they come in. She's a modern day Druid.

She fills me in on how the family are doing, offers me tea and cake, tells me how her daughters and grandchildren and great-grandchildren are getting on, and generally refills my spirit with that most holy of potions: TLC.

She writes me letters on a regular basis, telling me about the family and how they are doing.

I keep them all in a draw next to my bed. When the dark clouds loom, those letters act like a lighthouse and keep my spirit strong.

Just knowing she is there revitalises me.

We return home and I can feel my Samson's hair regrowing.

Next up: the Big Man.

Seeing my dad is like revisiting my childhood.

He concerns himself always with how I am doing, with the women I am seeing, and with how work is going.

He has, as always, a set of carefully prepared questions intended to elicit as much information from me as possible.

We stuff ourselves stupid with pub food and whisky and lime (the drink of the Gods), have a few laughs, and catch up. There is something wonderfully reassuring about our evenings out.

He's probably the single greatest orator and most naturally gifted actor I have ever seen.

He's just got natural gravity, to the extent that when he enters a room, it stays entered.

His command of his environment is a thing to behold. *Truly*. I get much of my (if I have any, as rumours would seem to indicate) natural Field Marshall-ness from him.

We've always done this - had drinks and food, and set the world to rights. And now, more than ever, I am filled with love for the man and am glad he is my father. It is not easy to have him as your dad, but it *is* immensely rewarding.

He sets a very high bar.

I get home and spend the rest of the night writing.

My next day is entirely couch-chilling. The mere presence of my mum is healing. I crack a few jokes and put on the Sean Connery accent, which has her rolling with laughter, and ironically "You Only Live Twishe" appears on the telly.

I can feel the chaos in my chest settling and reordering itself: all through the magic of a cup of tea, having your family around you, and a bit of TV with a dash of RnR.

When time to get back on the train to London rears its lovely head, it's all too soon.

"I don't want you to go."

I hold it together. *Just*.

"I don't want to go either."

But I have to.

We get to the station.

I get on board, heavy-hearted, and am caught a little off guard when I receive sex eyes from a group of blondes near the door.

"This the London train?" I check.

"Yeah," one smiles. "Come on in. There's plenty of seats... loads, really..."

Her friends laugh. I smile and take a seat opposite a well-built black dude who is chatting away on the phone: easier to write with no distractions.

I flip my laptop open and start writing.

"You an actor?"

"Hmmschgnlerlgghgrmmm?"

I snap out of the creative coma and look up. Built-like-a-school asked me the question.

"Oh. Yeah, actually, I am."

He smiles a megawatt grin.

"I knew it, man. Knew I'd seen you somewhere. Soon as you sat down. What you been in? Holby City?"

I laugh and nod; explaining yes I'm an actor and here's what I've been in.

"No shit!" he says. "I was meant to get an earlier train, man, and now here we are, and I've got me an actor friend!"

This is cool.

I normally speak to no one on a train unless they are very, *very* female. But this dude is so friendly and down to Earth it's impossible not to like him. He tells me he has to come home for a bit to get some of his mother's cooking.

I know the feeling, says I.

We talk for the entire rest of the train journey, during which time he tells me he is from London, visits Wolverhampton a lot, and has a missus.

"Why would you visit Wolverhampton a lot?" I ask.

"I play for Wolves. The reserve team. Used to play for England under-sixteens and under-eighteens."

"Erm, what?!? Dude! I was gonna get an earlier train too and now here I am with a mate who's a professional footballer!!"

Now the shoe is firmly on the other foot.

He tells me Wolves and West Ham offered him at the same time, and that he trains in the Midlands, and is gunning for his shot at the title. He's a Gunners supporter and will settle for nothing less than world domination.

I'm totally starstruck. This man played for my *country* when he was sixteen! And he plays for my *hometown* right **now**!

"Yeah but only the reserves man, I need to be on the main field."

That may be true, but I don't care! He says he works hard at his game, and that he plays striker. That he is good friends with Jermaine Defoe and that he has played on a field against Rio Ferdinand.

He listens to me talk about my music and tells me I should get in touch 'cause he's got loads of friends who make music and DJ and produce, and the like.

He's amazing, basically. And we swap numbers and agree to meet, after having a chat about how useless he finds his PR team. I tell him how to rectify the situation, and that if he likes I can help, and we say we'll grab drinks later in the month.

Legend.

I get back to the flat and Merlin, Rooster and LL are sat having beers watching "8 Mile."

Heh.

It's good to be home.

And yes, it's Mad Dog Casting tomorrow.

Let's see if we can make it three out of three.

Sunday. The day of rest.

I *wish*.

It's actually nice working on a Sunday; cause there's no pressure and no one nagging. There aren't many people who expect you to work on a Sunday, so it's pretty much easy street.

I head to Holborn and sit patiently by the Mad Dog office.

I receive an email on my phone from my agent advising me against extra work.

Sorry Bub: bills and dues both need paying. End of story.

Get me more work and I'm all yours. Until then, this is the right way forward.

I enter the Mad Dog office.

Fingers *crossed*.

Mad Dog done and dusted.

I come home from Mad Dog and a photo shoot for "War of the Sexes" and sit at home.

I write.

This week is coming up to a big event. It was my thirtieth birthday earlier this year, and now it's about to be someone else's thirtieth birthday.

And that someone happens to be our very own Brings The Pressure aka BTP.

Now, when most people have a birthday, they do big shit: have a night out, get drunk off methylated spirits, get high off shrooms, make out with a Giraffe, and so on and so forth.

BTP has hired out an entire hotel in Soho for all of us to party at while her celebrity DJs spin all night and we blow the top off the city.

This.

Spells.

Trouble…

And here it is.

My studio is finally set up. I'm making my first track all on my lonesome.

And you know what? I couldn't be happier.

Except I'm heartbroken.

I've just had drinks with Maya De La Fente, and she turns out to be:

- An actress

- A can-model-anytime-I-want-but don't-want-to model
- A MENSA member and therefore a genius
- An heiress who gave her money away to fund a hospital in Africa
- An amateur quantum physicist
- An only child
- A Lifeaholic (you should *hear* what she's done to get her latest film role)
- A singer; she was previously in a girl band at the tender age of fourteen, and one successful enough to tour Spain for three years
- A half-Spanish half-Mexican mouthwatering beauty who swears like a trooper and likes her rose wine

And of course, it goes without saying, she has a boyfriend.

What doesn't go without saying is that it's long distance.

What does go without saying is that she's been with him a year and a half.

I'm half-elated and half-heartbroken.

Heartbroken because of the obvious. But I'll survive that. I'm elated because it's things like this that make you realise there are indeed women out here of that calibre.

It's almost like having coffee with a unicorn.

So in a sense, I'm still celebrating. I'd recount you the whole thing, but I'll not because it might embarrass her. Suffice to say, even us actor rapper ex-soldier men can come home after being told "no" with a smile on our faces.

And besides, there's always tomorrow.

So.

"Eastenders" approaches tomorrow, and BTP's thirtieth the day after.

And then the week after it's "Love Tomorrow," and more work for Casting Collective.

And then only one more month of the book to do, and we're close to a finished album.

And then the money from "War Horse" comes in.

And then a finished edit of what we have so far of "HOTHouse."
It's almost too good to be true.
It seems impossible.
Except it's *not*.

Next, life takes a turn for the bizarre.

Smugz Malone is a line producer, like Rooster.

He also used to be an International Smuggler, moving stuff from the Bahamas into Cuba. So rumour would have it.

He's also run his own strip club, met and slept with celebrities, and filmed me a tad worse for wear nearly give myself concussion and collapse on the coast of France.

Hey *look*, it was a heavy weekend, all right?

He's basically one of the most interesting people I've ever met in my life.

And he has a daughter he hasn't seen in over ten years.

He comes over one night and he, Rooster and I have a drink or two.

Now, I can hold my liquor (occasionally), but Smugz has a BA in drinking.

When God invented alcohol, it's Smugz he got to field test it.

He can talk non-stop, and still has twenty-year-old models following him round when he's almost sixty himself.

He's in this country because his daughter is here. And we've spoken of this many times.

We drink. Then we drink some more. We talk about his daughter.

We drink a *lot* more.

I wake up in the morning with a hangover from Andover and find Smugz walking into my room.

My mouth needs a jet hose and my brain needs washing.

"He's found my daughter."

"Nrrghflmp... *what*?"

Smugz walks out.

I make a genuine attempt at dressing myself and almost succeed.

I get upstairs.

"What the... wat... nrg... wazzgoinon?"

Rooster, it appears, has somehow located Smugz's daughter.

God *bless* the internet.

Well, I say located. He's found her on several sites.

"And you're not gonna believe this, Steve..." Smugz starts.

"Show me her picture," says I.

"She's a runway model," Smugz finishes.

I stop. I consider.

"OK. I take it back. Don't show me her picture."

Rooster shows me anyway. And, predictably enough, she's a beautiful young girl.

"Do we know where she is?"

Rooster shakes his head.

"But we do have a previous address and birth certificate."

I look at the birth certificate. I think for about two seconds.

My phone's already in my hand.

I'm calling a Private Investigator company I used a while back.

My family has some history with Private Investigators. However, I won't go into that here and now, or I may not be here tomorrow.

They tell me it'll cost £200 to locate her.

I get my card out and pay it.

I've done a lot wrong in my life.

Hell, I've done a lot wrong *today*. And to a lot of people.

Most of whom didn't deserve it.

But believe you me; I have a heart the size of Kansas. And not for nothing do my friends consider me loyal as a dog.

So I pay it gladly.

I hope, in return, to reunite a good friend of mine and a fellow cinemusician with his long lost daughter.

And I hope also, it may buy me a little good karma, and help to atone for my sins when I come to meet the Great Creator.

I head out to pick up BTP's birthday present. I've got her a card, written her a letter, and had my design team help me design the image on the next page.

Think she'll like it?

;)

I've designed thirtieth Birthday presents for some of my closest friends.

I find it both cathartic and enjoyable making them.

Again, perhaps this is some kind of karma-trading.

But I'd like to think it's just me.

I walk from the gym, exhausted but feeling better.

My lower back and my core have been weak for the last ten years after I damaged my back in a powerlifting competition in the States.

The gym is an absolute must for me to maintain my strength.

"War Horse" and work meant I haven't been for about three months. This is not good.

Any self-respecting actor or PUA will tell you: you need to be a gym addict. Staying in good shape also contributes to a healthy mind, which I'm in dire need of in general.

And I'm losing weight again, which is good. I put on nearly a frickin *stone* over the course of "War Horse." That needs to come off, asap.

And I'm back down to thirteen and a half. Which is better, but still not right. I need to be thirteen, and ideally twelve and a half.

I get to Bank station when things go fruit-shaped. A voice comes over the tannoy (wicked word).

"Would all passengers please exit the station due to a reported emergency... would all passengers please exit the station due to a reported emergency..."

In the Age of Terrorism, this kind of announcement is met seriously and with no small measure of panic.

A tube station can house thousands of passengers, and while I'm no terrorist, I'd imagine that makes it a decent target.

And, as any Londoner will verify, the tubes get overcrowded, warm, and sweaty. They are fertile grounds for colds, flus, and all manner of shit that can mess up your sinuses.

I'm in an Alton Towers queue, except there's no cool ride at the end. We're zombie-shuffling, step by drudging step out to the cool air.

Down here it is muggy, sweaty, and you can feel people's tensions rising...

"Would all passengers please exit the station due to a reported emergency..."

Yeah, I get the point mate.

Hundreds of people massclog the tunnels. Individuals take weird turns off down other tunnels, thinking to find a shortcut. They fail.

People start muttering how pointless this is, and wondering at what the danger or disruption might be.

I start daydreaming about Tattgirl, and find myself gradually getting angrier and angrier at the fact that all the exits in a station are *miles* away.

"Would all passengers please exit the station due to a reported emergency..."

I grit my teeth. The air down here isn't even air. It's all regurgitated CO_2 and people's burps, farts, sweat and bodyheat.

Children are getting uncomfortable and starting to cry. Even the buskers are packing up their kit and G.T.F.O.H.ing (Get The Fuck Outta Here) en masse.

Elderly people are taking out old copies of their will and making final alterations.

"Would all passengers please exit the station due to a reported emergency..."

OK, we get it, asshole. And my blood keeps on rising, my mood like a storm cloud on the horizon, threatening to unleash hell at any second.

Passengers start complaining to tube staff, demanding to know what is going on.

The tube staff, predictably, refuse to answer and just keep on telling us to leave the station 'in an orderly fashion'.

Lucky, that.

I was going to come out cartwheeling while singing Bohemian Rhapsody. *Imbeciles.* This must be what purgatory is like.

"Would all passengers please exit the station due to a reported emergency..."

Fuck. *Off.*

I see a simply stunning girl in the peopleswamp ahead of me. I swear to myself in the name of taking opportunities that if she is

367

anywhere to be seen outside and if I don't die in Bank tube station, I'll be getting a date with her.

"Would all passengers please exit the station due to a reported emergency..."

I swear to *God* it doesn't need to be said *that* often, you insufferable...

Ahhhhh...

Finally I almost burst out into the real world and suck in a lungful of cool air. I feel nauseous, but the feeling subsides quickly.

Christ, that was unbearable.

I force myself to remember I am in one piece, am healthy and alive and not dying of starvation. I am however running *very* late for BTP's thirtieth party.

I see the girl at a bus stop. I walk over and say hi.

"Sorry, I don't espeak emuch Ingleesh..."

I look at her. She's beautiful.

"Espanol?" I ask.

She smiles and nods.

Heh.

I was *hoping* you'd say that...

I'm smiling in the cab on the way home.

Spanish women are some of my favourite on the planet.

I tell you, God outdid himself with Spanish Girls.

I get home and prep my clothes for the night, and halfway through eating a 300-calorie micro-meal I get another call from Princess Paloma.

Princess Paloma is a blonde-haired girl from the UK who worked on a short film with me earlier in the year. We never actually met onset, or at all in fact until on a recent photoshoot.

She turns out to be, after we meet on Facebook:

- A model and actress
- A yoga instructor
- A writer
- Studying to be a psychologist

She's interested in my work and belief system, and also by my music.

The fact that she is boxer-rippingly attractive does no harm at all.

We agree to meet for coffee, and then before I know it I'm out the door en route to the second BTX crew thirtieth birthday of the year.

BTP's party is a hit, as it was always going to be.

She's hired every inch of this slickalicious hotel just off Regent Street, and almost all our crew are in attendance other than Metis, who was outta town.

Loki, Merlin, LL, Snoops, Lady Pinzella, Rosemania, Shanghai, Adz, and Blitzshorty are all in the building and dressed to kill.

Hops walks in dressed like the Queen of Socialites, and TG arrives like Top Cat with his usual retinue.

BTP's got a constant flow of champagne from every corner of the room, with black tie waiters refilling your glass the moment it hits the table.

Five star food appears in the form of Asian fusion cuisine, and before you know it there's about a hundred or so of the world's young up and comers all at the same venue.

She's got internationally acclaimed DJs, one of whom is her boyfriend and a real gent to boot, playing at her birthday.

You have to give the woman points for style.

It's all top end bubbly, stir-fried beef, "may I take your coat, sir?" "no-let-*me*-refill-your-glass," first-rate Italian architecture meeting Victorian English interiors, and "have you tried the seasoned spring rolls?" along with DJs from Barcelona, women in designer dresses, and more.

The toilets look nicer than my entire *flat*. It's a stunning, stunning location.

BTP's in her element.

She looks stunning, works the room like a pro, and absolutely shines.

Shanghai and I give her the present, and I pass her my card and letter.

The lads got her everything from designer bags to glowsticks.

You couldn't make up a better party.

The crew doesn't get to see enough of each other, so we relish nights like this. It's a free bar & free food affair, and it couldn't have come at a better time.

It still guts me to see LL in his leg brace, but he's moving much better and looks like he's coping well.

There's a cinema downstairs with guitar hero, a roof terrace upstairs with a jacuzzi, and a restaurant on the first floor.

It's mental.

There are people here who could probably buy my secondary school and turn it into their garden. But the cool thing isn't that: that's just money.

The cool thing is that you'd never know from the way they act.

They're as down to earth as you could want.

Rosemania rocks up and we know at that point we're in trouble.

When Rosemania comes in, the night is going downhill. Merlin ends up drunk as an animal but dances himself into a near coma.

The crew is back together and getting more and more a-gonner.

"Is it a free bar all night?" someone asks.

I confess I don't know.

"How many drinks, heh, how many drinks, *heh heh*," someone else asks, "do you reckon they'd give us free...?"

This is a bad move.

Because given a choice between being the paragon of acceptable behaviour and taking the flagrant piss to see what we can get away with, I'm the latter all the way.

"Gimme a sec and I'll find out," says I.

I head to the bar.

Several people get their drinks, and I end up at the front.

The barman looks at me. I look at him. He looks at me some more.

"Twenty double jack and cokes and twenty double vodka red bulls please."

I say this with some conviction because, well, as you know I can't help myself, and because, well, why not?

PUA teachings state that whatever you do, do it with confidence.

I reckon the barman's just going to tell me to fuck off anyway.

To my utter and complete bafflement, I see what looks like fourty double or triple drinks poured and placed on the bar.

To the uninitiated (or the sane), that's about two to three to maybe four bottles of spirits. At this point we've already had almost five hours of drinking.

The crew cheer me like a hero for getting them enough drinks for the rest of the night.

To be honest, I should've known better.

In my defence, I did hit the bar once more to procure H2O for young Merlin. Or what was left of him.

I have a long chat with Pinzello, and then I make sure Merlin drinks two glasses of water, and then it all goes hazy.

I make a sharp exit and get two bags of McDonald's on the way home.

I stuff myself silly and then pass out.

For the record, I was "designated driving." As in, looking after others. Around 30 to 40 people stayed up till 1pm the next day.

I'm not *always* the madman. Just sometimes.

What a night.

Until, that is, I am elbowdropped at six O'clock in the morning.

I think I am having some kind of nightmare.

I get elbow-dropped again.

"Nrflfghghjmmmmfuck*off*..."

I get elbow-dropped *again*.

And then *again*. This time by more than one person.

I am *not* dreaming. I can tell this, because I can hear at least two people laughing.

"Nrrhghglgmgmgm FUCK *OFF*..."

I open my eyes.

Merlin, LL, Chow Bella and Rosemania have appeared from somewhere.

My duvet is dragged off me and I am freezing.

And my head hurts. The elbowdrops also were not a vacation.

Surely, no one is this stupid?

Merlin leaps onto me again as LL removes all of my bedding.

Now, I'm not the nicest of people at the best of times.

But if you wake me up when I'm deep asleep and take my bedding from me, and elbow-drop me, *repeatedly*, when I am hungover, then you're going to *get it*.

So I grab Merlin in a headlock and chuck both of us off the bed.

I then grab a flip-flop and begin smacking Merlin in the head as hard as I can.

371

At some point I feel LL drag me off him. Merlin doesn't look like he's in pain. He's that drunk he just seems really, really confused.

The look he gives me as I flip-flop him in the head is that of a man who loves his friend dearly but does not comprehend why said friend is assaulting him with an item of casual footwear.

They leave.

Chow Bella then kindly informs me that Rosemania is now passed out drunk in her bed and will not leave.

I am likely to have to physically drag this man out of Chow Bella's bed.

I don't know what the woman does, but somehow she has some kind of drug effect on men and has them chasing her round like she's Aphrodite.

I ask.

I plead.

I threaten.

No use.

I sigh.

I unbuckle my trousers and threaten to both urinate and dump on the man. And yet he still will not leave. I threaten to shag the man.

He finally leaves, drinks a JD and coke, and then drops to the floor and passes out, totally uberflunted.

And the man I drag out of her bed up the stairs is *not* a lightweight.

I may have broken his belt and my wrist in the process, but get him out of the bed I do.

Chow Bella goes to bed.

Merlin appears at the balcony window.

"Why is there a footprint on my head...?"

I manage to stop laughing after about fifteen minutes, head to bed and collapse.

My name is Peter J. Clements.

My life partner Cal and I run a dance course. We are at the Laban school of movement and dance.

My mother, a former dance instructor, would be green with envy.

Not many people know of Laban's theories of movement, and this I deem to be their loss.

His work was highly additive to the literature on dance and musical physicality, on which much has been written heretofore.

I watch a young man call Oriel dance like a storm. His cause, however, is a lost one: his attitude does not befit our studio's ethos.

He has the necessary talent; he merely lacks the necessary discipline to make that talent into a craft at our hands.

Eva knows of what I speak.

I await Cal.

I love the man like none other, and the kiss I plant on his lips when he arrives tells him so...

"Love Tomorrow" is a great film.

For a start, Andy Serkis is now the executive producer.

This means the movie is going places. And I'm Peter J. Clements on set.

Secondly, the cast and crew are amazing. There are people on here from "HOTHouse," "Ham and the Piper," and "Morning Tea."

There's a community here that I am becoming part of.

I'm starting to get to know people in this business.

And I like it.

Director Chris Payne is as I thought: careful, considered, and passionate about his work.

And although I'm only on for a few days, I'm glad to be here.

I missed out on the "Cock Tales" part, but I'll *not* miss this.

Day two on "Love Tomorrow."

I'm up at six in the morning, which makes me *muy* miserable.

I have a twenty-minute shower, stretch out the kinks, and have some cereal and a cup of tea to pretend I'm alive.

Which I'm not.

I have a shit and wonder why I have an upset stomach. I've eaten nowt but salad and soup, and still my kidneys feel like I've had a big night out.

I watch the morning news and grumble about the ludicrous airtime Prince Harry and Kate Middleton's wedding is and is going to receive for the next few days. I have a smoke.

I have a second shit. I've been awake a total of thirty minutes.

This does not bode well.

A stag pond disguised as Rooster staggers out of his room and zombies into his bathroom.

He's not in good shape. His back is about as bad as mine is and he hasn't seen hide nor tail of a gym in too long simply because of his work schedule.

Our cab rocks up at 07:15. We jump in and head to set in the middle of buttnuck fowhere.

We've been driving ten minutes when I hear the rumble in the jungle and realise I need toilet trout number three. This is not good, and bodes very, very ill for the rest of the day.

Maybe it'll be lucky number three and I can rest till lunch...

For those who do not know, London traffic is a ticking time bomb.

See, the city was initially constructed for horses and carts, and for river commerce and boating.

Playing host to hundreds of thousands of cars on a daily basis was never part of the plan. And yet here we are.

Unless you are bombing around at three in the morning, whereat driving can be a real pleasure, the city's trafficdom is a nightmare; like the veins of a human who's suddenly been injected with ten pints too many of blood, their coronary waterways overclogged and swollen under a heaving burden with which they cannot cope.

The population will increase.

The roads and tubes and buses and cabs will groan and buckle until they are completely strangled.

I wonder at what it will take to solve or even ease the problem.

And then we get to set.

And then I'm in the bathroom. *Again.*

"Love Tomorrow" has Rooster's handiwork all over it. Eduardo's doing locations, Louie Louie's doing DTI, Steven Cornaccia is involved, and Smugz shows up to do lighting.

The day goes amazingly: everyone is friendly as hell and the crew is just overwhelmingly polite and welcoming.

The director's in good spirits, despite the fact that earlier in the day someone nearly chopped his head off with the clapperboard.

I spend a good deal of time with Sam Barnett, who is a fascinating young man and a wonderful actor, but one with a broken heart. He's recently had a difficult breakup but is managing to hold his spirits high.

He's also fascinating company, and we spend a lot of time on set discussing philosophy, sexuality, and just ripping the piss out of people who are just as game as we are.

I have a nice time acting opposite Cindy Jourdain, an immensely talented and beautiful dancer-turned-actress from France who has an enchanting smile and a characterful face.

We laugh, we joke, and we work as one.

And then I see her.

The woman I lay my eyes upon is gobsmackingly beautiful.

She's one of the salsa dancers for the main scenes of the day, and even in a room of forty actors, actresses, models and dancers; she stands out like a lighthouse in the night.

She's tanned, has dark hair, has emerald green eyes, and dances like God himself is a dancer. Her body is straight out of married women's nightmares, and her smile is an indicator that I'm in trouble.

She's dressed casually but elegantly, her outfit sexystylish but allowing her plenty of room to do her thing. And when she does do her thing, I find myself mesmerised.

She's Portuguese, a dancer, is here for three months, and is absolutely stunning. I ask her for her number and we book a date for coffee.

I get home with Rooster in a cab journey, and Smugz comes over with a girl called Giselle.

He brings us drinks; we have a chat, we discuss work, and then he fishhooks me and punches me in the face.

C'est la vie.

Chow Bella has a new man.

And she's fond of him.

The Mahatma era may well be coming to a close, if her reports of this new man are anything to go by.

The only major downer is that he has a tattoo on his back of three naked women, a guitar, and a load of flames.

Not the classiest. But we'll see.

Watch this space.

Back to the gym.

Perfect hangover cure.

And we're back on "Captain America" tomorrow, and we have "Luther" (the TV programme) next week.

Now we're *talkin'*.

Till the end of November, I'm on:

- A "Direct Line" commercial (today, already met a fellow "War Horser" called Barnaby)
- "Luther" (some TV show)
- "Captain America" (again)
- "Miranda" (some other TV show in which I play a fecking Carol Singer...)

So work is looking A-OK.

This is a whole new feeling to me.

Both Ray Knight and Casting Collective are, I repeat are, worth their weight in gold without doubt.

Mad Dog I've yet to experience but it still leaves me with the same essential problem: my feature work.

All this background work is great, and anything that pays my bills is fine by me.

On the other hand, it's the foreground work that makes you an actor's actor, and right now that's in short supply. I need to get my application numbers back up.

And on the other hand again, I've still to see or have a screening of my four major films of the year. And if any of those make serious headway, then I should too.

But we'll see.

Days like today make it harder.

The Direct Line commercial looks good, and stars one of my favourite comedians who makes regular appearances on "Mock The Week" (best quiz-com on TV) and who plays a wicked character in "The Thick of It."

I'm literally five feet away from the man, who's about seventeen feet taller than he looks on a TV set.

However, the entire day (freezing) has involved sitting around in a warehouse (more freezing) in Galleon's Reach (wicked name, but *freezingissimo*) on set in an industrial estate (nad-crackingly freezing) and has been pretty devoid of what you might call 'a point.' Since we've done bugger all for six hours.

But I'm being paid about 90 'points,' and have another credit on my CV, so one must take these things in one's stride.

Or at least try to.

It's Tuesday.

I rise.

I clean the flat. I take out the trash.

I apply to ten more films. From one I get an email back almost immediately offering me an audition.

I go to the gym. I work out for two hours. I shop for food. I return home.

I receive a call asking me to book a film wrap party.

I agree to do it. I make another call. The party is booked.

An Eastern European woman I have never met ends up in my flat.

We say hello. We talk. She tells me she has brought me food. I thank her.

We end up in my bed.

Eventually, I sleep.

I walk in the flat from shooting on "Law and Order."
The weather has taken a turn for the fucktastic. It's shit.
It's so cold the frost called and asked us to turn the heating up.
I've two auditions tomorrow, one for a presenting gig, and another from my agent.
Then we're back on "Captain America" on Saturday, and after that it's the "Love Tomorrow" wrap party.
I feel soul-tired. It's been a stupidly long year, and all I want to do is go home for a fortnight, hit the gym, and get as fit and healthy as can be for next year.
My dad calls and tells me he's coming to London for a meet and a stayover next week.
It sounds serious.
I think this is the first time he's ever done that.
I need the home-time to recuperate. To become myself again.
There's only one more month to go before the book is done, and Lord Buss is reputedly finishing my album off soon.
"Radio London" should be done soon, as should "War of the Sexes." And "Love Tomorrow" ought to be in cinemas next year.
I'm starting to build a little momentum, and if I can return sufficiently recharged after Christmas then we have a real chance.
Was good today to get my first day's work done for Ray Knight.
It'll be even better to get one of the auditions tomorrow.
Cringers fossed.

I get to Wapping for the audition.
For a change, I walk in and say something totally unexpected...
"Can I use your bathroom?"
I bite my lips to stifle the pained noises and pray to the God of excrement to make this swift and painless.

He's apparently busy and not taking calls, as I end up having to chew on my hand to avoid yelling in pain.

OK, call me crazy, but something's possibly wrong with my bowels.

Plus I don't sleep properly, I'm losing my hair, I can never wake up in a good mood, and I have all kinds of addictions.

I'd go see a shrink, except last time I went out with one, after two months she needed to go see a shrink herself. Go figure.

Maybe I should just scrap all this and go volunteer in Rwanda.

There are guys at the audition who came all the way from Norwich. 'Course I have no idea where that is, but it sounds fucking far.

The lure (good word) of fame and fortune proves too much for some people as always.

"What do you all do?" says I.

And of course, they're all aspiring actors.

I dice-rolled for today.

My options were:

1. Don't go to any auditions and go sarging (pick up)

2. Go to the auditions as a woman (was kind of hoping for this)

3. Go to the auditions dressed as a rock star having done no prep whatsoever

4. Turn up but say "hi" and leave after five minutes, citing some unhealable medical issue, like a random attack of involuntary anal leakage...

5. Sack it all off and go ice skating

6. Turn up as a Russian gangster. Telling everyone involved that I "haf their dowter and she vill be reterned ven ve are convinced ze money is transferrrred to ze sviss benk akkahnt..."

I rolled a three.

Disappointing. So, here I am in my stage outfit, with four other hopefuls who want this job.

Myself, I could care less.

My character for the day is a Rock Star and they can take it or leave it.

As it also is for my next audition, where they may not be so forgiving.

Still. Like Johnny Depp says, as an actor you have to take risks and make decisions. And the one route I *always* take is to be different.

Plus, dice living is a smart move.

Ordinarily as an actor you would turn up in the same shit, give the same spiel, say the same shit, be the same person.

Not me. Every time I rock up it's different.

I make sure I keep my auditioners more on their toes than I am. 'Cause why not? Reverse the system and make it work for you.

Much better.

As per usual I end up chatting with my four compadres here and giving what assistance I can to help them career-wise. I'm not sure why I do this except that it's polite, and that I figure it's what my mum'd want me to do.

Ultimately they keep me there two and three quarter hours and don't even audition me.

This sounds ludicrous but it's actually pretty common. Time is always against us in movieland, and this is no different. It isn't the first time and it sure won't be the last.

Time to leave and get to audition number two. I head to Old Street, stopping only to drop my guts for the third time that day.

I get to the audition.

And see several kids lining up getting ready to audition. By kids, I mean six to eight-year-olds with their parents.

How much of a leg up will these youngsters have on their competition? A significant one.

I make a mental note to put my kids up for this kind of work from a young age. Get them earning their own money, and get their confidence sky high.

It's a good idea.

You know: if I actually live long enough to have any, that is.

My name is Wade Garrett.

I work as a technician for S.H.I.E.L.D., and we have just made the most amazing discovery of the age.

I stand in the frozen wastelands of the Arctic. I am clad head to toe in a red ski suit. Despite how thick and bulky it is, I am freezing.

My boys on Omega Squad and I have just found a terrorist plane crash-landed in the ice. It is in a bad way.

There is a stirring glow to the sky, a lot like the Northern Lights. It's real pretty, as Mama would say. The land is a deserted white, a solemn field of crystalline glitter beneath the wreak of howling wind.

The wing of the plane juts insolently from the ground. My glow-light provides little illumination.

I signal the boys to cut into the plane so we can see what the hell this thing contains.

The landscape is staggering.

I ignore the sound of the lasercutters searing through the steel and focus my eyes on the beauty before me. The winds screech past me and nearly take me off my feet.

This is Mother Nature on her period. Mistakes out here are expensive.

They cost lives.

My goggles mist up with my own perspiration. I am a red man alone among the dunes of white.

"Captain! Holy *Jesus Christ* Captain, come here now!"

Malone's voice crackles across the radio. It's unlike him to sound panicked.

I crunch my way across the powder and into the inner sanctum of the plane. I shiver a little as the winds drop. I see Malone and Edwards pointing towards an object in the ice.

I drop my rifle in shock. That cannot be what I believe it to be.

"No way... no way... Malone... Edders... that looks like..."

It looks like what it is.

It is a shield of red and white and blue, with a star in the centre with more meaning attached to it than that of David's.

"Sir. We have to call POTUS. This is a call he'll take, even if he's having the wettest dream of his dry life."

"Shut your yapper, Edwards," I command.

My mind will still not process that which my eyes perceive.

It is the weapon of the Patriot; it is the arms of the Son of Liberty; it is the shield of big ol' red white and blue:
Captain America...

The set is beautiful.

I'm at Shepperton studios and the timing for this couldn't be better.

We're getting near to Christmas and I'm ankle-deep in snow.

Of course, it ain't really snow. It's salt. And we're in another aircraft hangar of a set at Shepperton.

The days are long and what some might call boring.

But care I do not.

It's another Hollywood feature and it's amazing.

I feel lucky.

Punk...

The end of November.

It seems impossible. It's only five minutes since we moved *in*, for fuck's sake.

I grab some Mexican food in Hammersmith. Food before drinks is usually a good idea.

We head to the "Love Tomorrow" wrap and as usual, the wrap party is a mess.

Rooster walks in tipsy, Russia-Ukraine girl tells me she's not coming, and I walk into the pub with about fifty people there.

One of the leads heads home with a member of crew, Smugz walks in with Catherine, and the whole cast and crew are in the best of spirits.

Big T the A.D. and I have a chat about where he has worked and what he has done, and the director and producer give a speech, followed by the two leads.

I speak to the director and producer and they thank me ever so kindly for my work. I thank them profusely for the opportunity.

Smugz tells me a ludicrous and yet amazing story, the wardrobe and makeup girls are the talk of the night, and everyone ends up heading to an after party in Camden, apart from Rooster, me and Big T who all head home for further drinks and a chat.

Wrap parties.

You gotta love 'em.

I see Jenna and we spend a relaxed evening chilling out.

She orders Chinese, and I'm eating salad again.

I now weigh thirteen stone three. This is *better*.

I have maybe two or three more jobs and then we're home for Christmas.

At which point I should be thirteen stone and can then work on getting down to twelve stone seven in the New Year. Provided I don't eat a whole turkey farm over Christmas.

You might think it's soft, all this self-monitoring and calorie counting. If so, you're wrong.

As an actor it's absolutely necessary, and as a person it's highly beneficial. Your body is your engine. The kind and quality of fuel you put into it determines a lot about you and your health. Trust me.

I know what I'm talking about.

I'm out at an audition when I get a message off Louise telling me she is now considering a proper relationship with her other man, and that we may not see each other for a while.

I am not upset.

I am glad for her.

I also receive another message from my father reminding me he is still coming to London to see me.

Hmmm. Wonder what that's about?

And then a third message arrives from Lady Chow Bella.

"Hey Steve it's Flow... I've just fallen on the tube and my knee has popped out of its socket. I'm getting a cab home asap, just wondered if you or Rooster were home as I'm gonna have issues getting in the flat...and also can you bring a bag of ice or frozen peas so I can deal with the swelling...?"

383

I gasp.

She must be in *agony*.

What has happened this year with all the leg breaking shit?

First mi madre, then LL, and now Chow Bella. I tap the nearest table to touch wood for luck it doesn't happen to Yours Truly.

Rooster's in foul spirits from being dicked around by two nutty women who seem insane.

The end of this month is a real mixed bag for us.

"Anyone heard back from the estate agent?" I ask.

We sent a request in almost a month ago to renew our lease for two years instead of one. We like this place. We want to stay longer.

"Yeah. Bad news:" a pissed-off Rooster tells me. "The agent no longer manages the property. It's just the AD2 group (who own the building) we have to deal with..."

This *is* bad news.

The lead manager of our building hates both me and Rooster due to several run-ins earlier in the year and at least one phone argument that went severely fruit-shaped.

The notion that we'd have this flat taken away from us seems totally fucked.

This is *our* flat. And we're good tenants.

A feeling of dread tendrils its icy way up my spine.

To lose our flat near the end of the year would mean we all have to move house in a matter of weeks.

And Chow Bella has a dislocated knee.

And Rooster is working every day of the week.

This is not good.

I fall asleep late, but again; my sleep is fitful and my dreams are dark, and the sky ahead looks stormy and black.

DECEMBER 2010:

"EVERYTHING THAT HAS A BEGINNING, HAS AN END..."

"Lay - that - little head of yours down to sleep,
The hair around your head looks like a crown to me,
The last thing I want for you before you sleep
Is that you are the Master of all you perceive..."

- Talent -
"Bedtime Story"

- IMMORTALENTED 2013 -

It's the beginning of December, and the snow has fallen.

London and England are now covered in a white blanket.

The land is cold, and staying indoors makes way more sense than going out.

I head to Old Street to film my second commercial.

Direct Line was over a week ago, and today we shoot for Engel radios. I play a fireman and a lab technician.

It's the first paid gig my agent has gotten me and I'm chuffed to bits about it.

To be fair, given the weather and with all things considered I'd rather have stayed in bed. But work is work and money is money.

And it's important to get off the mark with my agent and the whole paid work situation.

You don't turn your nose up at paid work.

Christmas is now all over the TV and people are already gift shopping. The snow falling puts a nice full stop to things: we're now officially in the festive period.

I'm looking forward to going home to see the family and evaluating my year. And also to finishing my book.

Plus, there's always the view to consider: looking back over the year to see how far we've come.

My masterer is still sending tracks over, so we're on course to have all products finished by year-end.

I'm almost excited, but as always, I'll believe it when I see it.

Travelling on the tube is now a nightmare. The trains are people-clogged and are always delayed. The city will be choked in no time at all.

I feel for people doing the daily commute. I feel for the City, buckling under the weight of the tsunami of people out doing their Christmas shopping.

But it is good that the snow has fallen. There is a calm and a peace, a kind of relaxed serenity to things.

I look out the window and wonder how the tribesmen of old could have survived such weather without our modern technology.

It must have been hard.

The things our race has gone through to keep itself going simply *amaze* me.

On the slightly shittier side, I'm running out of money.

I've got a load coming in from "War Horse" still, but I need it for next year's rent. This is not good.

Being broke is shit. Let's be honest.

None of us like having no money.

And in this game especially, it sucks. It's the main reason so many people fail, or don't get where they need to be. It's hard to chase your dreams when you can't afford to pay your bills or buy food.

Surviving in this game is next to impossible: triumphing in it seems a million miles away.

So here I am: playing several roles over about twelve hours for 250 quid, having water tipped over me in a paddling pool in a factory in the worst weather possible.

Still.

Better than a kick in the nuts.

Dad comes over and we have an absolute *ball*.

He talks to Rooster and Chow Bella, and we head out for food and drinks.

Loki rocks up and shatters the world with news that he has an actual *job*. He works as an intern at a steel trading company.

I'm completely stunned, and am overwhelmingly happy for him. Dad's glad to see him too.

He looks sharper than a machete factory.

We drink, and then we eat, whereupon the waiter brings all our food out at once instead of starter first, main second.

Is this some idiotic new tradition I am unaware of, despite living here for ten years? I hope not, yet the phenomenon is to repeat itself the day after when Pops heads home at a different pub.

This concerns me. People in my country are not supposed to be this stupid.

At least, not without a prior eight pints.

We hit a pub. We drink some more. We have laughs, jokes, swap stories, and have a cracking time in general.

Rooster and Pops start a conversation about the country and the government and the future and we've drunk so much by this point that I decide to hit the sack.

Rooster and my dad stay up on the whisky until three in the morning.

Not me. I'm out like a light.

I've skipped over something that happened here, a not-so-minor request my father makes to me, and the very reason for his trip.

It's so mind-bendingly unexpected that I have to shelve it for the minute and just wait to see what I think once I've ruminated on it for a bit.

But fucking *hell*, he knows how to keep things interesting.

My dad and I had a difficult time communicating for quite some time.

It took years for us to work out how best to co-exist with one another. And now, finally, we have a good relationship.

As a man, he is about as alpha as it is physically possible to be.

When he enters rooms, they stay entered, as we've already stated. People take notice of his presence and adjust their position to permit him more room just to breathe. It's bizarre to observe. And he denies it strenuously.

My mother says I have a similar effect, but I don't see it. I deny it strenuously.

His gravitas has been extremely helpful with my work, however.

Playing certain characters just involves me re-imagining him and making a few tweaks, and suddenly you have an immensely watchable character.

I owe him a great deal.

Still, the request isn't a small one. This is going to take some thinking about.

He leaves thanking Rooster for both his hospitality as well as a scintillating conversation, and thanks Chow Bella as well.

As he goes, all three of us tell him to stop by more often.

Liam Heath comes to see us to show us the first mini-cut of our Behind-The-Scenes show on "HOTHouse."

It makes me laugh, and I have to admit, is interesting viewing.

It makes me want to see the whole thing, and to just get on with sending it out and seeing if someone will back us.

So tonight it's back to watching "HOTHouse" rushes.

We made a final Hail Mary play to see if the footage was retrievable via one specialist we hadn't yet tried.

And his news was as we expected: it was fucked.

So.

We have to make the best of what we have.

Just to keep the record straight, I've missed out on two girls this month already that I crashed and burned with.

And I'm not happy.

At *all*.

However. That's life. I'm not bitter. I am annoyed at myself, however.

They were both stunning, and precisely my type. Still. I have enough of my own so I can't complain.

But failure, despite how necessary it is for success, never tastes any better to me.

It's at this point I should state for the record: you never, ever, *ever* give up.

When you want something, when you have set your mind on it, when you realise that is what you want, you never, ever, *ever* submit, give in, let go, or give up on it.

You chase with all that you are.

And then you chase some more.

You'll see why in a moment.

I'm at the BBC centre in the freezing cold on a Saturday.

And what do I get to play? A fecking *carol singer*.

I'll be fair: the BBC centre is phenomenal.

It's located next to White City tube station on the West Side of London, and it's a stunner.

The studio we end up in is enormous. There's industrial lights hanging from the ceiling, fake walls and fake rooms and fake buildings all over the place. The ceiling has got to be sixty or seventy feet high.

There is so much history in this place that I am honoured to simply walk the halls.

I see Alan Shearer, Gary Lineker, Alan Hanson and all the footie crew walking in and out of a studio, no doubt for some kind of commentary work.

And I'm here to dress up like a snowman and sing "Ding Dong Merrily On High."

Fucking *typical*.

Still, it's another day's work and it's paid and I'm not complaining. I want more of this work.

The bills aren't gonna pay themselves.

I end up as a carol singer doing the damn "Ding Dong Merrily on High" song with three other poor unfortunates. And, as luck would have it, to keep my morale up, the Lord has seen fit to put Adam Bone (a lovely dude) off "War Horse" on this same shoot.

Just seeing one of the crew lifts my spirits.

I belt out the Carol for all I'm worth after having waited around for almost four hours. I'm dressed in my usual getup, so costume and wardrobe see fit to add some tinsel to my outfit. I'm not sure I've ever felt stupider, but who cares? For the first time in my life thanks to Ray Knight and the BBC, I may just be on national television.

I send a mental thank you to the Great Creator.

And to the Ray Knight agency.

I have a fitting next week for "Sherlock Holmes 2."

Yet another feature film to add to the CV.

And possibly my last job of the year.

We'll see.

It's Saturday night, and I spend four hours picking out the best "HOTHouse" takes.

It's soul-destroying work, partly because it's Saturday night and partly because I know we have an uphill struggle with all this.

We won't have a completed episode. And that means I have to get it commissioned with only trailers, script, and press pack.

Don't met wre gong: it's doable. And do it I shall.

I also have a strong tete-a-tete with Merlin, who, as expected, chews my ears off for leaving BTP's party early, as well as for neglecting my friends, as well as for general negligence.

I check my instinct to rip him a new one and keep the conversation as civil as I can.

No man living has put more time and effort into those he loves, and having my amicable and professional integrity called into question does not put me in a good mood.

See, the issue with having such gifted and intelligent friends is that they are notoriously difficult to mind-fence with.

Their ripostes and parries are of a higher calibre than the average, and it means you don't just stay on your toes; you live on them.

If I've made any mistakes (and I most certainly have), it's that I've been overly easygoing on people. I should probably be ripping a friend of mine a new one here, but I'm not. I reckon it's easier to crack open a few cervezas.

We resolve our issues and we drink some beer.

Textbook.

The next day we get a visit from Ben Sharon, our lead on "HOThouse."

He's about to go travelling for three to six months, has just starred in a feature, and has another pending for next year. Hearing his success inspires me, and reminds me to stay on course.

Merlin's words had a ring of truth to them: my focus this year *has* changed. I am, if possible, more obsessed with work now than I have ever been.

I can see how close we are all getting. We are all of us inching nearer the prize, and in my book you don't slack off when you near the finish line.

You accelerate like a mowfowe. But yes, without doubt, for months now I have seen less of people. And that rankles.

I walk from the house to visit Princesita, the Irish actress come yoga instructor who is also a writer, along with being a magnificent human being. She has a nice habit of calming me down.

My head is full of "HOThouse," work, and agents, and I require some human time. A dangerous chord is struck in my head that perhaps I have had too much human time this last week, and that I may be slacking off.

I check this line of thought as quickly as I can, and then crush it utterly. If there are people out there who work harder than me, they're called soldiers.

And I've been one, and not met many since who worked as industriously or took as much responsibility.

Self-doubt is not always beneficial. Self-surety almost always is.

Remember this.

I take Irish Princesita out for a drink.

We talk. I have such a lovely evening that I wonder how I survive with so little of this.

She tells me I need to eat more, and that my calorie levels are dangerously low. She tells me that I am unusual, and asks me what it was like to be a PUA and an escort.

So I tell her.

She asks if I am using PUA tricks on her. I tell her I am not. And also more importantly, that I would not.

She looks at me.

"You're very good," she observes.

I look at her.

"Thank you," I reply while shrugging.

She looks at me with suspicion in her eyes. But I care not.

I'm not the World's greatest at taking compliments. But I appreciate her honesty. Especially since I can see the lack of certainty in her face.

She is not sure whether I am being real with her or gaming her.

I am as my self as I can be, and leave the decision to her.

If being honest and being yourself is gaming someone, then I'm guilty as charged.

I hit the "Sherlock Holmes" fitting and find out to my delight that I am to be a Parisien artistic type from Holmes-era France.

The outfits are wonderful.

I check the latest mix of "Parimosita" (a track on my album) on my ipod and sigh as I hear the last thing I needed to hear.

More work needed.

And we are running out of *time*...

Ma nemme eez Jacques Francois Clousteau.

Ah em eh Ferench Peinteur at le wedding of monsieur Watson, oo eez a kollegg de monsieur 'olmes, le grett Eengleesh superslooth of Bekker Streeeeet.

Oh la la la la *la*.

Eet eez a wonderfull daiy to be alave, wis le Sonn shaniiiing, and ze sky so bleu it 'erts to look at eeeet.

Ah shall report beck more efulleeee, afteur I 'av sin ze wedding and ze events zereof.

I 'opp you aff a jour tres bien, mesdames et messieurs les tous.

Au revoir, mes amis.

I watch injustice take hold of "The Apprentice", as Liz Locke is dismissed when Bagsie so clearly should have gone that it is almost embarassing.

Plus, have you *seen* Liz Locke? Finer than a strand of *hair*...

I also go for the most cultured night of my whole year to an art show with Jenna, who is there to support her best friend and flatmate showing her new collection on "Fashion and its Practicality."

I almost freeze my ass off in a warehouse in Shoreditch, and sip white wine while I look at a variety of "artistic endeavour". And it leaves me a tad confused, to be honest.

Some of the displays are quite interesting; amongst them a woman who encourages guests and visitors to write or draw on plain white trainers, and a lady who has filmed a bunch of older people, naked.

I also see a board game in which players have forty-five minutes to tell a story which ends up reflecting on the tellers themselves.

Most of them are quite thought provoking.

On the other hand, some of it is shocking. And not in a good way.

And that same day, Rooster messages me to tell me that he thinks, given the state of our lease, he has to move out.

I'm so stunned by this that I think I'm in a state of shock.

Er, *what*???

I stand in the cold reading these messages getting steadily angrier and angrier.

And Jenna remains calm and unperturbed, bless her.

None of this is to do with her, so I shield her as much as I can from my own wrath, and leave her to dinner with her friend. No point in me pissing on other people's parades.

I stalk home, a belly full of fire and a head aching from concern and the cold.

I ended my last year homeless.

I'll not do it again.

And here was me all worried about December being boring.

Rooster and I decide to have a random night out.

We head to TK's place, where TK, Lulu and Clark are having a mad girl's night in.

I know off the bat this is fraught with landmines.

TK and I haven't spoken in a while. And adding Rooster and me to a party of singers, models and actresses before then adding alcohol to *us* is *not* a good idea.

But we get in the cab anyway. My spider sense tingles the entire way.

Sometimes I question my own sanity. I really do.

We arrive, and it's beautiful carnage.

Hip hop plays out of massive speakers, there's drinks everywhere, and the girls are dancing round the living room like God's finest creations. Which, of course, they are.

TK also still has our key fob, and I reckon the odds of us getting that back this evening are not good.

She puts it down her bra and disappears into another room. Nope, we're not getting it back anytime soon.

And it's while I'm listening to Katy Perry's "Firework" and hearing Lulu talk and drinking a Rockschool, that something in my head clicks.

There's a girl I know called Unia who is a very talented woman.

I've known her more than two years, and not once have I thought about her other than as a friend and a really talented young woman.

She's always been someone I am fond of and admire, so to speak.

Suddenly, sat there with a drink in hand, I hear the words "I'm the female you, innit?" in my head again, and then I actually laugh out loud at my own stupidity.

And instead of a friend, what I see in my head (infuriatingly) is a beautiful, exotic, gifted, intelligent, feisty wild-child of a woman; one with a sharp mind, a coma-inducingly delicious figure, and a face designed by the Gods of *amore*.

This image stays in my head as TK reappears with more drinks before heading to her room to pass out. Rooster and I pile into a cab with Clark, and we vamoose to Brixton for more nonsense.

It all gets *ugly*.

We eventually arrive home round four or five in the morning.

Rooster waves at me and passes out. I tell myself the image in my head is about to go away.

I pass out.

The image in my head does not go away.

It begins to drive me up the wall.

I can barely sleep. It makes me crazy. Admittedly, it's also probably the lack of sleep.

Occasionally I am prone (especially as a diceman and artist) to bouts of extreme randomness. I don't think, I just get out the house and go somewhere to do some mad shit.

It's the war inside me, you see. And the thought in my head is like a splinter I cannot get rid of.

I walk out the house and call Unia.

"I'm coming over," says I.

I'll not go into details, but I end up going to see Unia and have the kind of day I'll not repeat here.

Or ever.

But to all my fellow hombres, suffice to say, sometimes being a dude is just about that: being a man.

I love that.

It lets me know I am not a coward.

Rooster and I sat hunched and collapsed in front of the computer. We're both so exhausted that our actual *clothes* need rehab.

But after almost eight hours of solid editing, arguing, debating, more editing, all on a fucking Saturday, we have a five minute roughcut of a "HOTHouse" trailer.

And by 'arguing' I mean it's a miracle (again) that we didn't kill each other.

And it looks pretty good.

A weight the size of Manhattan releases itself up off my shoulders. I can see how, if we added this to the Behind The Scenes, the press pack and the script, we give ourselves a shot at the title.

And that means we've let no one down.

I'd still prefer to have a full episode, but if we can get funding or help off people then I'm not going to care about the full episode.

Because then we have a TV show.

My innards feel like someone melted a goat in there. I take nurofen. I curse my own appetites, my own idiocy, my own flaws and my own weakness.

And then, before you know it, I see my reflection in the mirror, and three slash marks on my face, and I remember Unia shaving my stubble, and then shock on her face, and then blood, and then...

You're sick, maggotfeed. Your body is on comedown. You went rampaging round London to fuck yourself up after working for four months straight with only two days off, and you succeeded.

Heh.

You're doing my job for me. Remember what Reith told you:

"You should be in a mental institution, with your background."

But it ain't gonna be that easy, chickenwing. You think you're gonna end this year on a high?

With your 'work' to send out?

Not if I can help it. You will kneel and scrape in the dirt before I permit you success...you hypocritical fuck...

Kneel.

*In the **dirt**...*

What's left of me raises itself from the dead and heads to my studio (yep, on a Sunday) to record the last bits of ADR (additional dialogue replacement) for Michael Andrews' "War of the Sexes."

I'm in no shape to work, but fuck it.

I have only days remaining until I leave for home. So one way or another this is getting completed.

I see Kofi Lefty in my studio, and we spend about four hours finishing off the ADR.

I love my studio. I haven't even been here in about five months, which in itself is criminal, and being here makes me feel like being home.

But not yet. Just a few more days.

I walk out and get the bus home.

Gonna treat myself to pizza and chips and a beer. We find out tomorrow what Rob (our building manager) says about our flat and paying for it and next year's lease and all that crap.

And I still hear nothing back yet from Unia.

Fuck it.

Junk food and beer it is.

Monday.

I meet Shanghai for coffee and then hit the gym.

Rooster and I get a dude called Manoj over who helps us grade and colour the trailer and then teaches us how to do basic sound design.

I sit up script editing till five in the morning and check the director's diary.

I'm so beat I'm practically an egg.

"You know what?" Rooster says. "I think it looks good."

My look says, "*are you paking the tiss?*"

But he isn't. And he's right.

Hours later we are in our estate agent's office discussing our lease.

We cannot do the one-month extension thing we wanted to do.

We cannot do less than a six-month contract.

We cannot renew for two years, as we wanted to do.

The Estate Agent is adamant that we should renew for a year.

But we have cashflow problems and need to have a chat.

Rooster and I head out to the coffee shop to have a chat. We call Chow Bella to see what she thinks. She gives her assent.

We walk back in.

"Fuck it," we go. "We'll do the six month thing."

Thank Jesus.

Rent and lease sorted.

Another weight comes off my shoulders.

And finally, I'm on the way home. It is snowing. I am in a cab and it feels like I am on the way to the airport to go on holiday.

Except of course, I do not have my passport because I am not on the way to the airport.

I am headed to my favourite station to go home. This feels good.

My mind is full of work and women. I try to ignore it. I look out the window at the snow and rain, and I think how lucky I am to be alive.

And! Rooster and I have managed to edit "HOTHouse" down to a five-minute trailer. It looks *wicked*, blad.

And I think it is good enough. Good enough to get us in. And by "in," I mean into the bigger leagues. I want it signed.

End of.

I message and call Unia. It's all fucked up. Which makes me all fucked up. But so what?

I can take it.

And then some.

And then I am home.

And the whole world has gone white. It is beautiful. The snow grinds the country to a halt.

But to my mind, it's worth it. It's absolutely stunning to look at.

I see student protests on TV about the rise in tuition fees. I experience mixed emotions as I watch the usual ruckuses and violence erupt.

Students or rent-a-mob scum (faces hidden by masks, faces *always* hidden by masks) smash up windows, government buildings, culturally iconic statues, the works.

One exemplary imbecile, a history student from Cambridge, would you believe, is seen swinging from a Union Jack flag off the cenotaph, as his 'colleagues' lay waste to London.

He apparently "did not know" the significance of the cenotaph.

And he's a history student.

At *Cambridge*.

It is a disgusting display.

Before you know it I am at Kev's playing "Call of Duty 2," ordering pizza and having a snowbeer.

Incidentally this is the second day I have not smoked. And while it is easy, it is also not.

I like smoking.

"Ha. Haha. You're not *too* dead. Dead? You? Oh, dead *you*? You're what? Deeeeeeeeaaaaad..." Sharv exclaims proudly, as his avatar grenades mine through a window.

I wanted to talk to Kev to find out why it is I actually do this, to uncover all my own secrets and get it all out in the open. But apparently that's not happening.

What matters is we're into Day Three, and I can talk to Kev any time. There's no rush. I'm in the chillzone.

Snowbeer, for those of you who don't know, is the most refreshing drink on earth.

You take your cans of beer and stick them in the fridge, as per usual. But then you take some more cans of beer and stick them outside in the snow.

The resulting temperature of the beer after about thirty minutes is just divine, so long as you are indoors, warm, have video games, and have just ordered two super-sized pizzas with chips and dips.

You will almost certainly feel ill, but it'll be worth it.

"Eat lead salad, *beeeeeyaaaaatch*! It's lead city. Nah, fuck that, it's lead *world*..." Kev cries.

The man is a teacher. He is responsible for educating the young.

Apparently.

The snowbeer goes down a treat as Sharv, Kev and I send each other hails of bullets on "Call of Duty 2," which is one of the sexiest-ass games of all time.

We've all known each other and killed each other on video games for fifteen years.

There will be beatings later as I dish out much whup-ass on Street Fighter.

This is how chilling out is *meant* to be done.

So.

Smoking.

I am a recovering drug addict. That much is clear. And I said I'd give it up, and here I am, trying and succeeding. For four days now.

Three more days and we're onto a week.

But why did I do it in the first place? That's the question.

Well. The only way to answer that is with the Truth.

Personally, I reckon there's an addictive gene to my DNA, which is hardly detective work since both my parents smoke.

But that ain't it. It sure as hell is no-one's fault but mine.

I *also* reckon I have a naturally consumptive bent to my genes. If I were given an infinite metabolism, I'd wolf down pizza, chips and beer before I even thought of the word 'salad.'

I also have, like my mother, a form of organisational psychosis, a kind of "prefer things to be going at a hundred miles an hour" adrenaline junkie thing.

I sit on the edge of my seat, not far back in it. And smoking, as science states, far from chilling you out and lowering your heartbeat, raises your heartbeat, blood pressure, and stresses you out.

I'm a nicotine-addicted, over-consuming adrenaline stress-junkie.

Add to that a decade of habit, and that's all the reason you need.

Plus it doesn't help that I actually *like* smoking.

None of this is good enough reason to continue it, however. It is damaging. It is against everything I believe in.

Therefore it must stop.

The old me, the one who smoked, must be updated. Therefore, he must be executed.

End of.

I sign up to Jacqui Lawson to get all my cards sent out online.

I've not done proper cards for a long while, and that changes now.

2011 needs, if anything, to be more ordered and structured than 2010.

This way madness may lie, but so does success, in all likelihood.

And I reckon 2011 is make it or break it year. I type up my email for this book.

I type up my email for my album. I type up my email for "HOTHouse."

I'm telling you, Ladies and Germs, in 2011, we come out *fightin'*.

Monday the twentieth of December.
Just five short days away from Christmas.

And I have just seen myself on national television for the first time ever.

On the Christmas Special of "Miranda Hart", on BBC 2 at 20:30pm. And there's a repeat Christmas day at 10:45pm.

Now *this* is what I call progress.

"That was surreal, watching you on TV," says Mum.

"Er, yeah," says I.

Inside, somewhere deep, somewhere no one ever gets to see, in a secret place I seldom share, somewhere long forgotten, a cheer erupts like a volcano...

Album done.

Guy Buss sends me several SendSpace files with the files attached.

I can hardly believe my eyes.

And I'm a happy chappy.

There's more work that needs doing but it'll wait. I can start sending my stuff out and that's what matters.

I go see my nan and life begins to make sense again.

Her home is the nexus of calm I need.

Christmas Eve.

The day before Christmas.

And I am done.

No more gym, no more work, no more anything.

I can relax for a couple days and just forget there's a world outside. The idea seems nice.

I'll believe it when I see it.

I've got my dad the new Tom Clancy book, which is what he wanted. I got my nan the Judi Dench biography, which to be fair I wouldn't mind reading myself. Kev gets whisky and "The Expendables." Steve H gets Glen Duncan's "Life of an Ordinary

Man" and the movie "Legion" (see, I'm a decent friend. I get good pressies for people. *Kind* of.)

Rooster gets a bottle of whisky.

Chow Bella gets, well, I'm not sure yet; I'll work that one out.

Metis may get a book on Quantum Mechanics. Merlin, I have yet to decide. And mi madre gets:

- The Leonard Rossiter biography (fascinating man)
- A massive mug with "Best Mum" on it
- A huge bouquet of flowers delivered to the house
- Some dark chocolate
- A drinks mat I can't resist with "World's Best Mum" on it
- The two most beautiful cards I can find

See, in our house, Christmas is a big deal.

We make a fuss of each other. We go to the proper level when we do festivities here.

When you get the chance to be kind to others, take it.

I sit and watch "War of the Worlds."

It is a film by Steven Spielberg starring Tom Cruise.

I feel disconnected and not really here. Time to fix that. Can't be disconnected at home over Christmas.

I end up messaging with Irene Stephans, a girl we nearly cast in "HOTHouse." Her banter makes my mood rise and I feel better for it.

Tomorrow is Christmas Day, folks.

Almost survived year one of Dreamchasing.

And Lifeaholism.

Christmas Day.

And I wake to be hugged like a long-lost son, cause I've just seen that my mum's seen her presents and is fairly chuffed.

Good.

Now, for a cup of tea.

This is how to start Christmas.

See, to all you feckers who think I'm complicated; I'm actually quite a simple dude.

A cup of tea, my family around me, some shit TV, and I'm a content individual.

And after excavating through all my presents, I have been given:

- Running shoes
- Money
- Two bottles of whisky
- A book on philosophy
- A book on mathematics
- More money
- An Ed Hardy shirt
- Two books from JHBrown
- And the offer of a date from a woman in Kentucky who likes my song "Lost Tribe"

Helping to cook settles me.

I take a long conversational trip down memory lane with Mum, talking about school, about betrayals, about long-gone loves, about losing those who meant a great deal to me, about A levels and GCSEs, and about family and how I felt I was doing.

It felt cathartic.

When we got round to having Christmas lunch it was more like Christmas dinner, being about 5pm early evening. I love that about Home.

Convention can just go out the window and we do things our way.

I find myself messaging Unia and booking a date.

And messaging all my friends to wish them a Merry Christmas.

And then I see myself again on National TV on Christmas Day, sat on my couch, with a single malt whisky and lime.

Boxing Day arrives.

It's one of the days of the year when I am most grateful for my Family.

Carol's food on Boxing Day is so good it's almost rude not to have a nap immediately afterwards. The Family all gather in the same place, they eat, they talk, they laugh and tell jokes.

It's a wonderful day. You can't get better than this.

I go running for half an hour.

Ayan, Karl Bayliss, and Kev come round.

We chat shit like only old friends can, and we have a few drinks.

I'm always amazed when I see my friends holding such conversations.

We've known each other over a decade and a half.

It brings you right back down to Earth, and reminds me why I do this in the first place.

I return to London.

I spend my first two days still in the Chillzone having drinks with Rooster. The second night we talk almost all night and have a great catchup.

And then Merlin arrives the Day before New Year's.

And now it's time for New Year's Eve preparations. We end up buying:

- Four bottles of champagne
- Ninety beers
- Four bottles of vodka
- Four bottles of whisky
- One bottle Malibu
- One bottle Gin
- Ten bottles of mixers

- Four bottles red
- Four bottles white

Plus, for foodstuffs, we get:

- Twenty pizzas
- Ten quiches
- Enough crisps to kill a mule
- Dips
- And sausage rolls

We lock doors and put the valuables in the storage cupboard. We do a basic flat clean. We move all major breakables out the way.

Let's see if we can start the New Year on the right note.

Welcome to New Year's Eve 2010, Ladies and Germs.

We spend a load of the day prepping the flat and putting the food out.

Rooster can't decide whether to be "The Crow" or Neo from "The Matrix." He thinks "The Crow" face makeup will inhibit his pulling skills.

I think otherwise.

Chow Bella is Lucy Liu out of "Charlie's Angels," a smart call for a girl cause it means she's basically looking hot in a red dress: no inhibited pulling there.

Jita reckons she's going as Amy Winehouse, which looks to me a lot more like going as "Jita," but she's still looking good.

Merlin decides to go as Jesus, and his costume, to be fair, looks wicked. There's a crown of thorns and everything.

Me? I'm dressed as Captain Jack Sparrow. And it's actually not a bad costume.

Gandhi is apparently coming as Enrique Iglesias, which means he's dressed like Gandhi except with his shirt a bit unbuttoned and with someone having drawn a mole on his face.

Chloe arrives with her charming friend Tom and after a few drinks she warns me she sometimes gets "overly friendly," and in which case my recourse is to "tell her to fuck off."

Also we have a conversation about her character and how important she is. I am gobsmacked when she informs me she feared I intended her for only one episode.

JHB comes over early and brings weasel. He dresses as a space barbarian and looks amazing. Rosemania and his brother also show up early *sans* costume but *avec* JD and coke.

Amanda brings eight women, some of whom are very attractive.

Smugz leaves early, drunk, because of a woman. He wigs out whilst leaving at the injustice of it all.

Steve South and Sean of Ibiza Pacha fame DJ their socks off and we screen the "HOTHouse" trailer at 11:30pm in Merlin's flat.

This is a big deal to me.

We've worked, failed, succeeded, striven, fixed, and laboured at this for months.

And now we are screening it at a penthouse by the Olympics on the line of Time.

To all our friends and colleagues.

Everyone cheers and applauds, and people the rest of the night come up to Rooster and me and congratulate the shit out of us.

We have thirty bags of alcohol on the balcony.

We do a midnight countdown at Merlin's and then everyone legs onto the balcony for Firework City.

I end up playing designated driver and keeping an eye on the flat, and also giving a female guest a foot rub.

In a night of inane and incestuous hookups, Vix hooked up with Rosemania, then with Rooster, who then hooks up with Teenster, before then hooking up with some random, and then with our beautiful makeup girl.

A lady in the bathroom does Charlemagne whilst discussing the niceties of anal sex.

Loki then rocks up with his Angel, just before Benos and Richard from "War Horse" turn up. Winehouse's friends rock up and nearly kick a fight off.

I manage to get them out the flat with a minimum of fuss, despite a drunk and lairy Rooster exacerbating the situation.

Sean and Southie arrive and DJ the night away.

We live on the nineteenth floor.

We somehow get noise complaints from the *eightth* floor.

That's over halfway down the *building*.

On the greatest New Year's Eve I've ever had, in the same year as the greatest 30th and *night* I've ever had, this is *big*.

We have:

- DJs from Ibiza
- A "HOTHouse" screening
- Enough food to lay out a T-Rex
- Enough alcohol to fill Lake Windermere (everyone's entry fee was a bottle of spirits or two bottles wine)

We get Kid Ant arriving as Mr T and Lady King as a Ghostbuster.

The General arrives, style personified, with Neil, who is a lovely guest.

The party is by all accounts an absolute hit.

People are telling Merlin and me that this is the best party they've ever been to.

New Year's Day and we're watching "Inception."

Me, Chow Bella, Rooster, and Rosemania end up ordering pizza and somehow I've still not slept.

Me? I'm still going.

Somehow I'm awake at seven am in the morning, whereby Sahota comes over and we talk for hours about relationships and life.

I watch "Robin Hood" twice in a row.

I eventually go to bed at eight am Sunday morning after cleaning the entire flat and collapse into an immediate sleepcoma.

I spend the entire next day in bed.

I realize, dimly, that I have survived my first year as a full-time actor.

I realize, dimly, that my album is now finished.

It dawns on me that I have written a book this year.

I grasp that I have played the lead in two TV pilots.

I smile as I recall two month's solid work on a Steven Spielberg movie.

I feel with pride the elation one can only feel at playing the lead role in a feature film that actually has something to *say*; in this case, "Radio London."

I realize I am a represented actor, and that I have built a better film CV in 12 months than many actors I have met have in 12 years.

I consider that Rooster and I have our own TV show to shop around.

And there's still more to come, 'cause this is only the start.

I know not if it was foolishness to leave a six-figure job to chase one's dreams, but right now, I wouldn't change a thing.

It's now about to be Tuesday, and I have to be back on-duty, dear Reader.

I have managed to have a one week holiday and a New Year's that was the best I've ever had, topping off the best year I have had, which included the best night I ever had.

I start my 2011 feeling like the luckiest man in the world.

I wish nothing less for you.

May these writings find you in the best of Health, those you care for well and warm, and may the skies stay clear for you, wheresoever you may set sail.

Fin.

NEW YEAR'S END

NEW YEAR'S EVE 2010 - At the HOTHouse

GODDAUGHTER'S WEDDING 2010

WAR OF THE SEXES - Promotional Shoot 2010

BTP'S 30TH BIRTHDAY 2010

OUTRODUCTION: "ONWARD AND UPWARD"

HOW THE HELL DO WE TOP *THAT*...?

So that's yer lot.

That was the year that was. It was the year I turned thirty. It was the year I grew most fully into manhood.

I now have: -

- An album ("ImmorTalented")
- This book ("Lifeaholic")
- A TV pilot ("The HOTHouse")
- A film ("Radio London")
- A clothing line ("BTX")
- Another film ("Morning Tea")
- A documentary ("Talent 2008")
- A music single and video ("Everyman")
- And another TV pilot ("War of the Sexes" / "Going Commando")

All to promote and sell to someone. I have no idea how this will go.

Although my track record gives me some indication, it's no guarantee.

I've no idea how I even survived this year, but somehow I did.

If hard work equals payoff then someone should be handing me a winning lottery ticket at some point.

OK not quite, but you get the point.

And, I suppose it's only fair to look here at the end back at there where we started.

My New Year's resolutions, remember?

The trick is, see, you score as many Q1 and Q2 as you can. Get some out the way. So, here's how we did off the original list:

WRITTEN - To Write (4) 3/4
- ImmorTalented / Lifeaholic (my book)   DONE
- A TV show (TBC)   DONE
- My first short (Loveblind)   DONE
- My first feature (RiotBrawl)   --------

MUSICFILM (9) 7/9
-   Finish album mix   DONE
-   Master album   DONE
-   Sell album / get signed / get management   ---------
-   Do 5 feature films   DONE
-   Do a Hollywood Feature   DONE
-   Do first film score music   DONE
-   Get your own agent   DONE
-   Complete your album art   DONE
-   Write a Clubland Treatment   ---------

HEALTH (4) 4/4
-   Quit smoking   DONE
-   Stay at 13 stone   DONE
-   180 gym visits   DONE
-   1000 calorie a day diet   DONE

LIFEAHOLISM (7) 3/7
-   Bungee jump   ---------
-   Go LA for a fortnight   ---------
-   See a Darksky   DONE
-   Do a standup comedy show   ---------
-   Have a 30th bday holiday   DONE
-   See the Cannes Film Festival   DONE
-   Take Driving Lessons   ---------

FAMILYWOMENMISCELLANEOUS (6) 6/6
-   Make 6 trips home minimum   DONE
-   "Meet" 12 new women   DONE
-   Sign up to Ray Knight extras agency   DONE
-   Sign up to Casting Collective   DONE
-   Sign up to Mad Dog extras agency   DONE
-   Save 10k for next year -rent & bills   DONE

TOTAL RESOLUTIONS = 23/30 = **77%**

Which isn't bad, if I say so myself.

I still have acres of shit to work on, but I'm getting better.

As much as I have lost this year, which, given who got married is a lot, I gained even more.

I got footholds and handholds on the cliff-face that were not even *there* before. And now all I need do is sell any one of five products to allow me enough *time* to sell the other four.

I need more work as an actor, and more work as a director.

And which of those two paths will I choose to do more of?

Or will music or writing be more popular with Joseph Public?

I've no idea the answer to that either: but like I said, I'm not dumb enough to claim I have all the answers - only bravestupid enough to have the guts to ask certain questions.

You should be able to see by now that I'm not in the business of trying to make myself look like 'the man.'

I've told you about so much stupid stuff that I've done that I'm going to be amazed if I have any fans or friends *left* after this.

What I do want you to see, is just how much you can do with a year when you put your mind and your will to it.

I haven't "made it" yet, according to my own ludicrous standards, but then that's both subjective, and more importantly, just a matter of time.

I'm in the game and *that* is what matters.

And you can do *exactly* what I have done.

You wanna write a book?

You can do it.

You wanna make a movie?

You can do it.

You wanna get with a glamour model or a Miss Country or an actress or a celebrity?

You can do it.

You wanna make and sell an album?

You can do it.

You wanna be in a Hollywood feature film?

You can do it.

You wanna build a house, paint a picture, stand on the moon, fly a plane, be the President of the United States?

You wanna achieve everything you ever dreamed of?

YOU.

    CAN.

        DO.

           IT.

That's why I did what I did this year; to make sure you knew, not thought, not believed, *knew* that you could do *everything* you want to do.

It simply comes down to how bad you want it, and what you are willing to do for it.

So.

Just to give you an idea, the beginning of the year has been more mental than last year.

I've had:

- A new lead role in a feature film "The Android"
- Got in the top 1% of 2012's "Britain's Got Talent"
- Appeared on National TV on "Harry Hill's TV Burp"
- Appeared on National TV on the "10 O' Clock Live" show
- Acquired a music manager called "The Man In Black"
- Seen "Love Tomorrow" win Best British Feature at the Raindance Film Festival
- And finished this book…

I repeat.

Whatever it is that you want to do, you can do.

Just decide what kind of life, what kind of wife, what kind of home, what kind of job, what kind of career, what kind of adulthood, what kind of existence, what kind of daily routine, what kind of love, what kind of friendships, what kind of thing you wish to have, and work out what it will cost you to get it.

And then pay that cost.

Gladly.

Every day.

And it will be yours.

"My wife is my life, but my life is my wife." - Stephen "Talent"
Brocklehurst - March 2011

How is the album gonna do?
How is the music video gonna do?
How is "Radio London" gonna do?
How is "HOTHouse" gonna do?
How are "War of the Sexes", this book, my short films, and "Love Tomorrow" gonna do?
I'll be honest with you. As I promised at the beginning.
I've no idea. I can only tell you this.
No matter how they do, I'm not stopping.
I've got an idea of how close we are, us risk-taking London folk, us BTX, us cinemusicians, us HOTHousers.
It's so close I can taste it.
So. Do your thing.
Don't *believe* anything is possible.
Know. That Everything is possible.
And hopefully, I'll see you on set one day.

Oh yeah, the escort thing?
You'll just have to wait for the next installment, amigo…

Just remember – we do this because of our love for others, as much as for the love we have for our self.

My love to one and all.

S

Stephen "Talent" Brocklehurst is an actor, writer, director, singer and model based in London, England. He claims no animals were harmed during the making of this book, and apologises in advance for any lack of offence he has caused. He works freelance in the United Kingdom, and occasionally wonders how that can be the right name when, *actually*, they have a Queen. He is uber-tall, dark-haired (thanks to the wig from "Angels"), has a GSOH, and is available for tea. But *no* sugar. He was formerly a TA Parachute Regiment soldier, a dance instructor for JRP London, a male escort, and a waiter. Allegedly there is a warrant for his arrest in Nacadoches, Texas. *Allegedly…*

www.stephenbrocklehurst.com
www.twitter.com/talentbtx
www.facebook.com/talentbtx
www.myspace.com/btxistalent
www.reverbnation.com/talentbtx

MORNING TEA

A Milan Sebo Film

When Milan Sebo decides to take his life into his own hands, and the lives of a self-help group, all of whom are terminally ill, will he convince them all to take their own lives as an act of reclaiming control, or will he be uncovered as the psychotic he might be…?

The controversial feature film from first-time director Milan Sebo starring Stephen "Talent" Brocklehurst and Simon Humphries, "Morning Tea" deals with Milan's struggle to lead a group of people to retake control of their lives after they were diagnosed with terminal illnesses...

The story follows Milan and a group of terminally ill people, all struggling to make sense of their lives in the city that forgot them…

Directed by: **Milan Sebo**

Written by: **Milan Sebo**

Produced by: **Roopesh Parekh**
Alex Macaulay

Starring: **Stephen Brocklehurst**
Jamie Addicott
Simon Humphries

IMMORTALENTED

The highly anticipated and critically acclaimed forthcoming album from two-time EMA (Exposure Music Award) nominee Stephen "Talent" Brocklehurst.

A three-time UK Unsigned finalist and top 1% of the 2012 Britain's Got Talent roster, Talent has been working on his first album for over 4 years.

He has opened for Memphis Bleek at Café De Paris, hosted the 'Respect The Mic" show at Baker Street, and is part of the collective known as the 'BTX'. The album is part of a 360 degree project, including: -

- **"Radio London" – the feature film**
- **"Lifeaholic" – the book**
- **"HOTHouse" – the TV Series**
- **"War of the Sexes" – the Mike D'Rews TV Series**

"His name says it all - he is hugely multi-Talent-ed and knows no boundaries, involving artistically pushing his limits and exploring new roads of discovery. Musically, comparisons could be made to Eminem as a British version - but adding a touch of class. He really is pure Talent." **– Natalie Neri, owner and founder: NN Models**

"Over the last couple of years, we have witnessed a new talent enter the music scene in London. Talent (the artist, & he fits his stage name perfectly) has been performing across a string of underground clubs and has grown a solid fan base. His acts combine power, a touch of raw talent (there is that word again) and absolute love for the music. There is no doubt that this performer will be entertaining larger and larger audiences in time to come." **- Roger Birch, co-founder of Cartel Clothing**

421

RADIO LONDON

A Rehan Malik Film

Can Tariq Solomon, an innocent man accused of a heinous crime, ever return back to society? What are the secrets that bind him to the refugee girl and the street preacher he encounters under the shadow of intense media scrutiny?

The highly anticipated feature film from breakthrough director Rehan Malik starring Stephen "Talent" Brocklehurst and Ziad-El Hady, "Radio London" deals with Tariq Solomon's struggle to prove his innocence in a society that believes him guilty already.

The story follows Tariq, Abdullah the Preacher, and an Afghani immigrant girl all trying to survive in the Great British Capital.

Directed by:	**Rehan Malik**
Written by:	**Leon Hady**
	Ziad-El Hady
	Raydolph Amponsah
	Rehan Malik
Starring:	**Ziad El-Hady**
	Albert Clack
	Stephen Brocklehurst

"I directed a feature film with a hugely talented ensemble cast. Stephen's was that one breakout role that makes you sit up and take notice. His blistering performance as a complex multilayered and troubled character stands out like nothing you've seen before…"
Director Rehan Malik March 5, 2012

www.ingramcontent.com/pod-product-compliance
Lightning Source LLC
Chambersburg PA
CBHW031030030726

47497CB00004B/1080